MW01248115

# PICTURE
# OF ELIZABETH

JENNIFER D. BARRY

Quantity sales and special discounts are available on quantity purchases by corporations, associations, and others. For details, contact the publisher at the address above.

Orders by U.S. trade bookstores and wholesalers. Email info@ BeyondPublishing.net

The Beyond Publishing Speakers Bureau can bring authors to your live event. For more information or to book an event contact the Beyond Publishing Speakers Bureau speak@BeyondPublishing.net

The Author can be reached directly at BeyondPublishing.net

Manufactured and printed in the United States of America distributed globally by BeyondPublishing.net

New York | Los Angeles | London | Sydney

ISBN Hardcover: 978-1-63792-375-7
ISBN Softcover: 978-1-63792-376-4

*"For my mom, Linda."*

# CONTENTS

# PROLOGUE

The law is cruel.

*What is the law?* She thought to herself. *Is it just some pointless scam to con the American public into believing that its citizens matter? Or is it an unbiased system of government to help and comfort those in fear of being wronged?*

Those she once trusted seemed to be plotting against her. What could she have done to warrant such treatment?

*These bars are cold. This cell is cold. God only knows how many convicts have passed through this dungeon-like room.* She was terrified of the future.

I wonder where my darling James is this minute. Will I ever be able to touch him again, unobstructed by these damn bars?

She decided to concentrate on her inner thoughts. She wouldn't dare listen to the everyday noises of where she was, the constant echoes of screams and yells, wood against iron. What a dark, uncaring place. This aching mental tension was working its way into her brain, gradually entwining itself with each cerebral fiber and thought, until strength surrendered her into a state of absolute fright.

*This place is a place of punishment, of penalty. A place where the worst and foulest of people go. No, you are innocent, Lisa. Innocent until proven guilty. You're stronger than this.*

Her inner voice gave in to the pouring rain as it trickled down the barred windows. The drops bore resemblance to tears, casting reflections upon her face as she vacantly stared out the window into the prison courtyard. The single light bulb above her head flickered for a few seconds. She hadn't eaten in days.

How could she eat when she had possibly lost all that she held dear?

She ran to the door, clutching her velvety hands around the worn, black metallic rods. "Please let me out of here!" Her voice reverberated down the long, ghostly corridor.

*How long must I stay in this dreadful hell? I've been here for weeks and have not heard or seen any sign of ever getting out.*

*Could this be my new home?*

*One year and six months earlier...*

# CHAPTER ONE

February, 1958

She struck her knuckles against the door.

No one answered.

Overhearing an argument, she positioned her ear up to the door. Their voices were muffled, but every harsh word between the spouses could be heard through the paper-thin walls. She knocked louder this time. Their voices stopped simultaneously.

The door unlocked and she stepped back. She peeked around to see who answered, but the chain obstructed the door. All she heard was a clearing-of-the-throat on the other side coming from what sounded male.

Not expecting to see his sister standing on the other side, he licked his lips in irritation before realizing it was Lisa. A pleased smile came across his face. He unfastened the chain and greeted her with a much-longed embrace.

"I've missed you," Donald whispered. "Come in. Please."

Lisa was a thirty-seven-year-old petite woman with a buxom figure and shoulder length russet hair. Her most valuable feature was her smile; alluring, delicate, yet simple. Sometimes there's beauty in simplicity. She had lived in the growing metropolis her entire life and found it took strength and willpower to keep up with the thriving beast. It was all she knew and couldn't fathom living another way.

She entered the Wells home. The drab wallpaper was a creamy hue with tan lines. A carpet once a vivid white had become pale from foot traffic and spilt food and drink. Contrasting these features of the home were paintings of glorious landscapes and handsome still lifes.

"Where're Simon and Julia?" Lisa asked.

Rebecca was sitting rigid on the sofa's edge. Stanley the cat massaged Lisa's ankles as she scoped the room for her niece and nephew. Donald nodded to his wife to get them. Lisa was mindful of the tension within the room, which is why she made asking for the children her first priority.

"What is going on, Donny?" She spoke in a soft manner. "Are you fighting again? This makes the second time this month that I've come by and overheard some sort of dispute."

Donald gazed down at the floor. Embarrassment or shame? Lisa couldn't tell.

"You heard," he muttered.

"I'm certain the whole tenement heard. Donny, it's me. You know you can *always* come to me, right?"

Lisa laid a firm finger beneath his chin and raised his head to show him the comforting smile he dearly needed. Upon hearing her reassurance, his eyes met hers.

"Lisa, I..." Donald was interrupted.

Rebecca entered with their two children. Simon and Julia, each holding their mother's hand, shrieked in delight and ran to the legs of their favorite aunt. Six-year-old Simon was the eldest and resembled his father. Julia, nearing three, inherited her mother's long henna curls. Being too young to acquire any distinct personality traits, it was obvious Simon was the more rambunctious child, always making it a sport to knock his sister down to get to Aunt Lisa first.

Lisa obliged them both in their childish ritual, wrestling them to the floor to tickle and bombard them with affection. "How is my Strawberry today?" Lisa asked Julia grabbing at her sides.

They kicked, screamed, and pleaded for mercy. Lisa treasured every second. The couple, though, didn't find the scene as rewarding. They watched recalling those missed sentiments. Afterward, the adults chatted in the kitchen over coffee while the kids played in the next room.

"So," Rebecca began. "How have you been?" she asked with a sigh out of pure common courtesy.

"Same old grind. You know I'm always at the diner." Lisa turned to Donald to find him with his head limp, staring into his coffee. "Donny, how...how are you holding up?" She laid her hand over her brothers' resting on the table.

Rebecca interjected quickly, "Did Donald tell you I'll be taking the bar exam next year?"

"No, he didn't. If it works out the dough you bring in will really alleviate the tension around here." Even as she said it, Rebecca becoming a lawyer was open to question, but if it boosted their spirits, or lack of, that's what mattered.

Donald raised his head. "I help her study whenever I can."

Lisa spoke to Rebecca in admiration. "I'm proud of you. To be frank, I never expected you'd make it this far. If I was twenty-five again, I wouldn't have the wit or pluck to pull off an achievement like this."

Lisa raised her mug. "I wish you all the luck in the world, girl."

"I haven't passed yet, but it'll pay off."

Donald exhaled from his nose as he peered across at his wife. Lisa sensed much more than their everyday infighting. Donald was keeping something from her.

ALMA GEORGE – There was never before a woman who holds a grudge as strong or as pitilessly.

Lisa returned to her small Midtown Manhattan apartment. Knowing Alma was the old busybody she was, attempted to be as discreet as possible, but tiptoeing on the creaky floor did not abet the silence. The hinges of her next-door neighbor's apartment door screeched. Lisa fumbled with her keys.

Alma, believing she was undetected, only revealed an eye between the thin cracks. Lisa threw her head back and implored to the ceiling in hopes the good Lord above would be merciful.

"Hello, darling."

Lisa shut her eyes.

Alma opened the door nonchalantly. Holding her signature cigarette between her bony fingers, she leaned against the door and presented an elevated, penciled-on eyebrow. Alma fussed with her dyed scarlet red hair as if her appearance was man's finest gem. For some reason, Alma never bothered to alter her hairdo, still exhausting an early 1930's finger wave style.

"Hard day at work, dear? You look beat." Alma crossed her arms, hinting of resentment that complemented the crooked smile.

"I didn't work today, but I had a rather pleasant day, thank you. Sorry, can't chat, Alma. I *do* work tomorrow."

Lisa started to leave and Alma seized her left shoulder, somewhat jerking her to her recent position. "Tell me, that brother of yours, Donald is it? How is he these days?" Alma propped her body up against the wall with her shoulder.

"Yes, it is Donald, and he's doing fine...*thank you*." Lisa answered this time through clenched teeth.

Alma had studied Lisa's frailties and knew what her brother meant to her, and kept pressing until she saw red. It made no difference to Alma what Lisa did, but she lavished in her work.

"He's still married to that redhead, isn't he?" There was a brief silence as Alma anticipated a verbal response that never came. Lisa stared at the gray roots peeking from Alma's scalp. "Well, I guess some of us stay married."

Alma took a puff from her cigarette. Her voice was deep and hoarse. "It must have been true love with Donald. I mean, who in their right mind would be willing to bestow their entire life to someone they didn't truly love?"

Lisa fumed as the witch's vicious remarks took root.

"The truth of the matter is, we've been neighbors for, oh my, roughly a decade now. I haven't seen you with anyone since Robert, my dear, and I'm worried about you. Now darling, you're approaching forty, don't you think it's time..."

"Good night, Alma!" Lisa slammed the door, leaving Alma in the hallway with her cigarette butt and a grin.

# CHAPTER TWO

"**M**orning," Larry greeted Lisa as he wiped down tables in preparation of a frantic Monday. "Better get movin'. We've got a line out there."

Lisa opened the blinds to illuminate the diner with early-morning sunlight.

"Hurry, get the burners going."

"Alright Larry, relax. They're not going anywhere," Lisa said tying her apron around her.

Lisa, a waitress and cook, received over a hundred customers a day coming in to pamper their stomachs to a hearty breakfast and lunch that only Larry's Diner could provide.

Louis Jacobi, or better known to his friends as "Larry", was the owner and manager of his charmingly crafted establishment: A cozy, bright little restaurant with red swivel chairs at the counter and cushioned booths lining the windows. He was a kind, overweight man, who devoted the latter half of his life to his lifelong dream.

Breakfast at Larry's consisted of cereal, oatmeal, doughnuts, pancakes or waffles of many sorts, and whatever a customer had an appetite for that pervaded the air with its scrumptious aroma. Six days a week the atmosphere was hectic, jam-packed with the noisy resonance of clanking silverware, perpetual chatter, and jukebox music. Larry and Lisa were always in sync. With them at the helm the diner ran like perfect machinery.

Lisa hopped from table-to-table as people babbled and begged for service. Three hours of heat emitting from the grill and hot fare formed a shine on her skin. In another hour the lunch rush would arrive. The masses that passed the modest restaurant consisted of the same people. The same nine-to-five crowds that worked in the area and kept Larry's Diner the success it had been those many years in the heart of Manhattan, or perhaps the stomach that gave it its energy.

Larry observed in fulfillment as the customers devoured their food. Lisa served freshly squeezed orange juice to a feasting man at the counter. With all the people she met, numbered in the thousands, in the eight years she worked at the diner, she knew not one.

LATER THAT NIGHT Lisa was busy closing when her brother paid the diner a rare and unexpected visit.

Donald, a resident of the Bronx, worked two jobs to keep his family afloat, a cabdriver by day and a stock clerk at a grocery store by night. Twenty-eight, tall, with a thin frame and black hair, he was drained of the vitality a young man should have.

"Lisa, are you here?"

Donald pressed his lips together. With trembling nerves, he pushed aside his pride and stepped in. The bell on the door rang. It was being secretive that harassed Donald's conscience. He couldn't shake this feeling of injured pride and guilt.

Donald scoped the room. The diner was dark and empty. Its minimal light came from the kitchen in the back.

"Lisa?"

Lisa ceased washing the dishes when she heard her name and peeked around the door. "What are you doing here? Aren't you supposed to be at work?" Lisa threw the dishtowel over her shoulder and went to him.

"I'm on my break. I needed to see you."

His refusal to look at her told her something was wrong. "What's going on? It isn't the kids."

"No. I-I need your advice on something."

"Donny, I'm a little busy. Larry went home early and left me in charge of closing."

"I-I don't have anyone to turn to. I'm desperate. Look at me, I'm shaking," Donald said, revealing to Lisa his hands.

"Everything is going to be alright. You sit down over here." Donald gave a hesitant nod as Lisa led him to a booth.

Donald asked, "Did I catch you at a bad time?"

"Don't worry about it." She patted him on the back. "Stay here while I go fix you something to eat."

Within minutes Lisa returned with hot chicken soup and a sandwich to find Donald with his head in his hands. An empty atmosphere surrounded the diner and all that could be heard were sighs of worry. It appeared her brother, with each visit, was developing into a different man.

Lisa set the food in front of him, placed a napkin in his lap, and sat across the table. With a low register she spoke to him, the soft lilt of her voice helping to calm him. "Come on, I've heated you some soup. It'll make you feel better."

Donald tried to eat to please her, but found the burden too big. "I don't think I'm gonna make it, Lisa. It's too much." He threw the spoon into the bowl and shielded his face with his calloused hands.

"What's too much?"

"Don't be stupid. That's one thing I know you're not." Lisa di- dn't respond. "Look, the damn landlord raised the rent $10 last month *and* they're docking my pay at the store." Donald wiped the fresh sweat from his brow and folded back his sleeves.

"Why?" asked Lisa.

"I don't know. You can't begin to imagine what I'm forced to deal with. The public will spit in your face and look down on you like garbage. Every single day I'm forced to deal with it, Lisa."

Donald softened, "I'm sorry. You just don't know how bad it is out there. Last week a man and woman in heat hailed me down and played some back seat bingo between Central Park South and Amsterdam." Lisa exhibited a look of disgust.

"Rebecca...she doesn't understand." His tanned skin progres- sed to a red tint, and the restless bags beneath his eyes turned white. "She's been so caught up in her studies that she expects my hard-earned money to fall out of the sky. And when I tell her we have to cut back on certain things, she...she henpecks me."

Donald took her hand and stroked it with his thumb. "If I had my way, I'd make Rebecca drop out of law school, but every time I think of bringing it up, I tell myself, "Hey, if she does, all of the money you've invested might as well have been thrown into the incinerator." What do you suggest I do?"

Lisa huffed, "You may not think so now, but Rebecca going to school will be better for the whole family. That was the plan, was it not?"

"Assuming she passes, *and* if we can make it till then. That re-dheaded vixen is bleeding me dry." Donald toyed with his soup as though trying to acquire hunger. "Maybe we should move to the Adirondacks or something. I don't know."

"Don't be silly."

"We're as poor as Job's turkey. Oh, and I forgot to mention the car. I had to put the piece of junk into the shop again."

"Attorneys make loads of money these days, Donny."

"Well, to be honest, it's not all Rebecca...it-it's the kids. I don't want them to endure the troubles you and I had."

"I know." Lisa didn't care to open the conversation to those particular memories for either one of them and changed it to a happier one. "Do you remember the time that..." Lisa fought to speak through the laughter. "That Mom made me pick you up from school and I got sidetracked on the way."

"Because you had a crush on that Peter character." Donald scoffed. "I was eight and we lived more than twenty blocks from the school."

"I'll have you know Peter Nesmith was an upstanding young man."

Donald dug deeper to get a rise out of her. "If I remember cor-rectly, you were grounded because I walked home alone."

"Big deal," Lisa shrugged.

"It rained you know. All the same, Peter Nesmith was a no-class bum and only dated you 'cause he wanted sex." Donald's stomach jerked as he held in his laughter.

"You better watch it, you little..."

They both chuckled. Donald looked on her with idealized affection for a brief moment. Lisa flipped open the notepad she used to jot down orders. Donald spoke no words as he observed her writing down numbers, but a grin began to grow at the edges of his mouth.

Lisa slid the pad in front of him. "Will this be sufficient enough for your needs?" Donald was fortunate to have a sister such as Lisa. This wasn't the first time he had delighted in said fortunes of her generous heart.

"Yes, it's quite sufficient, but Lisa…"

"It should get you by for now. It's not a lot, but it's all I can afford. At least you won't be scraping the bottom of the barrel."

"Lisa, I…" Donald was grateful, but his guilt remained. He wanted to put these feelings into words.

"I promise you, Donny, even if I have to give you every paycheck I receive from now until the day I die, I won't let you go under." Donald leaned over the table and kissed her cheek.

"Lisa, um, could you keep this from Rebecca? I don't want her to know, because…you know."

"Sure, Donny. Just eat your soup before you collapse." Lisa smiled at her little brother whose mood and appetite had changed for the better.

DUE TO DONALD'S PRIDE, REBECCA WAS NEVER TOLD of Lisa's generosity. Since their talk, his relationship with his wife had furthermore improved. So much so that he surprised Rebecca with a bouquet of lush red roses. He couldn't afford them, but they were necessary.

"It's a beautiful day," Donald began. "Do you have any plans?"

"Lisa and I are going shopping," answered Rebecca primping her flowers.

Donald assisted Rebecca with her coat. "Maxine should have the kids back long before I get home," he said.

"We'll be finished by then."

"And could you pick up some milk while you're out?"

"No, I thought we'd browse in some of those designer shops." He ceased in movement for a split-second. "I did say "browse".

Donald kissed her and opened the door to leave. "Okay...well, you two have a good time then."

Rebecca kidded him. "Be careful not to run over anybody. Oh Donald, can you give me a lift to the subway?"

Donald glanced at his watch, "I'm ten minutes late as it is. You'll have to take a cab." He dug into pocket and placed some change in her hand. "Here. For the fare."

Rebecca met Lisa at the corner of her place where they started off. Upon their arrival, casing the assorted stores, they became one with the abundant activity of thousands of New Yorkers: Constantly hurried people shoving one another to get to the place they needed to go as if their lives depended on getting there. The beauty of the majestic skyscrapers as sunshine bounced off the glass and profuse bedazzling lights are facets that one could never ignore, but flourish within man's greatest creation of commerce and culture.

The air was thick with the constant hum of engines and honking horns. Lisa's mind succumbed to deep thought, leaving Rebecca to chatter at the wind. Her mind, focused on the common madness encircling her, leapt to a prudish aristocrat arguing with the negligent cabbie who had backed into his prized automobile, a woman disciplining her fussy child, and the large pack of leather clad teenagers drinking and shouting profanity.

The two women kept up with the rushing crowd. "Which store do you want to go into first? A furrier!" Rebecca grabbed Lisa's hand and pulled her in.

Donning furs of the upmost quality, they dreamt of strutting down Sunset Boulevard emerged with the celebrities of the time. Other patrons saw them as intruding parasites they didn't have the legal authority to dispose of.

"Rebecca, this fur is $600!" Lisa was astonished and held the costly ermine as if it were some deadly toxin. The sensation of the fleece lying across her arm was silky and inviting.

"Too bad, you look, oh...what's the phrase the teens use?" Rebecca snapped her fingers. "Gas! Your outfit is a gas."

Lisa turned back-and-forth in front of the three-sided mirror. "Do I look Grace Kelly gas or Deborah Kerr gas?"

"Neither. You're more like Judy Garland gas."

Rebecca glided her hand upon each mink coat and stole with envy as though attempting to remember every stitch simply by touching the luxury she would never have again. "You know, Lisa, it's a shame when a woman has to struggle for the beautiful things God intended us to have." She practically stated this to herself as she ran her hand down a snow-white sable.

"I know better than to go into all these shops."

Lisa uttered not one word, but prepared herself for the rant she heard many times before.

Rebecca walked to the mirror and felt of the bargain fabric she was wearing. "I don't know if Donald has told you this, but... God." She couldn't look at herself in the surrounding mirrors as she told Lisa of their deep financial woes. "You see, my husband and I are having difficulties with our marriage."

Lisa exhaled. *This is why she asked me to go shopping with her. She wants to unload on me, too.*

"I didn't want to tell you, but I have no one else. For the past six years Donald has badgered me about going to college and if it was the right thing to do."

Lisa shook her head. She understood why Donald was upset to the extent that he was. Rebecca was spoiled, and Donald had done all within his power to keep her as satisfied as financially possible.

"Rebecca, you of all people should understand what he's going through."

"Yes, and every night when he gets home, I have to hear about how *hard* he has it."

"He does have it hard."

"Maybe, but I have it no less. Do you have any idea how much shit I would catch if I happened to fail the exam? I don't think he would ever let me live it down."

Lisa felt it her duty to defend her brother. "You act as though you think Donny doesn't love you anymore."

Rebecca drew a coat from the rack and held it in front of her. "Lisa, feast your eyes on this coat." Lisa was becoming angry. "My grandmother once owned a coat such as this. My mother, by the time she was fifty, owned four of these.

"I owned two. I grew up in a luxurious neighborhood, was taught in a private school. The Du Plissé's were at the top of the social ladder. Then my father died.

"We were forced to sell everything, with the exception of a few paintings we managed to hang on to with a death grip. My father would roll over in his grave if he found out I was living in the Bronx on Melrose."

Rebecca's voice cracked, "Do you remember my mother?" Lisa took the coat from her and hung it back. "When I married Donald, I didn't care that he was poor. I knew I wasn't going to live the life I'd previously led. I tried making the adjustments, but I thought that I would at least have total support from him."

"Have you told Donny this?"

"He wouldn't understand. I tried to get him to move us to Massachusetts once. Mother wanted me to go to Harvard, but *no.*" Rebecca mocked Donald's voice. *"We can't go to Massachusetts. It's not practical."*

Lisa pulled a handkerchief from her handbag and handed it to Rebecca. "I know my brother. I practically raised him. And I know for a fact he works like a dog. Not just for the family, but for *you.*

"That man adores you. I remember when he'd come home from school and all he could talk about is the gorgeous redhead with the blue eyes. You're his wife for God's sake."

"I don't think Donald could ever love me as much as you."

"Stop it. Dry your eyes and listen." Lisa turned Rebecca around to face her. "You go to school and study all that you need to pass the exam.

"In the meantime, you let Donald worry about the bills and expenses. He'll see to it everything will be fine. I'm sure you miss the old life, but you'll have to make do with what you have for now."

They took a taxi down Fifth Avenue into Tiffany's, a boutique filled with women's delights and caprices. Walking along the glass cases, they became enthralled by glistening visions of tiaras, diamond necklaces, brooches, and rings of all fashions and carats.

At least Rebecca could reminisce.

# CHAPTER THREE

It was the first of the week. Lisa dragged herself out of bed, made her regular cup of black coffee, and sat at the kitchen table draped in her robe before going to work.

She brushed the hair out of her eyes and a familiar feeling came over her. In a moment of weakness, she longed for Robert. It was the voice of Alma that kept creeping into her head, screaming, *"I haven't seen you with anyone since Robert..."* In her mind, those words were nails on a chalkboard. It was painful serving all those couples every day.

11:00 a.m. crept up. She had already served seventy people at most. It advanced to the time of day when the diner would be mostly empty until lunch at noon. She breathed a sigh of relief and fell on a stool.

The bell sounded. She lifted her head.

Standing in the doorway was a man she had never seen. He was a fine-looking gent with a stocky build, glossy, dark flaxen hair, about forty. He fashionably bore a white turtleneck and dark blue blazer, lovingly intermeshed with white trousers and fedora.

This was not one of the regulars.

Six-foot-two, stout – the muscles on his arms were apparent through the thick material of his jacket. He stood with one hand in pocket, scrutinizing the restaurant. He ambled in and took a seat in a far booth next to a window facing the street. Lisa rose from the counter and pulled out her pad and pencil.

"What can I start you off with, sir?" Lisa asked, using her waitressing charm as she presented him with the menu.

The gentleman grabbed the menu from her hand. "I'll be ordering breakfast," he demanded.

"Breakfast ended fifteen minutes ago. Sorry."

"I happen to be in the mood for breakfast."

"Well, I'm afraid I can't. Lunch is being fixed as we speak. The most I can do for you now is a cold snack."

He had a clipped style of speaking. "I understand, dear lady, but a customer should be able to order...what he wants." He finally looked up to see Lisa's delicate face and grinned in the pleasures of his view.

"What is your name, sir?"

"Mallory," he spoke in a much softer tone, painting every visible inch of Lisa with his eyes.

"I'm sorry, Mr. Mallory, breakfast is closed and if you want..."

"I'll take whatever you have on the lunch menu then."

"What?"

"I'll take whatever you have."

"Well, what is it you want?"

"I really don't care, Ms..." He checked her uniform for her name tag which stated her first name. "Ms. Lisa. You are a Ms., aren't you? I do hope so."

Lisa gave a hint of a smile. "I don't see how that's any of your concern."

"You know, Ms. Lisa, I find your behavior inacceptable."

"I beg your pardon? You won't tell me what you want. I'm not here to make assumptions, Mr. Mallory."

"Please...call me James."

In exhaustion, Lisa's head fell to the floor. "Please understand, James, I'm running on a short leash and do not have the energy to argue with you or anybody else."

James leaned over the edge of the booth closer to her. "Want to tell me about it?"

Larry stormed out of the kitchen after observing the scene. "What's going on here? Lisa, I have never known you to argue with a customer. I apologize for my employee's conduct, sir. Let *me* take your order."

James looked at Lisa. "No need." James stood; her eyes followed. "Forgive me, Ms. Lisa.

"Let me make it up to you by treating you to lunch. When is your break?"

Larry answered for her, "Not for another hour."

"Well, I'm sure you won't mind if she takes it now. Go get your things, Ms. Lisa. I'll be outside."

Lisa couldn't stop watching her employer as he exhaled fiercely. She was torn. She wanted to go, but dreaded later having to come back to an irate boss.

James stood on the corner farther up the street. *What the hell are you doing, Lisa? No customer has done this before.* She walked towards him.

James reached out and grasped her elbow. "So, Ms. Lisa, where do you dine for lunch?"

"Nowhere. I whip me up something in the diner."

"Alright then, where would you like to go?"

"Look buster, I don't know you. It's your fault I got into trouble in the first place." Lisa turned away from him and faced the stone buildings as if the rejection would cause him to leave.

"I see. Well, why don't we go back into the diner and you can whip up something for the both of us?" Lisa still ignored him.

James took a step closer. His warm breath touched her hair. "Please?"

Lisa gazed into his sapphire eyes. They appeared so gentle and so firm. After all, it wasn't every day that she got picked up by a man like this one.

"Alright, but you pick the place."

"How does The Château sound?" James puffed out his chest in pride, prepared to flex his financial stability.

"I've never heard of it."

"Oh. It's a posh club for the upper-classes which offers the best cuisine and wine assortments. You must be a registered member to get in."

"I'm not a member."

"You're with me. I'll register you in as a guest. We'll need transportation." Lisa walked to the curb to hail a cab. "No, no, there's no need for that.

"I'm parked about a block away. Follow me."

When they reached the next block, Lisa's jaw plummeted in response to the eye-catching, blue 1957 Mercedes-Benz sedan tucked away from the public. James opened the passenger door and held out his hand for her to accept it. A warm smile came across his face as she placed her petite hand into his. She stepped in adoring the white upholstery and fragrant interior.

James pulled into the long train of traffic. He would occasionally glance at Lisa in amusement to find her acting as if this was her first ride in an automobile. The stunning impression James left was equally matched once arriving at the club.

They strolled inside arm in arm. Lisa had never before been subjected to such riches. They passed through the revolving glass doors and a blast of exquisiteness stole her breath away. The well-mannered Maître d' greeted them and relieved them of their coats. A second man dressed in a black tuxedo then appeared to show them to their table and obliged Lisa by pushing her up to the tables' edge.

The Château, with its dim lighting and soothing atmosphere, gave Lisa the equal feeling of a fish out of water. It was not the decorative flowered walls or the striking chandeliers that dangled above the polished marble floor. Nor was it the pianist gliding his hands up and down the Steinway beside the fireplace. It was the attire of the wealthy patrons, and their heads were turning.

Compared to other women, Lisa, in her black turtleneck and plaid skirt, was underdressed. She began noticing each woman in the club peep at her from the corner of their eyes. She felt self-conscious and hid behind her menu, not discerning all the arrogant Almas in the room with their cigarettes.

"James, I wanna leave."

James lowered his menu. "What's the matter?"

"I don't like it here. Please, can we leave?" she asked in a beseeching manner.

He was puzzled at first and then noticed her eyes shifting. "You don't have to worry about them, Ms. Lisa. They may be rich, but they've no variety in their lives. You're something new to gawk at."

Lisa rose out of her chair. James caught her wrist. "One lunch – that's all I ask."

How could Lisa resist him? She was nervous as hell, but it felt nice. She smiled faintly and sat back down.

James asked, "Have you decided what you want?"

"Whatever you're having, I guess."

"I having shrimp."

Lisa grimaced. "In that case I'll have this...specialty hamburger here."

"A hamburger? That's what you want?"

"Yes, ham-bur-ger."

"Sam?" He waved at the waiter nearby.

"James Mallory!"

"Hiya, Sam."

"It's good to see you again." Lisa noticed the classy waiter wore satin pants. "It's been some time since you've paid us a visit. This must be a special occasion. Well, well, well..." He saw James's lady sitting across the table.

"Sam," James cautioned.

"Gettin' back on the horse again?" Sam whispered. "Well, what can I get you two?"

James ordered for the both of them. "I'll have the crevettes and the lady will have the specialty hamburger. And we'll each have a glass of Chablis from France, please."

"Right away. I'll be back with your orders in a few."

Lisa could feel James staring at her. She did her best to ignore it.

"Tell me, Ms. Lisa..."

"Why do you keep calling me that?"

James kept folding and unfolding his napkin. "I don't know. It fits you. I mean, you're short, or compared to me you are anyway, and the freckles on your turned-up nose, I find it adorable." Lisa covered her mouth with her hand to hide her smile.

"But never mind. Tell me about yourself."

"What's there to tell? I work as a waitress in a small diner. I live in a fair apartment here in Manhattan, and, as I'm sure you can tell..." She leaned in. "I'm not all that rich."

James hung on her every word as he studied every curve and ridge of her face. "Why would I care about that? By the way, what is your last name?"

"Frisco."

"Lisa Frisco. Different. I like it."

This man was different. This man was special to a woman like Lisa who was susceptible. He was attractive, conceivably rich, and polite. Of course she had met many a gentleman prior to this day, but this one was showing interest. She wanted to find out more.

"What is it that you do?"

"I'm a doctor. Been in the profession for, oh, going on twelve years now."

"What kind of doctor?"

"An M.D. I'm from St. Louis. But I enjoyed New York so much that I decided I might as well live here. I also must keep an eye on my clinics."

"You have your own clinic?"

"Yes. I have a smaller one in St. Louis, but I'm fonder of Manhattan so I've been working on refining this one."

Lisa exhaled, "I'm sick of the Big Apple myself, all the way to the core. I've thought about leaving, but I have a family."

James froze. "A family?"

"Yes, my brother and his kids. I could never leave them. They're all I have."

James laid his warm hand on top of hers. She delighted in it for five seconds or more and retracted it and laid them both timidly in her lap.

Sam returned with the food and set it before them. "Does everything appear satisfactory?" asked Sam.

James placed a napkin in his lap. "Yes, Sam. Thank you."

"Good. Let me know if you need anything."

"Wait a minute," Lisa spoke out, dissecting her hamburger. "What is this? This...hamburger is soggy and draped in mushrooms."

"That is the only burger on our menu. Would you like me to take it back?"

"It's just not what I expected." She spoke to James. "I suppose my palate is not adapted to upper-class food."

Lisa knew she revealed too much to someone she didn't know. Never before had she divulged such personal information to just anyone and couldn't understand why she told him. It had been years since Lisa had been with a man.

Robert was the last. This promise that she repeatedly reminded herself of continued to creep into her mind on the ride back. It was, upon her finger, the indentation of her previous vow. As she held her hands in her lap, she couldn't help but stare at it, as it remained a constant reminder of what was.

When they returned to the diner Lisa sat motionless attempting to conjure up the precise words to express her gratitude for the kindness he had shown her. James stepped out to open her door. She wanted to see him again regardless her mind was congested with thoughts of what could be and what shouldn't.

James was attracted to this woman he knew little about and wanted to see her again. What he was unaware of was her similar feelings toward him, but what was he to say to a woman appearing to have no interest at all?

Lisa walked away as leisurely as she could in the optimistic hopes that he would stop her. James hesitated one moment too long.

Lisa was gone.

There he stood, still contemplating what to say. In frustration of his delay, James slammed the door shut and drove away, leaving Lisa to wonder why he didn't follow her in.

LISA, ACTING THE PART OF THE WOMAN SHE HAD BECOME, refused to let her heart take control. It took years of heartache to get this far. She worked hard to take her mind off this latest fixation.

Morning, noon, and night he dominated Lisa's mind. She couldn't seem to forget the velvety resonance of his voice, the luster of his blond hair, and blue periwinkle eyes. Or above all: His picturesque smile. She dwelled on the welfare of her heart as she hoped this was another foolish fancy that might return one day.

*Why did I let him go?* Lisa asked lying in bed one night, tossing and turning with mental discomfort. *He can't be worth all the worry and bother.* She recalled her past mistakes and threw this upon the stack of experience.

With this new commitment fresh in her mind, she refused to let James Mallory have any further effect. Within the short time she spent with him her feelings were somewhat identical to those she felt when she met Robert. She had been to that movie and didn't care to see it again.

But this day James came into the diner, taking a seat in the same booth as before. Lisa knew the moment he entered the room. She was never happier to see anyone's face. He hadn't forgotten her.

She pondered what to say and how to approach him, but the surrounding distractions were too much. Lisa dashed to the restroom and splashed cold water on her face. *What am I going to say?*

"How can...how *may* I help you? – No. – Would you like some breakfast? Hey James, what can I get you? – God, that's awful."

Lisa's rehearsal only made it worse. She stood so rigid that, had she fallen, she might have broken into pieces. His booth drew closer with each passing table. His head turned suddenly and she panicked and veered in another direction.

"Excuse me?" James vied for Lisa's attention.

Lisa turned. He caught her pretty face in that instant. The pleasures of his view had not dwindled in their week of separation.

Lisa was pleased also, but neglected to display similar feelings. Three years of practicing her poker face was paying off.

"What'll it be?" Lisa wiped the table with a drenched rag, raking water on James's suit and wingtip shoes.

"How have you been, Ms. Lisa?"

"Do you need a minute or do you have a preference?"

"I apologize for waiting so long to see you."

Lisa made a special point to look at her wristwatch. "It's half past ten. Would you favor some breakfast?"

James grunted in frustration.

"I have other customers. You have thirty seconds."

"You're timing me?!"

"Twenty-five."

"Fine. I don't want breakfast. I actually would favor some lunch." Lisa had not yet looked him in the eye until that moment. "Maybe when lunch rolls around, I'll order dinner...dessert first."

That did it.

Lisa blushed like a teenager. It was hard not to succumb to youth's coyness. Her pink cheeks lifted in alignment. She opened her mouth to speak, but all that departed was air. This was enough for James.

"You know what, Ms. Lisa, I'm not that hungry. Sorry I bothered you." James stood up from the booth.

"You're leaving?"

"I'm afraid so." He tipped his hat to her and left.

She couldn't believe it. Lisa tore off her apron and stomped into the kitchen. As far as she was concerned her shift was over for the day. She marched past Larry who was serving a customer.

"Fill in for me, Larry. I'm going."

Larry excused himself and chased Lisa outside. "Wait one minute. What is this nonsense? How stupid do you think I am?

"Did you think I wasn't aware of that guy coming in again, or you running around like a lunatic?"

"Larry..."

"No Lisa, you've worked for me too long to fall to pieces because *one* handsome man out of millions happened to show a tiny interest in you. You're stronger than that."

"You're right. I've only been out with him the once." Larry put his arm around her and led her back inside. "Keeping your mind busy is the best medicine."

"Waitress!" yelled an old man from across the room, flagging her down as if she were a cabbie.

Lisa walked past the table where James once sat and took notice to a white card on the floor. There was writing on it.

*Across the street when you get off work. See you then, Ms. Lisa James, the breakfast man*

Turning over the card, Lisa saw that it was a business card containing James Mallory's clinic information. She worked as hard as ever, for there was something at the end of her shift that she could look forward to, a real reward to say the least. Unfortunately, it was Saturday – the one day of the week the diner served dinner, which meant she wouldn't get off until late.

9:00 p.m. arrived. Even at that time there were still the select regulars, all men, either finishing their orders or postponing going home to their wives. Larry was conversing with one of them. This was something she wanted to deter. She had something just outside waiting for her.

"I'm leaving, Larry."

"Hey!" Larry yelled. Her body was halfway out the door. "You have yourself a good night and I'll see you on Monday."

"See you Monday."

She rushed across the street and scanned each head that came to view. Back-and-forth she turned in search of that handsome blond-haired man. The suspense of being in his company was taking its toll and she couldn't wait.

The street was much visible by ongoing neon. It would have been impossible to miss him. Thinking she may have read wrong, she pulled the card from her handbag and read it again. *"Across the street..."*

Two large hands came from behind and grazed Lisa's waist from both sides, proceeding then to a soft embrace.

"Hi," James whispered in her ear. She smiled, turning her head upwards. He turned her gently around. "Come, Ms. Lisa. Walk with me."

Lisa remained captivated as he began to speak unlike before. "I thought you would never come out. I've missed you."

"Did you, James?"

"Yes, and you know what else?" They both stopped. He took Lisa's hands and held them to his chest. "I've been thinking about you every second that I've been away."

He took her head and leaned in to kiss her. Nearer he came where the heat of breath was felt, only to be obstructed within inches of tasting them. Lisa turned away. She would not look at him.

"Lisa?" James turned her head back. She tried turning away again, but his masculine hands would not permit it.

"Something isn't right. There's something inside me that's telling me this is wrong."

James released her. "I-I don't know what to say."

Lisa pulled her purse strap onto her shoulder in despair. She tried to think of something, anything to say. She wasn't even certain what she meant.

After all the fretting and wondering if he felt the same, now that she knew the feeling was mutual, she turned on him. The sudden reject was an instinctive reflex. Lisa became accustomed to living without a man's touch. Bouncing back would not be easy.

They walked in silence. Soon they came across a bench and decided to sit. James laid his arm on the back behind Lisa. "Are you alright?" he asked. "I mean, have you been doing okay?"

"Why didn't you come to see me?"

"I did! I swear I came to see you every single day since that day I met you. I was afraid the feeling wasn't mutual." James put his hand to Lisa's cheek. "I would rather remember that precious smile you gave to me across the table at The Château."

"I wouldn't have rejected you." James placed his other hand upon her face, embracing, admiring. "James, before we take this further, there are things I must tell you, things about me you should know."

"In time, Lisa, in time…you're worth the wait."

TWO WEEKS LATER – Lisa and James had become a genuine couple. The solitude had become a way of life for Lisa. Now she dined in the most elegant restaurants, visited the picture show, browsed in the finest art galleries, and attended the orchestra.

The Palladium, The Imperial, and Roseland were developing into a haven. Lisa had a companion to share with her all these merriments; two weeks of becoming acquainted with one another to the point of tranquility.

"Surprise, my darling," said James as he withdrew flowers from behind his back. Lisa gasped at the sight of the lavender orchids. "…a little something special for a little someone special." He gazed on her favorably top-to-bottom. Her chestnut hair tickled the gold chain necklace resting on her collarbone.

How sophisticated and wealthy she appeared to be was novel, and she savored it like fine wine. James led her to his new Rolls-Royce Silver Cloud, purchased in part by trade a week before. Such an automobile glistened under evening light with its burgundy finish.

In all the time they spent together, she so desired to kiss this man, but always an alarm inside her was triggered, causing her to halt her advances. What if he was like Robert?

This had gone on long enough. It was time to move on and move in. His real intentions, whatever they were, no longer mattered. Tonight was the night she was going to face the man she believed was a better man.

They browsed the lineup of different films showing at the cinema. Lisa scanned the marque, keeping in mind her plan, and saw *South Pacific*, a beautiful romantic musical possessing all the facets needed to set an ideal mood. Lisa had difficulty paying attention all through the picture. All she could think about was the man sitting beside her.

It wasn't until Emile starting singing "Some Enchanted Evening" that she felt a tingling inside and her heart raced like never before. She was almost scared to set her eyes on James. What a wonderful man he was to have been so patient.

This was the time. Lisa inhaled deeply to ready herself. But before she could move, James pulled her to him and kissed her.

Is this really happening? He's kissing me.

Her mind became blank, occupied in relishing in the damp sweetness of James's warm and silky lips. They parted. He was so calm and Lisa trembled like a baby.

He swept the bangs from her eyes. She shimmered as an angel from heaven and he couldn't resist. His hands come up from the chair onto her shoulders and they kissed again.

Whether she knew it or not, James had her. For the remainder of the movie their hands were locked. Still, Lisa could not focus. Their first kiss kept replaying in her mind, like the song, again and again.

Afterward, James drove around until he found a secluded place to park, beneath a large sycamore tree where the moon gleamed in long strips of white in the car. James leaned over and situated his arm around her. Lisa leaned in slowly for another kiss, hoping he too would move in until their heads met. Instead, he pulled her down onto his lap and kissed her passionately.

"Lisa, I-I want to be a part of your life." Lisa stroked his smooth hair as he spoke to her. "You have no idea what you've done – what you're doing to me. Never in my life would I have thought I'd fall for a waitress, and how I'm falling fast.

"I'm concerned that I may hit the ground too hard." James pulled her closer. "Lisa...I...I...God, I love you."

Now all that flooded her mind was if she loved him back.

"I understand that what I *do* know about you isn't much and I want to rectify that. I want to meet your family, your friends. Don't be afraid to open yourself up to me. Nothing in this world can keep me away. Not even you."

*Nothing in this world can keep me away.* His words wouldn't leave her that night as she tried to sleep. However, they caused her to remember what she had to tell him – Robert Frisco.

Would he stay knowing she had been married? The longer she waited, the harder it was going to be for both of them. This was the one subject Lisa dreaded. She couldn't bear losing this man.

Lisa tossed and turned all night. All she could think about was Robert, a man who betrayed her, a man she hated.

# CHAPTER FOUR

❝...and this is my little brother, Donald. Donny, this is James.”

James held out his hand. Donald scrutinized him. He was hesitant. “Nice to meet you,” Donald said sharply, grabbing his hand rather forcefully like it was a dreaded chore he wanted to be done with.

“Come in and make yourself at home,” Rebecca invited. “Dinner will be soon.” She motioned for them to sit. The sofa on which they sat was a yellowish hue that had become pallid through years of use.

James couldn't help noticing the clash of conventional and opulent décor. At the bottom of the wall were cartoon drawings, obviously drawn by children. Donald and Rebecca sat in the chairs across from them.

Donald began, “So where are you from?”

James was interrupted by children's voices as they came running out of their bedroom.

“Aunt Lisa!” Simon and Julia yelled in unison. Simon, once again, knocked down his sister and jumped into Lisa's lap.

“Ouch! James, these are my niece and nephew.” Lisa nuzzled them close to her body. “This here is Simon. Say hello to the nice gentleman, Simon.”

“Hello.” Simon leapt off Lisa and grabbed Stanley who mewed for help. “Hey mister, have you met Stanley?” Simon shoved the furry feline in his face.

Donald yelled, “Simon, get the cat out of the man's face!” Simon jumped back on her lap with Stanley.

"This pretty girl is Julia. I call her Strawberry. What do you say?" Unlike her brother, Julia was very shy, especially around male strangers. All she did was bury her face in Aunt Lisa's chest.

"Hey princess, you don't have to be afraid of me. I'm your friend." James pulled out a Life Saver from his pocket and gave her his irresistible smile. Julia smiled and a little "thank you" came out.

"Come on you two, get off Aunt Lisa and go play in your room," Rebecca ordered. Julia wouldn't take her eyes off James. Even in the eyes of a three-year-old he was something special.

Donald continued, "Anyway, you were about to tell us where you're from."

"St. Louis, Missouri."

"I was there once," added Rebecca. "My father was flying down on corporate business of some sort, so he took my mother and I along; such a charming town, St. Louis."

Donald was observing James's apparels closely. His own trousers were worn and his shirt was a faded white, unlike James, whose suit smelled of class.

"What is it you do for a living?" asked Donald. "My guess would be something nice." Lisa was slightly startled by this.

"I'm a doctor."

Lisa added, "He owns two clinics; one on the Upper East Side and one in his hometown."

Donald was polite but indifferent. "I guess we'll know who to turn to if one of us gets sick then."

Rebecca left the conversation, or grilling as the direction seemed to be heading. "I'll get things set in the kitchen."

"Would you like some assistance?" James uncrossed his legs and scooted to the edge.

"No, you're our guest, Dr. Mallory." Donald folded his hands in his lap and stiffened his demeanor as if preparing for an interrogation. "A doctor!" he exclaimed. "Tell me, how long did it take you?"

James was puzzled.

"I mean the two clinics. That is quite an accomplishment. I'm not smart enough to go about doing that even if I wanted to. You must be a smart man."

Rebecca poked her head around the corner. "Donald, get the kids washed up...*please*?" Lisa figured Rebecca was giving her a hand. She must have picked up on the tension. Donald hadn't spoken to his sister yet that evening, almost like he was avoiding her.

Lisa waited until he was out of the room. "What do you think?"

James sweetly picked the loose brown hairs from her blouse. "I like them. That Julia is a darling, and beautiful."

"She looks like her mother. Her disposition though is not that of Rebecca's. Rebecca can be stubborn, and she isn't shy. What... what about my brother?"

Rebecca appeared at the kitchen door. "Time to eat."

The table was small and draped in a red and white checkerboard cloth. Because the table could seat only four, Simon had to sit away from the adults at a card table while Julia sat next to her mother in a highchair. The meal was simple fare. They each began to serve themselves.

"I made my ever-special pizza with mozzarella and tomato and a tossed salad. I hope you like it, James."

"I'm sure it's delicious."

Lisa stared at the food on her plate and grinned. "You know, I was just thinking about the time Donny decided he would make dinner. I recall you were pregnant with Simon and D-Donny..." Lisa laughed. "He attempted to make a meatloaf.

"Donny, I didn't know meatloaf was black." Donald rested his chin on his fist, throwing out a sarcastic chuckle. "That was before little brother learnt to cook."

"How did you meet?" Rebecca asked taking a bite.

"James was a customer at the diner. He came before the lunch rush wanting breakfast."

"She wouldn't feed me. I begged and pleaded but she wouldn't give in. So I treated her to lunch."

"Where'd you take her, James? Somewhere romantic?" Rebecca laid her fork down. Donald lifted his head up from his plate taking an immediate notice to his wife's sudden interest in his sister's love life.

"I took Ms. Lisa to The Château."

Donald's eyes widened with Rebecca's.

"Oh, I've always wanted to go there," said Rebecca. "I once read an article on The Château, about how elegant a restaurant it is." Donald's silence was broken by clanking silverware and deliberate throat sounds.

James followed Rebecca's lead. "How did you and Donald meet?"

"I was thirteen. Lisa just moved Donald and herself to Manhattan, where I was living at the time. We often took the same bus to our schools. When it was cold out, he would lend me his jacket."

Lisa interjected, "Donny, bless his heart, was an annoyance talking about Rebecca all the time." They all chuckled except Donald who no longer ate, but played with his food like his son. The veins in his head protruded as James found amusement at his expense.

Rebecca said, "Our anniversary was last month. Seven years." She pondered briefly then changed the subject. "Dr. Mallory, I find running two clinics so far apart a miracle.

"I don't know how you manage it. Neither have I ever heard of a doctor doing it. You must enjoy your profession."

Donald took a large gulp of water and slammed the glass down onto the table. Lisa drew her attention away for an instant.

"It puts bread on the table with a little to spare. But it takes a lot of planning and time management. Of course, I have supervisors to my aide, as well as doctors, but the constant running from state-to-state can be mind-numbing. I often recall one earlier patient of mine..."

"Just how much do you make in a year?" Donald blurted out, his hands bracing the tables' edges.

"Donny!" Lisa jumped up, shoving the chair back with her legs. "The living room. Now." Donald pushed the hair out of his eyes and obeyed.

"What is the matter with you?!" Lisa yelled through a hiss, not waiting to see if he was behind her. "What have you got to say for yourself?

"Mom and Dad taught you better than this. *I* taught you better than this." Donald showed that he was beginning to realize the insolence of his actions. "I'm waiting."

He put his hands in his pockets and scuffed his feet on the floor like a child. "I'm sorry."

"That's it? No explanation?" She crossed her arms as she looked up at her brother in search of reason.

"Lisa, I-I...I can't stand this guy." Donald lifted his hand before she could respond. "If you need the whole song and dance...I work like a dog, even with your help, and I hate his arrogance. *"It puts bread on the table,"* my ass. His employees work while he rakes in the proceeds."

Donald moved aside, "Look at my wife. She's eating all this up. Go ahead, take a gander."

Rebecca was smiling head-to-toe with a perpetual gleam. She was probably recollecting her past life of abundance and wealth that she could now relive through this handsome guest.

Lisa poked his chest with her finger. "How could you be so selfish? This man means a lot to me. I never said anything against Rebecca, did I?"

"No, but..."

"But *what*?"

"You liked Rebecca and she liked you. To compare the two is one-sided of you, Lisa."

Rebecca yelled from the kitchen, "Is everything alright in there?"

"In a minute!" Donald turned his head back around. "Look, Sis, I'm sorry. I don't know what more you want me to say." He gestured a big shrug, then let his arms fall down onto his pants with a smack.

"You just watch what you say from here on out."

James hadn't understood the specifics of what was happening, but knew it was because of him. The table was silent. There was the possibility that her brother and the man she might love may not get along. Lisa felt helpless.

Donald threw a quick glance at his sister. By resuming the dialog between him and her boyfriend he thought he could lighten her discomfort. She would be expecting it. In truth, Lisa was hoping he wouldn't say another word for the rest of the evening.

"James...it's uh, good you make a decent living."

Lisa tensed up, preparing for another jab. James smiled and took a bite of the chocolate cake Rebecca made for dessert.

"It's good to know you have a better financial status than Robert did anyway."

Lisa dropped her fork.

James looked up at Donald. "Who is Robert?"

Lisa was panicking inside. He knew. She couldn't lie. She waited too long.

"Uh, James, I-I never told you."

Donald covered his mouth.

Lisa couldn't bear to look at James. "I was married. It was a long time ago and it didn't work out. Robert was..."

"Do you love him?"

"What?"

"You heard."

"I assure you there is nothing to worry about."

"The hell there is."

Everyone was silent. Julia began to weep. Rebecca wanted to say something, but knew this was more important.

"I don't care that you've been married, Lisa. I don't even care that you kept something this important from me in the month we've been together, through all the quiet moments when you could have told me. All that matters is if you still have feelings for him."

Lisa's hands shook in her lap. A warm hand grasped them from beneath the table. It was going to be okay.

She looked into his blue eyes and spoke the word she knew to be true. "No."

James leaned over to kiss her cheek and she met him halfway. James finally knew, and what a relief it was. There was no need to tell him of their relationship and why they busted up.

They each resumed eating their cake, except Rebecca who had taken Julia into the kids' room for a nap. Donald couldn't stop gnawing his lip. He wanted to apologize, but knew it would be no good, as he understood the odds that were against him.

Lisa peered across the table at her brother knowing what he said was intentional. *How could he? I've never asked anything of him.* She grew angrier the more she thought of his egotism. But she maintained her temper by refusing to speak or even glance at him.

There still remained something strange about this Mallory guy that Donald did not like. This was a hunch. No matter how hard he tried, he couldn't bring himself to even smirk in his direction. But the probability this was brought on by jealousy was high.

James saw Donald as being an overdramatic adolescent with a huge temper and green envy.

LISA AND JAMES saw each other every day. Even though his was the best relationship she ever had, she still contemplated if she loved him or if she liked him immensely. Perhaps she couldn't remember how new love felt.

Was it simply the idea of love that lured her into his arms? James hadn't a doubt in his mind, but he needed to hear one of the oldest, long-lasting, and most beautiful phrases ever uttered to a fellow human being.

It was a sunny day in Central Park, which invited many diverse groups out onto its land; young boys playing baseball in the fields, old ladies exchanging their favorite recipes, aristocrats walking their purebred canines, and Lisa riding her bicycle amongst majestic saplings. Lisa peddled through cool shade and warm rays as the sun gleamed through the many thousands of leaves and twigs. A refreshing and peaceful wind blew past her ears and down her back.

James stood erect, tinkering with his finest tie as she made the last bend. A small group of kids ran in front of the path and Lisa nearly ran into the youngest one lagging behind. She pushed the break, lost her balance, and fell to the ground. James rushed to her aid. The kid scurried away seeing James charge at him.

"James!" She was surprised to see him coming out of nowhere like her knight in shining armor.

He saw she was holding her ankle. James removed her shoe and delicately flexed her foot in different directions.

"Don't do that!"

"Shush." He winked. He lifted her into his arms and sat her on the bench next to the walkway.

"I am glad you happened along."

"I didn't happen along, Lisa. I know you ride here every Sunday morning." James lowered his head; not what he'd planned, but nonetheless successful. "I uh...got you these." From behind he pulled out a bouquet of pink roses.

"Oh James." Lisa took them and breathed in their aroma.

"Well, it's not broken," said James holding her foot. "I was gonna invite you to see a great jazz band in the Village with me this evening, but we better get an icepack on that ankle. Come on, Ms. Lisa, I'll take you back to my place."

"Now, wait a minute."

"That is, unless you prefer to limp home?"

"What about my bicycle? Someone will steal it."

"I'll buy you a new one."

James placed her in the back seat of his car where her foot could rest upon the leather. Reaching his high-rise residential hotel, Lisa, bedazzled at its stunning distinction and panache, nearly leaned out of his arms trying to see the top. The doorman greeted Dr. Mallory and the pretty woman he was carrying. He grinned at Lisa to convey she baited a good catch.

The lobby voiced that of the wealthy and the spoiled. Bellboy's sported red suits with white gloves and catered to rich old men with twenty-three-year-old wives. The marble floor glistened beneath the shimmering colossal chandelier. The exquisite two-way double staircase curved to meet at the top and was dressed in a garnet carpet.

It's funny that people didn't seem to pay much attention to the uncommon spectacle. James decided to take the stairs instead of the elevator, given that he was on the second floor anyway, or maybe he wanted to show Lisa that he was that strong. He set her down to get the key. When Lisa entered a jolt of wonderment froze her body cold.

The apartment was vast. The walls were adorned in a red and gold silk wall covering, with the gold formations interweaving within the red. It was in perfect harmony with the apartment's bursting of the latest designs. Lisa even noticed there was not a speckle of dust on any of the furnishings. This wasn't an apartment; this was a house.

"Holy cow, this place should be put in a museum."

"Quiet." James guided Lisa to the sofa. He stooped down to her ear and whispered, "I don't think we're alone."

"What do you mean?"

"I didn't need a key. I have to check."

"What if they're still here?"

"Be still."

He crept over to the wall and peeped into the master bedroom first. He inspected each closet and behind every door. Clattering resonated from the kitchen. He snuck across to the entrance and thrust opened the door, slamming it against the wall. A heavyset man was bent over with his head in the icebox.

"Hey! What're you doing?" James kept his distance and examined his surroundings in search for a potential weapon.

The intruder turned around holding a sandwich. "I'm eating. You got a problem with that, kid?"

"Joe?" James took a couple steps forward.

"And if I'm not? Were you planning to kick my ass?"

"Joe Norris, I haven't seen you in-in..."

"Eleven years." Joe took a second bite of the sandwich and it was gone.

James scratched his head, "How...how did you..."

"One of the maids around here let me in." Joe closed the icebox door and leaned against it. The icebox creaked from the weight of the large, bulging man. "So, Jimmy, still doing the physician thing?"

"Twelve years. I don't believe you were sober at the time of my graduation."

"How old are you now? Thirty-five?"

"Forty-one."

"Well, you look great. I'd like to know who your Avon lady is."

Lisa was still sitting on the sofa in anticipation with her foot propped up on the table. Joe entered the room with his fierce gate. The moment her eyes met the sixty-three-year-old, gray-haired man, she neglected her pain and stood to her feet. He was as tall as James, but doubled him in mass and muscle.

"Lisa, darling, I would like you to meet an old friend of mine, Joe Norris. Joe, this is Lisa."

Joe's black eyes drifted to her. Actually, they weren't black as much as they were so brown that they might as well have been. He reached out to shake her hand, but she was reluctant to do the same. This feeling prompted her brother to cross her mind when she was faced with the same circumstance that he was days before. His was damp and clammy as he squeezed her fragile hand.

"Hello, Lisa," acknowledged Joe. His voice was gruff and husky from forty years of chain-smoking and hard drinking.

"Have a seat, Joe, so we can all get better acquainted?" Lisa was having unkind thoughts about this friend of James knowing she didn't have cause.

James asked Lisa, "Can I get you anything to drink?"

"I'll have a beer, Jimmy," answered Joe. "Schlitz will do."

"Lisa?" She shook her head.

James left to fix an icepack. An awkward silence befell the room where Lisa and Joe were left. Lisa rifled through her handbag pretending to look for something as Joe violently bounced his leg.

James returned with Joe's beer. "All I have is Ballantine, Joe."

"It'll do."

James bandaged Lisa's ankle. Joe didn't pretend to ignore Lisa's exposed leg resting on the table. She got a sense of this hole that was being bore right through her. Even when Joe was talking to James, he was looking at her.

James took a seat in the corner. "What are you doing these days?" he asked. "Still on the force?"

"Not for nine years. I'm a salesman now."

"What is it you sell?"

"Shit. No, life insurance. Don't knock it. I get a damn good percentage from each shit policy I sell."

"Joe, there are ladies present." James indicated to Lisa.

"There's only one. Fine." He grabbed Lisa's hand, "Forgive me, madam."

James's knuckles grew white. "Do you live near?"

"What is this, *The $64,000 Question*?"

Lisa drifted from the conversation. This man James introduced to her was strange, unpredictable at best. This vulgar man also appeared to have a fascination with Lisa. No matter what James tried to distract Joe from this woman he cared for, he ignored him and undressed her with his eyes.

"What's your name again?"

James answered for her. "Her name is Lisa."

"Was I talking to you?"

James hit the arms of the chair. "Joe, I would like to speak with you in the next room." Lisa couldn't help to notice this bizarre parallel between this surprise visit from Joe and last week's family meeting. The only difference was the overprotective sweetheart role had been switched from Lisa to James.

James stomped to the entrance of the bedroom and held the door open. Joe turned to say something to Lisa, but James shoved him in. "Now you listen to me. I'm in love with that woman in there, and you will *not* do what you've done in the past."

"And what is that?"

James swallowed hard. "Elizabeth Moran. You remember. I *know* you remember."

"She was too much for you, kid. A man can't eat an entire buffet, but he sure can try." Joe laughed somewhat.

James seized his shirt collars. Each man stood nose-to-nose, breathing in the other's face. "If you ever lay one finger on my Lisa, mark my words...I will kill you. Do you understand?"

Joe's warped smile died. He took hold of his wrists and threw them aside. "Jimmy, I'm staying in New York for the foreseeable future. Let's try and get along."

Joseph Norris was a man James hadn't seen in eleven years and then returned without warning. Why?

Lisa was unable to hear the exchange taking place in the next room, but knew it was heated. She had an unshakable feeling about Joe, only she didn't know what it was. Her first impression of him was not a good one. Those first impressions that people deem are most always wrong, well, Lisa was sure she was justified this time.

If Joe was going to hang around, Lisa would have to learn to endure his questionable nature.

WITH EACH BILL DONALD PAID ANOTHER TOOK ITS PLACE. From 2:00 to 10:00 p.m. he worked at Greta's Grab 'n Go. The store was miniature in size and convenient for local Manhattanites who wanted the trivial knick-knack or essentials, such as milk and bread.

Donald worked for Greta Schiller or "the Nazi" to former employees, a big-busted German immigrant with whitish blond hair. The majority of his income depended on Ms. Schiller's salary, so when he went to work, he made sure he worked hard and that she saw it.

Greta wore her hair in a tightly wrapped bun and paced each aisle with hands behind her, inspecting every item to its perfection. This night there were only two on shift: A teenager with grease-saturated hair mopping the floors and Donald managing the cash register. He was counting the day's earnings when he spotted Greta watching him. She tried to cover by arranging an already-fixed magazine rack and then made her way over to her diligent employee.

He gazed up at the clock above the door, anxious. "Um, ma'am, it's almost eleven."

"So?"

"Well, can I take off now? I haven't seen my family today."

"And that is mein problem because..." Greta said in her deep voice, lapsing into German as she did frequently.

"Well, I've put in a lot of overtime this week."

Greta beat her brawny fist upon the counter as she contemplated. "Alright, Don, you can go home...und you can take off tomorrow since I have made you to work extra this week."

"Ms. Schiller, I didn't mean..."

"Go. Leave. It's okay."

The family was in bed. Donald changed into his pajamas, fixed his TV dinner, and listened to WINS late-night music on the radio.

He hadn't taken one bite when there was a gentle knock on the door. Donald moved his tray to the side and switched off the radio. He cracked opened the door. It was Greta Schiller.

"What are you doing here at this hour?" he asked her.

"Am I not welcome?"

"I'm sorry, come in." He noticed a strong fragrance overwhelming her person.

She threw her coat on the sofa and walked to the other side of the room. "You don't like me here, do you, Don?"

"Why are you here? Is there something wrong?"

"To be frank, I have come to give you a...a vorschlag?" She couldn't think of the word and Donald had no clue. "Offer is the word, I think."

"Alright."

She decided to continue standing, needing to obtain a sense of authority. "You may sit, Don." He did as he was told.

"What offer?"

"How does a $1.00 raise und a week vacation sound?"

"That would be fantastic!" The elation passed as quickly as it came. Donald thought about it. "What do I have to do?"

Greta moved to the other side of the room; her eyes locked on Donald as she crossed. She switched off one of the lights. She removed her black gloves and rested her large hand on top of his head, running his jet-black hair between her thick fingers. This was more than awkward and made him more than uncomfortable.

Donald stood, "Ma'am, are you asking what I think you are asking?" The lighting crafted a dim and intimate setting which did not assist his nerves.

Greta shrugged, "Come Don, I crave a little fun and passion. She stepped closer to Donald who was stepping away. "We each have what the other wants. I need a man who is sinnlich."

Donald was able to guess what that probably meant. He was terrified. What if his family were to wake?

"You want me to leave my wife. Is that it?"

"Good heavens, nein. I'm asking for one night." It seemed this woman wanted a cut-rate exotic fling.

"Yeah, I bet you've had many an employee, eh?"

She unbuttoned her blouse and threw it aside. Donald was not attracted to this woman in the slightest, but he had to look at her breasts. Each was crammed inside its cup that was about three sizes too small. Her nipples could pop out at any second. She stepped out of her skirt; it dropped to the floor.

Greta shook her hair down and tossed her head side to side, permitting her graying mane to fall wherever it pleased. He had never seen her with her hair down before. Greta was evolving into this animal with immense carnal urges. Donald stepped back in fright or disgust until the door obstructed him.

"You'll wake my family."

"I won't make a sound. We can go into the bathroom. My name is Greta, Don. That means great...with a few altered letters."

Greta continued to advance while removing her slip and pressed her bare body against his. "Mach Liebe zu mir," hissed Greta, raspy and low. No promotion was worth this, not worth the guilt that would follow. She took hold of Donald's hands and forced them on her breasts.

Donald's head struck the door as he struggled to free himself from the strapping Nazi. "No!" He shoved her off of him. Donald licked the sweat that had fallen onto his lips.

"You refuse?" Her German dialect took control of her English as lust surrendered to humiliation, then subsided to anger.

"Dummkopf! Damn dummkopf! Ich hasse dich!" Greta picked up her blouse and shielded her chest. Donald lowered his head. Even before it happened, he knew his employment with Ms. Schiller was finished.

"I want you out of my home." Donald bent down before Greta to pick up her clothes. She spit on top of his head. He wanted to strike her, but handed the rest of her garments to her instead.

Stepping back into her slip and skirt, Greta said, "You are done!"

"I quit anyway."

Greta, holding the remainder of her clothes, left and slammed the door so hard the wall shuddered. She was now walking down a public hallway only half dressed.

Donald Wells had gone from a respectable hardworking citizen to a sacked fool or dummkopf to those "Germanly" inclined. All of this was too massive to swallow at once.

"What will I do? Goddammit!" He picked up his dinner on impulse and threw it across the room. It hit the wall and fell face down on the carpet. Donald turned to find the door to his bedroom shutting quickly.

"Oh no."

"ARE YOU COMFORTABLE?" James asked Lisa as she lay in his lap listening to Dean Martin's latest single "Return to Me" playing on the turntable.

"Of course," she answered. James looked to his left at a silver-framed photograph of a young Lisa and Donald on the table beside him.

"That was taken outside our tenement in Brooklyn. Donny had just turned five." Lisa took the picture and slid her finger across her brother's smiling face.

"How old were you?"

"Thirteen. It's funny. We were hungry, yet we were happy." Lisa held the picture to her chest.

Lisa kissed the picture before softly placing it back. "James, is something the matter? Your mind seems to be elsewhere tonight." Lisa lifted his hand and held it to her delicate cheek. "Tell me."

"Lisa, are, um, do you...feel anything for me?" Lisa let go of his hand. "Dammit, Lisa, do you not love me at all?"

This hot seat was very uncomfortable for Lisa and she wanted to get up, but James stopped her. "No Lisa, no more stalling. Tonight will determine if what we have here is to continue. Robert is gone. *I'm* the real deal."

"Oh, she is that important to him, eh? Ha-ha," Alma chuckled, moving in closer to the small hole she had crafted connecting the two apartments. "Aw, isn't that sweet? She's lying in his masculine lap." Alma took such unmitigated pleasure in watching her long-time neighbor.

James felt if he revealed something about himself that it would make it easier on her. "Since we're being honest with one another, now is a good time to tell you, if you haven't gathered it already, I'm wealthy." Lisa nodded. "I have achieved this through my business of course, but mainly by inheritance.

"My old man was rich. I had no brothers or sisters, so I inherited everything – millions." She shied away. "A little over three million."

"I've had to be sensible with it, placing it in stocks, bonds, timeshares, and a couple winning investments. Believe me, I'm far from becoming the businessman who lives and breathes for the exhilarating game of buying and selling."

"Why...why didn't you tell me before?"

"I didn't want my money to be the crux of our relationship. But please, no one must know. This is between us."

Alma whispered in surprise, "Well, well, well, that little gold-digger."

Lisa stroked the sides of his face, "Oh James, this is too much." The song was over and the needle was scraping the end of the record. She wanted to kiss him but it was as if her feelings stopped dead in their tracks and begun the trek back. He imposed his kiss on her anyway and noticed it was not as lovingly reciprocated.

James searched for the candor he needed dearly. "I don't know what he did to you to make you distrust men so, but..." Lisa hugged her arms as if growing cold. The mere thought of Robert always made her feel abandoned. "I have so much to offer you.

"I want to pamper you with the finest comforts, I want to protect you, and I want to hold you when nights are cold. I can do that, Lisa. And you are the woman I want to do it for."

"What are you saying?"

James breathed softly, "Marry me." All movement within her ceased, even her own heartbeat. "I won't break your heart like he did. Your heart is safe with me. I'll take good care of you."

All was still as Lisa absorbed the moment in its beautiful entirety. *Could this really be happening? It's too good to be true.*

Alma stomped her foot, "Answer him, stupid."

Lisa squeezed him so forcefully it took the wind from his lungs. "I love you, James, so much."

"Is that a yes?"

"Yes! Yes, I'll marry you, James Mallory!"

He pulled from his pocket a small black velvet box containing a two-carat diamond ring and slipped it on her finger. It was like he plucked a star from the sky, and now the twinkling of that star that countless women have admired on a lonely night, wishing silently for the love of a lifetime, rested on Lisa's plain finger.

"I'll probably make a dreadful husband."

Lisa embraced him tight. "You'll make a magnificent husband."

After losing everything, now was her chance at a new beginning.

# CHAPTER FIVE

Donald took a deep breath as he stepped into Lisa's flat. Rebecca and the kids followed closely behind.

"This is a pleasant surprise," said Lisa.

Donald replied, removing his soft felt hat, "Yeah, while we were out, we thought we'd pop by for a bit."

"James is here, too." Donald's face fell. "We haven't seen you for a couple weeks." James came out of the kitchen holding a teacup and wiping his mouth with a napkin.

Donald said with little enthusiasm, "Dr. Mallory, good to see you again." James bowed his head in response. They looked at each other from opposite sides of the room. James was there very early and Donald pondered momentarily of this man spending the night there.

Lisa felt a light tug on her skirt. "Aunt Lisa, I have to go to the bathroom."

She took her niece's hand, "Alright, Strawberry. Make yourself at home in the kitchen, Rebecca. Fix Donald and the kids some French toast or something." Donald sat down on the sofa and began thumping his hat against his leg. James returned to the kitchen with Simon by his side.

Rebecca sat down next to him. "When are you going to tell her?"

"When the timing is right."

"Today, Donald, I mean it."

"Alright, alright."

"Do you have any clue how deep the hole is that you've dug us into?"

"You know damn well this wasn't my fault. Unless you think I should've taken her up on her offer?" Rebecca lowered her head. Donald may have gone too far with that comment, but it got her off his back.

Groveling was never an easy duty for those forced to practice it. This was a situation that had to be resolved with immediacy or let their pride interfere with their children's soon-to-be-empty stomachs. For Donald to beg for more money at the feet of his sister who dedicated a good portion of her life to him already was developing into a growing ache in his heart and stomach.

With a sigh of concern, Rebecca clinched her knees together and rubbed the palms of her hands against them.

"Lisa will come around." Donald glided his hand across her back. "There's no need to worry." He scoffed. "That Mallory in the kitchen, I believe, will be our ace in the hole."

"He probably wipes his ass with gilded toilet paper wherever his mansion of residency is." Donald leaned over his wife to get a glimpse of James in the kitchen.

"I suspect he will. Anyways, sponging off your sister more than you already are would be cruel."

Donald wasn't quite sure what she meant, but hoped it wasn't what he was thinking. How did she find out?

Rebecca crossed her arms. "I'm not mad. Still, I would've preferred you told me about the whole ordeal instead of sneaking around."

She knew.

"What else was I supposed to do? We needed the money for rent, groceries, and the car. It's not like the bank would've loaned me any. And if they had I couldn't pay it back. How did you find out?"

"That's irrelevant. The point is her petty amount isn't going to help us pay the bills. We need money now. A lot of it. Who's going to tell her?"

"My sister – my problem. I'll handle it." Donald flapped his hat near his face for cool air.

Julia came running in and crawled up onto the sofa beside her mother. "So, how'd you do?" her mother asked her.

"Aunt Lisa said I was a n-national."

"No, sweetheart, I said 'natural'," Lisa corrected with a chuckle.

Donald gestured with a cock of his neck for Rebecca to leave.

"Come, Julie, let's go into the kitchen and see what your brother's up to." As Rebecca led Julia into the next room, she turned to catch Donald's troubled eyes lock on hers. In that second, theirs was a look of hope, anticipation, and even hatred of each other due to the situation.

"Boy Donny, do I have news for you." Lisa took a seat on the right of him. She flipped back the hair from her neck with her left hand so he would see her diamond ring, but he wasn't looking.

"As a matter of fact, I do too, Lisa." Donald pushed the hair from his forehead and out of his eyes – a recurring habit he developed in childhood during times of stress and anxiety.

"What is your news?" She placed her left hand on his leg.

"It's not good."

Lisa should've known as soon as she saw her family standing in her doorway, a rare occurrence, that there was something bringing them there. The past couple of weeks had been simply wonderful for Lisa. She was able to overlook the daily burdens and seek shelter under James.

"Nothing serious, I hope."

"I lost my job."

"Jesus Donny, which one did you lose?"

There was a long pause before the dreaded response. "The store." He covered his eyes.

"Dammit! If you had to lose either of the two, why did it have to be that one, Donny?" She smacked her hands against her bare knees in frustration.

"I don't need to hear it!" Donald jumped up. His sudden burst of temper took her by surprise. "I'm fully aware of the seriousness of the situation. If you aren't going to help, I'll take my family and get outta your hair."

When he realized Lisa was going to let him go he crawled back. "Sis look, I didn't mean to yell at you, it's just...I understand that you're the only person who can help me. I don't know what came over me."

Donald sat opposite her on the coffee table and took her hands and held them tight. He spoke facing the kitchen where his wife was occupying James to buy him time. "Lisa, I don't ask that you give me any more money. I would appreciate your help in finding another job. Maybe your boss could use an extra pair of hands."

"Does Rebecca know about this?" Donald nodded. James and the others came into the room. Rebecca mouthed an "I'm sorry" to Donald who was vexed by the intrusion.

"What's new in your world, Mr. Wells?" James put his arm around Lisa and kissed the top of her head.

"Nothing much."

"Well, your sister and I have a world of good news to tell you."

Lisa muttered, "Not now, James."

Donald's chances of discussing the matter in private were blown. He had to go out hunting for a job. He would have to drive the cab of a day and job search of a night, if not pick up a part-time job in-between.

"I'm sorry, we have to go. I'll have to talk to you some other time, Lisa. Come on, kids, say goodbye to Aunt Lisa." Donald seized his children's hands and led them to the door.

Simon fought to free himself from his father's grip. "James, when can I see you again?"

Donald stood firm behind his son, peering at James with a boiling hatred. "Not now, Simon. The doctor has *patients* to see to, I'm sure." He pressed his fingers into Simon's back and nudged him towards the door.

Lisa was able to throw out an "I'll call ya" before the door closed.

Just then it occurred to Lisa the reason he brought the whole family. One word: Sympathy. Her niece and nephew's presence would soften her up, or would provide adequate backup if his own tears didn't do the job. The visit became far less meaningful in her mind.

Rebecca jumped on Donald in the hall. "That was dreadfully impolite."

"I refuse to grovel before my sister with that Mallory feasting his eyes on my pain. I told her what happened. She'll come through."

"I hope so...for our sake." Rebecca told her husband as they entered the elevator.

Lisa displayed to her fiancé a look of major concern she had exhibited many times whenever her brother was within her midst. Lisa always worried for Donald in a way that only a mother could. Was it because she had to assume the role of mother that she felt she always had to be there for him in any situation?

One might even go as far as to say Donald Wells was too young and inexperienced to raise a family. Could it be that he was spoiled, totally nurtured into thinking that under any circumstance he would be taken care of? Could it also be Lisa blamed herself for letting it get that far?

James asked, waiting for them to leave. "What was that about?"

"Oh, uh, my brother's just having some financial trouble."

"It must be serious then."

Lisa turned, "What makes you say that?"

"Well, Rebecca kept asking about my two clinics. She asked questions concerning the salaries of my staff. She didn't even attempt to cover. What's going on?"

"Donny lost one of his jobs. Look, since we're getting married let's get something straight. I have never left Donald to face this wilderness alone. It's a cold, harsh world out there. And by "world" I mean this godforsaken city."

"Are you saying you want to help him? As generous as that is, Lisa, you can't. You're a working-class woman yourself."

"He's my family, don't you understand?"

"He's also a grown man. It's pretty sad when a young, able man has to be supported by a woman, especially if that woman is his sister." That remark hit too close to home for Lisa, considering she did it for five years in her previous marriage.

"But he needs me! He has a wife and two children to support. You saw how distraught he was a few minutes ago."

"He looked like that last time I saw him. I'm assuming you've helped him before. Lisa, you must put yourself first."

"Where the hell do you get off giving me advice on *my* brother? You don't even like him." Lisa rose quickly and faced James who now looked at her in shock of her sudden display of justification.

"When did I say that?"

"You didn't have to say it. I can see it." Lisa folded her arms and turned away.

In her mind, she knew she was behaving like her little niece would in an argument, or her brother does when he is angry, but her emotions were something her mind couldn't always control. It had to be genetics, pure and simple – a family trait.

James stared at her back. He walked to her slowly, rested his hands on her shoulders and kissed her neck. "I never meant to upset you. I want what's best for you. That's all."

"I know you do. My brother is a responsible man. That's why when he comes to me, I know it must be for good reason. I can't lose him. He's all I have."

"You have me." James took Lisa's hands and kissed them. "As you are to Donald, I am to you.

"Ms. Lisa, you can come to me whenever you're in need. If you feel compelled to help your family with their financial difficulties, come to me." James took the handkerchief from his jacket pocket and dabbed her nose.

"Are you saying you will help Donald?"

"Until he gets back on his feet."

"Oh, James!" As a burden was lifted, Lisa leapt to the tips of her toes to embrace the circumference of his shoulders in their entirety. "I'll call him tonight and tell him the good news."

"No, no, I don't want him to know."

"I meant about the wedding. Donald was in such a hurry he never gave me a chance to tell him."

GRETA SCHILLER was still adamant in her decision in letting Donald go. It was an easy-to-fill position, and the Nazi would have no trouble filling her achingly needed prescription. Always Greta was able to get what she wanted. One way or the other by means of bribery, blackmail, or sexual talent, they all agreed in the end.

Donald was the exception.

Greta sat at her office desk at the back of the store. The room was barren, containing a few pictures, a potted plant, and a desk that swallowed the majority of the room. Sweat trickled down her chubby cheek, making its way onto her chin in the form of a droplet.

It was quiet except for the perpetual drone of the city and Greta's exasperated huffing. So immersed in thought, she took aback when her office door opened. A humble Donald Wells stood in her doorway, his posture bent and staring at her through tousled hair.

Greta's eyes narrowed as she smirked and removed her glasses. The realization of his visit came the moment her eyes caught him before her. Donald was scared. He wasn't positive this was a good idea and knew it would be wrong. But these were desperate times.

"I must say I'm shocked. I thought you were a man who means what he says." She chuckled and stood, pushing back the chair with her legs.

Greta spoke in her native tongue. "So eine traurige Welt, in der wir leben, wenn ein Mann alle Moral und Anstand verliert." Donald swallowed hard.

Translation: Such a sad world we live in when a man loses all morals and decency.

Greta shook her head. "I must admit, I thought you were a man of some dignity."

"Alright. I came here tonight with the intent of getting my job back. If you aren't going to listen to what I have to say then I'll leave."

"Nein, nein, do not act so hasty, young Don. You do not know yet what I will say. I may surprise you." Greta pressed her glasses between her teeth as she sat half of her body on the edge of the desk.

"I want my job back. What more can I say?"

"What more can you *say*? Don, did you think that I would just *give* you your job back for nothing? Nein."

Donald stepped away from the safety of his only exit. "Come, ma'am, surely you can find it in your heart to be kind." The nerve-wracking situation he had thrown himself into began to reveal itself more and more. Donald fussed with his hair, licked his lips, and stumbled over his tongue.

"Ma'am, I...I have two children, a son and a little baby girl, a wife I'm putting through college. My, um, my bills are way above what I make, let alone ends meet. Can't you help me?"

Bobbing her leg, she smiled and laughed. Donald crumpled his hat in his fists and gnashed his teeth. "It's not funny! Stop that!" He dashed over to Greta.

"Oh, cool off."

"What the hell do you want from me? Get down on my hands and knees and beg your forgiveness for doing what was right after putting me in the predicament in the first place? For God's sake, do you have any idea what you were asking of me?!"

She shrugged and spoke perfect, unbroken English. "Did you come here to tell me off some more or did you come to get your job back?" Donald took a deep breath. He wanted to avoid this, but he also knew it would make her happy.

He threw his hat on her desk and stooped to his knees. She arose with her eyes fixed on his. She took several steps back. Donald knew what was expected of him.

He placed his hands on the carpet and forced his right calf forward to crawl to Greta like a child would crawl to its mother. With each advancement Donald made she would take one step back. He could feel the coarse texture of the fabric of the rug through his trousers and between his fingers.

Donald never felt so degraded. "Please, I beg you." He took her hand and held it to his cheek. "I swear I'll do anything, just please...*please*. No more."

She could feel the warm tears, but they didn't warm her heart. Greta lifted his head. He felt so weak, so dejected. When he stood he was able to look down on her, but even so, still felt insect small. Donald had to fight to keep from sobbing and wished he possessed the strength to take up for himself.

"I don't think so."

"What?"

"I will not give you your job back. Sorry." Greta playfully slapped his face and returned to her desk. Donald marveled at the sight. She had sat her glasses back on her nose and was actually working as if the last five minutes never happened.

"You Nazi bitch. You already made up your mind before...didn't you?" Greta snubbed him. Like a time bomb, tick, tick, ticking away the seconds, Donald was ready to explode. "Answer me!"

"Leave me!" Greta threw her finger at the door.

Donald stomped around her desk, yanked the heavyset woman out of her chair like a doll and kissed her. His kiss was forceful and rough, and as fervent a kiss he could muster for a woman he loathed. Almost instantly Greta relaxed. Then, recalling her intense lust, he made the decision that the one kiss would not be enough. He worked over to her ear and felt around its dips and ridges with his tongue.

Greta dug her nails into his back. It hurt, although his anger made him numb to the scratches. He made his way down to her neck where he caressed and bit the fleshy skin that was not in any way like his wife's. She groaned and sighed at the sensation of wonderful pain until she could no longer contain. Greta threw Donald onto her desk, ripped open his shirt, and unfastened his belt.

Even if Donald had doubts, he had thrown himself into a cage and given her the key. Furthermore, he was more than willing to go through with the deed, but he had to make sure he would get what he needed out of it.

"Does this mean I have my job?"

Greta paused kissing his bare chest when he asked the question she was unprepared to answer. If she said yes than she would lose all control. If she said no, she would have to give up, at that moment, what she wanted more than anything.

Donald was leery of her silence. "I will do this under one condition. That you give back my job with equal pay I was receiving before."

"I-I can't, Don."

"Very well," said Donald, drained and irritated. He lifted Greta off his legs and tucked in his shirt. He made a bee-line for the exit he should never have left.

Greta blocked his way of the door. "I can't because I already filled it."

"In one week? I need cash, Greta, and I refuse to work for free." Donald shoved her aside.

"We can come to terms on something." Greta was pleading as Donald had minutes before. "I am willing to make a deal, any deal. What have you got to lose?"

"WHERE HAVE YOU BEEN?" Rebecca asked. "Lisa phoned while you were out. Great news!"

"Oh? Who died?"

"Your sister is getting married. Lisa phoned about an hour ago and told me the good news. She and James are getting married, Donald. Aren't you excited?"

Donald lumbered to the sofa and fell flat on his back with deadweight. "I've lost my sister...again...to an asshole...again!"

Rebecca went to him and crouched down. "Don't you understand what this means?" Donald humored her by listening. He pushed himself up with his elbow.

"James equals money. Lisa marries James. Therefore, Lisa marries money, and money is something Lisa gives to brother."

Rebecca continued, "Aside from everything else, you should be happy for her. Did you expect her to remain lonely for the rest of her life to appease you? And she *is* going to help us. She didn't say how much, but said it will be enough to sustain. I've got a feeling James is behind this."

Donald grabbed one of the pillows, mangled it within his hands, and threw it to the other end of the sofa. "I'm not begging anymore. It's making me sick to my stomach."

Rebecca was puzzled by his reaction. Donald stepped outside to smoke a cigarette of relief, his first after a year or more of successful abstention. What was to transpire within the coming weeks was unknown, and journeying into this foreign territory frightened him.

# CHAPTER SIX

**I**t was the day!

After a month of preparation, it was the day Lisa was to become Lisa Rose Mallory. Even so, she was not as happy or enthusiastic as she should have been due to one factor: Donald. It was because of him that she wasn't completely cheerful on what was supposed to be the happiest day of her life.

Many times, Lisa called and no one answered. Many times, she went to visit and no one was there. It was breaking her heart knowing her little brother wanted nothing to do with her, all on account of falling for a man he disliked. She wasn't even sure he would come.

James wanted to pamper her with illustrious nuptial music and bombard her senses with large assortments of breathtaking flowers. As far as the reception, he had planned an elaborate display of fine cuisine and entertainment on their night to remember forever. In his sight, this was a day not to be frugal, but Lisa chose to keep it personal.

She donned her new bridal gown. Rebecca watched with interest and envy as her sister-in-law practiced her walk. Lisa fretted over her ivory dress, her hands struggling to smooth each wrinkle and the lace tiers to lie perfectly. With each tick of the clock her heart beat faster, which made relaxing a challenging plight.

Rebecca sat in a chair and motioned for Julia to come over. "Turn around and let me fix your bow. Lisa, you're going to rub a hole in that dress. Leave yourself alone. *My* wedding day I had the girth of a tree trunk."

Rebecca tore her eyes away from her daughter to see Lisa and her hands that were at war with each other. "He gets off work soon," she said.

"It's not his work that I'm worried about. What if he just decides not to show?"

"Oh, he will always render time for you, especially today. I know they don't get along as well as we'd like them to, but James is soon to be a part of the family."

Julia moaned with discomfort with her knees clasped. "Mommy."

"Julia, I swear. Didn't Mommy ask you if you had to go before we put the dress on?"

Lisa followed them. She didn't want to be alone. She was thinking of Robert. She couldn't help herself.

She wasn't about to tell Rebecca that. He was quite a man. The bitter divorce didn't change that fact; thick, wavy brown hair, blue eyes, a casual smile that made the women swoon, and an English accent that reminded her of royalty.

Lisa recalled her first wedding day. It was a day of heavenly splendor on earth, and it was much simpler than this one. A woman never forgets a wedding, even if the following years have dimmed the memory of said splendor. The splendor, that is, was nothing material, but it was Lisa's state of mind and how she perceived the world around her.

Rebecca came out of the stall holding Julia's hand. Lisa was still fussing with her dress. Within her mind was a multitude of varied thoughts and feelings, interrupted by the abrupt entrance of Simon.

"Mommy, Mommy that big man wants to talk to Aunt Lisa."

"Does he have gray hair?" asked Lisa.

"Uh-huh."

"It's Joe. Tell the big man he can come in. Rebecca, I would feel better if you and Julie left."

"Mr. Norris is kind of intimidating. Why in God's name is *he* the best man?"

"Don't ask. James and I argued about it."

They met Joe coming out of the ladies' room. The light grew dim as the large shadow came over the room. "Excuse me," said Rebecca, timid as she and her daughter went around him. Joe examined Lisa head-to-toe.

"What can I do for you?" Lisa asked, crossing her arms in apprehension. She was nervous enough and this wasn't helping.

Joe shoved his hands in the pockets of his tuxedo. He looked like a giant penguin. "I wanted to talk to you about Jimmy before the ceremony started."

"Oh?"

"Strictly my opinion – you are exactly what Jimmy needs. You're good-looking, polite, you seem to hold your own, and you're the right age. No offense."

Lisa shook her head. "I appreciate that."

"Jimmy and I had quite a few sordid adventures in our younger days. You know the kind where you wake up in a motel with no money, a dame, and a hangover? He was a player. I guess those days are over and done. Now that I think of it, you may be *too* good for ol' Jim."

"Out with it. What're you trying to say?"

"No more bullshit. Are you sure you aren't jumping on the bandwagon with this guy? Haven't you been married before?"

"How dare you?!" Lisa took a brave step forward.

"Not that I care, but...why did you get divorced? Was it his fault?"

*How did he find out? James must have told him. How could he?*

"Leave me alone!" Lisa walked away from him.

Suddenly she felt him come up fiercely behind her. Never before had she allowed herself to be this close to Joe. Lisa spun around to find him breathing heavily above her and backed away.

"Don't marry him. You will regret it if you do. It's not too late."

"You better get away from me or-or I'll scream." The window behind Lisa was nearing closer and closer as she receded.

"Listen to me. I know Jimmy, and he's not what he seems. You don't know what he's done, what he's capable of."

Lisa's back touched the windowsill. She trembled in fear as Joe's large body forced hers into submission. His thick, muscular fingers pressed into her shoulder blades.

"I-I thought you were his fr-friend?"

"Why do you think I'm here? Heed my warning, lady. If you marry James, you're taking one big risk." Without looking back, Joe turned and left.

*Risk? What does he mean?* Lisa stood trembling, her mind a frenzy on her perfect day.

It was like Joe to do something this cruel. That bastard enjoyed causing turmoil where there was none. Lisa was determined to keep this day special, a day that not even a Joe Norris ploy could ruin.

"2:55 – five more minutes," Lisa muttered to herself clipping the flower-accented headband veil to her hair. She made her way to the vestibule where Rebecca and the kids were waiting.

Rebecca put her hand over her mouth to cover her smile. "Lisa, this is the most beautiful I have ever seen you. Isn't Aunt Lisa lovely?"

"You're like an angel," said Simon.

Rebecca adjusted her veil. "I can't help but think of my own wedding day when I look at you. I recollect you saying in a room similar to this one, "Don't be afraid. You will make an ideal mother." You primped and fussed over me like a mother."

Rebecca spoke softly, "With my mother being gone, it meant a lot to me. I don't know where we would be without you."

Lisa sighed, "Donny..." She stared at the floor. "I can't believe him."

"I'm sorry, Lisa."

"I raised him after our parents died, helped him with his homework every night. I have denied him nothing. *Why*?" Lisa's frustration evolved to a soft whimper.

"No, no, don't. This is your special day." Rebecca pulled a tissue from her bag and handed it to Lisa. "If it will make you feel better, I'll kill him when I get home."

Pastor Mulligan poked his head through one of the large double doors. "You girls ready?"

"Yes," answered Rebecca.

"And the little man?"

Rebecca saw Simon had torn off his bowtie a second time. She stooped to one knee and clipped it on with frustrate-driven force. "Ouch!" Simon yelped.

"He is now."

Mulligan noticed Lisa was upset. Rebecca covered for her. "Pre-wedding jitters."

Rebecca took Lisa's hands after the pastor left. "No more crying. There is a handsome, wonderful man in there waiting for you." She then began whispering in her ear as if attempting to entrance. "Now, shut your eyes and forget everything.

"Forget Donald, me, work, everything. As you walk down that aisle, set your eyes upon him. Nothing else in this world exists."

"You're right. This is my day. I'm getting married today."

Rebecca pointed to her watch, "You're getting married now."

"Oh no. Oh boy."

"You're not going to start pacing again, are you?"

"Jesus, I am so scared. This is it, Rebecca. I'm going to be a wife again."

REBECCA OPENED THE FRENCH DOORS holding her bouquet of white roses. She gave Lisa a swift wink before marching in. Her auburn hair sparkled as the sun's rays struck it. The cerise hue of her dress was perfect for this August afternoon, as well as for little Julia, an exact replica of her mother. Simon wrestled with his bowtie, hating every second he was forced to keep it on.

Lisa nudged him through the door. Her heart was beating in her ears. She didn't want to deal with the children. This was one time she wanted to be selfish.

"Are you ready, Strawberry? Do you have your basket?"

"Yes, Aunt Lisa." Julia started down tossing the white petals.

Lisa embraced her pale pink roses and baby's breath when a hand came from behind taking hers.

"Donny..."

"Would you mind if I gave you away?"

With a smile and a tear, she gave a consented nod. He wasn't dressed for the occasion, but that didn't matter to her. She took several deep breaths before they faced the sanctuary. The piano cued and everyone stood. Donald took her arm, wrapped it around his, and held her hand in place.

"Okay Sis, let's do this. Let's get you married."

The bright light shining from the window above the altar was blinding. Lisa smiled up at Donald before taking her first step. Lavender flora lined each pew. She observed some of the faces staring back at her; several employees from James's workplace and friends from Rebecca's school, Larry and his wife, Genevieve. They all beamed as she passed them.

Slowly she marched, each step bringing her closer to the man soon to be hers who stood firm with his hands behind him. He wore a dark suit and silk white tie with a white rose peeking out from his lapel, and his golden hair glistening below the brightest light her eyes had ever seen.

"If you marry James, you're taking a risk." Those words she dismissed as lies returned for not even a second and vanished. Joe wasn't worth it, not when she could look ahead and see what she was so ready to receive.

Lisa glided towards him as an angel in ivory, this waitress of Manhattan. Donald lifted her veil, kissed both her cheeks, and gently placed her hand into James's. James saw the livid animosity in Donald's face. Lisa felt the butterflies flying like mad inside her stomach and the tingle radiating down the nerves of her legs to her knees and back up, all from the warmth of his large hand engulfing hers.

The congregation sat. All was still. James peeked down at her from the corner of his eye.

Holding his Bible, the pastor smiled at them as he tapped the back of the book with his fingers. "Love is patient and kind. It isn't envious or boastful or proud. It doesn't demand its own way.

"It isn't irritable and doesn't remember any wrongdoings against it. It delights only in truth. Love never gives up or loses faith, and is always hopeful, and endures through every circumstance...I Corinthians 13: 4-7."

James stroked Lisa's hand with his thumb.

Mulligan continued, "May you two feel this way today and for years to come. Repeat after me: "I, James Mitchell Mallory, take thee, Lisa, to be my wedded wife, for better, for worse, for richer, for poorer, in sickness and in health, to love and to cherish, for as long as we both shall live."

As James spoke the vows, Lisa felt a touch of guilt for thinking of Robert earlier. Now it was her turn to recite. Though James was the second man she had given herself to, she spoke with sincerity.

"Now: The giving and receiving of the rings."

They all looked to Simon. Simon was fidgeting in his uncomfortable tux.

Joe nudged the boy, "Gimme the ring, kid." After wriggling his fingers down into his breast pocket, Simon finally pulled it out. An idea of Rebecca's after it kept falling off the pillow.

"This ring is the symbol of marriage. The golden circle represents the enduring union of two people. May it be an emblem to remind you of the vows you have pledged." James placed the ring upon Lisa's tiny finger. "James, do you give this ring as a token of your love for Lisa?"

"I do."

"Lisa, will you accept this ring as a token of James's love for you, and will you wear it as an expression of your love for him?"

"Oh, I will."

"Oh brother," Donald scoffed.

Rebecca passed the ring to Lisa. "Lisa, do you give this ring as a token of your love for James?"

"I do."

"James, will you accept this ring as a token of Lisa's love for you, and will you wear it as an expression of your love for her?"

"Oh, I will, too." Faint chuckling followed his response to Mulligan's question.

Lisa couldn't help but trail off, hearing a mere drone from the pastor. Seeing and feeling this band upon her finger felt so strange and yet so pleasing. Three years since she donned such a ring and it already felt better than the last.

"You may kiss the bride."

"My pleasure." James kissed her ringed finger first and then her lips ever-so-tender. Rebecca instigated an applause that rose up from the pews to the high beams of the nave.

"I present to you Mr. and Mrs. James Mallory."

They faced everyone as they clapped. As happy as she was, Donald was still on her mind. He was applauding, but not smiling. Not until he discovered Lisa watching him did he force a minor grin. She had a new husband offering a fresh new start and she wanted to include him in it and everything it had to offer.

Lisa and James, arm-in-arm, began their walk down the aisle together until she was unexpectedly hindered by Simon who rushed over to hug her legs. Lisa laughed and rubbed his head.

Outside the sunshine warmed Lisa's face. There wasn't a cloud in the sky or in her heart. The fragrance in the air was that of a garden. Patchworks of flowers planted around the picturesque chapel embraced the building like a Monet painting being held within an antique frame and it's hard to tell which is more beautiful.

One of James's employees parked his Rolls-Royce out front with "newlyweds" written on both sides. Joe obnoxiously laughed about something he told James and was beating him on the back. Lisa was shaking hands with Larry when Donald came up timidly behind her.

"Well, I guess this is it," Lisa said. Donald did not look at her. "Donny, did you want to say something?"

He embraced her and lifted her off her feet. Since James entered the picture, this was the first they had been affectionate, and both siblings missed that.

"I hope he makes you happy. I want that for you." Donald leered over Lisa's head at James. "I can trust Mr. Mallory?"

"Yes," replied James.

THE NEW COUPLE WAVED GOODBYE as they drove away. James dropped Lisa off at her apartment to change clothes and pick up her luggage for their trip to Niagara Falls while he did the same.

Lisa kept thinking of insignificant things, such as getting accustomed to a switch in residence and having Mallory for a last name. She couldn't have been happier.

Lisa was in the middle of dressing when she heard knocking on her door. *It couldn't be James,* she thought. She threw on her dressing gown and peered through the peephole and saw Alma. *Nothing could ruin this day. What the hell?*

"Lisa," Alma acknowledged.

"Alma."

"May I come in?"

"I guess, but not for too long. I'm kind of in a hurry. I'll be in the next room."

Alma studied Lisa's apartment having not been in it for some time. It was fair. Not as nice as hers. Bright with a few flower accents, and tidy. However, it lacked the special touch that only an experienced decorator such as herself could contribute.

She crossed over to the mundane sofa and spotted Lisa's wedding dress draped over the back. "I noticed your luggage beside the door. Are you going somewhere?"

Lisa spoke from behind the door. "James and I are leaving for Syracuse." She knew she wouldn't be able to keep James from Alma entirely, but to keep as much from her as possible was strived. She did not want to tell her she was married to him, despite the fact Alma already knew.

"What is it you wanted to talk about, Alma?"

"Since you're leaving, I will make this short. Would you care if I had a smoke, dear?"

Lisa's tone expressed her growing annoyance, "No, go ahead."

"I just hate bringing up bad memories, especially long forgotten ones. But I can't, for the life of me, remember the name of the girl Robert ran off with. It's been preying on my mind." Smoke escaped Alma's nose when she smirked.

As malicious as the question was to even be posed, Lisa wasn't all that shocked. She remained calm. "I think her name was Stacy...something-or-other."

"Do you know if they got married?" Alma was staring at the door to Lisa's bedroom anticipating her to come out.

"Yes, I believe they did."

"When?"

Lisa exhaled, "I'd heard about four months after the divorce; February of '56. At least that's what he told me last time I saw him."

"I liked Robert. He was distinguished, suave, attractive, and damn good in the boudoir, if you catch my drift. Ha-ha."

Now she had gone too far. Lisa dropped everything and threw open the door. "Explain that remark!"

"There is nothing *to* explain, dear. I was merely stating a possible fact. That doesn't mean I slept with him. Oh, and incidentally, her name is Stella, not Stacy."

Lisa wetted her lips. "Why did you ask then if you already knew?"

"I wanted to see if you knew."

Lisa was returning to her room. *How does she know this?* "Wait a minute. You never met her, not to my knowledge."

"She is my niece. Stella Henderson was her name at the time I introduced her to Robert. Poor darling, she was recovering from a nasty breakup, and Robert was just what the doctor ordered to get her back on her feet."

Lisa was in shock. It wasn't anger or sadness. But she grew lightheaded and thought she might faint. "I'm assuming you were the doctor."

Alma pressed her cigarette into the ashtray and sauntered over to her. She forcibly lifted Lisa's left arm. "My, my, that is quite a ring.

"He's wealthy." Lisa swallowed hard. "What, may I ask, is your name now, um?"

"Mallory," Lisa answered feebly. Any elation from before was gone. How would she recoup in time to enjoy her new husband and their trip? "Why are you telling me this after all this time?"

"Believe me, I wasn't planning to. Then I saw your dress over there and changed my mind. I figured it doesn't matter anymore." Alma gawked at Lisa's ring.

"Ms. George, you have sunk to a new low, even for you."

"Not at all. I simply introduced two people to each other. It's not my fault Robert chose Stella over you."

Lisa withdrew her arm from Alma's grasp. "You have overstayed your welcome. Did you really care if I knew that girl's name or not?" Lisa asked Alma as she was almost out the door.

"I needed an opening line. I couldn't attack your little brain all at once, now could I?"

"Why, Alma," she asked, almost begging for a reason even if the reason was clear. She needed to hear it.

"Simple. Because I despise you." Alma took one last glance at Lisa's ring. "You have a nice honeymoon, dear."

ALMA HAD BEEN GONE no longer than fifteen minutes when James returned. It was his idea he and Lisa dine at The Château before departing.

Lisa dressed her finest, wearing an off-the-shoulder lilac taffeta frock and jacket, tight in the bodice, with sable trimming, that she'd purchased at Bloomingdales, and her new Cartier watch. James spoiled Lisa to every extent known, maybe because he saw her as a damsel in need of spoiling. To spend innumerable amounts of money on frivolous items was of no hindrance to him.

James requested they sit at the same table as on their first date. Lisa did not mind the arrogance of the aristocrats this time, given she was now one of them. Dinner at The Château was more elegant than lunchtime. As more experienced waiters carrying black rounded trays darted around tables with perfect precision without fear of colliding, Dick Hagen and His Orchestra played a soft instrumental version of George Gershwin's "But Not for Me".

The Mallory's white-covered table glowed with subtle candlelight. Serviettes were in a mountain fold at the center of the china. Lisa, a simple soul, examined the menu and found the cuisine to be above her standard knowledge. She did her best under the circumstances for James's sake.

Sam came up to the table wearing a friendly face. "Sam, my good friend," James said standing up and putting his arm around him. "I want you to meet my new wife. We're on our honeymoon."

"Congrats, both of you! I hope we can make your day a bit more enchanting, the cherry on top in a manner of speaking. Speaking of cherry, dessert is on the house. Our special today is the Raspberry Peach Clafoutis."

"Splendid!" James's face gleamed.

Sam poured water into their glasses, "Now, can I start you off with an appetizer or would you prefer to dive into the main course?"

"I am going to start with the stuffed escargot and my wife will have the stuffed mushrooms. For the main course, we'll have the pork tenderloin and a bottle of your most expensive white Burgundy." James looked at Lisa as he handed Sam the menus. She was wearing an unsure expression. "Don't worry, darling, you'll like it."

"Excellent choice. I'll get your appetizers out to you as soon as possible."

James asked her, "Tell me, do you feel different?" Lisa didn't answer. James leaned in closer. "You are the most gorgeous lady I have ever known."

Lisa took a sip of water. She wasn't hearing him. "Lisa, I didn't want to have to tell you this. I'm dying. I have three weeks to live."

Nothing.

"I knew it!" He struck the table so hard it shuddered and the silverware clattered. "Did he say something to upset you again?" He had her full attention now.

"Bashing me? Let me guess. He needs more money?"

"What are talking about?"

"Donald. What did he do?"

"I don't know what you're talking about. I haven't spoken with him since the wedding."

"What is wrong then?"

Lisa twisted her engagement ring around her finger. After all, he was her husband. But this was their night. "It's not important."

"It *is* important if it's important to you."

"Don't make me tell you, James. It would go against my better judgment." Lisa focused on him across the soft glow of the candle and smiled a big smile. It was a gift for him because her heart wasn't in it.

"Whatever you think is best, Ms. Lisa. Or should I say *Mrs.* Lisa?"

Lisa blushed.

Lisa spoke. "I wish my parents could have been there. They would have loved you. I'm sorry your mother couldn't see you getting married today. It's important for a mother to see her child on their wedding day, don't you think?"

James grumbled beneath his breath. "I wasn't all that upset."

"I've never met her. I've never met any of your family. She *is* my mother-in-law."

"Not this again," James muttered to himself and scratched his head in irritation. "I have not seen my mother in over twelve years. If I wanted you to meet any member of my family, I would have introduced you to them. Leave well enough alone."

"What is wrong with me wanting to meet your mother? It's not an unreasonable request."

"Drop it, I said!"

The restaurant got quiet. Lisa sank down in her chair. After what seemed like an eternity, the precious noise began to crescendo back to its original volume. James went too far and he knew it.

"I wonder what's keeping Sam. I'm getting hungry," said James. It was obvious he was trying to rekindle the affection at the table. Lisa didn't want to look at him or anyone else. "There is no excuse for me to talk to you that way."

James walked over to the other side of the table. When Lisa still wouldn't look, he kneeled down to one knee and embraced her waist. "I'm sorry, Lisa. Please forgive me."

Lisa gently reciprocated by grasping each side of his head between her hands. "Don't I always when your temper gets the best of you?"

"Come, I have a surprise for you."

"What is it?"

"You'll see."

James led her to the center of the dance floor, which was surrounded by the many round tables. Dick Hagen was relishing in a cigarette by the piano when James approached him.

After a brief exchange he gave a few nods and returned to Lisa on the sleek parquet. "This is for you."

"Ladies and gentlemen," Dick Hagen announced. "Permit me to introduce a new couple, married today." He pointed to the Mallorys with his baton and the club applauded. "With that said, the groom would like me to play a special song for the two of them on this, their special day. Everyone, give them another round of applause."

Within the clamor, the melodious "Mona Lisa" began. All other thoughts that consumed Lisa's mind before melted away. James took her waist into his hand. His warm fingers tickled her back. Lisa giggled like a girl of fifteen. It was a giggle that was more a feeling than an audible sound. It was a giggle that only her soul could feel.

James sang along with the music. He sang so low and only to her. He was slightly off-key; in her eyes he was Dean Martin.

Every woman watched as this dashing man guided Lisa around the lustrous floor. She mirrored his every move with the slow beat of the music. James twirled her smoothly around and dipped her. As his left arm held her weight, with his right hand he ran his fingers through her hair that dangled.

"I love you," she said.

"You know that's the second time you've said that to me. I may start believing it." Lisa laughed and James twirled her around and off her feet.

# CHAPTER SEVEN

They reached Syracuse around ten that night. James had made reservations at the Night and Day Bed and Breakfast.

James tapped the bell on the front desk. Within the dim lighting, Lisa observed this charming two-story house. Its lace curtains, fruit-decorated wallpaper, burnished wooden floors, and crown molding made this a much warmer place to spend the night, as opposed to a mammoth-sized grand hotel.

An elderly woman wearing a full-length quilted robe entered from the back. "How may I help you?" asked the lady as she yawned.

"I made reservations for tonight two weeks ago."

"Name?"

"Dr. James Mallory. This is my wife, Lisa. I apologize for our late arrival."

The woman flipped through her reservation book, scanning down the names with her finger. "Oh yes, here you are."

Lisa added, "We're on our honeymoon."

"That's wonderful. Well, sign in and I'll show you to your room." James collected the suitcases and followed the lady upstairs. "There is no one currently staying here; you're our only guests.

"I get up at six, so any time after I can leave you a wakeup call. Breakfast is at eight. It's quite a meal if you're interested in joining Glen and I."

"Seven will be fine," said James.

She handed James the key. "If you need anything just ask for Mrs. Franklin."

"Thank you very much," said Lisa as Mrs. Franklin walked carefully back down the steps. "Have you ever stayed here before?"

"A long, long time ago. This house has been here for many years." James opened the door and placed their suitcases inside the doorway. "Come. Let me carry you across."

"You're not serious. They only do that in movies, don't they?"

"So? Don't movies reflect the human heart's desires?" James started to turn, "Of course if you don't want me to..."

"No, no, I would like it very much."

James lifted her into his arms and stood in the hallway holding her close, gazing down at this fragile flower in his grasp. Lisa wrapped her arms around his neck and he stepped into the room. The room was charming with its simplicity. He laid her down upon the Queen-sized bed.

Lisa straightened her hair in the mirror of the antique bureau facing the bed. She glided her hands over the white diamond-pattern stitched quilt. "I never would've thought of staying at a bed and breakfast."

"I thought the peace and quiet would be a welcome change."

Lisa watched him as he pulled back the beige curtains to see the view. *I wonder what he's thinking.*

Lisa arched her back and neck and allowed her head to dangle. James smiled and rattled the keys inside his pocket. He crawled to the center of the bed behind her and massaged her neckline.

"Are you sleepy?" he asked. Lisa groaned at the pleasure of his fingers contracting her skin and muscle. James took the base of her chin and turned her head so he could taste her lips. The simple kiss never became more than what it started out as. An introduction.

He held her neck and he could feel her warm and gentle pulse along the sides. "My little waitress."

"I'm going to take off these uncomfortable clothes," she whispered, with the heat of her breath touching his face.

James remained on the bed while she slipped out of her dress, and with vigorous anticipation, braced for what was to come. An absolute tranquility took hold of him when Lisa stepped into the bedroom draped in her powder pink see-through negligée with lace trimming. Her alabaster skin, blushed, and cheeks of rosy hue complemented her hair that she'd unpinned from her head and let fall to her shoulders.

"Oh, my Lisa," breathed James as he took her. "Look at you."

James loosened the ribbon which held the negligée in place, exposing her cleavage. He lifted her onto the bed. Her breathing was erratic. It was then that he decided he would display his affection accordingly.

Lisa laid there in suspense. He switched off one of the lights, leaving only the lamp beside the bed to guide their vision. He stood high above her and unbuttoned his shirt and tossed it aside. There was an eager rise and fall of her chest as she admired his firm and strapping body.

Bending over, he connected his mouth with hers. She then felt the weight of his body softly come over hers.

THEY RELAXED BENEATH THE COVERS. The soothing cold sheets quickly warmed from their bodies. James stared at the ceiling as Lisa ran her fingers through the hairs of his chest.

"Didn't I meet you at a wedding?" she asked.

James rolled over and rested his head on Lisa's stomach. "What did you think?"

"Pretty good."

"Are you telling me I worked especially hard tonight for 'pretty good'?"

Lisa laughed and gave in with afterglow's fulfillment. "You got me."

"You were amazing."

"James, I have a question. It's not major, but...what did you mean by making me promise to never leave you?" Lisa stroked his head as it moved with her diaphragm.

At the time, Lisa didn't think much of it, but the more she mulled over it, the more it bothered her.

"I don't remember saying that."

"You did."

James moved back over. "I didn't mean to upset you."

"You didn't, it's just peculiar to me why you would pick while we're making love to bring it up."

James exhaled. "Why do you do that?"

"Do what?"

"Make molehills into mountains." Lisa sat up, resting her arms on her knees. James caressed her back seeing he insulted her. "I meant to tell you that I like your nightgown. Did you wear that on your first honeymoon?"

Lisa quickly got out of bed. James didn't know what to do. She threw her negligée over her shoulders and tied the bow tight in anger.

James darted out of bed and took Lisa by the shoulders before she reached the bathroom. "You listen to me. What happened here tonight happened out of love, and if you want to turn it into something else, well, we both know you're able." The slight drop of her head told him he'd reached her.

She knew he was right, but that didn't make it easier. "You see, anything having to do with my previous marriage...that's why I sometimes react to the littlest things."

"Don't you think it's time I know?"

Lisa walked over to the mirror in dismay and watched James across the room in it. "You must promise me that once I tell you, the subject of Robert will never arise again."

"Alright."

Lisa wrung her hands. Still, there was no greater act of trust and love, and then the painful memory was easier for her to reveal.

"It was November, 1949. I just moved into the apartment that I live in now. At the time, Alma – you know Alma."

"I've stumbled into her."

"Anyway, she was quite popular in the complex, well known for giving small parties. And since I was her new neighbor...of course she invited me. I was hesitant to go at first, but decided it would be good for me to meet new people."

James's eyes followed her. "She was a damn know-it-all, but did know a lot of people and how to amuse them. Nobody paid any mind to me. I sat in the corner sipping cold duck watching everybody pass me by."

It had been some time since Lisa permitted herself to revisit the memory.

*She sits in a chair with her drink on the small table within the cramped alcove. She pulls back a corner of the peach-tinted curtains. The black skyline and long horizontal glow of the city gives her the chance to escape from the chatter saturating the room. A woman dressed in red passes her. Lisa tries to grab her attention.*

She rests her head on her hand, bored, wondering why she agreed to the invitation. A loud cackle comes from the next room, Alma's cackle. Everyone quiets and chuckles in response.

"It was then that I looked up and spotted a dark-complected, sophisticated young man eyeing me from the next room. I even remember what he was wearing. A dark blue pinstripe suit, with his brown hair smoothed back. When he saw that I'd noticed him he made his way over to where I was."

James was relaxed on the bed engrossed in Lisa's story.

"So warm and cordial, he introduced himself and offered me another libation. The *good* stuff, not the cheap bubbly Alma was serving to her least favorite guests. He was so charming, James, and he was from London."

*"I don't believe we've met. What is your name?"*

*"Lisa," she replies, admiring his stunning smile and soft voice. "And yours?"*

*"Robert. Ms. George enjoys these frivolous little get-togethers quite often and I've been to every one of them. You must be new." Robert unbuttons his jacket before he sits opposite her. His accent captures her instantly.*

*"I moved in a week ago. Alma introduced me to pretty much everyone on this floor. Which floor do you live on?"*

*"Oh, I don't live here anymore; moved out a month ago. Yes, she still invites me." Robert looks around to make sure no one's eave-*

sdropping. *"To be honest, I don't care for these modest gatherings."*

*"Why?"*

*"Well, I've known Alma for a couple years now and she always seems to have a motive behind them."*

Robert's tender blue eyes gaze at her for a moment. Lisa's brown eyes do the same. "I noticed you were new and thought I could help alleviate some of the tension that comes with the territory."

*"That's very kind of you," says Lisa. "No one has paid any attention to me all evening. Alma let me in and then disappeared. I'm glad you came over." Lisa looks down and fiddles with her watch.*

*"This may sound forward, but I would be obliged if I could share in your company for a while."*

*Lisa straightens her necklace. She already knows the answer she is going to give, but pauses as to give the impression she's pondering. "I would enjoy that very much."*

"What happened after that?"

"We talked all night. Everything went so fast. It was great in the beginning, like us. He treated me like I was his entire world. He took me dancing every weekend.

"It would have stayed that way, too, except he was an alcoholic." Lisa struck the wall. "I disregarded many warnings and married him anyway...like us, four-months-later."

"Why, Lisa?"

"Because I loved the bastard. Oh, he tried to defend his drinking with a troubled youth story. He wept and I wept with him. He couldn't hold down a job for longer than a month before his employers grew sick of him coming into work late and hung over.

"He worked for Larry for a couple weeks and even *I* couldn't convince Larry to let him stay on. Soon after, he gave up working altogether."

"I'm getting the picture."

Lisa walked over to James and sat beside him. "You don't know the half of it. Living with that man was like *The Lost Weekend*."

He put his arm around her. "Donny fought like mad to get me to leave him, but I couldn't bring myself to do it."

"Your love for him was pretty strong, huh?"

"It managed to last through brutal rows and plastered nights when I'd have to wait up for him into the wee hours of the morning wondering if he'll come home. Still, I would've traded that for the times I had to pick him up at the police station."

"He must have loved you, too."

"I suppose, for a while. But...it was *Robert* that divorced me. He found someone he liked better, someone different...younger. I waved goodbye to my husband of five years and the girl who would soon take my place."

James never expected that. Lisa could read it on his face. He laid her back, using his hand as a pillow for her head. He empathized if she held any uncertainty towards him.

"It was Alma that introduced him to that girl. It was Alma. She did it." A tear inched its way down the side of her nose. Lisa wept pitifully with a still-broken heart as James held her near him.

"So that's why you were so down at the club this afternoon. Everything is alright now." He used the bed sheet to dry her eyes.

"I feel so foolish." Lisa rubbed her itchy reddened eyes. "You've seen me at my best and now you've seen me at my worst, and you're still here. That's promising."

James led her to the bathroom to wash her face. He propped himself against the doorframe and watched as water streamed down her face and neck. "If it were me you fell in love with nine years ago, and me that became an alcoholic and left you..."

"James."

"Considering all we've been to one another these few short months, well, I would beg your forgiveness so that I could make it right." Lisa smiled. "Robert didn't appreciate the gem he had and I'm glad for it."

IN EACH OTHER'S ARMS THEY SLEPT for the remainder of the night until Mrs. Franklin woke them at 7:00 a.m. And though they acquired less than three hours sleep, they both awoke refreshed and full of alacrity for the coming day ahead. Mrs. Franklin prepared a hearty breakfast for the new couple to nourish them for their 150-mile trek to Buffalo.

Before they made their way down, Lisa requested James go on ahead so she could take care of a couple things. Without delay, she went to the telephone and called home. It rang once, twice, three times...

*Come on, answer the phone.* – Four times, five....

She tapped her fingernails against the receiver until the operator's voice emanated from the other end. "Damn." Lisa slammed the receiver down. *Not even Rebecca? They can't all be gone.*

She speculated if they were choosing not to answer. She felt she needed to speak with Donald due to his current state-of-mind, but was now doubly bothered. It was ridiculous to try to contact her brother after one day, but it was a habit, this constant fretting over him since childhood. His existing predicament worried her as much as him. Each day was crucial to their survival in that merciless city.

The exhilaration of Niagara's cascading falls, with its translucent surge, rising mist and mighty wind, kept Lisa spellbound at this once-in-a-lifetime experience. The atmosphere was cool and moist, and their skin became damp. Each breath her lungs inhaled was fresh and crisp compared to New York's dense and laden oxygen. This was heaven.

She felt open and emancipated, free to do anything, even fly away if so inclined. The roar of the falls surrounded them. Lisa placed her arm around her husband. He kissed the top of her head.

Soon the dream would end and reality would take over. All of what they shared would be a memory. Even as Lisa savored this moment with him, the changes that were to transpire crossed her mind.

It was exciting, yet vague, and she imagined the best.

# CHAPTER EIGHT

Six months later.

Lisa's new life felt spectacular. At the beginning of each day she anticipated what new experience was to come for an absolute new woman of class and distinction.

Cos Cob, Greenwich, Connecticut is where they opted to purchase their home. Being a wealthy area, and remembering Lisa told him how tired of the city she was, it was nothing short of what James was hunting for. Thirty miles away from the stone forest on ten acres of land rested their luxurious two-story dwelling. Within this vast 8,000 sq. ft. house made of stone were six bedrooms, three full baths, formal dining room, and gourmet kitchen with breakfast bar, a spacious patio, recreation room, office, attic, and basement.

Lisa entered through the private entrance and called out to her husband. Her voice echoed throughout like sonar, stretching past the crystal chandelier of the twenty-foot foyer to the furthest bedroom on the opposite side of the house. Her new home seemed to be alive and beckoned her to come in.

Each room was busy with incoming furniture; large carpets, drapes, and décor. While James helped the movers transfer the furniture, Lisa walked up the long, curved, beige-carpeted staircase carrying a satchel. She rotated the brass knob to the wooden door of the master bedroom at the left end of the hall.

Lisa pulled out the only item the satchel contained: The silver-framed photograph of her and Donald. "I miss you," she sighed and placed the photograph on the fireplace mantle.

"Darling?" she heard her husband speak from behind her.

Lisa adjusted the picture. "He and I have nothing to say."

"You haven't spoken since Christmas. It's because of this that I detest him."

She sat down on the King bed. "Do you think he will profit by this new job?"

"Nightshift motel clerks don't make that much money. But that, in addition to the cab driving, should support the family."

"And us?"

James rubbed his nose in frustration and sat next to her. "We both agreed that as soon as he got back on his feet, we would stop the charity. Will it ever be enough?"

That bothered her. Not his gall to ask, but the question itself. When would it be enough?

*What about Julia and Simon? Would Donny deprive them of their aunt? And why hasn't Rebecca helped?*

What was going on over there? Would James cause that much turmoil?

WITH DONALD NO LONGER IN HER LIFE at present, though she missed him dearly, was able to breathe. No more having to run to his apartment during work to calm another marital spat. No more of his surprise visits to the diner drenched in sweat and tears to discuss the monthly rent he didn't have. Above all – no more having to cope with Donald's relentless insults and slander towards her husband.

By mid-March the Mallory home was nearly finished. All that was left was to paint the den which was in the old section of the house. Lisa's schedule had not changed for the most part. She arose at five instead of seven, drank her cup of black coffee, took a quick shower, and dressed for work.

James was the boss of his business and could make his own schedule. He opposed Lisa's agenda, telling her, "You are a wealthy woman and do not need to work." Lisa didn't want to quit. She wouldn't have felt right leaving Larry and the diner with some other supervisor who couldn't handle the strain.

The least James could do was see that his lady had a safe mode of travel from Point A to Point B. She found that her powder blue 1959 Buick Lesabre Convertible was a lavish essential. Lavish for its make and essential because she never would have known the headache of not having a car until she had one.

James opened the car door for her. "You be careful. It's a long way."

"Don't tell me you're worried about me."

"Of course not. I don't want you wrecking your new expensive car I bought you." James bent down into the car to kiss her.

She drove out of the hedge-lined, cobblestone driveway. That was the first feature that attracted her to the house; it reminded her of an old London street. She watched James wave in her rearview mirror. By the time she reached the station she realized he was right.

She would be driving her car to the station and then the train for the one-hour trek to Grand Central, and after work back to the New Haven Line for one hour, and then to the car, and then home. This was just the first day and already the idea of doing this day in day out sounded exhausting and tedious. Besides, this was a new chapter in her life. As Act II begins, Act I must close.

Lisa observed her hardworking, reliant employer, remembering all the years they put in to make his modest little diner operate. Now that she was contemplating leaving, she was more appreciative of him. With the passing of her parents and the subsequent war, she was not able to qualify herself. Then Larry came along and gave her a chance.

What Lisa didn't know at the time was that he needed her just as much. The diner was drowning in debt and sinking fast. He was searching for one loyal employee who could follow orders and take the heat and make others do the same. He never anticipated she would become his equal, let alone his friend. The diner seemed to be the jewel in the crown of this mid-sixties man who devoted the majority of his retirement to his business.

Lisa watched as Larry laughed while he took the order of his favorite regular. His big belly jiggled, his pudgy face turned red, and she almost shed a tear. This was going to be hard.

It was dusk when she made it home. The house was dark. James wasn't home.

She stopped at the entrance to retrieve the mail before parking in the two-car garage. She rolled her eyes at the sight of "Frisco" printed on the envelopes addressed to her.

All accept one.

It had no return address. She set her things down on the island in the kitchen. It was flimsy and bent as she broke open the seal across the top with her finger. Inside was a small piece of paper folded in half.

Lisa gasped. The rush of air entering her lungs chilled her throat. She read it again. Her heart thumped against the wall of her chest as she read the typewritten note aloud to herself to make sure her eyes and ears were in agreement.

> *You are hated.*
> *I am hated.*
> *Be ready.*

Lisa pressed her fingers into the paper. Whoever sent it was aware of her name change. She looked to the top right of the envelope for the post mark – *"March 17, 1959 – Yonkers, NY."*

"I don't know anyone in Yonkers." Nothing whatsoever tipped her off as being conspicuous, not even the four-cent postage stamp.

*This has to be a joke,* Lisa assured herself. *No one would...Joe? But why?* The more Lisa thought about it the more she seethed. She tore the paper down the center and froze halfway.

A voice from deep within made her stop. *What could it hurt?* She stuffed the note back in its envelope and in her handbag.

"I DON'T KNOW IF I LIKE THIS COLOR," said Lisa.

James shook his paintbrush at her from on top the ladder in the den. "Darling, this is the third time you've changed your mind. Besides, I've already painted half the wall. What's wrong with beige? It goes with the furniture, doesn't it?"

"You needn't get mad at me. The color we pick is the color we'll have to live with." Lisa turned lamps on and off around the room.

"I was hoping we could spend a little quiet time together and..."

"And you think *that* would be more relaxing?"

"Definitely more fun than painting a wall for the third damn time."

Lisa went over to the phonograph. "Come here. I'd like to play you something." James rushed down the ladder, throwing the dripping brush into the paint can. "It's a new hit song from Bobby Darin."

"Never heard of him."

"I picked it up a couple days ago. He's a very gas celebrity among the teen crowd."

James looked at her. "Gas?" She placed the needle to the record as he listened with pending ears.

"Don't you keep up with the times, Grandpa? "Gas" refers to whatever is popular or cool...I think. Rebecca told me." Lisa thought she would try twisting and shaking to the beat. James stood back. He wanted to laugh but loved her too much to do it out loud.

"What is that you're doing?"

"Dancing."

"Are you sure?"

"Come on, give it a try." Lisa grabbed his arm and pulled him to her. "Do what I'm doing."

James followed her lead and reluctantly gyrated. He was stiffer than her and embarrassed by this. "Forget it. I'm too old for this kind of dancing." James hit the reject button. "I'm more of a Rachmaninoff man."

"What's wrong with trying something new?"

"Nothing...if you're young enough." James blew her a kiss and left down the hall.

The doorbell rang. She pulled back the curtain of the sidelight window and cursed when she saw the back of Joe's gray head. So far it was a good day, but now it seemed that hung in the balance. Lisa opened the door in time to catch him flicking a cigarette into the magnolia tree next to the house.

"Ahem."

Joe turned around. "Hey sorry, I know it's late. I need to see Jimmy." He started to enter.

Lisa was not in the mood to deal with him. "James is not here," she said sharply, blocking him with the door.

"I can wait." Joe tried to come in once more, but Lisa again used the door as a blockade. "I'm getting the impression you don't want me here." His voice was subtle yet sinister.

James shouted from the top of the stairs. "Who is it, darling?"

Lisa closed her eyes tight. "It's Joe!"

"Tell him I'll be down in a bit!"

"I guess I'm coming in." Joe used his forefinger to push open the door. With Lisa following behind, Joe went into the den and sprawled out on the golden sofa. She observed this so-called man in disgust.

Lisa listened to the grandfather clock tick away the uncomfortable silence. For such a large room, the ticks were loud. The threatening note returned to her. Perhaps it was Joe's company that triggered it.

"Ha-have you been to Yonkers lately?" she asked. Joe clinched his eyebrows. Asking him this was nerve-wracking. Like balancing on a tightrope, it was bound to go wrong. "What I mean is, um, do you know anyone from there?"

"What's your point?"

*Get it over with, Lisa.*

"Did you send me the note?" There was a long pause as Joe glared with his black eyes. This hastened Joe's apparent guilt in her mind. Lisa put a hand to her mouth. "You did."

"I don't know what the hell you're talking about, lady."

"It came in the mail a couple days ago. It's probably nothing. Don't tell James; he doesn't know."

"Ha, he probably does. I warned you." Joe relished in a devious grin, his lips curved and warped with delight.

"Joe, you *better* think twice if you intend proceeding on that notion." Lisa stood her ground.

Joe advanced, massive and cross. Lisa staggered behind the sofa. "I don't give a damn what you do. I tell it like it is, and if you can't take it, that's no problem of mine."

Like his alleged warning before the wedding, she refused to believe him. He must have sent it. Despite his not admitting to it, why would he? And why accuse his friend?

"Tell me, what did it say?"

"Honestly, I don't feel comfortable telling you. You claim that my husband sent it, yet you have no proof. You advise me to watch my back the *day of* my wedding. Why should I believe you?"

"Why shouldn't you believe me?" Joe made his way around the sofa. "A dishy number like yourself married to a man she really doesn't know." He stood right next to her.

"He doesn't talk about his family, does he?" He placed his hand on her shoulder. Lisa stopped breathing. "Did you think for one instant that I didn't know you were sticking all of your uncertainties on me? Why is that?

"Because you, the former Ms. Frisco, found a handsome, rich man who happened to find you attractive, and losing that would send you right back down that goddamn mountain that took you years to get up. Tell me I'm wrong." Lisa couldn't bear to open her eyes. Joe's thick, hairy hand brushed the side of her face.

"Loneliness is one of the deadliest poisons. It could have easily been me in his place and that wouldn't have mattered to you. Except I would've made you glad to be a woman the first night, I bet."

Lisa could feel his lips touch her earlobe. Inside she trembled. His presence, his words, and his accuracy were almost too much to bear. She wanted to scream, but felt invisible hands were clasping her neck.

He placed her hair behind her ear and breathed low, "I know you fear me. When Jimmy introduced us, I sensed it. I don't blame you for thinking I sent the letter. I don't blame you for not believing me when I tell you Jimmy is a threat to you, but I'm not the one being threatened, now am I?"

He withdrew and peeled off the shoulder of Lisa's lilac blouse. His hot breath moistened her bare skin. "My..." Lisa swallowed hard. "My husband will be down any minute." Her voice quivered so much that she managed to speak only through exhaling breaths.

Joe returned her blouse to its rightful place. "I'm a patient man." He walked back around the sofa. "Relax. I think I hear him coming."

Lisa opened her eyes to find she was digging her nails into the fabric of the velvet sofa.

"Afternoon, Joe." James put his arm around Lisa's waist. She was startled at first and then was calm. Every inch of her body was frozen. There Joe stood, still in front of her, composed.

"I apologize for the wait," said James. "I had to wash up. I've been painting."

Out of the blue, Joe shut his eyes into tight slits and grabbed the back of his neck.

"Joe?"

Joe bent over. "I'll be fine, Jimmy. It'll pass in a minute."

"I don't like it. These attacks of yours are becoming more frequent."

Lisa was in a trance. *What happened? God, what just happened? What will James say?*

How will I tell him? He has to know; it may happen again. What if those things Joe said are true? They can't be true. My husband has never laid a finger on me.

"Lisa, are you alright?" James was holding her up. Lisa hadn't realized she nearly fell to the floor.

"It must be the paint fumes. I-I need to go upstairs and lie down." Lisa started to leave, but James wouldn't release her hand. "I'm okay, James. Let me go."

She grabbed hold of the banister and looked back. James still watched with concern, and behind him was Joe, smiling. At this point she was too tired to know what to think. It was not a question of what to believe, but more a question of principle. Joe's status hit rock-bottom and her husband of seven months had earned her confidence and devotion.

All she knew was she loved James and hated Joe. That made sense to her.

# CHAPTER NINE

**"W**hat are you doing in my office?!"

Lisa backed into the bookcase and a single book fell over. "James, you startled me."

He glared at her from the doorway. "Step away from the bookcase."

"I-I was just doing some light dusting."

"We have a housekeeper for that." She wasn't moving so James rushed in, took her by the arm, and ushered her out. "I told you before I don't want you in here. My office is the only restriction I've given you, Lisa.

"You can go anywhere you please, but you must respect my privacy." James closed the door. He stood in front of it with one hand gripping her wrist and the other on the knob. "I will make this clear one more time for you. This door stays shut unless I open it, understand?"

"I forgot."

"See that you don't again." James released her and went downstairs.

Lisa was shocked. It was her house as much as his. But she would respect his wishes.

"I CAN'T BELIEVE YOU'RE LEAVING. After nine years?"

"Yes, Larry. I-I feel that it's time." Lisa leaned over the white countertop that she had cleaned hundreds of times, a look of pain etched across her face.

That little diner that bore witness to the laughter, the hard work, and the meeting of her sweetheart, had become her home away from home. And Larry was her pop, never ceasing to supervise his loyal employee that kept his diner afloat.

"I'll give you time to find a replacement, of course," said Lisa.

Joe put his fists on his hips with a long sigh. "No one could replace you. I don't want you to go, but if you must...leave whenever you're ready.

"If you take care of James the way you've taken of me all these years, he will love and appreciate you that much more." Lisa recognized how true his words must have been for him to speak them aloud. The discussion was overdue and the burden felt good to release.

Lisa got off work at 5:00 p.m. sharp when the veins of the beast swarmed with people, and she merged with them, taking her place amid the crowd. Wind hoisted her hair from her shoulders as she quickened her pace. She spotted a cabbie lounging against his taxi, but a man helped himself to the backseat.

Every yellow that passed was occupied. Impatient people lined the sidewalk as far as the eye could see, throwing out their arms. Lisa walked to the edge to join them.

*I would like to get home before James does so I can start dinner,* Lisa thought.

She looked to her left at the approaching Greyhound bus looming over the encompassing vehicles. Her body aching with fatigue she let her head fall back to the blackened skyscrapers above.

*I think...*

Two hands pressed deep into her shoulder blades. Her neck cracked from the force shoving her body forward like a doll. Her head slammed against the pavement. Everything went dark. She scraped her nails against the road as she tried to pick herself up with her bare knees that were bloody from the coarse asphalt.

All she could see was a massive dark blur approaching from her left. She cupped her hand over her right eye as a trickle of blood dripped over it. The mass grew larger, engulfing her completely.

A woman screamed and the noise of the city ceased. Lisa looked fast at the intercity bus. The rubber tires screamed in agony to stop the 40,000-pound giant. Lisa's legs were submerged beneath the bus and she could feel its heat.

Two men lifted her up by her shoulders and pulled her out. Lisa stumbled over her feet as she held her hand over the gash. She knew that she felt two distinct hands push her. Her eyes darted to each of the spectators. Whoever it was escaped through the crowd.

The men rested her on the curb. Another man removed his jacket and placed it under her. People gathered around her, some gawking and some shouting questions. Lisa moaned from the constant burning of the open wound.

The driver of the bus parked the next street over and prodded his way through the people. "God, I am so, so sorry! Is she okay? She's bleeding."

A woman answered, "I don't know. It doesn't look good."

One of the men that carried her bent down to speak to her, "An ambulance is on its way to take you to the hospital." He held a handkerchief to her cut.

"What happened?" asked Lisa very shaken.

"You stumbled into the street and were nearly run over."

"Some-someone...pushed me." Lisa looked up at the faces that gazed curiously down at her. "Why are you looking at me like that?"

"There was nobody near you, ma'am."

"I didn't see anyone except you," added the driver.

Lisa tried standing until the buildings started to spin and the man sat her back down. "I-I need to call my husband."

6No, ma'am, you *need* to go to the hospital. You can call him later."

The ambulance soon arrived and carted Lisa off to the nearest hospital. All she could think about as doctors assessed and stitched up her wound was James and how she was going to explain to him what happened. No critical concussion evident, they released her the next morning with a headache and a prescription for pain medicine.

A rays of sun peeked over the horizon as she pulled into the driveway. Most every light in the house was on. Her head was throbbing and she rested it against the steering wheel, so looking forward to finding comfort in her husband's arms.

"Where in the *hell* have you been?!" James hollered. Lisa stood in the doorway taking the key out of the lock. James charged out of the den with his hands clinched into fists. "I've been up all night, calling everyone I know to call – Donald, Larry.

"I checked with Grand Central, a handful of hospitals. I even called your old neighbor. Don't just stand there! Say something!"

"James, please...I-I have to lie down. I'm so tired." She grasped her head and fell against the door.

James rushed to her. "Darling, what's happened? Your head!" He held her head in his hands.

"They tried to get a hold of you, but couldn't get through. I need to lie down."

James carried her up the stairs to their bedroom and placed her gently on the bed. He lit the fireplace so its golden embers could work its warming and relaxing magic on the room. He then slipped off her shoes and stockings.

"What did they tell you?" James lifted up one side of the white bandage and examined her stitches. The wound was an inch long and there were about six stitches that he could see through the red and inflamed skin.

"Just that I need to go home and rest."

"No concussion or head trauma?"

"No."

"That's a relief." James returned the bandage.

Lisa took his hand from her head, kissed the inside of his palm, and held it to her cheek. If only he were there when it happened, she thought. He would have made everything better, or it wouldn't have happened at all.

"You're here with me now," James breathed and laid his head on her chest.

"I was pushed."

James rose up. He didn't have to ask. His reaction did that for him.

Lisa pushed herself up with her arms. "I was trying to get a cab and somebody pushed me into the street. That's how I got this gash on my forehead. It happened so fast I wasn't able to catch myself."

James began stroking her leg. "Who pushed you?"

"I didn't see."

"Darling, the streets are overflowing with people every day."

"What do you mean?"

"What I mean is someone probably bumped into you." Lisa stared at him. He didn't believe her. "Lisa, I visited New York numerous times before I met you, and when rush-hour came, I felt like I was playing bumper cars, sidewalks like schools of fish."

"James, look at me! Look at my head!"

"I don't doubt that you fell, but for what reason would a person have for pushing you into the street?"

"I *know* when I've been pushed! I felt his hands!"

"It was a man?"

"I don't know. I guess. Or a woman with large hands." James shook his head. "Someone pushed me in front of a bus, dammit!"

"Hey, hey, calm down."

"I will not calm down! I could have died today had it not been for the alert reflexes of the bus driver."

James took her hands, "And I'm so thankful they were. You must rest. Please, lie back." Only because she was so exhausted did she follow his instruction. Not wanting to see him anymore, she turned over and closed her eyes.

"If you need me, I'll be downstairs." He turned out the light and left. The morning sun could not penetrate the dark curtains. The soft glow of the fire lit up half of the room, leaving Lisa's half and the bed she was in in darkness.

Immediately she drifted off, but it was far from peaceful. She relived the experience again, but in this dream she saw who pushed her.

James stood erect, bearing a sneer only Joe Norris could display.

All was silent and life went on as normal as her death was inches away. Fear paralyzed her. The shadow came over her once again. She knew what was coming, but the glint of malevolence behind those once-loving eyes caused her to forget the oncoming monster.

Lisa gripped the covers, her face scrunched and distorted in anguish as the dense tires rolled on top of her, smashing her legs one slow inch at a time. She screamed for James to save her. He *had* to come; he was her husband. She tried calling out to him one last time, but the mass flattened her lungs and the remaining air that was inside them.

James did nothing.

Joe's deep voice emanated from nowhere. It was a voice only she could hear as if her own conscience had assumed a different tone. *You knew this would happen. I told you. I told you.*

The very last thing she saw before the bus covered her completely was her husband grinning.

"Lisa! Lisa, wake up! Wake up, Lisa!" James was holding her up and shaking her when she awoke from the nightmare.

"What-what's g-going on?"

"You were screaming for me. You sounded frightened as if someone was hurting you." James wiped the sweat from her brow. "I'm sorry for what I said. I shouldn't have doubted you, darling."

"No, I wasn't thinking straight. Everyone that witnessed me fall told me they didn't see anyone."

James embraced her, holding her body as near to his as possible.

It was wonderful for Lisa to know that he cared for her enough to apologize, even if she was wrong. If someone actually pushed her into traffic, a bystander would have seen. If her own husband deemed it as melodramatic nonsense, then that was good enough for her.

"It's after twelve. I've made us lunch if you're hungry."

"I'm starved."

"Good. We'll eat out on the patio."

Lisa did her best not to dwell on the accident or the nightmare. The image of James grinning at her from the sidewalk was burned into her brain.

SARDI'S, so elegant, enthralled Lisa with its luxuriant ambiance and continental food. Be it dining there quite an experience, it almost surpassed The Château, except for her it didn't share equal sentiment.

They sat at an arched booth that touched the side of the next. The wall behind and around them was masked with back-to-back caricatures of movie stars.

"I've eaten here several times," stated James straightening his russet tie.

"I haven't. But I did see the *I Love Lucy* episode. You know the one with William Holden?"

"I must have missed that one."

Lisa observed her surroundings and the people as she sipped her Bronx Cocktail. When James suggested Sardi's she jumped at the opportunity, hopeful she would catch a celebrity, but no Bill Holdens dined there today.

"Is there anything particular you would like to do after dinner?" James asked.

Lisa glanced at the far corner across the room at a gray-haired man sitting at a table with his back to them. She did a double take. Even from behind the guy looked familiar.

"Lisa?"

"Oh, I don't know. Maybe we could see a movie or...something." James turned around to see what she was looking at. "I think I would prefer to spend a quiet evening at home."

"Fine with me. I would much rather curl up in front of the television next to you any day." James entwined his fingers with hers on the table.

"James, I've been meaning to talk to you about my job. I discussed it with Larry and I've decided to quit."

Lisa glanced at the corner in time to catch the gray-haired man swiftly turning his head back. He was checking her out, too. A waiter came up to his table and the man spoke. She recognized that voice.

It can't be. Not in a restaurant like this.

"Do you know when your last day will be?" asked James.

Lisa shifted her focus back to her husband. "When Larry finds a replacement." She quickly looked back at an empty chair and a moving figure that managed to drift with the current of hustling servers.

"What is going on with you tonight?" James released her hand and looked behind him a second time.

Lisa scanned the restaurant. "I'm sorry. Since I hit my head, I haven't felt right."

"Do you want to go home?"

"No, we came here to have an enjoyable evening together."

As they ate, James conversed about his patients and their ailments. Lisa paid attention, although she was fixated more on all that had transpired – the threat, the fall, and even Joe's speech. It was taking its toll.

They strolled down the sidewalk to the car that was parked a block away. Lisa nestled beside her husband's cozy arm. James lightly kissed the top of her head.

"I was thinking," Lisa began. "The other day when you didn't know where I was and you said that you called Donald looking for me..."

"Yes?"

"I was wondering what he said."

James sighed. "Your brother...um, let's just say he was abrupt."

"What did he say?"

"Lisa, I don't see the point..."

Lisa let go of his arm. She had to know if Donald was worried about her.

"He hung up." That she did not expect. "I told him you hadn't come home and that I didn't know where you were. When I started to ask him if he knew anything, he hung up."

Lisa couldn't stop the incoming destructive thoughts. *He doesn't love me anymore. He doesn't care.*

James pulled her to him. For the first time, his touch, his voice didn't take away the pain and disheartening thoughts. This heartbreak was something new.

"You did everything for him. That was your mistake. You feel betrayed? You have every reason in the world to feel that way. Your brother is a self-centered bastard."

"You were right all along." It was taking everything in her not to fall apart.

"What are you going to do?" asked James.

"I'm going to have to..."

Lisa didn't know if she could say it. Everyone, except Lisa, saw Donald the way she sees him now. To her he was the boy in the photograph; he was the little brother who followed her everywhere. As the years passed, she found she needed his dependence. No longer.

Lisa huffed. "I'm going to stop."

A single tear escaped when she closed her eyes. She embraced James and rested her chin on his shoulder. She saw the silhouette of a man dash from an entryway into the alley behind them.

They continued down the path. Lisa peeped over her husband's arm. The same time a head emerged out of the alley. She accelerated her pace.

James asked, "We're not in any hurry, are we?"

Lisa didn't slow. The silhouette followed and was keeping its distance.

"What is wrong with you, Lisa?"

Lisa stopped dead in her tracks and turned fiercely around. "Whoever you are..." She couldn't see the person, but knew they were there.

James grabbed her arm. "Stop this."

"I know you're there!"

"Lisa, let me take you home."

A voice came from behind them. "Having troubles keeping a hold of your old lady?" Lisa spun around. Joe Norris appeared.

*How did he get ahead?*

"What a coincidence that I run into you two." Joe relocated his eyes to Lisa. "That's a nasty cut you got there." He reached for her. "I hope you're okay."

Lisa seized his hand, jabbing her nails into his flesh. "Don't even *think* about laying a finger on me. I know that was you at Sardi's." Lisa pulled away from her husband. "I don't know why you've been following me, but I'm tired of your malicious nature."

Joe's grin diminished. "Look lady, I haven't seen you for a week to my good fortune. I was with a client."

"And what was the name of this so-called client?"

James interceded. "Her head took a good blow the other day and she's been in a lot of pain. I tell you what, drop in tomorrow and..."

"No, no!" Lisa shouted at the top of her voice and stomped her foot. "He's no longer welcome in my house! Anytime you're around things happen. I do not think it's a coincidence."

Lisa stepped in close. Providing James was near she felt safe. "Anyone who would purposely try to frighten a bride the day of her wedding is a lousy excuse for a human being."

"What?" James asked.

"And as if that wasn't enough, to continue frightening her is just plain evil."

Rid of Joe – rid of the problem. That was Lisa's approach. Confronting him face-to-face and verbalizing her thoughts made her feel strong.

"If you want to see my husband, you will have to meet somewhere where I'm not. Do you understand?"

"Yes, ma'am," Joe solemnly replied.

"I haven't yet gathered what you're up to, Joe, but I won't be a sitting duck waiting around to find out what that is."

The tension between Lisa and her husband's friend could not be strained any further. Lisa inhaled the fresh air as the 220-pound weight was lifted off her shoulders.

James took her arm and led her away.

"Goodbye, *Mr.* Norris."

Joe watched them until they were no longer in sight.

# CHAPTER TEN

Rebecca, with a special enough reason to celebrate, relished in its limelight. It was the killing of the fatted calf – a time of joyous occasion.

Lisa draped the stairs with long, colorful strips of garland. Multicolored balloons hovered high above the chandelier, gliding across the coffered ceiling with the slightest draft. Larry and Genevieve assisted with the food and refreshments that they were arranging on the dining room table. James was keeping watch, ready to alert the guests.

"James, can you help me raise the banner? They'll be here any minute."

The Wells family were in the back seat of the cab on the way to Lisa's filled with uncertainty.

"I wonder what's going on, Lisa asking us over," said Rebecca. "We haven't spoken in months," she uttered with a glint of blame aimed at him.

Donald returned, "Beau Brummel probably has a bone to pick. I bet he wants his money back."

"I expect you to be nice. They've helped us quite a bit. Accepting their invitation was the least we could do."

Donald combed Julia's ponytail as she sat on his boney knee; her fluffy dress made it comfy. "I'll be nice for the kids. Driver, are we almost there?" he yelled, impatient and on edge.

"Lisa gave me the directions, dear. There should be no problem finding the place."

They pulled into the driveway and drove a ways before the path curved and the stone mansion came to view. Donald swallowed hard at the sight of it. It was outstanding. Rebecca was reminded of one of the works of art hanging on her wall: A distant mansion on a Sunday afternoon where the most opulent people are gathering for a soiree and in the foreground a handsome gent assists his lady with her pink parasol out of the carriage.

"Donald, oh Donald, *look!*" Rebecca clutched his arm, her eyes huge. Donald could hardly focus to pay the driver. Holding the tiny hands of their children, they walked up the steps.

The house appeared to reach high into the clouds and blocked out the sun. Donald couldn't fathom his sister living in such a place. She was just Lisa after all. He breathed deep and rang the bell. They could only imagine what was behind those giant wooden doors.

"Surprise!" every person shouted with their hands held high.

Rebecca grabbed her chest. A large banner reading: 'CONGRATULATIONS REBECCA: ATTONRNEY AT LAW' hung from the stairwell with everyone standing before it applauding.

Lisa came out from behind the door. Rebecca embraced her. "Lisa, you did this for me?"

"Did you think I would pass up a big achievement such as this? Not on your life."

Lisa bent down to Julia and kissed the child. "I'm glad you came." Though she spoke to her, it was directed at the man beside her. Donald cleared his throat.

Lisa turned to her guests, "Okay everybody, before we begin, we'll toast Rebecca's passing of the bar exam. Refreshments are in the dining room. Once you've taken a glass please return to the foyer."

James said, "Follow me and I'll show you where everything is." Lisa watched Donald lagging behind the guests with his hands stuffed in his pockets.

When they returned with their drinks Rebecca stood atop the stairs, her family and friends below. "I-I didn't prepare. I don't know what to say."

"That would be a first!" teased a girlfriend from school.

"That'll be enough out of you, Betty!" Rebecca gazed at all of the anticipating faces and ran her finger around the contour of her glass. "I, um, would like all of you to know how much I appreciate you being here."

Lisa glanced at Donald whose glass was already empty.

Rebecca continued, savoring and prolonging the accolades. "I remember the night before I took the LSAT, Donald told me I could accomplish anything I put my mind to, and he knew I would pass. With four years of undergraduate study, three years of law, and my residency at Benson and Abbott, I proved myself worthy of graduation."

Rebecca was erect like a statue representing valor. "I would like to thank Dr. Mallory's coworkers for taking time out of their hectic schedule to be here to help with the preparations. Betty, Madge, Lucille, I'll miss you. We shared some interesting chats. I know the three of you will make it, especially you Betty, so don't worry.

"Mr. and Mrs. Jacobi, thank you for coming. I would also like to mention how appreciative I am of my devoted husband, without whom I never would have made it, and my two babies."

Rebecca then looked straight at Lisa. "Finally, my sister-in-law, Lisa and my new brother, James for holding this party for me." She was eating this up and it tasted good. They lifted their glasses high with hers and drank.

"Give em' hell, girl!" yelled obnoxious Betty.

"Before we eat, Rebecca," started James. "If you will come into the living room with us we have another surprise." She came down the stairs and James led her and the others into the living room.

Lisa peeked back into the foyer. Donald was sitting on the bottom stair. It was quiet except for the echoing voices emanating from down the hall.

*Why did he hang up on James? Why is he acting this way?* Lisa so wished for the return of that happy little boy she grew up with. Even the glum, downtrodden man would be better than this. She couldn't help remembering...

*Lisa walks in and brushes the snow off her shoulders. "Hi, Mother."*

*"Don't "Hi, Mother" me." Lisa knows that tone. Mom's hair is wrapped in a white head scarf. She crosses her arms, with the top*

*half of the broom wedged in the crease of her left arm.* "You've been seeing that boy again."

Lisa wipes off her pink lipstick with her glove. Some of it smears on her skin.

"Right after we warned you."

Lisa looks behind Mom's waist at a smirking Donald. There is no doubt in her mind now. "I'll strangle you!"

She chases him around the table. Mom is in the middle. The table's flimsy legs wobble. Donald makes wet smooching noises with his lips as he runs side-to-side to avoid his sisters' vengeful wrath.

Mom grabs Lisa by the wrist. "Stop this!"

"I'm seventeen!"

"I don't care if you're twenty-five."

"Why can't I see Peter?"

"Because your father and I said so. Both of you go to your room until your father gets here. We're going to have a talk." Lisa and Donald scowl at each other. "Go on."

They lay flat on their beds. Lisa tries to relax, but repetitious cartoon visuals of her brother getting punched in the face are preventing it.

"Fink." Lisa quickly raises herself up to the side of the bed. "Why did you tell on me?"

Donald shrugs, "I don't know. I don't like him. He's always all over you."

"We're in love, Donny. That's what people do when they're in love. What do you know anyway?" She throws her legs back up on the bed. "You've ruined everything."

"No, you did," he mumbles.

"What does that mean?"

Donald lets loose. "We don't do anything anymore. It's been months since you've taken me to a movie. We don't talk.

"You used to walk me home from school and we would talk." Donald takes the pillow from under his head and throws it. "It's like...like I don't matter anymore."

Lisa hears a sniffle. She steps across the room to Donald's bed. He is facing the wall. "I'm sorry, Donny. See, when you're in love you just know, you know?

*"Your mind and body are turned upside-down as the feeling consumes you and becomes all that you are." Lisa puts a hand to her heart at the very thought of Peter. "It's not that you don't matter; you're just put on hold. You will see what I mean some-day." She returns to her bed.*

*Donald turns over. He speaks so low Lisa barely hears him. "I'm sorry I told on you. I-I'll tell Dad I lied. He'll believe me."*

*Her eyes warm to him and she smiles. "I guess you didn't mean any harm."*

*"So... you forgive me?"*

*Lisa nods.*

A grave sob from Donald awoke her. She considered going to him until a shriek of excitement came from the living room.

James swung from the doorway calling to her. She glanced back at her brother, beset at the sight of him, this stranger, on the stairs. When she entered the lounge Rebecca was standing by the stone fireplace holding a plaque. Her eyes bounced to each person.

"Do you like it?" Lisa asked.

"Oh Lisa, I adore it!" Rebecca ran to her and kissed her.

*To Rebecca Wells for Outstanding Achievement and Dedication to Her Family.*

> *I Love You Like a Sister.*
> *Lisa*

Donald came around the corner in time to witness the bit-tersweet moment. James handed Rebecca a gold box adorned with a red ribbon. Lisa soon realized Donald was standing next to her. She stared down at his hand wanting to take it, but he moved to the sofa with his wife.

"What is it?" asked Simon, climbing up the sofa behind his mother.

"It's a typewriter...from Larry and Genevieve."

Larry stepped forward. He had replenished his champagne glass. "We figured you could use one now that you're a lawyer to type up contracts, wills, and things of that nature."

"That's very kind of you. Now I won't have to use the schools' anymore."

"Wow! What's this, Mommy?" Julia was studying the giant rectangular shape draped in a white cloth amongst the other gifts.

Rebecca read the card. "This is from Lisa and James." Lisa put her arm around James's.

James pointed, "Pull off the cloth there."

Rebecca screamed. Donald bounded to his feet. The kids jumped up-and-down.

"Lisa and I bought it for the whole family. It's a Silverstone." Under the tablecloth was a 23-inch television set with mahogany finish. Donald sat back down sluggishly, like an old man insecure of himself and the existence of the seat under him.

Rebecca ran her hand up the side. "This is too much."

"No, it isn't," snapped Lisa. "You guys have had that old radio for years. It's time you had a television set."

Donald was troubled by this, and also with himself for being troubled in the first place. Rebecca receiving and accepting all of this charitable attention made his blood simmer. Was he not good enough to give good gifts to his wife? Paying the bills was one thing, but this was emphasizing his inability to maintain a standard within his family as a whole.

"Isn't this wonderful?" Rebecca whispered to Donald as the others talked amongst themselves. "You haven't uttered so much as one word. Aren't you having a good time? What's wrong?"

"Nothing at all. Everything's *peachy*."

Lisa clasped her hands together. "Okay, we still have a few more gifts to get through. This next one is from...Madge."

Rebecca tore into the small box. "You're wonderful, Madge. Hum, a gift this size gives the impression of jewelry."

"You always told me you liked earrings," stated Madge.

"They're charming. I can't wait to wear them." Rebecca held the gold-plated loops to her ears.

"What the hell are you doing here?!"

Lisa stood rigid guarding her territory. In silence, everyone stared at her until they saw she faced the door and then looked to see what caused the outburst. Joe was leaning against the doorframe. No one noticed him.

Lisa maneuvered around her guests. "You are no longer welcome in this house. I thought I made that clear."

She was furious. Her nerves were eroding as a result of this man, for she had taken the brunt of his bad manner. There was the pungent odor of alcohol emanating from his clothes. Everyone was watching with uncertainty.

"I'm not afraid of you," Lisa muttered. She pulled on his arm, but his muscle impeded her from moving him. "James, help me." James was trying to keep his guests calm.

"Somebody?" Lisa sounded desperate. Not one person made an effort to help or say anything.

Joe looked down on her and grinned. Lisa shuddered. He uttered not a sound, verbal or otherwise.

Lisa took a large gasp of confidence. "Either you leave *now* or the police will come and *make* you leave!" He still wasn't moving. "Get out you bastard!" she yelled at the top of her lungs. Her voice cracked on the last syllable.

She pushed against his chest with force to little effect, except to anger. Joe let out a monstrous growl that emerged from deep within his throat and he shoved her aside. She hit the wall with a hard thud.

Lisa ran to the door to confirm he was leaving. This was her home and he was an intruder. She wasn't thinking about anybody else. She made it in time to see the bumper of his black '52 Ford exiting the gate.

She stood between the entrance and the outside and laid her head against the frame of the door. "Damn you."

God, how she hated this man. And the feeling was growing stronger. How embarrassing this was for Lisa who wanted so bad to reestablish a rapport with her family. As she made her way back down the hall, she met Donald in the doorway. His face was blank, void of any visible concern or puzzlement.

No one brought up the bulky, daunting man, at least not to her, though she figured they had formed an opinion within the secrecy of their own minds and would talk about it when they returned to their homes.

She reasoned with herself on what to do about Joe. He was a problem that was not going to go away.

"ROBERT?"

"Hello, Lisa." Robert rotated his hat in his hands.

Lisa put a hand to her mouth. "Oh my..."

"May I come in?"

"Yes, yes, come in, please."

Lisa closed the door and faced him. She couldn't help smiling. There he was. His brown hair parted on the side and curl dangling above his left eye. He hadn't changed.

Those pools of blue sparkled like two stars in the night sky. Neither time nor indignation had altered her view of him. He was courteous and handsome as ever.

"Can I get you anything?" she asked.

"No, thank you. I can't stay."

"Oh Robert," Lisa approached him. "How long has it been?"

"Three years and... two months. It was a week before my wedding."

"How is she?"

Robert fumbled somewhat. "Stella's-um, she's...fine."

"Let's go into the den so we can talk. It's cozier."

Robert grinned softly, "Alright." Lisa hung his hat and coat on the rack beside the door.

Robert began to sit next to Lisa on the sofa, but she relocated to the armchair across from him. "You carved out an attractive lifestyle since we parted ways," spoke Robert, observing the sizeable room. "I'm glad for you."

Lisa failed to recall how he damaged her, yet there she was delighting in his company. For years she wanted to tell him off, rehearsing the exact words she would say to him, and dreaming of that improbable chance. As he sat before her, looking as he did when she first spotted him across Alma's apartment, she seemed to forget. Whatever it was about that man that demanded she desire him ten years prior he still retained.

Robert removed a pack of cigarettes from his jacket. "May I?"

"Be my guest. How has life been treating you?"

"Very generous," Robert declared, crossing his legs. "I'm living in Yonkers now. I'm two and a half years sober and haven't so much as looked at the stuff. It turns out all it took was a little incentive, a reason to want to quit, and I found one."

*Just ask him, Lisa. There has to be a reason.*

"What brings you all this way?"

"Well," Robert exhaled the smoke. "There is no way I can tell you and still hang onto my dignity. I, uh, was talking to Alma..."

"This isn't about my accident, is it?"

"Accident?"

"Never mind, go on."

"She divulged to me where you lived. She also told me about your recent marriage."

"I see." Lisa held her arms and walked away from him to the other side of the room.

Robert pressed his partially-smoked cigarette into the ashtray. "I know what you're thinking. I agree with you. It would be a defamation of character to help the man that hurt you so. I wish I could give you a good enough reason other than the truth."

There was a pause. "Stella is pregnant." Robert stood close beside her. "I manage a small haberdashery. I can support us, but a third?"

"How far along is she?"

"Two months. Lisa..." Robert laid his hand on her back. She knew it was a tactic. It was all too familiar.

"Say no, say yes. It doesn't matter. But I *have* to try."

With all that was happening in her life this threw her for one rollercoaster of a loop. She never thought that marrying James would cause everyone to emerge out of the woodwork. There is such a thing as acquiring too much money too quick, and Lisa was learning this lesson hard.

"I couldn't be happier for you, believe me. And it is good to see you again, but you must realize how uncomfortable this must be for me." Robert now looked at her in such a way that indicated he wasn't as comfortable or self-confident.

"Dammit," Lisa shouted. "I keep forgetting what a crafty bitch Alma is! I see it all now. She knows I have money, so she tells her niece hoping her husband is still on good terms with his ex."

"Lisa, that's not true."

"Like hell it's not. I know that woman and so do you." Robert lowered his eyes. "I don't know if you know what she did to our marriage, but it would be senseless going down that path anyway. The damage has been done."

Lisa didn't know what to do. This had to be a first in history that an ex-husband importunes his ex-wife for money due to an unborn child that isn't hers. For her, the sheer absurdity of it all, and what desperation he must have been in to enter the residence of the woman whose heart he broke, she had to consider.

"Robert," Lisa began, her cheeks moistened and red, "why am I standing here? Why in the name of God am I standing here with you fighting right and wrong when I should never have let you in?"

Robert transitioned both hands to her shoulders and met her forehead with his own. She could have parted from him if she wanted to.

Upon the stairs James stared down into the den, spying at the manifestation of old feelings. Were those feelings truly dead or were they dormant, perhaps brought back to life by this reunion?

Lisa looked into Robert's earnest eyes that resembled adoration of former years. He was so affectionate, so convincing. "Robert, I-I can't. I just can't." Lisa lost control and cried into the palms of her hands.

"I understand." He wiped away her tears with his sleeve. "Lisa, dear, I will exit your life and I'll never hurt you again." She withdrew a tissue from her pocket and blew her nose. "I'll show myself out."

"Wait. Must you leave?"

"Well, Stella may need me."

"What-what will you do?"

"I don't know. We'll work something out. I wish nothing but the brightest future for you."

He kissed the end of her nose. Her heart raced at the simplest touch. The taxi was waiting. She hugged the door as a part of her was sad to see him go. Robert threw out his hand before stepping in.

Then Lisa saw something. If it hadn't have made sense, she could have sworn she imagined it. A redhead coming from the side of the house jumped into the backseat with him.

It was her. Alma's eyes wouldn't surrender the house as the car disappeared down the driveway.

Even in a different state Lisa couldn't escape her clutches.

# CHAPTER ELEVEN

**D**onald stared into his coffee, more specifically the swirling cyclone of cream in the center. The palms of his hands were damp as he grasped the sides of the mug.

James banged his knuckles on the table. "Well?"

"Give me a minute. This isn't easy."

"It's always been in the past. Why should now be any different?" James leaned back and folded his arms. "Because I'm not Lisa?

"I know why you called my office to meet you where Lisa works. You've got some nerve."

Donald took a careful sip. "I, uh, got my bank statement in yesterday. Lisa discontinued the checks."

"Yes, I know."

Donald looked across the diner at Lisa as she sat lunch in front of a family. "Why did she?"

"I think you know." James made sure Lisa wasn't anywhere nearby. "You, Donald, are a narcissist. *That's* why. You care only about yourself.

"I'm fed up with your perpetual down-on-my-luck attitude. No matter what trouble you get in, you insist on dragging my Lisa down with you. I will not let it continue."

The muscles in Donald's face tightened. "Hey pal, I have my pride."

James remained calm, pushing his drink aside. "If you had even an ounce of dignity left in your bones you wouldn't be here begging for money again." He pointed his little finger at Donald from his elbow. "Find a way to make the money yourself."

Donald slammed both his hands flat on the table. The dishes clattered. A few nearby heads turned. "You know what you are, Mr. Big Shot?!"

"Quiet."

"Possessive! *My* Lisa" you call her!"

"Quiet, I said."

"I don't give a damn! Lisa and I looked out for one another until you came along. Sure, you flash your expensive teeth and your expensive suits. At least I love Lisa for who she is, not for *whose* she is."

James resumed his casual posture, rubbing his nose in irritation as he tried to collect himself. "Well, it's better this way. Stay away from her."

"Look, James," Donald smoothed back his hair. His temper had got the best of him again. This was not the way to get what he wanted. "We appreciate your help. We really do.

"But working nights at the motel is dragging me down. I work twelve hours a day. Without your help I have little time with my children. I don't wanna fight with you. Out of respect for my sis I want us to try and work things out."

James shook his head and smiled. Donald's faded as his grew. "Kid, you're good. You're familiar with all the strategies. Who are you trying to fool?

"I do not like you. I didn't want to hold that party for your wife, because I knew you would show up."

"I didn't want to. It's not like I couldn't."

James's eyes turned cold. He took a sip of his tea, peering at Donald from over the cup. "But you did."

It took all of five seconds to hit him. "No. God, no. You can't."

"You attended the party. Lisa was at the party. The deal is off."

"*Please.*"

"I gave you precise instructions that under no circumstance were you to come into contact with or speak to Lisa other than a grave emergency. In return, I would your give you double on top of what Lisa was giving you. I do not recall an emergency prior to or following the party."

"But James, I never said a single word to her!"

"You were there. Besides, it was Lisa's decision to cut her share."

"Because of you! You've filled her head with lies!"

"I made you aware of the consequences if you broke our agreement. Anyway, you consented." James was relaxed. He almost seemed to be enjoying it.

"I-I, but…" Donald knew he had lost. He felt truly alone.

Lisa came up to their table and sat beside her husband. "James, Donny, I didn't know you were here. I've been training Susan."

She looked side-to-side at the two men and wondered what they were doing there together, and at Larry's of all places. Donald was subdued. He appeared so feeble, as if at any given moment he would fall out of the booth. Lisa took his hand. She felt the dampness underneath. He sniffed and turned his head to the window.

Lisa pleaded softly, "Talk to me, Donny." If only he would have looked to see the obvious suffering in her eyes. It spoke louder and more clearly than any word's meaning could impart.

He retracted his hand and stood. "I'm sorry." The way he said it sounded more to her like, "Mother died last night. I'm sorry I didn't tell you." Those words would have fit the tone.

A weak curve formed on James's maw. When she heard the bell of the door sound, she had a feeling she would never see her brother again. Lisa's hand was still in the same place where Donald's once was. She stared at it, pondering his words. *"I'm sorry?"*

James finally spoke, "While I'm here why don't we take advantage, um?"

"Why was Donny here? What's going on?"

"It was nothing." Lisa gave him a look that told him she knew that was a lie. "He-he wanted more money and I refused."

"You did what?"

"You made the decision a month ago. He is a master Machia-velli."

"I may have decided to discontinue his money, but I never intended on cruelty."

"That's what it entailed. I thought you understood that."

"Excuse me?!"

"Oh, I'm sorry, darling. Does Robert speak in kinder tones?"

James just stared at her. It felt like a test. Whatever this was she did not like it or his mentioning Robert.

James caught her wrist. "I didn't mean that."

Lisa shook off his hand. "I'm going to resume Donny's money. I'll bump it up a hundred for a few months. That should make up for lost time. But don't worry, I'll take it out of my paycheck."

Larry yelled for her from the kitchen.

"Wait." James took back her wrist and led her to the farthest side of the diner away from the people. "I was out of line."

"Lisa!" shouted Larry, sticking his head out of the kitchen door.

"Coming! I have to go." Lisa turned to leave, but avidly again he caught her.

He grasped her shoulders tight. "Not until you kiss me."

James wrapped his arms around her whole body. "Let me go," she murmured with their mouths adjoined. She pushed against his chest until she broke free.

AND SO, IT APPEARED LISA WAS CORRECT.

Donald was gone.

She called him soon after. He answered the phone, and unexpectedly she was speaking to Rebecca. Rebecca proceeded to explain that Donald voiced quite plainly he felt it best to have no further affiliation with her, that by reason of inevitable circumstance, their different lifestyles could do damage if he remained. And yet he stated it wasn't either of their faults, and he would always love her for the wonderful sister she was to him.

James and Donald were too different, and Lisa was the referee in this endless boxing match. Donald came to realize the negative impact this was having on her. It was getting to the point where she would have had to choose. To make things easier, he made the decision for her. Donald had become a barrier on Lisa's road to happiness and he realized that.

Lisa, like a twig bearing the weight of heavy fruit, was unable to stand any longer. She was in tears when she hung up the receiver and fell in the chair beside her. She rested her head on her fist, dabbing her cheeks with her lace handkerchief.

Granted he couldn't have broken her heart more, she did grasp his reasoning, however wrong he was, and his selfless intentions behind it. For years she told him he was a grown man and could make it without her. She would have to prove she believed that by abiding by his choice.

Within that vast house, the lone sounds were maddening to her ears; the ticking of clocks and nothingness. *Donny*, she thought, weeping into the arm of the chair.

Lisa felt confined, so she grabbed the keys to her Lesabre and went for a drive. She couldn't help wondering as she passed through Greenwich that if she and Donald grew up in such a tranquil town their parents would have been okay. Lisa cranked down the window. Nature provided its own air conditioning with swift streams of wind from the Mianus River. This solace was all she needed.

Soon she was venturing out onto a barren two-lane road. She was surrounded by dense trees and an occasional house. Before moving to Fairfield County all she had was Central Park. This simple drive, in what could be compared to as a thousand Central Parks, was the first time she felt isolated and free of burden.

There were no other vehicles in sight. Her Lesabre was a vanishing streak of blue in the green countryside. Donald's face seemed to melt away as she closed her eyes, if not but a second, when an earsplitting car horn broke the precious silence. Her rearview mirror was swallowed by a gray vehicle tailgating her and incessantly honking.

Lisa stuck out her arm and motioned for him to pass. He drove so close her bumper was tapped.

"Hey! Watch it!" Lisa had no choice but to accelerate. She left them far behind.

Peace restored. Lisa lifted her foot. *Teenagers. I hope they didn't dent my car.* She figured she would go no further than New Canaan. That's as far as she's traveled without needing a map to get back.

Her chest hit the steering wheel. The fierce jolt thrust the car forward. The motor revved as her foot involuntarily hit the gas.

Lisa's hair whipped around her neck as she looked fast behind her – it was the gray vehicle.

She had no time to think except to get away from this lunatic. There was a junction ahead. She sped up. Anything to get to that crossroads before the mystery driver did.

She disregarded the stop sign and turned sharply left, pulling the steering wheel with both hands. Dust and rock flew up from the tires. It felt as if the car would topple. She looked behind to confirm.

The gray car came plowing through the wall of dust.

"Dammit!" Lisa struck the wheel. He was accelerating so fast the driver must have had the pedal to the floor.

He crashed into her bumper again. She felt her neck would snap like a matchstick. He swerved into the next lane. She saw he was driving a Chevrolet.

The Chevy pulled up next to her. They faced each other the same time. All Lisa saw was their black silhouette staring back at her. This was no teenager.

The world came to a dead stillness. The falling sun peeked in, exposing the driver's arm; he wore a black leather jacket. The arm swung right and the car collided into hers. The tires of her Lesabre screeched as she hugged the side of the road.

"Stop it!" Lisa screamed. She slammed on the brake, leaving the leather-jacketed individual far up the road.

What to do...what to do...what to do...

How was she to elude them on an open road? Cat-and-mouse – was that their game? To intimidate, terrorize, or kill. She got that she was the mouse.

Lisa threw the gearshift in reverse and went back to the crossroads. Her time was limited. *I'll keep going straight. He'll assume I turned right.*

She passed the junction and looked over her shoulder – no one. She held her speed for a minute and looked again. It was hard to see because she gathered so much distance, but a gray car was flying down the anticipated road.

"Yes! Yes!" Lisa rejoiced. She deviated up the next road. She had to get back home and was contemplating another route. She was still new to the area and her knowledge of it was very general.

Lisa shrieked and hit her brakes.

The gray Chevy sat in front of her blocking the road. Her mind was unable to focus on any one of a hundred thoughts in that brief second. She floor-boarded the gas determined to get around. She made the mistake of going around his front.

When she did the Chevy moved forward, forcing her into the grass. Her car went sideways as she dipped off the road. He was behind. She drove not knowing or caring where the road took her.

Panic settled into her bones. The Chevy was almost on her again. She had the foresight to swerve side-to-side to avoid being hit. A fork in the road up ahead proved more of a problem, for beyond that fork – a red tractor that consumed the road. It was some kind of a loader, with a bucket in the front.

It seemed her attacker had become aware of this also and was scheming to force her into it head on. Her speedometer read sixty mph and he was staying right with her. There was no way she could slow down in time.

They were approaching the lumbering giant. Lisa swerved, but the gray Chevy was there acting as a barricade. The tractor was getting bigger.

This was a hellish nightmare, just like the bus incident, yet far more perilous. With all the might she could muster, she crashed into her tenacious assailant, but he resisted against her. The farmer's head she could now see sitting high in his seat; he was an old man and wore a red cap.

She hit the brakes but her car kept going. She quickly switched to reverse. That's when Lisa felt her rear drift sideways. Her tires were losing traction as earth soared into the air.

The Chevy made sure she stayed on target. It was a maximum shove-of-war between cars. Lisa was losing.

That massive red scoop was upon her.

"Why are you doing this?!"

"Never in my life would I have thought I'd fall for a waitress, and how I'm falling fast. I'm concerned that I may hit the ground too hard. Lisa...I... I...God, I love you."

# CHAPTER TWELVE

**"S**top! Please!"

Lisa gripped the wheel and readied herself for the final blow.

She glanced to her left. The Chevy was no longer there. He was sitting way back and the tractor was stopped. She took her first real breath since this attack started.

*I'm still alive.*

She was partially in the ditch. Her car bounced as it rolled back onto solid ground. The Chevy's motor raced. The attacker wanted to intimidate as a punk would spring out his switchblade in a rumble.

Lisa was now more on the verge of anger as well as fear. She shifted into drive, and once she gained momentum, she sustained her speed at about fifty-five. To go faster might have caused her to lose control on the curvy road. The Chevy hurtled towards her again honking the horn. If she couldn't outrun him, perhaps she could outsmart him.

She waited until the Chevy was just feet away and slammed her brakes. The Chevy skidded to the side. She swung to the center so he couldn't regain the road. Then she hit the brakes again.

He went off into the grass. Lisa's face was dripping with fear. An innocent car was approaching and the attacker forced it off. Cars began peeking over the hill one by one in procession.

They must have been nearing a town. She didn't know where she was, but was certain the influx of automobiles would deter her attacker. Between each car, the assailant did his damnedest to get around. Lisa managed to get a few cars between them.

The Chevy hurtled over a medium and plowed into her now-severely dented door. Men yelled out their windows. Lisa lost control and missed another car by a hair's width. This action, and the force behind it, more intense than previous hits, told Lisa he was getting desperate. But she couldn't take much more.

Ahead was a conglomerate of buildings and houses. She was eager, but couldn't shake the fear. Thus far, any hindrance her mystery attacker traversed. Cars whizzed past as she maneuvered around to reach the haven. A loud siren wailed from behind.

Thank God! Yes!

She slowed to the side in front of a speed limit marker. Any other time she wouldn't have been so relieved to hear that sound. She looked back as the policeman was stepping out of his patrol car.

He was a big man with a slight paunch. The cop tapped his knuckles on the window. "What happened to your car, ma'am? Get in some sort of accident?" asked the deep-voiced cop in an irritated manner.

Lisa, still clutching the wheel, was incapable of answering him. "You were exceeding the speed limit by thirty mph. I need to see your license. That is, if you have one."

Lisa leaned over to pick up her handbag and contents from the floor.

The Chevy drove slowly past.

"Officer, I-I was being chased. A gray Chevrolet tried to run me off the road." The cop waved his fingers for her license. "Did you hear me?"

"I heard you, ma'am." The cop bent down to address her. All Lisa could see was her reflection in those alien-looking black sunglasses hanging on his ears. "Ah, you're from Greenwich. Nice. I thought you people prized your automobiles."

"Someone in a gray Chevrolet tried to kill me! Look at my car!"

"Getting old, ma'am."

Lisa snapped, "What sort of cop are you? Isn't it obvious? Why won't you listen?"

"Because I saw your blue Buick, not a gray Chevrolet, nearly run ten cars off the road."

"He was right behind me!"

"That's enough!" Lisa threw her head back in despair. "Here's your ticket." She snatched it from his hand and started the engine.

"Hey! You be sure and pay attention to these signs." He indicated to the sign above. The cop thumped the roof of her car.

Lisa no longer felt safe. After all the warnings, no matter how ridiculous it sounded, she accepted that someone wanted her dead. And that someone had to be someone she knew.

Lisa now believed, beyond a shadow of a doubt, the threat she received in the mail was no joke. She had no alternative but to think this was not the end. The future held something else in store, and consistent with the past, it was going to be worse. She had to vigilant, attentive, telling no one of her suspicions.

Therefore everyone: James, Donald, Rebecca, Larry, Alma, Joe, and Robert in addition, were placed beneath this blanket of uncertainty within Lisa's mind. Not because they didn't mean something to her, or some of them, but because she wasn't sure, and for that she *had* to be sure to play it safe.

Something was coming. But...

When?

Where?

What?

JAMES HUNG UP HIS HAT. "LISA! LISA, ARE YOU HOME?"

Lisa was upstairs in a chair in the bathroom, resting in her lavender robe as she toyed with the belt. Every square inch of her body was hurting in some form or another. She heard him calling, but chose not to answer.

Inside her mind an eruption of excessive and dreadful thoughts ran rampant, thoughts of people she loved, people she trusted to also love her wanting to rid of her, and fighting like mad to guess why in the hell they would. Was it by some miracle or massive stroke of luck that she managed to survive, or was it planned that way?

She tried escaping from these thoughts she was inflicting upon herself with disappointing results. Who could she trust? She needed to confide in someone, but what if that someone was the one?

Lisa flinched when the door opened.

James spoke, "Darling, I didn't know you were here." He lifted her face and kissed her. "What's the matter?" He bent down to her. "Talk to me."

She stared down at him with vacant eyes, saying nothing. "Oh. You're upset about Donald. You needn't be bothered about that anymore. I've been acting childish about the whole thing.

"That is why I have decided to allow you carte blanche to help him any way you see fit. How does that grab you?"

Lisa remained blank. Realizing something was wrong James took her by the arms. "Lisa, what's happened?"

Weakly, she managed to speak. "How...how was your day?"

"Better now that I'm near you." He began caressing her neck. Lisa closed her eyes in guilty pleasure as he clutched her body. She ran her fingers through his hair. It was a relief seeing him.

"James?" He grunted. "I-I'm afraid."

"Afraid?" James wasn't listening. Then he must have sensed a change in her body. He raised his head. "Lisa, where is your car?"

"Some-someone must have hit the side of it with their door while I was in town. I-I'm having it fixed. "

"On a Sunday?"

"I-I found a garage that's open." James lifted her out of the chair and laid her softly on the bed in the next room. "Not now, James." He untied her robe.

It was unfathomable. She wasn't able to comprehend the idea of her husband wanting to harm her. Logic tried to intervene. The seed that Joe planted was always there, but now it had taken root.

LISA WAS SHUTTING DOWN.

On the chance that something would actually be done, she paid the local police station a visit. She neglected to take the note with her deliberately to test the waters first. She spoke face-to-face with a policeman who made her coffee and put her words in writing with a guarantee that he would get back soon. But when would "soon" come?

One week had passed since Lisa's escape from the gray Chevy and she acted as though in a hypnotic stupor, having nothing to do with anyone. After reflecting on all that happened and trying to fit the pieces together night after night, it seemed a rational way to be. Her last working day at Larry's was three weeks away.

She kept her usual routine, going to work in the morning, coming home to fix dinner, and retiring. James recognized the immediate change, as did Larry. Lisa lived in her room, lying on her chaise lounge by the window for hours and absorbing the once perfect picture of her beautiful landscape. James did most everything he could to bring the old Lisa to the surface by purchasing her expensive gifts that once gratified.

She opened both doors of her armoire and slipped her hand into a jacket pocket. It was still there, her recently-purchased lady's companion: A derringer. One could not have comprehended how a small piece of chrome-plated iron would offer such security.

Lisa couldn't stay in that room all the time. She was ready for whatever drastic event that she envisioned occurring when she would have to leave it.

Rebecca poked her head in. Lisa closed the doors quickly. "May I come in?"

"I guess." Lisa returned to her chaise and picked up the end of her silk white peignoir that was touching the floor.

"How are you?" asked Rebecca, sitting on the bed across from her.

"What is it you want, Rebecca?"

"I, uh, got your check in the mail yesterday." Lisa reclined, staring out the window. "You know, Lisa, it isn't necessary." Lisa was hearing her, but didn't want to give her the satisfaction of her full attention.

"I make a decent salary now. Donald is considering quitting the cab company."

"You still haven't told me why you're here." Lisa's coldness confused Rebecca. She didn't know how to respond. "I can't believe you. You let Donald back out on his family."

"It was his decision not..."

"*Not mine* – hooey!" Lisa swung her legs around. "And I didn't give that check to you. I thought that by sending that money I could win him back.

"Wrong? Probably. It's more than you did."

"I am sorry it came to this." Rebecca rose and placed a hand on Lisa's shoulder. Lisa's head was faced down with her hands grasping the fabric upholstery. "Our husbands cannot get along. Maybe in time..."

Lisa patted her hand. Rebecca handed her the check. Lisa hesitated, then took and folded the paper.

"James has phoned me twice this week sick with worry. What is going on?" Rebecca helped herself to the upper half of the chaise. "He tells me you hardly talk, and when you're home you lock yourself up in here all day. You never want to go anywhere."

"Rebecca, that lawyer you work for...I forgot his name."

"Neil McGaffrey."

"What form of law does he practice?"

"Personal injury, divorce, but what does that have to do with... *Lisa*, you're not divorcing James!"

 Lisa paused for a moment. "I need help with a will."

"A will, Lisa? Uh, a will is a document that discloses the wishes of a person's estate after they've died."

"Yes, I know what a will is."

 "Well, you will need to choose an executor. For a will to be legal it must go through probate. Take Donald for instance. He does not have a standing will, so if he died tomorrow, he would die intestate."

Rebecca stopped. She could tell Lisa wanted more. "You'll have to make an appointment with an attorney. There's nothing more I can tell you without knowing the specifics."

The seriousness of Lisa's expression and the heartfelt emphasis of her words made it hard for Rebecca to understand what was happening to her sister-in-law.

Lisa inched her head close to Rebecca's and whispered, "Can you help me? I...I really need your help."

Rebecca put a hand to her forehead. "God, you're being ridiculous! What is happening to you? You're not dying, are you?"

"Oh, I'm being ridiculous." She stood slow and rigid. "Give Donald my love."

"Lisa!" Rebecca shouted to her as she left through the inner door.

James came in seconds after from the hallway. He scanned the room and frowned when he saw his wife wasn't there. He extended his arms in question. Rebecca indicated to the inner door.

"What in the hell is going on?" James gave the bedpost a good wallop. "What did you talk about?"

"Nothing. She didn't give me much time. Oh, except that she's contemplating a will."

"She said that?"

"In so many words."

"Why?" James asked.

"I can only guess."

"I can guess, too. I asked you here to find out." Rebecca was about to put her feet up on the chaise. "Lisa sits there."

"*Sorry.*" Rebecca took a compact from her clutch bag and checked her makeup. "One would think such a long trip could be rewarded with a drink at least."

"Her behavior frightens me, Rebecca. Maybe I should ask her about it."

"Not wise. I have found when it comes to marriage you must let the spouse come to you. You don't want to smother the girl."

"That's why you and Donald get along so well." Rebecca clasped her compact with force. James went to the inner door and turned the knob. He was more than ready to confront Lisa.

"You're right." He backed away. James scratched the back of his head and what he said next he said to himself. "Something has to be done about her."

NIGHT WAS DESCENDING. Lights were beginning to pop up around the diner. Lisa mopped the floor, blindly gazing out the window as Larry and Susan conversed in the kitchen.

This was her last day and she had been dreading it. Larry's was her escape from home. It was Saturday, and for Lisa there would not be a Monday.

She ambled into the back room. Larry saw her and followed. He watched her briefly from the doorway before he spoke. "Are you okay?"

Lisa wasn't certain enough to answer his question.

Larry came up behind her. "You know, you don't have to quit. We both know Susan can never replace you or your Omelet Surprise."

Lisa turned to him. The ache of her resigning was apparent. "You're sweet, Mr. Jacobi." She pinched his chin. "But I do have to go.

"Besides, I have a lot of things I need to take care of." Lisa pulled her handbag onto her shoulder. "I promise I'll come and visit." They shared an embrace. Larry took her elbow to escort her to the door.

Lisa looked at Susan standing beside the cash register. "Take good care of him, you hear?"

"I will, ma'am."

"Don't be nervous. You'll do fine. Well," Lisa exhaled. "I guess this is it." She hugged him a second time.

Larry held open the door for her. "Remember, you promised."

With a feeble smile she told him goodbye.

# CHAPTER THIRTEEN

**6**:38 a.m.
Loud banging sounded in fours through their apartment. The door shuddered from the force pounding it.

"What the hell?" Donald sat up in a panic.

"Someone's at the door," Rebecca mumbled, still half asleep.

Donald reached for his wristwatch on the nightstand. "At this hour?"

The banging persisted.

"Stay here." Donald threw on his robe and closed the door to their bedroom. "Who is it?"

"Police," replied a deep male voice.

Donald opened the door. The chain prevented him from seeing the other half of the man's thick-mustached face. "What do you want?" he asked.

"Are you Donald Wells?"

"Yeah. Who are you?"

"Lt. Robson." He reached inside his jacket for his billfold and presented his badge. "This is my associate, Sgt. Dodds. Would you mind opening the door? We need to ask you a few questions."

"Well, does it have to be *now*? I'm not exactly dressed."

"You're dressed enough, Mr. Wells."

Donald unfastened the chain and stepped aside. Both men separated to opposite sides of the room scrutinizing it in its entirety.

Donald marched over to the lieutenant. "Excuse me, but don't you think you owe me an explanation? It's the crack of dawn."

Lt. Robson removed his hat and threw it in the chair. "When did you last hear from your sister?"

"Lisa?"

The young sergeant snapped, "That's the only sister you have, isn't it?" Robson gestured for him to be quiet.

"I'm not sure. It's been over a month."

"You haven't seen or heard from her in the last twenty-four hours?" asked Robson.

Donald noticed Dodds writing in his notepad. "Is-is she in some kind of trouble?"

Robson moved to the sofa. "Why don't you tell us a little about your sister?"

"Like what?"

"You're supposed to tell us," Dodds added, picking up a photo of Lisa taken during wartime. He studied her face. She was full grown and fresh-faced, and wearing coveralls and thick gloves.

"What are you doing?"

"Never mind him. You just tell us about your sister."

"God!" Donald swung his arms around like a wild animal caged for the first time. "What is this? You barge into my home, wake my family, and ask questions that don't concern you. You won't even tell me the why of it!"

Rebecca poked her head out of the bedroom. Donald went to her. "Rebecca, these men are the police."

"The police?" She tied her robe and walked out. "Has something happened?"

"I'm afraid so, ma'am," spoke Robson as he approached. His eyes suddenly shifted to Donald. "There's been a murder."

Donald stopped breathing and swallowed. Now the questions regarding his sister made sense. His voice was weak and faint. "Whose?"

"A man by the name of Joseph Norris."

Donald closed his eyes.

"He's of no relation to you, but we have reason to believe…"

"Yes, yes, we knew him. My God! Donald!" She took his arm.

Donald noticed Julia standing in the room rubbing her eyes. "See to the kids. I'll handle this."

The detectives sat. Donald licked his lips and tossed the lieutenant's hat on the coffee table as he sat in the chair opposite them. "What does Mr. Norris's death have to do with Lisa?"

"What was your sister's relationship with the deceased?"

"Lieutenant, if this is your technique of getting information where with every question you follow it up *with* a question, then we aren't going to get anywhere."

Dodds snapped, "We ask the questions, Mr. Wells!"

"Alright, Sergeant. In the interest of fairness…We estimate the time of death between nine and midnight. That is when Mrs. Mallory gets off work on Saturdays, correct?"

"I guess, but…"

"And no one has seen her since. Not her husband, not her employer, not you."

"What is that supposed to mean?"

Dodds stood, "You tell us." He flipped back several pages of his notes and began pacing in front of a very nervous Donald. "The body was discovered in an alley ten blocks from Larry's Diner. Wounds on the victim include a bite mark on the lower lip, a stabbing in the right hand: Weapon unidentified.

"And ultimately the cause of death: A gunshot to the head. We know it wasn't a mugging, because he had his wallet and a substantial amount of cash on him."

"Wait. This is all very hard to swallow. Lisa doesn't even own a gun."

"Don't jump to conclusions," Robson interjected. "Your sister has been missing for about nine hours. We found Dr. Mallory's address in the deceased's wallet and notified him. He in turn informed us of his wife's disappearance."

"So the death of this guy and my sister isn't related?"

"I didn't say that either, just that there are things we would like to clarify. Forensics is going over the crime scene as we speak."

Dodds crossed in front of Donald again. "Now you know everything we know. How about clueing us in?" Donald crossed his legs as a hint for them to proceed. "To repeat," said Dodds. "What was your sister's relationship with Norris?"

"He was a friend of the family."

"Yours?"

"No. James Mallory's."

It was Robson's turn. "How did they get along?" Donald exchanged legs. The detectives glanced at each other.

"I, uh, can't answer that. You see, I haven't seen much of Lisa and I've only met Joe two or three times."

"Understand this, Mr. Wells." Robson moved behind Donald's chair. Donald could feel the detective's eyes on top of his head. "As detectives our problem is not so much deciphering whether or not the individual is on the level, but more so if they are pretending to be blissfully ignorant."

Donald looked up at him and over at Dodds. "I-I don't know what you could expect me to know. I assure you I know nothing of my sister's relationship with Joe Norris. Furthermore, I don't appreciate being grilled in my own home."

"We're not grilling you, Mr. Wells."

"No? What do you call this? I'm getting third-degree burns."

There was a moment of silence before Dodds spoke. "You mentioned that you haven't seen much of your sister. Why is that? Having problems?"

"No. On the contrary, we're very close."

Rebecca quietly came out of the children's bedroom. "Would you gentlemen like some coffee?"

"No thank you, ma'am," answered Robson. "We're almost finished."

Rebecca sat on the arm of her husband's chair. "Is everything going alright?"

Donald scowled at Dodds. "Uh-huh."

"Mrs. Wells, if you don't mind." Dodds took a more calm and tactful approach to his questioning the lovely redhead. "Did you know Mr. Norris?"

"Not too well, I'm afraid. The first time I met him was at a dinner party given by Dr. Mallory prior to the wedding. And he was best man. All that I know about his past was he used to be a policeman."

Robson turned quickly around like someone hit him over the head with a blunt object. "Norris was a cop?"

"A long time ago."

Robson and Dodds were quiet as if pondering the gravity of a case that had just escalated to a different level of severity.

Robson reshaped his hat and fixed it on his head. "We won't occupy any more of your time, but we *will* be in touch. Don't bother getting up, ma'am, we'll see ourselves out.

"Oh, and Mr. Wells? If you hear from your sister, you will let us know?" Robson waited for Donald's indication he heard.

The door clicked shut.

"Liar!" Rebecca shouted through a whisper. "I heard everything."

"Rebecca, I'm in no mood." Donald retreated to the kitchen. Rebecca stayed within inches behind him. He drew a glass of water.

"You lied to those men. First of all, you told them you didn't know how Lisa and Joe got along when you know they didn't."

He exhaled in increasing anger.

"You remember the party? She practically threw him out on his face in front of everybody. Betty thought she had lost her mind."

"Betty's an idiot. I doubt if she knows which end is up."

"Don't change the subject. You also told them Lisa and you were close. Ha, that's a laugh."

He slammed his glass on the counter. "Get off my back!"

"Donald, if...no, *when* they find out, you could be in trouble for lying to the police."

Donald stomped back into the living room. Rebecca scampered ahead and put a hand on his chest to stop him. "When were you planning to discuss it then? Tomorrow? Next week? Lisa is..."

"She'll turn up. This whole thing is ludicrous. I don't give a damn anyway."

"Donald, a man is dead!"

Donald pushed her aside and took refuge in the bathroom.

He covered his mouth and laid his head against the door. The towel on the hook fell on his shoulder. His hands trembled as he tried to absorb what had transpired. Lisa was missing and Joe was dead.

He rested on the frame of the bathtub. He couldn't stop shaking as he gripped the sink beside him. All he could think about was his sister and how he treated her.

# CHAPTER FOURTEEN

"**W**hy aren't you girl scouts down there doing anything?!" James shouted into the receiver as he jerked the cord further out. "It's been forty-three hours! This is the second time I've called and been given the same goddamn answer!

"I was told I would be kept informed...no I won't relax!" James took the phone and sat on the back of the sofa. In one swift motion, he took his hand and wiped the sweat from his brow, rubbed both eyes between his thumb and fingers, ending with the stubble on his chin. With zero sleep, an empty stomach, and frazzled mind, the consequence was emphasized by his face.

Outside, a man in a gray suit, beige overcoat, and hat walked up the steps to ring the bell, but heard James arguing. He couldn't quite hear what was being said. He checked the door – it was unlocked.

"This Lt. Robson, he's handling the case? – Well, when will he be in? I want to speak with him."

The man crept in. James's voice grew louder with each step. From behind the wall, he peeked into the den.

James meandered over to the window. "I understand there's a murder investigation in the works. – Alright, alright, but I expect to be notified the moment something turns up. Got it?"

James slammed the phone down. "Ah!"

With hands in pocket, the man addressed him. "Dr. Mallory."

"Let yourself in, why don't you?"

"Thanks." The man stepped down into the room.

James sensed a vague eeriness about him, and it wasn't just because he crept into his house without an invitation or a sound. The man wasn't afraid, because he didn't even attempt to conceal himself. He intended for James to see him.

"It appears I'm falling behind," said James. "You know who I am."

"Yes, I do know who you are." The man faked a big smile.

"You a cop?"

"No. Name's Mayfield. I'm a private investigator." He showed him his license. Edgar Mayfield was a man of average height and thinning hair who had found his niche in investigative work, over twenty years building his experience and skill.

"That gives you the right to walk into other people's houses? Who hired you?"

"That's privileged."

"Look…"

"Before you get all riled, friend, I don't wanna make trouble. My intention is to keep this pleasant. Not resort to name-calling."

James tried to be polite despite his mood. "Can I get you a drink?"

"Scotch and water would be nice." James walked behind the minibar in the corner, dropped ice cubes into a crystal glass, and began to pour, eyeing Mayfield as he removed his overcoat. His gray suit was faded and baggy, no longer clinging to his body, as if it had been worn and washed numerous times over the years. Maybe this was a favorite suit, a lucky suit, or he just couldn't afford enough suits to ever send this one to greener pastures.

"Thanks," acknowledged Mayfield, taking the glass. "This is a lavish house you have. Very nice."

"I didn't do it. My wife – she's the one responsible for these delicate touches. She turned this house into a home." James's face transformed to a look of sorrow. "Lisa," he whispered and finished his drink.

Mayfield took a sip. "Tell me, is Mrs. Frisco…"

"Excuse me? Mallory is her name! Mallory."

"Pardon me, my mistake. Is Mrs. Mallory in the habit of disappearing?"

"Of course not."

"Mm-hmm. She's never done this before?"

"We have a fine marriage. Something's happened to her. She has no reason to run away."

Mayfield sat his empty glass on the bar. "Seventeen years I've been married. It's never been easy mind you, but good, real good.

"The wife doesn't point out my faults like some. She puts up with them and says she loves me anyway. Ha-ha."

"Lisa's not like other wives, or other women." Part of James seemed to be leaving the room. His eyes were far away, seeing past Mayfield, past the wall, and into a dream he wanted to relive and put into words. Mayfield observed him closely.

"Every morning I wake up and open my eyes to that beautiful sleeping face. Some mornings I lie there admiring it, not daring to wake. With nothing more than her little finger she can make me feel no bigger than it, and then turn around and make me feel like I can carry the world on my shoulders.

"Her eyes. God, I get lost in them sometimes. In those brown eyes I...I can see...I can almost see..."

"What can you see?"

James shook off the trance as he returned to his body. "Forget it." He fixed himself another drink.

Mayfield was taking in the room; the white carpet, sheer curtains layered with room-darkening fawn drapes, antique furniture. "How long have you been a doctor?"

"Thirteen years." James threw his head back and swilled the shot down his gullet. "And before you ask, I run a clinic in Manhattan."

"For how long?"

"Since '53."

"Make good money?"

"That's none of your business, but I guess so. Are you going to be much longer?"

Mayfield threw his coat over his arm and extended the other to shake. "I never stay longer than tolerated. Thanks again for the drink." He had taken the first step out of the den.

"Hold on," James stopped him; Mayfield turned. "Just like that?"

James sat his drink down without removing his eyes from the mysterious PI. He didn't appear to be a dangerous man, so why did his very presence feel like a threat. James took one step. His weary face was tighter and alert than a moment ago.

"This smells funny. I don't like it." His voice had gone down an octave. Without warning, James charged at Mayfield and threw him against the door of the den. "Where is she?!"

"Let go of me!"

Mayfield tried to pull the strong hands from his jacket. He was a mere inch away from the face that was colored blood red with rage. It was indescribable. He felt the seams of his coat pulling apart from the shoulders and knew James would have ripped apart his skin if not for the protective layer of his clothing. His hands alone possessed the power to pound the five-foot-seven PI into hamburger.

"You know something! Tell me!"

Mayfield looked him straight in the eye and said in a brooding tone. "I said let go." It was all Mayfield could do. James's grip slackened. Following a look of sheer disdain, he bolted down the hall.

Mayfield wiped the sweat from under his hat with his sleeve and got out of there. The PI parked his car in the street a short distance away from the gate. Once he got situated, he took the microphone and hit the red button on the tape recorder in the passenger seat.

"It's Monday, July 20...4:52 p.m. and I'm sitting outside the Mallory residence. I've just completed a personality assessment of Dr. James Mallory. He shows obvious signs of a severe and brash temperament, as demonstrated this afternoon when he shoved me against the wall because he assumed I knew where his wife was and wasn't telling him." Mayfield watched the house as he documented his findings.

"As a result, I wasn't able to find out much. I checked with his office beforehand. His employees make minimum wage, except for the two GPs that work out of his clinic. They knew little about him. I didn't get to see much of the house up here in Fairfield County, but from my viewpoint it looks to be maybe 7-8,000 sq. ft., not to mention his Rolls in the drive.

"I believe he is rich by other means besides his profession. In regards to his wife, he is particularly sensitive where her first husband is concerned. He's difficult to read.

"Has your wife disappeared before," I asked him, and I ran into a wall for my answer. He has a violent temper, but is he a violent man? It's understandable under the circumstance. I suspect he may know something. I think I'll keep my eye on him."

James emerged from the house. Mayfield stopped the recorder. He got into his Rolls-Royce and pulled out of the driveway.

Mayfield whispered, "Get a call? Going to meet someone?"

He started his engine and kept his distance. All through Cos Cob James's bumper was in sight. James stopped at a corner pub that was doing a fair business. Mayfield parked across the street and observed him in the rearview mirror.

He allowed James time enough to order and get relaxed. Mayfield lowered his hat over his eyes and went in. Several men were lined up at the bar. The air was thick with smoke and chatter.

Mayfield scoped the room. He gradually walked down the center between the tables and bar. It was at the end, the last man at the bar, that he saw him. Mayfield took a seat at a table out of sight.

"What can I get you?" asked the barmaid.

"A beer, please," answered Mayfield softly. For ten minutes he sipped his beer and watched him. Nothing of interest. He just ordered one whiskey after another.

The bartender came up and patted James on the shoulder. James was a regular patron. "Haven't heard anything, huh?"

James gazed down into his drink. "I had to go down and identify the body this morning. This could have been avoided. She tried to tell me something was wrong. I could have saved her."

"You talk as if she's not coming back."

"Don't you have drunks to wait on?"

Mayfield pondered James's behavior. His thought process being, if his wife was missing and a friend of his was dead, would he be in a bar?

"You're lookin' blue." A young blond of well-endowed talent helped herself to the chair beside James.

"What if I am?" he replied, taking another swig.

"Maybe I can help. I'm a good listener."

James's glance changed into a take-in-the-view kind of stare. She was built and dressed to please any wandering eye.

"I can buy you a drink," James offered with a shy grin.

"A dry martini."

"Dry martini for the lady."

The blond noticed James's hand resting on the counter. His gold ring gleamed under the light until she placed her hand over it. "Wanna tell me 'bout your trouble?"

"It's my wife. She's disappeared."

"Left you?"

"I don't know."

She flipped her hair to one side and inched closer to him. "That's terrible. What kind of woman would hurt a man like you?" James glanced down into the darkness of her exposed cleavage.

She moved her hand down to his leg. "I'm very good company."

"Thanks for the offer, but not now." As a last effort she squeezed and James got that pleasant sensation that shouldn't have manifested. James removed her hand.

"What hold has the old lady got on you anyway?" The bartender gave the lady her martini and she pushed it over to James.

Mayfield went to a telephone booth nearby and dialed his office. "Gail, it's me. – Yes, everything's fine. I'm calling to tell you to cancel my appointments for the next couple days. This needs my full attention.

"– As it stands, I can't tell. I'll fill you in later."

"WHAT WOULD YOU LIKE FOR BREAKFAST, SIR?" asked Susan.

"I would like a talk with your boss," Mayfield replied. Susan's how-may-I-help-you smile fell and she left to get Larry.

Almost immediately Larry approached his table. This was a rude intrusion on his work, as his apron indicated he was quite the worker. "Is there a problem?"

"Not at all. I would like to ask you a few questions, Mr. Jacobi." Mayfield pulled out his billfold.

Larry put his fists on his hips. "As you can see, we're packed. I'm afraid it will have to wait."

"I'm afraid it can't. You see, I'm here to discuss Lisa Mallory."

"I've already spoke with the police."

"Yes, I know." Mayfield followed Larry behind the counter. "I also know you were the last person she spoke to that night."

"Look..." Larry threw a towel over his shoulder and hugged the laminate with his chubby fingers. "Lisa worked for me for almost ten years. *Ten years* of back-wrenching work. Then she decided to quit."

"Why?"

"Her husband."

"Spell it out."

"She never said. I'm certain it was because of that husband of hers. It was back in April that she told me she had."

"Had to?"

"Again, she never explained." Susan slid an order over to Larry. He glanced at it. "Come with me." Mayfield followed him into the kitchen.

"Mr. Mayfield, I want you to understand something. I care about Lisa very much. What I tell you is under the strictest confidence. I don't know who you're working for, so no blabbering to every Tom, Dick, and Harry that comes along."

Larry picked up a bowl filled with pancake batter and poured it onto the grill. "May I ask what your interest is in all this?"

"I've just been hired to snoop around, whether I find anything or not. It may help Mrs. Mallory or not at all. Either way doesn't matter to me."

"Fair enough. What is it you want to know?"

Mayfield removed his hat. "For starters, you can tell me about her."

"Well, Lisa the employee was a damn good one. Lisa the friend – even better. She came to work for me around Hanukah, I believe. Yes, Hanukah of 1949. I remember because I was preparing to close my doors."

Larry mashed the pancakes down with the spatula. "I admit the hours are long, but she never complained. She enjoyed it. She took pleasure chatting with old customers every day.

"And it's not like I held back on her pay. She and I were practically equals in that department. There was no reason on God's green earth for Lisa to resign."

"That's why you believe her husband had something to do with it."

"Absolutely. In fact, that was how she met James. He was a customer here and she tried to wait on him."

Mayfield's private thoughts became audible, though his mouth barely moved. "A man of his means would eat *here*?" Larry appeared to have heard him.

Larry stacked the pancakes on a plate and placed them in the pickup window. "Now this is my personal opinion. Between us, since James entered the picture, everything in her life seemed to crumble."

"Tried to?" asked Mayfield as if he hadn't heard a word. "She tried to wait on him."

"He was flirting with her and getting her flustered. He took her to lunch right after. Those next couple weeks were the only time that her performance in her work suffered. Her first husband had no effect."

"If I may," Mayfield crossed his arms. "All manners and decorum aside. What is your opinion of James Mallory?"

"Don't like him." Larry answered so quick it caught Mayfield off-guard. "I guess it's because of the way he treats her. Or it could be his frequent patronizing of others, which I have witnessed firsthand and been subject to once or twice.

"Haven't you ever met someone you didn't like, but had no reason for not liking them? Must there always be a reason?"

"I guess not."

Susan cleared her throat. "Boss? Four eggs, sunny-side up, and bacon – table four."

"That's Susan, Lisa's replacement. She's slower, but she works hard." Larry went to the icebox for the eggs. "The regulars seem to be taking a shine to her. She learned from the best."

"What about Joseph Norris? Do you know anything about him?" Larry was arranging bacon on the grill and froze abruptly as if one of the bubbles of grease had burst and landed on his sweaty skin. Maybe it was the mere mention of the name of a dead man, and the cold feeling that goes down your back when you hear it.

"I'm not interfering with the investigation," Mayfield assured him.

"I-I suggest you talk to Lisa's kid brother, Donald. He would know more. He can be temperamental at times, but he shouldn't give you any trouble. He lives…"

"I have his address, thank you."

"Um, Mr. Mayfield?" Larry wiped his hands on his apron, his face troubled with thoughts of impending news. "There's one thing I neglected to tell you." Larry stood close to Mayfield and licked his lips, speaking low. "Before she disappeared, about a month's time to be exact, she…changed."

"In what way?"

"She was aloof. She took orders and cooked the food as usual, but she wasn't right."

"You don't have any clue as to what was making her act that way?" Larry shook his head. "Mm-hmm. You wouldn't happen to know where she was going that night."

"Home, I assume. I doubt she would have been going anywhere else at that hour. There is one thing she said that sticks out to me. She said that she had a lot of things to take care of."

"Things?"

"Maybe it had something to do with what was causing her elusive behavior."

"And maybe she had an appointment with her hairdresser. "Things" is a very broad word." Mayfield donned his hat. "Is that all?"

"I think so."

"What may appear irrelevant to you may be very significant to me. If you think of anything..." Mayfield handed Larry his card and they shook hands. "Thanks again."

Although he barely scratched the surface of his inquiries, he was compiling it all in his head and taking everything into account. Mayfield was to familiarize himself with the people in Lisa's life and sift through the chaos and confusion in hopes of finding a clue that he could run with. Thus far, he could only speculate. With any luck, Donald would provide more insight.

LT. ROBSON AND SGT. DODDS RETURNED to their precinct. The continuous ringing of phones, halls congested with cops, offenders, and grumbling citizens was of the norm. Robson, an already worn out, easygoing homicide detective, did his best under the circumstances of what seemed an ordinary killing.

"Hey, has the call from St. Louis come in yet?" Robson asked a detective working desk.

"Not that I'm aware of, sir."

"They're taking their time."

"Would you like me to try and reach them for you?"

"I hate being a pest. Yeah, go ahead. They should've called by now." Dodds followed Robson into his office. "Transfer the call to my office."

Robson kicked back in his chair and propped his feet up on the desk. "You know somethin'? I get that nagging thought sometimes like moving here was a mistake. Kay nagged me to move the family here, expecting some kind of utopia. Evidently my line of work and her expectations don't mix."

"You know what I find odd?" asked Dodds opening the blinds and not focusing on the lofty, claustrophobic buildings. "How our guy was dressed completely in black. Head-to-toe like some cat burglar."

"Apple Grove Life Insurance – how long did they say he worked for them?"

Dodds flipped through his notes. "Um…ah, here we are. Norris applied in December of '57, acquired the position in January. Approximately one year and four months. He left in May."

"He was making 15% commission. Why did he quit?"

"The head of the firm said he was a diligent employee."

"I don't know, but…" The phone rang. "Lt. Robson."

*"This is Capt. Sanderson of the St. Louis Metro Police Department. What can I do for you?"*

"Yes, um, I called yesterday morning for some information regarding one Joseph Elliot Norris. He was killed Saturday night and we know for a fact he came from your town."

*"Yes. I have his jacket in front of me."*

"What do you have?" Robson grabbed a pencil.

*"Well, he was born in Springfield, Illinois, April 16, 1895. He's survived by three younger sisters. They've all been notified."*

"Married?"

*"Was, to a Ms. Teresa Cartwright, April, 1916. They divorced a year later. She died four years ago.*

*"Oh, you'll find this interesting. Norris spent twenty-eight years as a police officer here in St. Louis – Central Patrol Division."*

"I heard something about that."

*"That's not all. Listen to this. In 1948 was discharged from the force for brutality after nearly beating a Negro man to death. Charges were never brought."*

"I'll be damned."

"What?" Dodds asked. "What is it?"

Robson shushed him. "Go on."

*"In 1939, '41 and twice in '45 he was booked for drunken and disorderly conduct. Two suspensions."*

"What was he doing in New York?"

*"Could he have been visiting?"*

"No, he had a full-time job, an apartment. As far as we know he has no family here, just a friend he knew years back."

*"Well, Lieutenant, if there's anything more we can do to help, get in touch. Likewise, if anything comes up, we'll let you know."*

"Thanks. You've helped a great deal."

Dodds was impatient. "Well? What did he say?"

"It seems our guy was a not-so-nice person. He was a policeman, yes, but was kicked off for brutality eleven years ago. Not to mention a few arrests for intoxication."

"Where do we go from here, sir?"

"I think our next move should be to look into Dr. Mallory. The friend seems to be our only lead at the moment."

"What about his wife?"

"Let's not focus on her until we have something more concrete."

# CHAPTER FIFTEEN

**M**ayfield waited in his car outside Donald's residence. Four hours so far, he kept an eye out. Cigarette butts dropped in a small mound onto the curb. He had to come home sooner or later, and it seemed the latter was approaching.

Mayfield glanced at his wristwatch – 5:37 p.m. A taxi dropped Rebecca off thirty minutes earlier. He wanted Donald, but was willing to take advantage of the opportunity. With them together it would make his job easier and them less of a chance to prepare.

The sidewalks and streets spilled over like a shaken soda pop. Mayfield observed every head. He had only a minimal description of Donald to go by: Tall, thin, black hair. Mayfield leaned over to pick up a newspaper from the floorboard and when he rose, a tall, thin, black-haired man was coming down the sidewalk.

Donald lit a cigarette on the steps of his tenement. Given he slouched, he was between six-one and six-two. He was very slender, almost lanky. His hair, as black as night, was combed to one side. Mayfield pondered the thoughts of this young man whose sister was missing.

The tenement he was providing for his wife and two kids was merely a fair one. But for any man with a family, unless he lacked the young man go-getter spirit, would hunger for something better. Mayfield was reminded of that 8,000 sq. ft. house back in Connecticut and wondered if there was any malice between the two siblings.

Donald kept glancing up at a certain window. He was stalling. He crushed his partially-smoked cigarette into the concrete and meandered a ways down the sidewalk, twice pacing in front of it before finally grabbing the rail and hurrying up the steps.

Mayfield rolled up his sleeve to time. At five minutes on the dot, he would go up and aggravate the nest.

"What is a Mayfield?" Donald asked.

"*He* is a private detective."

Donald looked down at his license. "And does he want to come in?"

"I won't take up much of your time." Mayfield greeted Rebecca as he entered the room.

Rebecca searched Donald for an explanation. She whispered in his ear, "What's going on?"

"There's no need for that," spoke Mayfield.

"I beg your pardon?"

"Whispering." Mayfield faced them.

"We're confused. The police have already questioned us."

"I'm not the police."

"Mr. Mayfield is a gumshoe, Rebecca. Sorry, private eye."

"Believe me, I've been called worse. In any case, let's all relax. I'm sure you're both curious as to why I'm here."

Stanley jumped up on the back of the sofa behind Mayfield. "Oh! Hey, little fella."

"This is Stanley," said Donald. Mayfield patted the cat's head. "Anyway," Donald lifted Stanley off the sofa and sat beside Mayfield with the cat in his lap. "You were about to tell us why you're here."

Rebecca sat in the chair and crossed her legs. "Who hired you?"

"James Mallory hired me."

Both Donald and Rebecca shrieked, "What?!"

Donald smacked his leg. "I *knew* it!"

"Donald, please."

"That jerk is always up to something. I bet he knows where Lisa is."

"Donald!"

Mayfield didn't say a word.

"What? What could I have said wrong this time?" Stanley jumped down. "For God's sake, Rebecca, this guy is dangerous. Maybe this detective here can help."

"What is the matter with you? The man said four words. Now your guts are all over the carpet."

"You're the one who threw the hissy fit when Martin and Lewis dropped in on us at the crack of dawn."

"Because you lied right through your teeth."

"Whoa, whoa, whoa!" Mayfield flailed his arms. "Martin and Lewis?"

Rebecca relaxed. "Lt. Robson and Sgt. Dodds, the policemen investigating the death of...someone we know. W-why..." Rebecca was becoming flustered as she tried to make sense of Mayfield's statement. "Why would James hire a private detective?"

"Let's just say he's concerned."

Donald stood and stuffed his hands in his pockets. "Sure, he's concerned, but about what? His career? His reputation?"

And there it was. Mayfield's prediction was accurate. There was malice. Donald exhaled deep through his nose.

"I understand this must be a difficult time for the both of you and your kids. Where are they by the way?"

"Next door," Rebecca answered. "Our neighbor watches them for us."

"By the sound of it, the two of you don't care for James Mallory." They glanced at each other.

It didn't matter what they told him. Donald's eyes revealed something that could not be suppressed, no matter what his mouth verbalized, even if he'd convinced himself, it would surface another way, and it happened to manifest in his troubled eyes. Bitterness, jealousy, fear, and regret; it was all there.

"Ahem. Look, Mr. Mayfield, I'm not meaning to sound impolite, but where do you get off making our business your own?"

Mayfield thought hard. He couldn't make them talk. "Mr. Wells, do you have a favorite game?"

"I'm sorry?"

"As in mumble-peg, bingo, checkers."

"I fail to see the significance."

"My favorite game is connect-the-dots. I've gotten pretty good at it. Sometimes the dots are obvious. Lickety-split," he snapped his fingers.

"Some dots are almost invisible, but with a keen eye and careful study they don't pose a problem. Now, the ones you have to watch out for are the hidden ones, the ones that are under the eraser shaving or the blotch of mustard. But they're there. Sooner or later...I find them."

Donald ran his fingers through his hair and sat back down. "No."

"No, what?"

"No, I do not get along with Lisa's husband."

"He's not so bad," Rebecca added. "I've never had a problem with him."

"He's arrogant, smug, superior, or so he thinks, to everyone. Who am I kidding? I hate him. Haven't you ever met someone you just didn't like?"

"You're not the first to ask me that," Mayfield muttered to himself.

"What have you found out?" asked Rebecca.

"I can't answer that."

"How long have you been on the case?"

"Sorry."

"Can't you tell us anything?"

"Ma'am, it's what you can tell me that's important." Mayfield was good at maintaining his temper or giving the illusion he was, but he saw they were going to take a little more elbow grease.

He looked over at Donald. "You, um..." He paused for effect, and to let them think he needed a brief moment to catch up with his mind. "You said that he was dangerous."

"Did I?"

"Mm-hmm. Care to spell that out?" Donald pressed his lips together. Mayfield smacked his hands causing Donald to jump. "Let's go! Let's get this ball rolling, people!"

"James is domineering. He's possessive over Lisa. He-he goes behind her back, lies to her. He says it's for her own good, but it's so the son-of-a-bitch can tighten his clutches."

Rebecca scoffed. "Don't you think that's taking it too far?"

"How do you know this?" asked Mayfield.

"It was last Christmas. Before we always used to have it here, but since James was the *new* addition to the family with the large apartment, we had it there."

Donald hands a gift to Lisa. "I hope you like it," he says.

"I'm sure I will."

Donald watches as his sister rips through the paper. Rebecca is on the floor with her kids and their new toys. James seems uninterested and goes into the kitchen.

Lisa unfolds the tissue paper and pulls out a bathrobe. "Oh Donny, I love it."

"I was worried lavender wasn't your favorite color."

Lisa holds a sleeve up to her cheek. "It's so soft."

"I'm glad you like it. After James got you the Chanel and diamond bracelet, I wasn't so sure." Lisa kisses his cheek. Donald hears a "psst" from the kitchen. James motions to him.

"Excuse me a minute."

James is seated at the table. The chair across is pulled out.

"What's all this?" Donald asks.

"Sit down." Donald hears the kids laughing in the next room. "This won't take long." He doesn't want to but consents.

James reaches inside his back pocket, drops his checkbook on the table, and begins to write. Donald's brow furrows. James tears out the check and slides it over to him.

Donald studies him. Is James testing him? He stares down at the check like it's provoking him to accept it. He lifts the paper up to his eyes. The figure steals his breath.

"How would you like to receive that once a month?"

"Well, um, this would help us a-a great deal." Donald giggles and covers his mouth. "I-I don't know what to say, James, except thank you. Oh, thank you." Donald puts the check into his wallet.

"Wait," says James. "Can I see it one more time? I think I may have misspelled your name." Donald hands it over and James rips it in half.

"What are you doing?!"

James takes the halves and holds them up. "This can still be yours...for a price."

"What could I give that is of equal or more value?"

"There is only one answer and you know what that is."

Donald sits back, an expression of astonishment fixed on his face.

"Here's the deal. You keep away from Lisa. No further association of any kind. That includes phone communication and postal. Under no circumstance are you to communicate with her other than a grave emergency which entails an accident, hospital, or death.

"If something should arise and you're unsure, call me. If Lisa answers the phone, hang up. I'm mindful of her financial generosity, so I'm giving you double, and you'll still be receiving hers. So, is it a deal?"

For an instant Donald wants to kill James, but his eyes revisit the two halves of the check in his hand. "Why?" he asks.

"Is it a deal, or no?"

"Can I tell you something? This is shady business. You're asking me to sell you my sister's relationship, as if you can put a price on it."

James stands up from the table and heads for the door.

"Wait. This-this isn't some kind of joke?"

"I don't joke."

James returns to the table and begins rewriting the check. Donald licks his lips. This time he is eager to grab.

"If I learn that you broke our agreement, the money will stop immediately." Donald reaches for the check. James retracts his hand. "No breathing a word of this."

*"O-okay." Donald seizes the check; his fingers are trembling.*

*"Let's go back and have a nice Christmas."*

*"Lisa is in there."*

*"You can have today."*

*"How long must I do this?"*

*"Until I say otherwise."*

"Oh my God," Rebecca marveled in disbelief.

"Two months ago, the checks stopped. Come to find out it was because I attended Rebecca's surprise graduation party. It didn't matter that I didn't speak a word to Lisa, just the fact we were in the same room."

Rebecca was angry. "That explains a hell of a lot. What the hell is wrong with you? Lisa giving out of her salary wasn't enough?"

Mayfield asked, "He never said why he came up with this proposal?"

"Not straight out. However, I've always believed him to be an overbearing husband, possessive at the core. With me around he had less control."

Donald bent over like he was going to be sick, with both hands supporting his head. "I never imagined it would have got as ugly as it did." Donald closed his eyes and a small tear rolled down the side of his nose. "She truly wanted us to become friends."

"Can you prove this?"

"It's all in the bank statement. Hold on, I'll get it." Donald left and came back with a folder and held the papers between them. Rebecca was in shock, but was also feeling left out.

Mayfield flipped through each month. "Starting in January there's a moderate increase. By late April your balance is up $1,500." Mayfield looked at Rebecca in curiosity. "You didn't question this significant rise in your balance, Mrs. Wells?"

"She doesn't handle the bank statement. She only knew of Lisa's check."

"How much was James giving you?"

"$250 a month like clockwork."

"Five months. That's $1,250," said Mayfield. Rebecca stormed out of the room.

Donald paid no attention. "Can we hurry this up? I have to work tonight."

"The Sugar Maple?"

"Yes."

"Joe Norris – What can you tell me about him?"

Donald was short. "Nothing."

"Nothing at all? I think it would unnerve, Mr. Wells, the gravity of this case." Mayfield lit a cigarette. "I hope you don't mind. I saw the ashtray in the corner over there."

He bid his time, inhaling a few puffs.

"At any rate, a man has been killed and your sister's disappeared. She could be in deep water, chest high, my friend. And I feel compelled to add if you keep playing this little game with the police that you're playing with me, you could get burned by the same hot water."

Donald crossed his arms. "You enjoy threatening people, don't you? I only met him three times. The first was at a dinner party before my sister's wedding, then the wedding, and he interrupted the graduation party. They must have been having problems."

Donald ambled to the other side of the room, pensive, scrunching his jaw. "I was sitting on the sofa watching Rebecca open gifts when the room got quiet. "You are no longer welcome in my house."

"Those were Lisa's words. She went to him and..." Mayfield leaned in to hear. "She whispered something to him. I-I couldn't hear.

"Next thing I knew she was threatening to call the police if he didn't leave. Then she screamed, "Get out you bastard!" He knocked her against the wall. That scared me."

"Mm-hmm. After that?"

"He left."

"See? There was more you could tell me."

Mayfield checked his watch. He said nothing else. Silence spoke louder than any voice. Regardless of Donald's involvement, or lack of, it was wise not to ask too many questions. Divulging how much he didn't know could be chancy.

As Mayfield opened the door to leave, he noticed a wedding photo hanging on the wall behind, and an expectant Rebecca draped in undeserved white, clinging to her new hubby's arm. That one picture had the power to answer so many questions.

"Mr. Mayfield, wait," Rebecca whispered. Mayfield was at the end of the hall. She closed the door and tiptoed to him. "Not that I disagree with any of what my husband said. All of it was true, but...well I-I..."

"Yes, Mrs. Wells?"

"Well, I think he's jealous."

"Of James? Thanks, but I already gathered that." Mayfield turned to leave. Rebecca grabbed hold of his arm.

"You don't understand. Since that day Lisa introduced us to James Mallory, Donald has dissected every inch of him. Honestly, there is very little that would shock me."

"What about that gargantuan mouser your husband let out of the bag? That didn't surprise you?"

"We were in dire straits at the time. The money aspect of the deal didn't. Who offered it however..."?

"Mrs. Wells..."

"Listen, my husband would never tell you this due to his inbred male pride, but he idolizes his sister. He literally believes she's infallible, and he despised both men she married. Agreed, Robert was a dreadful husband, but that wouldn't have mattered. James is perfect. He has looks, personality, stability, and he *still* managed to find fault."

"Mm-hmm." Mayfield waited to see if Rebecca said all she wanted to say. "I appreciate the help, ma'am."

Even considering this last bit of information, Mayfield still didn't have reason to believe that Donald would harm his sister for whatever purpose. He hated his brother-in-law, true, but not enough to keep from selling out Lisa for a helping hand. The notion was placed on the backburner for now.

Why did James give Donald money to stay away from Lisa? Was he planning something and thought Donald would interfere? If that was the case, why lay down consequences? Perhaps the money was payment for something else. The story may have been a cover. What about the photograph behind the door?

Mayfield mulled over these questions into his recorder. From inside his car, he stared up at their window. He almost couldn't blame Lisa for running.

THE WORLD AROUND HER WAS BLACK. She could see nothing ahead. Where she was going, she didn't know. Wherever the destination, she was determined to get there.

As if underwater, silence consumed every sound. She walked in slow-motion, sluggish, dragging a great heavy weight. A distant light emerged at the end of what appeared to be a long and narrow passage. The closer she came to the light the more she was able to see a hulking dark figure standing beneath it.

The weight grew heavier and heavier until she could barely move. But she had to reach the light at the end. She dug her nails into the ground and pulled using all her strength. All else seemed absent of existence. The mounting weight and her difficulty breathing was all she could sense.

The figure stood still. Lying at his feet, she looked up at him, yet she could see no discernable features. The light above was blinding. A gun materialized within her hand. Without knowing why, she aimed.

Her forefinger twitched and the man dropped – the light went out.

"No! No!" Lisa's cheeks were moist with horror. The covers of her bed were rolled into a knot between her legs. She detached the damp hair glued to her neck.

Lisa wept, burying her head in her arms. Her wedding ring slipped down to her knuckle.

"Hey! You alright in there?" asked a female voice from the other side of the door.

"Go away!" Lisa rolled onto her side and grasped the thin covers like a teddy bear.

It was Friday, noon. The curtains were drawn and the only light in the room was coming from the crack at the bottom of the door. She wanted to go back to sleep, but was frightened of the recurring nightmare. This motel was a good but temporary retreat. To venture out may not have been safe.

Lisa thought about her family continuously, Donald most of all. Split-second flashbacks persisted of cheerful times before he married Rebecca, before she met Robert or James, when they were happy. She recalled the day she marched down the aisle, closer with each step to her husband-to-be, his back straight, hands clasped behind him and wearing a warm smile with which to receive her.

She caught herself off-guard when she laughed. Larry and the fat belly he would have to maneuver to get behind the cash register. That dear-hearted Jewish man was indeed a true friend. She felt she had left them all behind.

Lisa stepped outside the protection of her room. She was fearful of the unknown. Had he been found? Was there an investigation taking place? More importantly, were they searching for her?

"Excuse me?" Lisa vied for the attention of the front desk clerk reading the paper. "Ahem." He looked up. "Would you happen to have a newspaper?"

"Nope," he answered, even though he was holding one. "There's a stand down the street."

Lisa was terrified as she inserted herself into the moving swarm and attempted to blend in. Every person she passed, every head that turned, every eye that blinked was focused on her. She tried the nonchalant, casual demeanor, but worried she was trying too hard. This made her appear guilty of something.

*This was a mistake.*

A woman to her right pushing a baby carriage peeked at Lisa from under her broad sun hat.

*That's the second time she's looked at me. Why would she look at me twice? There it is!* Lisa pushed her way through.

"*The Times*, please." She moved to the side of the stand and frantically scanned every page top-to-bottom and was somewhat relieved not to see her picture staring back at her.

*"Ex-Cop Found Slain"*
– Lisa dropped the paper.

*Oh my God, they know. Be calm. Don't jump to conclusions. Pick up the paper and read what it says. It could be anybody.*

Lisa slowly bent down. Her ring slipped to her knuckle. Taking a deep breath, she opened the page.

Ex-Cop Found Slain

On Sunday, July 19th, a former St. Louis police officer by the name of Joseph Norris, 64, was found shot to death. The victim was discovered in an alleyway behind 24 Hour Washeteria. At present, details of the investigation have been withheld.

"They don't know," Lisa whispered.

A policeman stood ahead of her, keeping his eye on the traffic that whizzed by. Coldness crept all the way down her legs and her knees locked. Was this what it felt like to be a criminal? How could they live like this day-to-day?

Lisa didn't wait to see what he was going to do. She held the newspaper high to hide her face. From the corner of her eye, she watched him. She steadily moved back into the crowd, her eyes just above the paper to see where to go.

Once she passed him, she took off, by surprise and by accident, into the arms of a young man. Both went tumbling onto the sidewalk.

"What's the deal, lady?" asked the young man, dusting off his trousers.

"I-I'm sorry I..." Lisa glanced at the cop who was well aware of her existence. "I didn't see you."

Lisa's newspaper was on the young man's stomach. "Unless you're Superman with x-ray vision, I don't doubt it, lady." He threw the paper aside.

Lisa got to her feet. The officer was still staring. She fled before he could do anything else. By the time she returned to her haven she realized she left her paper on the sidewalk.

*What if the cop followed me?* Lisa ran to the window and peeked through the thin gap. She was ready for that knock on her door to come soon.

"LT. ROBSON CALLED; SAYS HE WANTS TO SEE ME. I'm James Mallory."

"Right through there," pointed an officer.

Robson sat at his desk, mounds of files and documents stacked along both sides. "Dr. Mallory, come in, make yourself comfortable." James took the chair opposite him.

"What a week! I'm buried in paperwork up to my eyeballs as you can see. How've you been holding up?"

"Let's drop the formalities, shall we? What have you got?"

Robson removed his glasses and folded them into his shirt pocket. "I got a tip." He leaned back in his chair and stretched his arms behind his head. "Your wife and best friend did not like each other." James poked his tongue against his cheek.

"You knew this and you didn't say a word to us. You're a smart man. Keeping information from the police is not smart, doctor. I understand, you know? You want to protect your wife."

His eyes focused away, James asked, "Are you making a formal charge?"

"Not this time. But for future reference, it would be wise not to keep anything from us." Robson got up to pour himself a cup of coffee. "Like some?"

In one breath Robson switched gears. "Were you aware your wife owned a gun? Before you answer..." He plopped down into his squeaky chair. "Remember what we just talked about."

"Lisa doesn't own a gun. That's the most ridiculous..."

"A Smith & Wesson .32 caliber derringer to be precise." Robson slurped his coffee. "Are you sure you wouldn't like some? It's common for city women to carry a pistol in their handbag-purse or whatever. My wife has one."

"You're suggesting I don't know my wife. I know Lisa, and she doesn't own any firearm!"

Robson pulled out the top drawer to his desk and dropped a little bag in front of James. "Here is the shell casing we found at the crime scene. We have the bullet as well." He maintained composure.

James was seething under his breath. "What the hell are you suggesting, Lieutenant?"

"Not a thing." James was getting that pinned in feeling and started to pace, rubbing the back of his neck. "Have you heard from her?"

"No. It will be a week tomorrow." James leaned on the desk with his fists. "Is this why you asked me here?"

"No actually, I asked you here to identify an item." Robson held up a second bag. "We found this underneath the victim." He dropped it onto the desk.

James rotated it in the sunlight coming through the window. "Do you recognize it?" asked Robson, taking another sip.

James studied every aspect of the tiny golden circle. "It's...this is my wife's wedding ring."

# CHAPTER SIXTEEN

As of Friday, there was a warrant for Lisa Mallory's arrest. Every policeman was given a description of her height, weight, hair color, and clothes she might be wearing. Black-and-whites sent out on a dragnet of Manhattan combed the streets for its wrongdoers, and Lisa was now on the list. Within the sea of concrete, would they be able to locate one potential killer on the run?

There were so many places she could disappear. The number of rocks to turn over was insurmountable. Was Lisa still in that dreary motel? Perhaps the risk was too great to stay in one place for too long. Or perhaps moving was the bigger risk and it was safer to remain.

Lt. Robson and Sgt. Dodds were en route to Connecticut. James was not expecting them. With any luck he would let them in since they didn't have a search warrant. He answered the door clutching a beer bottle. His once-silky hair was matted to his head as he reached the threshold of inebriation.

"Surely you didn't come all this way to tell me you found her. You could've done that over the phone."

"With your permission we'd like to take a look around." In contemplation, James tapped his fingers on the door then moved to the side. "You search the grounds, Sergeant."

"Yes, sir."

"You won't find her here, you know," said James.

"It's protocol. Won't you give me the full tour?"

"Oh, what the hell. We'll pretend it's the Circle Line. Shall we begin with the upstairs?" James led Robson up the curved staircase. His shirttail was sticking out of his trousers and he was in his stocking feet.

Robson told him, "You don't look so good, doctor."

"You're kidding me, right? I haven't been this blitzed since I graduated medical school."

"You don't act drunk."

"You're not in my head. I've been inebriated so many times my body has developed an immunity to the poison." James led him to the right end of the hall. "This is one of six bedrooms."

"Did you say six?"

"Yes. They've all been furnished. There're four up here and two downstairs. Lisa and I use the same room. The only time this and the other bedrooms have been used since we bought the house was when we gave that party for my brother-in-law's wife."

Robson inspected all of the upstairs, including two bathrooms and James's office. Thus far, he hadn't found anything significant. It came to his attention that James was avoiding one room in particular. Twice they came upon it.

The last time, Robson stopped in front of it. "I want to see this room."

Slowly James turned. In his heart he didn't want to, with everything in him he didn't want to, but his mind took charge and obliged the lieutenant in a seemingly calm manner. What he never told Robson was he hadn't slept in their bed since or even stepped foot in the room. He had taken most of his belongings out and was using another room.

Robson turned the brass doorknob and looked over at James. The lieutenant went straight to the window. The sheets on the bed were still outlined to the shapes of their bodies. The chaise lounge seemed to have assumed the role of closet. James waited in the doorway as Robson browsed through her clothes and her dresser.

Robson moved to her bedside bureau and found a significant piece of evidence in the first drawer. "Look, a bill-of-sale for the gun."

Robson found what he needed to link Lisa with the bullet and shell casing found at the scene. Two days ago, when he told James he knew Lisa owned a Smith & Wesson .32 caliber derringer he was bluffing in the hopes James would spill the beans.

"Incidentally, is there anyone else that has access to the house, such as a maid or cook?"

"We have a housekeeper that comes in three times a week to clean and do the laundry."

Robson took out a notepad from his inner pocket. "Name?"

"Doris Tilbury. She's in the kitchen now. It's no use asking her anything. Besides, I'm going to let her go – just too much going on."

James caressed his hands over the fabric of the chaise. "The very first day we went furniture shopping she spotted this and pleaded me to buy it for her. She had me place it right here by the window so she could look out at her new surroundings.

"The grass and sky seem so large from here. She would sit for hours." The appearance on James's face seemed a melancholy one, a blankness brought on by distant memories.

Robson moved in behind and jolted him awake. "What about your friend?"

"Until last year I hadn't seen him for over a decade."

"How did you come to know him?"

"He was a friend of my old man. When he died Joe never went away."

"Were you aware of his arrest record?"

"Yes, but I lost track of Joe after I left St. Louis."

"I see." Robson pushed back his hat to scratch his brow. "I think we've about covered everything up here." Dodds was in the den waiting for them.

"One moment," Robson told James as he went to consult his partner.

"I searched the entire perimeter – nothing. The garage was locked. I'm thinking her car's squirreled away in there." Dodds gazed over at James who was resting his head over the banister. "He looks awful."

"Wouldn't you be? Hey, check this out." Dodds looked down and saw the receipt in Robson's hand.

James knocked on the door of the den. "Excuse me? I'd like to get this over with sometime today."

James helped himself to a drink, observing the two detectives chat amongst themselves. "Can I ask you a question?" He moved around the bar towards the two men, churning the ice cubes in his glass. "Would you tell me if you had even the slightest hint of where she could be?"

"Of course."

"So, with all your resources and manpower, you haven't one damn clue?"

"She must really be off the grid," said Dodds. "We looked into her accounts at the bank and nothing's been withdrawn. She hasn't used her credit cards."

Robson added, "Unless she's using cash. How much cash does she usually keep on her?"

"I don't know."

"If she has ample cash she could easily disappear for a while, and since she's lived in Manhattan her whole life that gives her an edge."

"Not her whole life, Lieutenant." James smiled. "Lisa's a Brooklyn girl." It came to James's attention that Dodds was snooping in the corner by the phonograph and record albums.

"The point is she could be anywhere." Robson tapped James's shoulder with his finger to get his attention. "I'm confident she knows the streets as well as any officer. Do you think we could find her at her brother's place?"

"They don't get along anymore."

Dodds stated that instant, "Mr. Wells told us the opposite."

"He lied. They haven't spoken in months."

With James at the helm, the two detectives searched all of the downstairs and found nothing. Robson expected as much.

Doris was in the kitchen sweeping the floor. Her graying hair was pulled back into a bun and a few strands of hair had fallen over her face.

Robson approached the aging woman. "Mrs. Tilbury?"

"Yes?"

"I'm Lt. Robson. This is Sgt. Dodds. We need to ask you a few questions about Mrs. Mallory."

She glanced at her boss. "Alright." Robson pulled a stool out from under the breakfast bar for Doris to sit. She was a little stiff and apprehensive due to being put on the spot.

"Now, um, how long have you worked for the Mallory's?"

"Since February of this year."

"Do you like working for them?"

"I-I don't see either of them much. By this time Dr. Mallory would have been at his office and Mrs. M would have been at the diner."

"That's incorrect, sir," said Dodds. "Lisa Mallory quit her job."

"I know. Quiet."

"Now, surely you saw Mrs. Mallory at some point."

"The last time I saw Mrs. M was when she paid me my wages." Robson's face displayed he wanted more. "Oh, it-it must have been a Friday. That's when I get paid. Two weeks ago."

"That sounds about right," Dodds responded. "How did she act?"

Robson rephrased the question. "Did she act differently than normal?"

"Come to think of it, she did. Before she would take me into the kitchen and we would chat about all kinds of things over tea. I hate coffee, so she fixed us tea. Mrs. M is a sweetie. It did come to my attention when she handed me my check and walked off."

"Thank you, ma'am," acknowledged Robson. "You can get back to your work. Doctor, my partner and I would like to see your garage."

"Would you look at that?!" said a stunned Dodds gawking in awe at both automobiles. "That's a Rolls-Royce!"

Robson asked, "Which is her car?"

"The Buick. I bought it for her birthday. You won't find anything. I already searched it."

Robson took the front and Dodds the back. James leaned against his car and observed, sipping his drink.

"Did you bring the car back from the depot?" asked Robson.

"No, the towing service picked it up."

They inspected between and under the seats, the glove compartment, and under the floor mats. "What's he doing?" whispered Dodds.

Robson glanced over his shoulder. "He isn't doing anything. He's standing there."

"He *actually* seems bored. I don't trust him, sir. I think he's shielding her."

"There's nothing we can do about it today. Keep searching."

It was no surprise to either when they found nothing.

James belched. "No luck?"

"Did *you* find anything?" Dodds came around the car with brisk stride. Robson was glaring at James.

This made James nervous. "I-I gather you're implying something." James licked the beverage off his lower lip and directed his next words at Robson. "You know what? I think I've showed you all that I care to today."

Robson pointed at James, almost scolding him. "We have a ways to go, Dr. Mallory. Whether you believe it or not, *when* we catch her, it will be to her benefit. Do you understand?"

James gave Robson the look that many say could kill and forced a "yes" from his lips. He was happy to show the detectives to their car. He waited until they were out of the driveway then hurled his glass across the yard.

TUESDAY NIGHT – the thickening clouds hovered low over the city. Being no longer able to contain, Mother Nature cleansed its surface in the drops that fell in scattered billions.

The Sugar Maple was quiet. Donald was sprawled on the sofa in the parlor. Muffled raindrops hitting the roof lulled him to the brink of sleep until a road-weary couple decided to check in for the night.

They signed in and he carried their bags to their room. Donald hugged the side of the building back to the office. Stretching as he yawned, he turned the corner and saw two feet on the floor.

He inched closer.
"Lisa?"

# CHAPTER SEVENTEEN

"**L**isa!" Donald fell to his knees beside her and turned her over into his arms. She was unconscious.

He placed a warm hand to her cold, wet cheek. He barely recognized her. Her complexion was pasty and there were sagging dark circles under her eyes. Her neck bore a faint discoloration. Turning her head both sides he saw it encircled all the way to the nape.

The backs of her arms were severely skinned, as well as her legs. Through the soaked thin material of her blouse, he saw something. He inched up her blouse to examine her stomach and there was a large but faint bruise beneath the skin. Her expensive skirt was now tattered and frayed.

"My God," he whispered.

Donald lifted her up and laid her on the sofa. With a combination of gladness and despair he stared down at her, wondering what in the world he was going to do.

There were two choices he could make:

One: Call the police and take the advice of the private eye to stay out of hot, rising waters.

Two: Hide her.

One was the right thing to do and one seemed the right thing to do. He had to decide which was which.

He went outside to think. What could he do? Recent past wouldn't influence his decision. Donald grasped the post like a lifesaver in the midst of a sea of raging turmoil colliding into him.

He bit a ridge into his bottom lip and it became clear to him. A look of fear was replaced by determination. He went back into the office and took out the register book.

Donald paused before entering in The Sugar Maple's new guest.

He removed both #7 room keys from the rack and peeked in on Lisa once more. He didn't want any guests to wander in, so he turned out all the lights and locked the door. Donald somehow needed to divert suspicion to make it convincing for management and housekeeping. He left in his car for the nearest store still open that time of night.

Despite his outward appearance, he was a ball of worry and confusion. He was gone for a little over an hour and was fearful he would come back to flashing lights and a mass of spectators, but the motel was still dark and quiet as he left it. He grabbed the suitcase and overstuffed shopping bags from the trunk and reached in his pocket for the key, but not before verifying if curious eyes were peeping behind curtains.

Donald knew what he was doing was wrong from a legal perspective. It wasn't clear whether or not his sister murdered Joe Norris. However, he disregarded those feelings, deciding to pay more attention to the ones that reminded him of all those years Lisa cared for him. It was a matter of duty, but also devotion.

He organized the room in such a way to give it a lived-in appearance all while the consequences were being whispered in his ear by some disembodied voice. If he was caught, he would not only be fired from his jobs, but he would be thrown in jail. He might even lose his wife and his children.

Donald placed Lisa's new clothes in the closet and her toothbrush on the sink in the bathroom. He opened the window to welcome the rain's cool draft into the musty room. As he was about to leave, he switched off the light and looked both ways. No one was there.

Lisa was still out. Donald placed her dangling arm across her chest and took a deep breath before lifting her up. She was so limp as if nearing death, and light; weight loss was apparent. He made sure again no one was outside and quietly made his way down the boardwalk. What little noise he made was masked by the rain.

He kicked the door closed and laid her gently on the bed. Where had she been all this time? What happened to put her in this condition? Donald peeled off her shoes and noticed the bottoms and sides of her feet were red and blistering. He grabbed a towel from the bathroom and wrapped up her feet.

Donald sat on the bed and massaged them gently. "You're safe now. Everything's gonna be alright. I'll take care of you." He pulled the covers up to her chin.

Donald sat the suitcase next to the closet and placed the key by her on the nightstand. He was contemplating if he overlooked something when he spotted a gold ring on the floor by the door. He realized it was her wedding ring and slipped it back on her finger.

Then it hit him: Her handbag. He recalled seeing it earlier on the floor in the office. When he picked it up it was somewhat dense for such a small handbag.

He peeked inside. The tip of a silver barrel glowed at the bottom.

IT WAS DIFFICULT TO BREATHE. Again, she found herself dragging the weight towards the light far away. The dark figure stood beneath it. Lisa knew what was coming and fought the covers.

The gun materialized in her hand. She aimed.

"No! No!"

The man dropped.

Lisa buried her head in the pillow and sobbed. There was no escaping.

"Hey, hey, hey…" Donald put his arms around her to keep her still.

It took her a half a minute to come into focus. "D-Donny? *Donny?*"

"You've been out close to five hours now," he said. "You somehow found your way here. Don't you remember?"

"Vaguely." Lisa suddenly started looking all around. "Where's my…"

"Your purse is over there on the dresser." Donald pulled up a chair beside the bed. "Relax. You're safe here."

There was so much to be said, but neither cared to take the plunge. Lisa never thought she would see the day when they would be in the same room together, and talking. She sat back and studied every feature of the face she deemed she would never see again.

Donald started, "I don't know how else to say it, but to...say it. We've all been questioned by the police and some gumshoe sticking his fat, ugly nose into things. I didn't want to believe it, Lisa, but is it true?"

Donald was hoping she would respond. "The gun in your purse, um..." Lisa's eyes jumped to the bag. "I saw it. How...what happened to you?

"You're going to have to say something sooner or later." Lisa's silence was making Donald anxious. "You've been gone for over a week. I was beginning to think you...left for good."

"Donald, I thought you knew me."

"I thought I did...until the police knocked on my door." Donald hit the nightstand. "Tell me! If you're still mad, I got the message, okay?"

"You think I murdered that man?" Lisa tried to sit up too fast and fell on the bed. Donald seized her arm. "I'm alright."

"You're weak as a kitten. You better lie down. I'll go out and bring you back some food." Donald was halfway out the door.

"Donald," said Lisa softly. He stopped. "Do-do they know it was me?"

"They do now."

For the first time since that night, she was going to speak aloud what happened.

"I was leaving the diner. I-I hadn't walked far when I was pulled into an alley."

Donald closed the door and went to her.

"He took me by the throat and...." She felt of her neck, recalling the thick fingers wrapped around it. "I remember staring into those eyes until everything went black.

"I don't know how long I was out. When I woke up I-I-I felt around for something to hit him with. I managed to grab a handful of gravel and threw it in his face."

Donald said, "If it's too hard you don't have to tell me." Watching her anguish at reliving the night was harder for him than hearing the memory itself. It was a thoughtful way of asking her to stop.

She looked up at her brother and swallowed hard. "My purse was on the sidewalk. It was my only chance, but I didn't get far."

Lisa gripped the mattress. "I wasn't strong enough. Much about that night is a blur; I can only recollect fragments. He... he threw me down and kicked me. He was going to kill me for sure."

Lisa's nose was starting to run. "He-he grabbed my neck a second time and squeezed so much harder this time. God...my neck. I thought my pulse was going to come out of my eyes.

"Somehow, I broke free. I got the gun from my bag. He-he fell on me."

Donald intervened before she got too upset, and more audible. He held her tight to ease the memory of a nightmare come to life.

"Why did I shoot him? I shouldn't have shot him."

"You did what you had to do." Donald went to the window and scanned the outside. "Lt. Robson is handling the investigation. He's issued a warrant for your arrest. The police have already searched my home looking for you."

"How-how could they have *possibly* found out it was me. I left nothing behind."

"I don't know."

"Didn't they tell you?"

"Of course not. Why the hell would they tell me anything? If anyone knows anything it would be...never mind." Donald caught himself. He almost said James.

"Now, listen close. Here's what's going to happen. I get off at seven, that's an hour from now. I get to work around ten at night. Anytime between those hours you are not, repeat *not*, to leave this room.

"I work on Saturdays occasionally, never Sundays, but I may try to come in. I registered you as a guest, room #7. You're paid-up for one week in advance."

"What's my name?"

Donald smirked, "Frances Kincaid."

"I get Frances, but Kinkaid? The old landlady who used to curse out Dad? The same landlady who whipped you up four flights of stairs for dumping water on her cat?"

"Ha, I-I'm sorry. It just popped in there. Nevertheless, that's your name and don't forget in case something should come up. Housekeeping shouldn't bother you as long as you keep the marker on the door. I also went out and bought you a few belongings."

Donald went to the closet to show her. "I wasn't sure of your size, so I got you different sizes." He held out a blue dress. "Your pajamas and slippers are in the dresser, and a brush, toothbrush and paste are in the bathroom."

Seeing what all he had done made her feel loved. She wouldn't have cared if the clothes hung from her body.

Donald didn't know what else to say. "Well, if you need anything else let me know and I'll get it for you. I guess I'll get you something to eat now."

"Wait." Lisa found the strength to stand and shuffled to him. "Donald…"

"Donny," he corrected. The siblings smiled.

"Donny, how long do you think…"

He didn't know the answer and she could read it in his face. "We'll have to play it by ear. Don't worry. We'll cross each bridge as we come to it."

"And burn it, too."

"Right. Hey, I tell you what." Donald was excited to have his sister back. "Um, you take it easy and I'll be right back. We'll have breakfast together."

"Sounds good."

"Great. Great."

Lisa waited for the door to close and her genuine mood surfaced. Donald did cheer her up, but the hidden fear deep inside was too powerful. Lisa walked around the room to acquaint herself with her temporary home.

*I guess you never know what life will throw at you. You mosey through each ordinary day assuming nothing bad will ever happen, next you find yourself running around like a chicken for the gallows. Staring a first-degree murder charge in the face is one of those things you never expect to happen. That only happens to bad people.*

She saw the toothbrush Donald placed on the sink which made her chuckle.

*But it's happening to me. I never thought I would be hiding out in a motel, unable to take care of myself, but here I am, one in a city of millions, with just one to rely on. What a curveball.*

For an instant the notion that Donald was playing Judas assaulted her mind. Commonsense told her he wouldn't have gone to so much trouble if he had the concept of handing her over. However, stashing her away like this was dangerous. If this Lt. Robson he spoke of got wind of this he would drop a hammer on her little brother almost as heavy as the one he was saving for her.

For Donald's sake, she couldn't stay long. The clock was ticking away precious seconds, and it was a matter of time before police came knocking on door #7.

# CHAPTER EIGHTEEN

**M**ayfield didn't want to interfere with the investigation. In the past he faced many a confrontation with police. After many a trial-and-error he developed the know-how to keep from bumping into them. He made it a rule to move quiet.

Mayfield was on the outside looking in which gave him a clearer and broadening perspective. He sat perched on higher ground and could peer down on the activity of everyone involved. He felt he needed to see the crime scene since it appeared to be the location of the "breaking point".

"Mallory!" Mayfield shouted. James leapt up from behind the trash cans.

A forceful exhale expanded James's nostrils. "What are *you* doing here?"

"Funny. I was about to ask you that very same thing." Mayfield approached. "Of the many people I thought I might run into you were at the top of my list."

Mayfield had been tailing James for two days. It was no surprise. "You want to explain to me what you're doing?"

"None of your business, Mr. Private Detective."

"Mayfield," he corrected. "And it is my business, friend."

"If you must know, I'm sick of staring at the walls waiting for the phone to ring."

"Whoa, whoa, I know what you're thinking and it is not a good idea. There's been a warrant issued. The only thing you can do is get yourself in trouble. Why not go down to the station and..."

James kicked a can to the side. "I'm tired of people giving me their unwanted advice. People are so quick to say, "Well, I wouldn't do that, I'd do this. Don't do this, you should be doing that." You have no idea what this feels like."

Boxes, trash, and garbage cans filled the barren and narrow alley. Even in the daytime its seemingly harmless appearance didn't fool Mayfield who saw a much darker place, an isolated crevasse between buildings where an evil occurred. It was hidden from the rest of the world. The light source was pouring in from the street, but mostly lit the ground up to a point. The higher the elevation the dimmer the light became.

The two buildings that seemed to entomb them were no more than ten feet apart. Mayfield and James were nearing the end and standing in the shadows. And this was in broad daylight. What was it like for Lisa fighting for her life after dark inside this crevasse? In Mayfield's mind this alleyway was a fracture of what once was a whole structure.

James studied his surroundings trying to envision what happened with the little information he had. "Robson said the body was found behind trash cans like someone strategically placed them around the body." He walked to the spot where the body was found. "He was face up against this wall.

"We know how he died, but he had a puncture wound in his right hand. That leads me to believe there was a struggle."

Mayfield folded his arms; he wasn't buying it. Who did this doctor think he was playing detective? The PI's private thoughts kept telling him the entire persona known as James Mallory was nothing more than a performance. Deep in the doctor's mind laid the truth, the answer to every one of Mayfield's questions, except for Lisa's whereabouts, and that was the driving force behind this "act" of true love and concern.

James kept vocalizing his thought process. "There was blood found on one of these cans. I guess the police have it. There's no doubt Lisa was here. She was last seen when she left work around nine. So...she-she was attacked."

"By your best friend." Mayfield added. "And ran away after she killed him." Both sets of eyes drifted down to the ground.

James asked, "Why here?"

"Seclusion. The time between the gunshot and when Norris was discovered is significant. No one heard it."

James's expression indicated he was bothered. "I don't get it. This alley is in the opposite direction. Lisa takes the train home. Grand Central is east, not south."

"Maybe she wasn't going home."

James looked at Mayfield questionably and with intent, chewing on a request he wasn't sure he had the nerve to spit out. "I still don't know who you're working for, but I trust it's *for* Lisa, not against. Am I correct in assuming this?"

Mayfield gave no indication.

"Well, there are a few people that...let's just say Lisa had difficulties with. Alma George – have you heard that name?" Mayfield shook his head. "She was Lisa's old neighbor; hated every bone in her body."

"Why?"

"Not even Lisa knew. There's something else. Lisa's ex, Robert, they divorced back in '55, and this past April he came back. The way she described him to me, well, I never thought she would welcome him with open arms the way she did."

"Why the sudden U-turn?"

"I've been under tremendous strain. You're as intelligent as any police dick. No. Better, because you can go beyond the jurisdiction of the police department."

Mayfield thought for a second. "You want me to report back what I find...to you?"

James solemnly replied, "Whatever they're paying you, guaranteed I can match it. Whatever carrot your client is dangling I can offer two, or maybe three."

"That's not going to happen. I refuse to take on more than one client within the same case."

Mayfield's refusal angered James. "I don't need you anyway! I can find Lisa on my own!" He stormed out of the alley like Joe Norris's ghost was after him.

Was this new information credible given its source? James must have thought he could buy anyone. Mayfield was leery of him. Was Lisa in greater danger now that her husband wanted to find her on his own?

"LET ME IN, ALMA," barked James through the door. "We need to talk." He knew she was in there. He heard the TV just before she muted the sound.

"I don't have anything to do today. I can wait." The wind caught his hair as the door opened swiftly. James stooped to her height. "Oh, are we not happy?"

Alma glared, "Come in."

She lit a cigarette and plopped down in her chair. Her apartment was similar to Lisa's old one, except hers was messy and disorganized. Alma sat with one leg propped on the footstool. She returned her lighter to the right pocket of her thin robe and the left shoulder slid off, displaying her chunky figure that was stretching the stitches of her silky white slip.

"We need to talk, Ms. George."

"You already said that. Why aren't you with the wife?"

The atmosphere was quiet and unsettling. James wandered behind her. Alma felt uneasy when he didn't answer. Her eyes jerked side-to-side. Not being able to see him added to the feeling.

James moved slowly around her.

"It must be one hell of a something to bring you here."

James very slowly sat on the sofa across from her. His every move was slow and careful, like the calm before the storm. Alma could see no storm looming, but did sense one. James was trying to read her as well.

"That something you claim to have no knowledge of *is* in fact serious." He continued to search for an indication of anything – a twitch, a sigh, even a sniffle, but her face remained dour. "Do you read the paper?"

"Sometimes."

"In last Friday's paper there was an article about a shooting of a former cop." Alma puffed her cigarette. "He was a friend of mine." James leaned forward, "Lisa shot him."

Alma held the cigarette away from her mouth, sluggishly blowing the smoke from the corner. "So?" She stuck the cigarette between her lips.

"I don't know where she is." The edge of Alma's maw trembled as she struggled to keep it down. "The police have issued a warrant for her arrest. You hate my wife. There's no denying that."

"Point?"

"You hated her! Enough to kill, I wonder."

Alma rose up quick, "Now hold on a minute!"

James stood high above her. "Back in April when I called you to ask if you knew where Lisa was you revealed a great deal to me. Or did you forget?"

"I didn't forget."

"You begged me to call you back once I found out anything. "Nice little chat," you said. I lied to her for you, telling her I only called you the once when I was trying to find her."

"I'm not your scapegoat. *You* and *you* alone lied to her. She would believe whatever drivel oozing out of your mouth."

"Why did you? Why did you want so badly for me to call you back? Juicy melodrama?" The low, choppy way he said the last sentence revealed he had answered his own question. "Or perhaps the anticipation that something serious might've happened to her."

That had to be it. James couldn't stand to look at her anymore and walked to the opened window. He held back the curtain with one hand and braced the window jam with the other. He gazed down at the street below.

"I was wrong to go to you for help after she told me everything you did. It took her a long time to trust me."

Alma pressed her cigarette into the ashtray and went to him. "You really care for her, don't you?" He closed his eyes. "I don't know what's going on, but I commend your gallantry."

"You said you wanted to talk to me about my wife. You never mentioned gossip."

Alma chuckled, "If that helps you sleep at night..." She moved behind him. "I lived next door to your waitress for nine years. You think I don't know what I'm talking about?"

"What do you want me to say? If all of that were true then why didn't she tell me?"

"Ashamed, I guess. You did just say it took her a long time to open up to you."

Alma was digging her nails in deep. The sun shined through the cloudy glass onto his face, exposing his tired eyes and light stubble. There was merit to what she said. James nudged her aside to leave.

Alma rushed in front of him, acting as barrier. "I was thinking maybe we can benefit one another. Obviously, you don't believe Lisa murdered this friend of yours, but she is "on the lamb" as they say."

James reached for the doorknob. Alma grabbed his arm.

"I know things about Lisa no one else does. Don't you want to do all within your power to find her? If you're worried she will be livid about me then your priorities are in need of a little tweak."

James let go of the knob and rubbed his hand against his sandpaper cheek. He lumbered back into the room. Alma was learning how to use Lisa Mallory. She was turning out to be a powerful force that Alma could use on or against multiple people, sometimes without their knowing it, because that name used to be synonymous with someone they could trust.

LISA AND DONALD played Scrabble sitting on each end of the bed. Bags of food, paper plates, and cups were lying around the room. The lived-in appearance had been achieved.

Lisa peeked at him from behind her notepad. Donald's face tightened. Lisa took a long, deep breath and paused. It was fun watching her little brother squirm on the edge of anticipation.

"Well?!"

"Donald: 253." He smiled, preening at his highest score yet. "Lisa: 279."

Donald raked the tiles off the board. "One more."

"I'm tired." Lisa went to the bathroom and immediately poked her head out. "You've had three rematches anyway."

"Oh, shut up," Donald whispered. He straightened up, ridding the room of two days' worth of litter. "Did anyone bother you today?"

Lisa began washing her hands. As soon as they hit the water her ring fell off. "Dammit!" It nearly fell down the drain before she caught it.

"What's the matter?"

"No, no one's bothered me!"

Lisa held the ring up to the light. With so much going on she never gave it any thought, but her wedding ring never slipped off before. Lately it was doing it all the time. She placed it on her finger.

Lisa straightened her arm and shook it – the ring fell to her knuckle. "This isn't my ring."

She examined it closer and noticed a monogram on the inside – *"E.N."* Lisa came out of the bathroom in a daze. Donald saw something was wrong.

"This isn't my ring," she whispered.

"What?"

"This is not the ring James gave me."

"What are you talking about?"

Lisa yelled, "My wedding ring! This is not my wedding ring!"

Donald whispered in a demanding tone, "Be quiet."

"You don't understand. This isn't my ring. My ring hasn't left my finger."

"So, whose is that?"

"I don't know. It has "E.N." monogrammed inside. Have a look." Lisa fell in the chair in the corner. "It must have happened the night I was attacked.

"Remember I told you that I blacked out? Joe must have switched rings. I was certain I left nothing behind. *That's* how the police connected me at the scene – my wedding ring. James could identify it."

Donald bent down on one knee and put the ring in her palm. Lisa gazed down at the false ring longing for hers. Her ring, which was still so precious to her, was in the hands of strangers. That ring symbolized the promise she made to James.

The vow she pledged was dear to her. The idea of bearing another woman's promise troubled her.

"Oh, Donny..." Lisa was on the verge of breaking down. She was right on the edge and was hanging on by her finger nails. She could see James as clear and bright as day.

"Don't cry, sis. You're stronger than this."

"No, no, I'm not."

Donald put his hand beneath her chin, prompting her to raise her head. "Don't give up now. Not after all we've been through."

Donald was doing as Lisa did for him many times before. "You cared for me when Mom and Dad died. You were all the family I had in the whole world. And what if Joe succeeded?

"I would've had to live with the way we left things for the rest of my life." His warm and gentle gaze revealed the concern he felt. It was the best medicine.

"Thank you," she breathed.

Lisa was putting off asking Donald a certain favor, but this latest scare hastened her request.

"Donny, I've been thinking. There's a lot going on. I mean, with the police and the PI hanging around. I, um, I would kind of like to know what's going on. I'm in the dark here and you're my only source to the outside world."

"You want me to be your eyes? Oh, I don't know."

Lisa beseeched him, grasping both his shoulders. "I'm not asking you to shadow anybody. After all, I'm the subject of interest. Not you."

"Lisa, I work two jobs, not to mention watch over you now. You're a fugitive, and I am sure I have a bunch of blue eyes keeping tabs on me, if you know what I mean. If I go probing into Robson's investigation..."

"I have to know."

"Ugh, alright." Donald stood up and stuffed his fists in his pockets. "God forbid, if they find us out don't hold it over me."

"If they find us out, I won't be able to hold it over you."

It was something neither wanted to think about. "I'll be back. I have to check the office."

Lisa hugged her arms. The room was making her stir-crazy. She fell on the bed and, after a moment, held her hand up to her face and slipped the ring back on.

"I've been waiting for you!"

Mayfield was waiting by the desk.

Donald took aback. He was stiff, somewhat afraid, and unprepared. "What-what are you doing here?" He moved behind the desk at the same time Mayfield moved in front.

"Oh, I'm just making the rounds."

Donald hung the key to Lisa's room on the hook and said with a long exhale of annoyance and dread, "What is it you wanna know?"

"Have you heard from your sister?"

"No."

"I find it odd that she hasn't made some form of contact with you." Donald shrugged his shoulders a little bit. Mayfield leaned on the desk with his elbow. "I've talked to a number of people and none of them has a clue as to where she could be hiding. Do you?"

Donald tried to control his stammering. Mayfield was indeed perceptive. "I-I figure she's moving place-to-place; probably a different location each day. That's what I'd be doing."

"You don't seem concerned."

"I am...I immerse myself in other things to keep my mind busy, you know."

"Mm-hmm. I learned a new name today. Alma George."

Donald had to think for a second. "Lisa's old neighbor."

"Tell me about her."

"There's not much to tell. From the get-go they didn't like each other. I always chalked it down to personality clash. From-from..." Donald coughed. "From what I remember, Alma craved gossip.

"She was like *The New York Times* of rumor. Every piece of gossip in that building circulated from her apartment."

"Any about Lisa?"

"Only one I can recall. A long time ago Alma disguised herself as a friend of Lisa's and hinted to me that Lisa had come down with a bad case of syphilis. I-I talked to Lisa about it and she explained what was going on. Even then it had been going on for a while. You see, Mr. Mayfield, Lisa didn't always tell me everything."

"Why would she target her?"

"My sister's harmless. She would never harm a soul."

"Mm-hmm." Mayfield grinned. Donald was nervous, and the little man wouldn't take his eyes off.

Mayfield asked, "Do you mind if I have a look at your book here?"

"Why?" Donald started to fidget. "Well, I-I guess if-if you think it'll get you anywhere."

Mayfield turned the book around and leafed through the pages. "Mills...Dawson...Thompson," he muttered to himself. Donald was growing more edgy with the passing of each second and page as he kept in mind what was seven doors away.

"Kincaid – July 28."

Donald freaked with a burst of rambling. "Sorry, there isn't anything of interest. I do-do understand why you need to look. You never know, you know."

"That's right."

"I want to find Lisa as much as you do. I-I-I would tell you if I knew anything."

Mayfield glanced up and gave him a cunning smirk. "Sure, I know you would."

"Do-do you see anything significant to your investigation?"

Mayfield put a finger to his lips.

Donald was starting to glisten with sweat. He licked his lips and tampered with his hair as Mayfield studied the one page. What if he demanded to see the rooms?

"Well, Mr. Mayfield," Donald broke his silence. "If that's everything, I've got a lot of work to do."

Mayfield carefully closed the register. "One more question. Do you work alone at night?"

"Uh, y-yeah."

"What are your hours?"

A woman entered the office. Donald's rescue.

"I'm sorry but I must insist."

Mayfield got the message. "See you around."

Donald waited on the woman all while glancing out to make sure Mayfield was driving off.

The clock was ticking.

# CHAPTER NINETEEN

"I... I DON'T KNOW WHAT TO SAY." Robert slowly reached for the edge of the sofa. "You say Lisa murdered this man?"

"It was self-defense, I think," said Mayfield.

"I can hardly believe it. Is she alright?"

"I don't know."

Robert looked at Mayfield, and without words, asking the question, "What does that mean?"

"No one knows where she is," Mayfield replied.

Robert wetted his lips, his tongue helplessly fumbling around his mouth. "Why...what..."

Mayfield took the seat next to him with the intention of appearing less of an authority figure and to put him at ease. He gave him a moment to let it sink in and then pushed things along.

"I believe you can help me."

"Y-yes, of course, whatever you need to know."

Stella came out of the kitchen carrying a silver tray with cups and saucers. She was a golden-haired lady, voluptuous, beautiful, and pregnant. And she caught Mayfield's eye.

"Would you like some tea, Mr. Mayfield?" she asked.

"Tea?"

"This is a half English household," Stella said with a prideful glow.

"Please. I couldn't help noticing your accent, Mr. Frisco. What part of England are you from?"

"London. I came to America after the war. I lived in Boston for a year and then moved here."

Stella added, "We've lived in Yonkers for a couple years now." She handed both men a cup.

"What year did you and Lisa divorce?" Mayfield glanced at Stella. The look on her face revealed she was uncomfortable concerning her husband's former love. "I apologize if this bothers you."

"No, it's alright. I'll go into the kitchen and let you two talk. Holler if you need me."

Robert took her hand and kissed it. He waited until she was gone before he answered. "Lisa and I divorced four months prior to our marriage. I was unfaithful, yes."

"Mm-hmm, I see."

"It's not what you think. True, Stella is younger and a bit more...shapely, but that wasn't the reason. There are several "last straws" that triggered our separation."

Mayfield sat his cup on the table. "Tell me about the straws."

"It is rather personal, unless you think it would help."

"I can't answer that until I know, now can I?"

By his demeanor, whatever he had to tell him was not going to be good. "Well," Robert rubbed his hands together. "Alma introduced me to Stella. Alma is Stella's aunt. That is how we met."

Mayfield scooted forward. "Your wife is Alma George's niece?"

"You see, at the time..." Robert's head fell back. "God, why is this so difficult? I-I was an alcoholic. Bless Lisa's sweet heart."

Robert paused to gather his thoughts. "Stella was staying with Alma for a time. I never intended on being unfaithful, but she made me smile. Lisa was always angry and always yelling. I'm not condoning what I did, but the second I laid eyes on Stella I was hooked. It felt the same as when I saw Lisa for the first time. I guess some people fall in and out of love pretty quickly, eh?"

"So, Alma introduced you to her niece, because...why? I heard that she hated Lisa."

Robert poured himself another cup of tea. "That's true. It was abrupt animosity. A month before we married it was gossiped all over that Lisa was living rent-free." Robert chuckled inside his cup. "All the tenants were saying she was sleeping with the landlord.

"The man was a fossil. Alma's led a drab life. People are her hobby."

"Mm-hmm. Well, enough about Alma. Let's discuss your visit with Lisa back in April."

Robert froze in mid-sip. He lowered his cup down to the saucer and to the table.

Mayfield said, "What I don't know is why." Robert reached inside his pocket for his pack of cigarettes. "Nervous?"

He pulled a cigarette out with his teeth. "I, uh, manage a haberdashery. I put in for a raise, but it hasn't come through."

Robert exhaled the smoke and crossed his legs. Telling Mayfield wasn't easy. "My salary is adequate enough for Stella and myself to live relatively without concern, but Stella is six months pregnant."

Mayfield sighed in understanding, being reminded of that extravagant house in Greenwich. He knew what Robert was going to say.

"Alma phoned Stella up and told her about Lisa's recent marriage into wealth. I almost didn't go through with it."

Mayfield saw the kitchen door crack open. Robert continued, "I hadn't seen Lisa in years. I forgot how pretty she was...those big brown eyes." He whispered to himself, "There is something about that woman."

"What did she say?"

"No, of course. It was Stella's idea. I guess you can say I traded my self-respect for nothing."

Stella came charging out of the kitchen. "Tell him. Go on, tell him!" Robert threw her a cautionary glance. "Tell Mr. Mayfield the actual cause of your divorce."

"Be quiet, Stella."

Stella stood over Mayfield. Venomous saliva was spurted with each consonant. "The divorce wasn't consensual. Lisa didn't want it. She was still crazy about him."

Robert took Stella's arm. "This has nothing to do with you."

"Then you shouldn't have told me."

Mayfield snapped his fingers at the two. It was clear Robert was hurting inside. The whole truth behind his decision to leave Lisa was about to be revealed.

"In 1953 Lisa became pregnant. I didn't know. She made damn bloody sure to keep it a secret from everyone, including me." Stella sat beside him and laid her hand on his leg. "She had an abortion.

"She killed our baby. "Why," I asked her. Her answer: "We couldn't afford it."

"I take half of the responsibility for our failing marriage. I was a drunkard without a job, but it was still our baby. She had no *right* to do this terrible thing!"

This bad memory coupled with the news of his ex-wife made him feel like a spectacle, speaking his deepest feelings in an arena to an audience of one. Coping with the death of your child without ever having celebrated his conception is something you would never expect to talk about to someone you just met.

Robert moved behind his wife and placed his hands atop her shoulders. "Look at us, Mr. Mayfield. We can't afford a child, but we're going to get through it...together." Stella laid her hand over his.

"We tried to make it work, Lisa and I, but between her abortion and my drinking the damage was too great to mend."

"Who," Mayfield had to clear his throat. "Who else knows this?"

"No one knew but us. When I told her Stella was expecting she became very excited for me."

Mayfield was now thinking this gave Robert a motive, a definite cause to hate Lisa. He wanted to leave after being told this intimate secret. Stella opened the door for him.

Robert came up and put his arm around her. "I don't know if Lisa told her husband this, but she can no longer have children.

Whoever did the procedure botched it. Against her wishes, I took her to the hospital when she began to have stomach pains.

"Our child would be six-years-old."

Mayfield pondered into his recorder. "Robert may be holding a grudge. The brief visit tells me they must be desperate. I wonder. If Lisa had told him about the baby, perhaps it would have motivated him to shape up.

"I wonder if he's thought of that. With a baby in tow, they might have stayed married and she never would have met James Mallory, and in turn, never met Joe Norris.

"What about Alma George? Not only was she spreading lies, but she purposely handed her niece over to a married man in the hopes a relationship would blossom. Alma accomplished her goal of destruction, but did it stop there?"

# CHAPTER TWENTY

**1**:29 a.m.

Donald exited his apartment and drove away. Mayfield checked his watch. He was parked across the street under a streetlamp. Donald hadn't worked a Saturday since Mayfield started keeping tabs on him. He started his engine and slowly pulled out.

With Donald's bumper always within his line of vision, Mayfield concealed himself behind other vehicles, crisscrossing between them on occasion. He found himself heading down Hudson Parkway from West Avenue all the way down to Eleventh Avenue in Chelsea. He hadn't one clue as to what would bring Donald to that district that time of night.

Donald led him to a quiet residential area. The street was covered in shadow except for the occasional streetlamp. Mayfield switched off his headlights and slowed the car to a stop. Donald was parked in the driveway of a random brick house.

Mayfield shut off the engine and reached in the back for a small brown satchel which he kept his camera in. Donald's lanky outline walked up the steps and knocked on the door, and Mayfield began snapping pictures. There was a single light emanating faintly from the front window.

Mayfield cursed to himself when Donald blocked his view of the person. Less than a minute after the door closed the light went out. He reclined his seat and folded his arms, preparing himself for the probable long night ahead. He made up his mind he was going to know who Donald drove twelve miles to visit in the dead of night, and he was going to know before the night was up.

Time crawled by; hour stacked upon hour. To stay awake he downed numerous cups of coffee from his thermos and a club sandwich which was devoured by the second hour. It wasn't until the peach hue of morning sky was there activity from the mysterious house. After five hours Donald emerged, zipping up his jacket.

Mayfield lifted himself up with the steering wheel, and used his knuckles to eradicate the film of sleepiness from his eyes. Donald stood there gliding his fingers through his disheveled hair. The look on his face was one of remorse and anxiety. Mayfield took one last picture.

He had to find out whose address this was, and from that, decide if it had anything to do with Lisa. Mayfield would have plunked down however much money he had on him in a bet that the party in question was female.

Mayfield walked across the street to the house and rang the doorbell. He removed his billfold from his jacket. He would have won the bet.

"Beg your pardon, ma'am, Sgt. Gifford with the police." Mayfield flashed his license quick so she wouldn't see. "I'm here to answer complaints we've been getting from some of the houses in the area about a barking dog coming from this residence."

"I do not own a dog."

"I'm sorry, Mrs..."

"It's *Ms.* Schiller." Her whitish blond hair was pinned above her head and her face was moist and flushed. Mayfield could see her nipples poking through her thin robe.

"Are you sure?" he asked.

"I ought to know if I owned a dog."

"There must be some misunderstanding downtown." Mayfield tipped his hat. "My apologies for disturbing you, ma'am."

"Donald Wells is having an affair with a German woman named Schiller. Rebecca is a beautiful woman and this woman is not. Why?"

WHERE IS HE? HE SHOULD BE HERE?

Lisa threw back the curtain.

*What if the police got to him?*

That night came rushing in invading her brain, leaving her frozen at the window. She could see it clear on the movie screen of her mind.

*He climbs Lisa's back. The weight of his bulging stomach crushes her back.*

Lisa grabbed her handbag from the dresser and hurried into the bathroom. She took out the gun and set it aside. As she rummaged for her aspirin, she saw the glint of her nail file at the bottom.

*She stabs the file into his hand. He screams.*

Lisa tossed the pills into her mouth and washed them down with water. "Why won't this damn headache go away?" She grimaced, massaging her temples. "Three days straight."

Carefully, she picked up the gun, her intention being to put it back in her bag, but something stopped her. Joe's face appeared, his grin expanding the hole of his black mask. It was so real, Lisa thought he was on the other side of the mirror.

"No, no, no!" Lisa hit her head against the mirror as if that would drive the image out. Her headache wasn't going away. The vice was squeezing tighter and tighter.

*There is a loud pop. Wetness drizzles onto her face. He collapses on top of her.*

Lisa dropped the gun into the sink. She curled into a ball beside the bed and pulled the covers off and over her. Beneath the darkness of the covers, she struggled to remove the face from her mind. Now she could feel a pulsating from deep inside her skull.

*I think the aspirin made it worse. God!* Suddenly the handsome face of her husband morphed from the face of the other.

The covers were quickly peeled off of her. "Why are you on the floor?"

Lisa wiped the long, wet streaks from her cheeks. Donald gazed down at her with concern. She recalled her gun in the sink. She stood up from the floor and stepped around him.

"Lisa?"

From inside the echoing bathroom she remarked, "I can't do this anymore." There were definite cracks in her armor and her health was failing. She appeared at the door. "They're gonna find me."

Donald shook his head.

"They are going to find me if I stay. I've been here for a week now." Donald gave her a quizzical look. "They'll know it was you. I can't let that happen."

"You can't leave. If-if you leave then…then this will go away."

The earnest comment touched Lisa. Those weren't the words she was expecting to hear. She was anticipating, "You will be caught." Or, "Where will you go?"

It was a selfish yet caring approach to make her stay. One good thing came out of this horrible ordeal. Their relationship hadn't gone this well since before James entered the picture. At Lisa's expense, Donald got what he wanted.

Lisa hugged him. In that, he felt security that it was going to be okay between them no matter what happened.

JAMES WAITED FOR ALMA in his car outside the complex. He glanced at his wristwatch multiple times before she came strutting out. Alma caked on the makeup for some reason; bold blue shadow, pink cheeks, and flaming red lipstick. None of it matched her brown suit and hat. James couldn't figure out why if all she was doing was tagging along.

Alma ordered stepping inside the Rolls, "There are a few stops I need to make before we begin."

"No."

"I beg your pardon?"

"Let's get one thing straight. I'm in charge. It was your idea to come along. I would do perfectly fine without your delightful company."

"Okay then, boss. Let's get going."

James lagged behind the long, endless train. "Larry's will be our first stop. Lisa's been close friends with him for years."

"Oh, I-I had assumed you would look into Donald or-or Robert."

"Donald? Lisa wouldn't have anything to do with him."

"Are you positive?"

"He's a mouse. He would never help Lisa."

"What makes you say that?"

James glanced over at Alma; he didn't trust her. "Forget it."

He questioned his reasoning behind bringing Alma along, except that she knew things about Lisa that he didn't know, or so she said. Her presence made him uncomfortable, and her intensions could only mean trouble, but these were desperate times.

Alma lit a cigarette. James gripped the steering wheel tighter. It was better to say nothing.

Larry happened to look out as James and Alma appeared at the window. He rushed into the kitchen. "Susan, I need you to do me a favor. I know I told you to prepare for lunch, but I need you to go on your break now."

"Well, alright."

"I'll fix lunch. Go."

Susan scooted around Alma as they were coming in. "You think he saw us?"

"Let's find out. Hey Larry, you back there?"

Larry didn't answer.

Alma whispered, "Maybe he left."

"Larry!"

Larry emerged from the kitchen grinding his teeth and exhibiting a cold stare that revealed his dislike of the intrusion and the company.

James asked, "Why did you run?"

"Are you hiding something?" added Alma.

"I didn't want to see you." Larry turned to Alma. "And no, I am not hiding anything. Who are you?"

"Ignore her."

"This is my place, and by right of law, I have the legal authority to throw you out of it."

James smirked, "If you can."

The implied challenge triggered the two men to stare each other down, both anticipating the other to make a move. Alma inserted herself between them. "Come on, kiddies, put your backs down. James wants to ask you about Lisa."

Larry unclenched his teeth but not his fists. Soft yet terse, he replied. "You've got nerve, young man, to come to my place *now*...with Lisa...Leave, both of you."

"What is your problem?" asked James.

Larry set his fists on his hips. "Lisa's missing, a man is dead, and you're sticking your nose where it doesn't belong. I don't trust you." James lunged forward; Alma pushed against his chest.

"I'm not hiding anything from you or Lucille Ball here." Alma patted her hair in response. "Ever since Lisa met you, she's been sick."

"What?"

"You smother the poor girl! Because of you she quit the job she loved. I had to replace her with a fair but competent wai-tress who'd never fixed a flapjack before."

James loosened his muscles. He was amused in a puzzled sort of way. "You're mad 'cause I took Lisa away? That's why you're having kittens?"

"You couldn't stand to see her working. It was easier to per-suade her to quit and throw money at her, right? That way you could keep her at arm's length, and every second of everyday know where she is – at home, waiting for you."

"Look at this place! It isn't worthy of a woman such as Lisa."

Larry turned his back to him. Insults on his establishment cut the deepest. He muttered, "Lisa loved you."

"What?"

"You heard me." Larry spun around. "I said Lisa loved you."

James didn't know how to respond. Alma was taking in the whole scene as though she was watching one of her own lies unfold.

Larry kept at James speaking in a tender manner, "That child isn't property. Lisa is a kind human being and she wanted to include you in her simple life." Without a word, James's icy blue eyes dropped.

"What could I know that you don't? You're her closest friend. I don't know where she is. Believe me, I pray for her every night."

All the fight in James was depleted. "Let's go, Alma."

James opened the door and then thought of one last question. "Did you hire a PI?"

Larry struggled to recall his name. "May...May..."

"Mayfield?"

"That's it."

"You know him."

"But I didn't hire him."

Alma tapped her foot against the pavement. "That was a pathetic waste of time."

"I disagree. Larry's met the PI." James opened her door. "And if he knows him then Donald knows him. Get in the car."

It was close to ten that night when Donald arrived at the Sugar Maple. Parked in front of the office was a burgundy Rolls-Royce. There was only one person he knew of that owned such a fine piece of machinery. He moved in closer and saw a redheaded woman in the passenger seat by herself. He just saw Rebecca to bed, so it wasn't her.

Donald went around to that side of the car and tapped on the glass. "Hey! What're you doing here?"

Alma ignored him.

Alma's presence gave him an eerie feeling. "Where's James?"

Donald bolted into the office. His eyes darted all around searching, but all he found was his biggest fear coming to life.

"Oh my God." Donald grabbed the key to room #7 and nearly knocked James over on his way out. "James!" He gripped the key in his right hand behind his back.

"I've been looking for you," said James.

Donald looked past him at Alma. "And her?"

"She implied, more than once, reasons for why you could be involved, each one more convincing than the last. Lisa may have come to you for help. Current circumstances would cancel out any squabbles of late. Your previous problems would make the perfect cover."

James extended both of his arms to each side of the door. It was a subtle intimidation that was very effective and blocking Donald's only exit was a bonus.

James asked, "What have you got in your hand?"

"A key." Donald attempted to leave, but James wasn't budging.

"Why in such a hurry? You've got all night, haven't you?"

Donald didn't have an answer. His fear blinded the clarity of his thinking.

"Look James, we're adults. Let's be civil about this."

"Civil? When have you ever been civil?" James glanced down at Donald's left hand at his side that had developed a mind of its own. "Are you scared of me? Have I done something to scare you?"

All Donald could think about was if James had got to his sister. He had to know, but he didn't know how to make James leave. It was bad enough to be in this situation in the first place, but for her to be killed after surviving the first attack, and while in his care, he couldn't keep the gruesome imagery from coming.

James's threats did nothing. If he knew he wouldn't be putting Lisa at risk, he would have laid a right cross on his Prince Charming smile something fierce and smashed some teeth.

Donald tried to get him to back down. "Why come here? And with that woman?! You know where I live."

"I just want you, kid. Wouldn't want your wife and kids to see." James made a sudden jerk; Donald recoiled.

The clerk Donald was relieving came up behind James, "Excuse me."

Donald took advantage of the intrusion while James was looking away to stuff the key in his pocket. All the while the clerk was collecting his things James and Donald's eyes were locked.

"See ya tomorrow, Don."

James posed a much bigger danger than any cop.

"I don't know what you want from me. I have a lot of work to do, so either intimidate me some more, beat me up, or get the hell out. Better yet, come back tomorrow night without your guard dog and then we'll talk."

James was about to explode and left before the boom. The headlights blinded Donald as James started the engine and pulled out.

Donald ran to Lisa's room and banged on the door, forgetting the key was in his pocket. "Lisa! Lisa!" Every second that she didn't answer brought Donald closer to pure terror. Frances Kincaid left his mind also.

"Lisa, open the door!" He kept banging harder and faster. Guests started opening their doors and looking out their windows. A solid minute was gone and Lisa had not come to the door. Donald was on the verge of knocking it down with his bare hands.

"What's going on?" asked a gentleman staying next door. Donald was too engrossed to hear him. "Hey, bub, do you need some help?"

Donald dug the key out of his pocket and inserted it into the lock. As he turned the knob the door was opened from the other side. His heart skipped in fear because he was convinced that he would see the mangled body of his sister thrown across the bed.

Lisa was half asleep in her oversized pajamas, half expecting to see police accompanying him. "What's happening?" Donald shoved her inside and closed the door quickly.

Alma yelled, "You're a fool! You had him!"

"Shut up!"

"We watched him all damn day! We planned the best way to get at him! You're nothing but a coward!" James accelerated to a speed much too fast for the road. He darted around cars to prevent hitting their bumpers.

"Slow down!" He lowered his foot on the gas. "Are you trying to kill us?" Alma peeped at the speedometer at the needle rising gradually and eased off her brash manner. "Look, it's just the first day."

"I don't intend on wasting any more of my time on this guy or you. I have my wife to worry about."

They turned down the next street and the tire ran up on the curb. "Stop the car! I want out!"

There was a red light ahead with a long line of cars and James showed no signs of slowing down. Alma shrieked. James hit the brakes.

Alma jumped out and kicked the door repeatedly. "I hope you rot in hell!"

# CHAPTER
# TWENTY ONE

**M**ayfield didn't know how Donald was going to react.

Mayfield's philosophy was if you cook something on a stove when it's alive it will squirm. Those same rules apply in his profession. When the heat becomes too much, that's when the truth will reveal itself. This method may have been a slow and tedious process, and at times risky, but it got results.

"What is it this time?" Donald let him in, but reluctantly. It was getting to the point where seeing this man always meant bad news.

Rebecca bumped into Mayfield from behind as she came through the door with the kids. "Oh! What are you doing here?"

Mayfield smiled down at Simon and Julia. He had only seen them in photographs. "Hello, young man, what's your name?" he asked, offering the boy his hand. Donald sat on the arm of the chair.

"Simon." He shook the stranger's hand.

"Nice to meet you, Simon." Mayfield bent down to one knee. "And you are?"

Julia hid behind her mother's leg. "You'll have to forgive Julia," said Rebecca. "She's a little shy. Simon, take Julie into the kitchen."

"Beautiful children."

"Thank you. You didn't come all this way to meet our kids."

Mayfield turned to Donald. "Is there somewhere we can talk?"

Donald exhaled, smacking his hands against his legs as he stood up. He didn't even try to hide his let's-get-this-over-with look. He gestured for Mayfield to follow him to the bedroom. Anything that had to be discussed away from the significant other was never good. Rebecca was uneasy and kept her eyes on the closed door.

"Mr. Wells..." Mayfield walked around the bed rubbing his chin. Donald stayed by the door with his hands in his pockets. "Six years ago, your sister became pregnant, unbeknownst to her husband at the time. A short time later she had an illegal abortion."

Donald's eyes widened. He advanced. Horrified, he pulled at his hair.

He mustered the strength to speak. "Why...why didn't she tell me?"

"So...it's not the fact that she took it upon herself to remove the life growing inside her, or that she too could have died, but because she didn't tell you about it."

Donald lowered himself to the bed. "She-she...she's Lisa. She's a fighter; gets it from our parents. I was never like them.

"The depression hit us pretty hard. We barely had enough to eat some days, but we were a very close-knit family. Dad was a jack-of-all-trades. That was how he made the bread."

Mayfield leaned against the door and tossed his hat on the dresser beside him. He figured the news about his sister's abortion was the trigger.

"Before I could bat an eyelash or divulge my gratitude they were gone. No goodbyes, no I-love-yous."

"May I ask how?"

"Automobile accident. The cab they were in was struck by an off-duty cop. Mom died instantly. Dad made it to the hospital, but died before Lisa and I got there."

The couple died leaving two innocent siblings behind to fight the battle of survival in an America that was being ripped apart bit by bit.

The glass of the window muffled Donald's words as he spoke into it. "Lisa was thrust at the helm instantly. By 1942, World

War II and its hardships made the hurdles more of a challenge. She landed a job in the New York Navy Shipyard and became a welder for the war effort. She sacrificed everything for me, Mr. Mayfield, and there is nothing I wouldn't do for her in return."

Mayfield could see the relationship between Donald and Lisa had not declined in any way. Donald looked to his sister for comfort and counsel as he would in the mother and father that was taken from him. He meant every word.

"It shocks me to learn she would do such a thing, but it changes nothing. I appreciate your discretion." Now that his point was made Donald made his way for the door. Mayfield caught his arm.

"Oh, I'm not finished." Mayfield reached inside his jacket. "I have a picture here and I was wondering if you could help. I can't see too well without my glasses. Can you tell me who that person is?"

Donald grabbed the photograph of him exiting the house he visited many nights before.

Mayfield turned up the heat. "The person is tall, most likely a man, dark hair...kind of like yours."

"I-I-I can't tell. The picture is too dark."

"Mm-hmm. He kinda looks like you. I wonder why that is?"

Donald handed the photo back. "Don't know."

"A Ms. Greta Schiller owns the house. She used to be your employer when you worked at Greta's Grab 'n Go over a year ago. There's no chance that could be you."

Donald scowled at Mayfield from the corner of his eye. Low he murmured, "Why the hell should I tell you anything? You're just going to spill it all to James."

"You're sure going on the defensive for someone who has so much to hide. You're having an affair with this woman." Mayfield pulled out a second photograph of Greta standing at the door in her skinny robe. "You left at one o'clock in the morning to shake the sheets with Irma Grese down in Chelsea.

"Do you think I'm playing games?" Mayfield threw the photos at Donald and they bounced off his chest. "Step down off your high horse. Convince me you aren't involved in Lisa's disappearance. Start fillin' me in."

The bags under Donald's eyes grew white or it was his face that grew red. "I've been seeing her for a year now. We're not in love or anything like that. It's not even physical attraction. It's for purely fiscal purposes."

Mayfield couldn't believe it. Was there nothing this man wouldn't do for a dollar?

Donald felt he should have realized with a private investigator snooping around that he would be caught. "I keep the stash where only I can find it."

"How much?"

"The amount paid depends on the extent of the favor and how much it is enjoyed." Donald's anger subsided to shame. "This is a secret that I intended dying with and still do."

"EDGAR, I was beginning to think you weren't going to make it home for dinner."

"Ruth." Mayfield embraced his wife. "Sorry, I didn't get a chance to call. What're we having?"

"Pot roast."

"Ah, the famous pot roast and gravy. Delicious."

Ruth assisted him with his jacket. "It'll be a few minutes. Why don't you unwind in your chair and have a drink?" She gave him a peck on the cheek. "Gail phoned while you were out and left you a message.

"Something to do with the case you're working on." Ruth went to the desk and brought back a folded-over notepad. "She received an anonymous phone call."

"Male or female?"

"She couldn't tell. They must have been disguising their voice. Anyway, they have useful information pertinent to the case and to meet you..."

Mayfield did everything but jump out if his chair. "A meeting? Where?" She was hesitant. "Ruthie, I have to know!"

"In-in the alley at midnight. Come alone. What alley, Edgar?"

"Where Lisa was attacked."

Ruth held the notepad to her chest and closed her eyes. "I should have done it. I should have pretended the call never came." Mayfield didn't get her being so uptight over a message. "Oh Edgar, don't do it. *Please.*"

"A woman's life is at stake."

"So is yours. This is the most volatile case you've been on in a long time. There's a chance you've been conversing with a murderer."

"Attempted murderer."

"What difference does that make? "Attempted" just means they failed. What if you get too close? I can't go through it again. What if it happens again?"

Her imploring eyes softened him. "I'm more careful now. You and Perry mean the world to me. You know that. But this is what I do.

"I've been doing this for half my life and I'm good at it. You stood behind me when I chose to leave the military."

"This is different. In this profession you hide in the shadows, become a fly on the wall of these messed up people's lives, and..." Ruth's voice broke. "You find yourself getting stabbed by the husband of a woman who hired you to keep her informed of the philanderer."

When she said that Mayfield put his hand just under his left breast where the old wound penetrated his lung, and he didn't even know he did it. Mayfield tried to take her in his arms, but Ruth nudged him away. "I have to check on dinner."

This was a burden she had been carrying for a long time. She was accurate in saying this was his most dangerous case in years.

Ruth was wiping her eyes with her apron when he came in. She quickly returned to her pot roast on the stove. "Could you tell Perry to wash up for dinner?"

Mayfield rubbed the back of his neck. He was doubtful whether he should approach her. "Dear, I think it may take a little more time on this one. This is a very complex case and the police don't give damn about this woman. The evidence points to her; that's all that matters to them."

Ruth set the table around him.

"I don't think she killed that man in cold blood, but there doesn't seem to be any solid proof of that. I've considered quitting. Then I think about her controlling husband and money hungry brother, both of which I believe could be behind this. I refuse to let them get the best of me.

"She also has an embittered neighbor who hates her guts for whatever reason, and an ex-husband who resents her for aborting their baby...*and* has his hand out at the same time. It's an awful mess." Mayfield exhaled heavily at what he was about to say. "Ruthie, I must go tonight."

With every case Mayfield would trade his night's sleep for a possible resolve, whether he was shadowing someone or going over facts in his mind. The Mallory case was the worst of late. Fitful nights were evolving into pure insomnia. He had a gut feeling the answer was right under his nose.

Ruth could see the lack of sleep was taking its toll on her husband. "I'm frightened for you. I can't help it."

He met his wife at the stove, gently taking her waist. "You're something else." She chuckled in embarrassment. "You've always looked after me, haven't ya?" He tucked a loose brown hair behind her ear.

"Trust me," Mayfield winked.

Anonymous phone calls were seldom liable and meetings done in secret were always high-risk. This person knew something about the attack on Lisa's life and sought to keep their identity withheld. It's not uncommon when police are involved if said informant wants to avoid the hot seat, but also can't sit idly by saying nothing.

It also crossed Mayfield's mind this may have been a plot to bump him off, but he wasn't about to plant that seed in his wife's mind. The only way to find out was to show up at 12:00 a.m. in the alley of the attack.

Alone – not unprepared.

MAYFIELD STOOD BEFORE THE ALLEY.

It was too dark to see if he was alone or if the informant was waiting in the darkness. The only light to see by was the streetlamp above him, but the blackness of the brick cave swallowed what little light it created. Mayfield could only imagine what hell Lisa suffered on a night like this one. He slipped his right hand into his overcoat pocket and wrapped his fingers around the handle of his revolver.

Slow and vigilant he started down. Each sound was amplified to his ear. He could hear the crunch of broken glass and gravel under his beat-up leather oxfords. And if he could hear it so could someone else. When he neared a garbage can he would slow as not to give the possible attacker the opportunity to jump him.

Dead-end. He stomped the ground in frustration with the assumption he was stood up. He pulled up his sleeve – 12:17 a.m.

He turned back around and there stood a person at the opposite end. The streetlamp above them casted a heavy shadow and distorted his view of any distinguishable features.

Mayfield shouted, "H-hello?" They said nothing. "My name is Mayfield."

Mayfield approached very gradually. "You asked me to meet you here. What is it you want to tell me?"

Mayfield cocked his head, straining his aging pupils. The closer he came he was able to see they wore an oversized brimmed hat that hung over their eyes and a raincoat that went past their knees, but still the face was a black hole.

They opened one side of their coat and reached inside. Mayfield froze dead. Was it a gun? Mayfield gripped his tighter.

They pulled out a folder and held it out. Mayfield started to go to them, but they threw up their hand in an abrupt warning, meaning they wished to remain anonymous and to not get closer. The person dropped the folder and was gone. He ran to the entrance to catch a glimpse of them, but he was the only one around.

The file was under his right foot and now marked with the imprint of his shoe. He scanned the area once more. If they were on the other side they would be watching from some entryway. They were somewhere nearby; he knew that much. They disappeared too quick.

He bent down and opened it. Inside was a 1940 tax return for Henry Norris. He opened the first page and noticed a large sum on the W-2.

He flipped to the back and a small piece of paper flew out with the written words,

ASK JAMES

# CHAPTER TWENTY TWO

My Dearest Lisa,

*In the entirety of my life my heart has not beat as many times as I have thought of you since you've been away, even if it beats faster when your gorgeous face enters my troubled mind. I cannot help but wonder if you knew how truly I love you that you would come back to me or that I would come downstairs in the morning from another sleepless night to find you in our den...*

James tapped the tip of the pin against his chin. The single lamplight on his desk beamed down on a love letter that he wasn't sure would ever be read by its intended recipient.

"Lisa," he sighed. The phone beside him rang. "Mallory residence."

*"This is Russell Sheridan of McGaffrey Law Offices. May I speak with Mrs. Mallory please?"*

"She isn't here."

*"Oh. Well, what time will she be in?"*

"That's a bit complicated. I'm her husband. If you want you can leave a message with me."

*"The business I have with your wife is confidential. I am rather concerned. She made an appointment with me and then never showed, and I haven't heard from her since."*

James crumpled his brow. "May I ask when the appointment was for?"

*"I'll have to look in my book."*

"Could you do that?" James took the phone and stood up from his chair. He had no idea Lisa had a lawyer or why she needed one.

*"Mr. Mallory?"*

"Right here."

*"The appointment was for the 18th of July."* James knew instantly this was the day she disappeared. *"Odd thing though...she pleaded with me to make it on that Saturday at nine o'clock."*

"In the morning."

*"No, at night. I don't make a habit of scheduling meetings on weekends, but I was going to be here, so I figured one time wouldn't hurt. But she never showed."*

"You won't tell me the nature of the appointment?"

*"I'm sorry. Listen, when you see her tell her I called and I need to speak with her."*

He hung up the phone very sluggish. James was beginning to realize there was much more that Lisa didn't tell him. The line was crossed when he spent the remainder of the day rummaging through Lisa's things in search of anything bearing the name Russell Sheridan.

RUTH rolled over in bed and awakened when she didn't feel her husband there. Light was emanating under the kitchen door. Mayfield sat hunched over the table.

She wrapped her arms around his neck. "It's past two, you know?"

Mayfield grunted.

"Edgar." She peeled his glasses off his face. They had been sitting on his nose for so long there were deep impressions on the sides.

"Ruthie, I know I've ignored you and Perry all day, but I'm working desperately hard to make sense of this tax return. I've read, reread, and read it again and again in excruciating detail. I've gone over my recordings and notes and thought I might accidently stumble on to an aha moment. I have no clue, to be frank.

"This only confuses me more. More questions. Maybe that's what they wanted. They want me going in circles."

Ruth pulled a chair out for herself.

Mayfield stretched his arms back behind his head. "This Henry Norris is related to the deceased Joe Norris in some way. That's a given. He could be his brother, son, father. I don't know. I'll have to ask James Mallory."

"The friend?"

"Yeah. Although it's romantically optimistic of me to think he will be cooperative." Mayfield yawned. "Henry Norris worked for Moran and Brewer Banking and Loan of St. Louis in 1940 and made a whopping $15,488. He must have been an important man, most likely in a managerial position of some kind."

Ruth picked up the small piece of paper in front of her. Mayfield said, "That's the only real clue they gave me. "Ask James.""

"Wouldn't it be easier to tell you what they wanted you to know?"

"Clearly this Henry person is connected somehow, whether he's involved or knows somebody that is. But he couldn't be. Not if he's in St. Louis."

Ruth would stay up with him for the rest of the night if it helped, even though she wanted to lay her head on the table. She rubbed the palms of her hands together and asked, "What are you going to do?"

"I'm going to take the informant's advice first thing tomorrow." Mayfield yawned again. "I-I can't help but feel something bigger is going on. I fear Lisa is in danger.

"It's a good thing she's missing. I don't know, I just…"

His insomnia was getting the best of him this night. In what is an otherwise effortless staple of communication, his brain was having difficulty picking out words. Tonight, he would sleep. Not as long as everyone else or as long as he deserved, but it was precious sleep.

"Bed sounds good." He looked down at the papers one last time. Time away would do him good. As he crossed over the threshold into sleep, to Mayfield's displeasure, James and Donald were there. Each exhibited stern looks.

They approached. Donald held his hand out and revealed a key. "Ask James" was pinned to James's jacket. Somewhere a baby started crying. At Mayfield's feet was the white outline of a body.

Now Ruth was the one who could not sleep.

WHEN DONALD SAW ALMA, he knew she was up to something. What reason would James have for collaborating with Lisa's old neighbor, whose disdain for Lisa was common knowledge? He figured James was the brains behind their venture and was trailing after him to get a line on Lisa.

Donald's first order of business once his shift began would be to pay Alma George a quick visit. As he neared Lisa's old complex, he flipped the switch to the light above his cab to let people see he was free for passengers.

The plump redhead on the corner wearing a white skintight outfit waved at him. It couldn't have been anyone else. Donald darted in next to the curb. Before he could put it in park, she was in.

"St. Clare's Hospital. Make it fast."

Donald observed her from his rearview mirror as she toyed with her bangs peeking out from her hat in her compact. As if she could sense him, she looked up in time to catch him switching his eyes to the road.

Alma scooted up to get a better view of his face. Donald turned away. "Driver, do I know you?"

"I don't know. Do you?"

"Don't play cute, young man. What is your name?"

Donald stopped at a red light and spun around. "You did get a good enough look at me two nights ago." Alma liberated herself from the situation by getting out of the car in the middle of oncoming traffic. "You've *got* to be joking," Donald muttered to himself as Alma marched past the honking cars.

Once his light turned green, he turned the corner and pulled up alongside of her. Her nose pointed high, she continued to walk, not even making an effort to pass a minor glance at the yellow cab beside her. Donald called Alma's bluff and went after her on foot. He parked the car and ran to catch up to her.

"Wait, I wanna talk to you!"

Alma's pointy heels clacked beneath her feet. "Maybe I don't want to talk to you."

Donald had to jump a few steps to keep up. "Can't you stop for a second?"

"As you can see, I am in a hurry. I must find another way to work, thanks to you. "

"I know we haven't spoken in a long time..."

"Not all of us can take time out of the day to chat, Mr. Wells."

"Look, I just wanted to know if you knew what was going on and if so, how much."

"Your sister is not a bother of mine anymore."

"So, you *do* know."

"Pardon?"

"Lisa. You know about Lisa." Alma didn't respond. "I don't know how you would come to know about my sister. It's not like anyone close to her would have told you."

"Is it your intention to follow me?"

"Not at all."

"For someone who is devoid of the intention you are doing a good job."

"I wish I could say the same about you the other night."

"Please, don't hand me that sanctimonious nonsense. You've always been a washout."

Donald felt he'd been kicked in the gut with those echoing high heels. Alma excelled at ripping people's insides apart with a colorfully spoken insult. Other times she went straight for the jugular.

He managed to compose himself and catch up to her. "Listen, I got the impression that James talked with you. Maybe he told you things that could implicate him."

"Is there anything else?" asked Alma.

"Yes! I would like to know why the two of you showed up at my workplace Tuesday."

"You've got your nerve to hound and accuse me of conspiring with a man I've never met."

"You're dodging the issue."

"I'm not dodging anything, Mr. Wells. If anyone knew anything it would be you. And don't pretend you're not involved."

"I'm not pretending anything. It was you sitting in James's Rolls-Royce. How many people own Rolls-Royces? Huh?"

"I wouldn't know anything about the quantity of Rolls-Royces in New York City."

Donald shouted, "Oh hell! Hell! Am I wrong to have wanted a few straight answers?"

"You brought this on yourself, Mr. Wells. The sooner you leave this in the hands of the police the better." Alma halted abruptly, rather taking Donald by surprise. "I'm an aging woman.

"All I wanted was a comfortable ride to work and now I'm going to be reprimanded for being late, and it's all your fault."

"Then why don't you go for God's sake?!"

Alma ranted as she departed from Donald. "I always thought you were a nice young man. Go scream at your coward brother-in-law!"

Donald shook his head in disbelief. He didn't know what to make of the conversation. It felt more like a debate.

"YOU SHOULD HAVE BEEN THERE, LISA. It was maddening! I've never hit a woman before in my entire life, but..."

"It doesn't make sense why James would do this." Lisa raised up from the ruffled bed and held her arms in despair at the thought of the news Donald brought to her.

"She kept eluding the question at every turn. By the end she had me doubting myself and I was there. Oh, you know that gumshoe I told you about? He's still nosing around."

"Has he found out anything?"

Donald hesitated as a reaction to the lie, "Nothing substantial."

"Oh Donny," Lisa's jaw trembled. "I'm scared."

Living out of a motel with her brother bringing her food made her feel she was already caged. The fact that she had a husband and a home waiting for her return made her reality that much more painful.

*Maybe he thought he could find me through Donny. Yes, that must be it. He wanted to find me. But why with Alma?*

Lisa couldn't supply herself with an excuse, or it was that she couldn't think up a reason to justify it.

# CHAPTER TWENTY THREE

Mayfield was standing outside the Mallory residence. After a considerable amount of time and no answer, he went around to the garage to see if James's car was there.

James glowered from a window on the second floor. All he could see was the top of Mayfield's hat, but he knew who it was.

Mayfield peeked into the garage window. James was there alright. Mayfield had no legal authority. He couldn't make him come to the door, but this lead was his biggest yet.

Mayfield was determined to get James to that door. He rang the bell over and over again repeatedly so fast the bell couldn't keep up with his finger. James Mallory was becoming less and less compliant and more and more agitated as time went by.

James fiercely opened the door.

"I apologize, friend. I saw your car in your garage there and I need to ask you some questions." It was midday. James was unshaven and disheveled in his robe. He probably hadn't left the house in days.

James tied his robe and folded his arms. "One question."

"Right here?"

"Right here."

"Do you know Henry Norris?"

"I did."

"Spell it out."

"I met him once."

"Who was he to Joe?"

"One question."

Without missing a beat, Mayfield repeated, "Who was he to Joe?"

"I just know he was a relative."

"Was?"

"Henry left...sometime in the late forties. I wouldn't know where or why."

"Mm-hmm."

James took a very long pause. He wanted to say something, but was in conflict with himself. "You know, there is something I think I should tell you. The other day we were discussing where Lisa was going the night she was attacked."

"Yes?"

"Yesterday I got a call from Russell Sheridan." Mayfield had no idea who this was. "Apparently, he's Lisa's attorney."

Mayfield asked, "What did he say?"

"Like you, he gave me that client confidentiality crap, so I don't know what her business was with him. She made the appointment with him that Saturday after she got off work. That explains why she was on that street."

Mayfield stepped closer to James, "Your friend somehow found out before we did."

James jerked his head up. "I'm busy," he said in a curt manner. He was about to slam the door in Mayfield's face when Mayfield inserted his foot in the door.

"It's good to know you're still able to work. Tell me, was Henry Norris a rich man?" James slammed the door with so much force that Mayfield was pushed back.

Mayfield hung around for a few minutes thinking James might make a second appearance. James peered through the side window at Mayfield who was walking back to his car. He kept glancing back at the house as if considering going back.

"Just get in your car, you son-of-a-bitch."

When Mayfield returned home there was a car that he didn't recognize parked in front.

Ruth stood before him rigid and still as her body screamed a warning to him. Mayfield followed her eyes to two gentlemen sitting on the sofa in the living room.

One of the men stood. "Mr. Mayfield – Lt. Robson." He flashed his badge. "We need to talk."

# CHAPTER
# TWENTY FOUR

Mayfield sank his teeth into the side if his mouth. The shock of finding the police in his house had settled in his legs. He took notice of two empty cups on the coffee table. They must have been waiting for him for some time.

"Whenever you're ready, Mr. Mayfield," said Robson. Ruth helped Mayfield with his jacket. He could feel her hands trembling as she pulled his arm out of the sleeve. The way the two detectives sat around him told him that his living room was to be a temporary interrogation room.

Robson began, "Do you know why we're here?"

"I was ticketed for speeding last week."

Robson and Dodds glanced at each other. "This is no joking matter. I know you've been sniffing around my case. It's an open one, too, and I must tell you I wasn't too happy when I found out."

Dodds added, "We want to know who you're working for."

"Sorry," said Mayfield.

"Mr. Mayfield..."

"It's privileged. I don't have to spill a thing to you."

Dodds was ready to verbally cut into him, but Robson grabbed his arm. Robson spoke soft and calm, but his frustration was apparent in his taut jaw. "That's true. You have that right.

"On the other hand, as I said before, this is an open case. If I think you have information as to Lisa Mallory's whereabouts, I can take you in right now."

"I don't much like being threatened, Lieutenant."

Ruth retreated to the kitchen.

"I wasn't threatening you. But I must do my duty, and will. How long have you been on the case?"

"What about you? What have you found out?"

Dodds jumped into the conversation. "We're in no mood to dance, PI. We know you've been probing around the accused's family. You're treading on thin ice and if you continue your feet are gonna get really wet."

"You've been following me? Boy, you police love throwing away good tax money. Why waste your resources on me when you should be going after the real bad guy?"

"You are a resource."

"Enough," snapped Robson. Robson chucked slightly and then grinned at Mayfield.

"You're taking the good cop/bad cop thing a little overboard, aren't you?"

"I've heard of you before. Capt. Brandon has mentioned you." Mayfield rolled his eyes slightly. "Had a few run-ins when he was a sergeant, I hear."

"Perhaps if we both pulled our information. It seems a good time to do so. Then I'll tell you what you wanna know."

"The police do not bargain with PI's, smart mouth," said Dodds. "What can you tell us about Lisa Mallory?"

"Who is Henry Norris?"

"We can't tell you!"

"Wait!" Robson raised his hand. "Henry Norris? There's no such person."

"Yes, there is. He's a relative of Joe's."

"Mr. Mayfield, I've spoken to Norris' relatives and I don't know any Henry Norris. You're not going to budge, are you?"

"Nope."

Robson and Dodds got up to leave and Mayfield stood with them. "Mr. Mayfield, Lisa Mallory is to be charged with first-degree murder. Anyone with prior knowledge to her location will be arrested right along with her.

"That being said, don't make me pull your ticket. Stay out of it."

Ruth came out of the kitchen to show the policemen out. Robson fixed his hat on his head. "You've been warned."

Ruth fell against the door. "Thank God. I thought they'd never leave."

"I would have seen them." Mayfield rushed to the window. "They were asking too many questions to have been following me all this time. *And* I'm not that clumsy."

Mayfield witnessed Robson lift his hat to signal the man sitting in a car across the street.

"Damn."

"What is it?"

"I can no longer work on the case."

"Why not?"

"Do you see that white car across the street? That's an unmarked police car. Robson must have ordered him to monitor my movements. The cops were tipped, Ruth. Whoever it was, they're the one that wants Lisa dead."

# CHAPTER TWENTY FIVE

L isa couldn't sleep.

The room was too quiet. One thing Lisa could no longer stand was silence. It was when all was dark and still, when most people's minds would shut down, that hers would come alive with dreaded thoughts and ghastly flashbacks.

Lisa made sure the coast was clear and tiptoed down the boardwalk to the office. She peeked into the open door. "Donny? Donny, are you in here?"

Lisa walked into the parlor and found him asleep on the sofa sitting up, his head tilted back against the wall with his mouth open. She remembered even as a little boy he was a mouth breather when he slept. She touched his leg.

"I'm awake! Oh." Donald caught his breath. "What are you doing?" he asked, brushing the hair out of his eyes.

"I couldn't sleep."

"Uh-huh. What if someone comes in and sees you?" Donald adjusted his clothes. "Never mind. Can I get you something to eat?"

"No. I don't want to be alone right now." Lisa sat beside him and hugged her legs up to her stomach. "Can we talk until I get tired?"

Donald started, "Okay. Um, the cops phoned..."

"I don't want to talk about that."

"What do you want to talk about?"

"Anything else."

Donald thought for a second. "Thursday, I picked up an elderly lady with two yapping Yorkies popping out of her handbag. And she kept talking baby-talk to them like they were her children."

"Really?"

"Yeah. I got so ticked off at one point that I asked her if she would be so kind as to shut the mutts up and she got all huffy. It's hard to drive with..."

A bright light shined into the room. A car pulled up in front of the office.

Donald took Lisa's arm. "Quick! Over here." He placed her in the dark corner of the room. Lisa slid down to the floor.

"May I help you, sir?" Donald asked.

"Yeah, I'm lost. Quite a bit lost, actually. I was hoping you could point me in the right direction."

Lisa breathed a sigh of relief. She knew Donald wouldn't let her go. She would have to run away. Then there was the side of her that was scared to death to leave.

The idea of being cuffed for the first time in her life was so frightening, and she had enough time to think up every detail. The embarrassment. There was also the dread of family and friends trying to ease their minds with endless questions and then display their hurt for not feeling important enough for her to go to them for help. This was the motivation behind her staying, contrasted by the reality of Donald going down with her.

It was time. She couldn't keep this up for much longer. The dread of it was far worse. Capture was bound to happen. Why not on her own terms?

"False alarm. You can get up." Donald helped her to her feet. She stepped around him. "What's the matter?"

Lisa plopped down on the sofa. "I've been meaning to ask you. It's been on my mind for a while.

"How can you afford me? It's sure to be costing you a lot of money keeping me here; the room, the clothes, food every day."

"Well, Rebecca is making good money now."

"But Rebecca doesn't know I'm here, does she?"

"No."

"So all this must be coming from you."

Donald looked off to the wall. "I...come on, Lisa. I put some aside for myself, okay? You-you helped me, so now I'm helping you. That's all that matters."

"How is Rebecca? Two of you getting along?"

Donald exhaled, "The arguments have escalated since you went missing. Some days the second I walk through the door she jumps on my back, most of the time over nothing. Sometimes I get the feeling she's picking these fights."

Lisa scooted closer to him. "Tell me about the babies."

"Simon is excelling in school. His grades couldn't be better. And Julie's made a friend. Her first friend. Her name is Grace; she's a grade ahead, but a sweet girl."

"I miss them so much it hurts. I would give anything to be near them."

Donald recalled his unpleasant last meeting with Mayfield. "You love my kids, don't you?"

"God, I wish they were mine." Her eyes shined as she thought of them. Donald sensed the sadness in her voice.

"Simon reminds me of myself when I was a boy. The other day I told him to clean his room. A half hour later I went to check on him and it looked like the Japanese had raided. We're talking clothes in piles, toys everywhere. He was hiding in the closet fixing to attack Julie. I think she was the 50 Foot Woman or something."

"Donny...have you ever had the feeling that something was going to happen before it happened? A premonition?"

She switched gears very abrupt. It was no wonder she couldn't sleep.

"I don't think so."

Lisa stared down at the floor. "The day our parents died, Mom took my shoulders and told me how proud she was of me, and she knew she could trust me to take care of you." Lisa took hold of Donald's fingers and squeezed lightly. "That is my last memory of her."

She wouldn't look at him. Otherwise, she might get weak and change her mind. The way she was feeling, she didn't much care for being pitied.

Donald didn't know what to say. Lisa wanted to say so much. Her heart was full of bittersweet memories and a longing sadness that she was being taken further and further away from them.

Lisa kissed Donald's cheek and hurried out. He reached for her, but she was too quick.

ANY OTHER MORNING HE WOULD BE GETTING DRESSED FOR BED. While the family slept peacefully, he was at the kitchen table still fully clothed, bouncing his sister's words around in his head.

All through the drive home he couldn't escape them. The total lack of emotion in her voice conveyed something, and that something was masked behind the last memory of their mother.

Lisa threw her suitcase on the bed. Neatness and order gave way to urgency as she stuffed every piece of clothing Donald bought for her into one suitcase.

Donald became a statue. The complete use of brainpower froze his body cold. "She wouldn't."

With purse and suitcase in hand she took a deep breath and stepped out. It did feel good.

Donald's leg had developed a nervous twitch, bouncing up-and-down with involuntary commands. That intuition Lisa spoke of not hours ago was happening to him. To go back would provoke suspicion. All logic told him not to.

"Key, please," asked the clerk, fogging up the area with smoke from his pipe. Lisa placed the key to her room on the desk and slid it across.

Donald blasted the horn and beat the steering wheel. "Move it! Come on, move!" Damn early-morning rush-hour traffic.

"Cabin #7?" The clerk looked for her name on the register. "You're paid up for the remainder of the week, Ms. Kincaid. Let me refund the days you have coming."

"Oh. Okay?"

Donald punched the roof of his car. Of all days. He questioned if anybody ever stayed at home.

Lisa went behind the motel to a large garbage bin. It was her intention to travel light. With one great heave-ho, she tossed the suitcase in. There was no going back now.

Donald sped into the motel. The breaks screeched to a stop. The door to room #7 was open with the housekeeping cart in front. Donald jumped out and ran into the room startling the maid.

"Where's the woman that was staying here? Where is she?"

"She checked out."

Donald threw back the curtain. Lisa was gone. He pushed the maid out of the way and ran across the parking lot and into the street. A car whizzed past him. He spun around, lost like a child missing its mother.

Lisa wandered aimlessly going in and out of stores, bars, and restaurants pretending to be a customer. Dusk began to fall and she was in a fog. She didn't have a clue as to where in the world she was going, except she had to get away from the Sugar Maple.

She made the decision to turn herself in. All day long she stalled and strained to talk herself out of it. She couldn't take the plunge.

Lisa was dragging her feet along the side of the road with her head bent over.

*Where is the nearest station? Should I give Donny a call? You have to do something, Lisa. You can't wander the New York streets all night.*

"Ma'am," spoke a deep voice to her right.

*I wonder what time is it. Will I go to prison for the rest if my life?* Lisa pulled at her hair. *God, this has to stop!*

"Hey, ma'am?"

The voice alerted Lisa. A police car was creeping alongside of her. Lisa saw the two men in uniform. "Can we help you, ma'am?"

Lisa imagined this moment many times and worked out in detail how it would go. The opposite occurred. She bolted.

The two policemen glanced at each other and switched on their light. Lisa bumped into people trying to get by them. The soles of her shoes slipped on the pavement as she turned the corner.

She resisted the temptation to look back. To look back would be her forfeiture, sacrificing one second that could have been spent on her escape. Her mind was in a frenzy.

Lisa darted into the street and a dense mass collided into her.

# CHAPTER TWENTY SIX

Saturday, July 18
     9:17 p.m. – Lisa left Larry's Diner.

It was eerily silent except for a siren that wailed in the distance. It could have been an ambulance or police car; she couldn't tell. Streetlamps were few and scattered. She studied the street that curved into blackness, trying to recall every nook, alleyway, and passage. Clutching her purse strap tighter, she set off down the isolated path.

She passed under a lamp. She anticipated the next. The brief light was brief relief. Her steps were quick and short. She glanced cautiously into cars parked along the side.

A shuffling emanated from behind. She stopped – the shuffling stopped. She waited. Nothing.

She resumed. Again, the dragging of feet scraped the pavement behind her. She jerked around swiftly and saw a figure moving behind a car.

*Oh God. What do I do?*

Lisa hastened her pace, steadily increasing to a dead run. A vehicle's engine starting from behind prompted her to stop. The shuffling figure was no longer there and was most likely in the car that drove away.

She rested against a lamppost. "This is ridiculous," Lisa panted. Below the broad beam of light, like a protective shield no attacker could penetrate, Lisa felt safe.

Two gloved hands snatched her by the neck. Into an alley of unknown she was pulled.

HIS GRIP TIGHTENED.

He growled from the pit of his gullet. Lisa could feel finger-nails digging into the back of her neck and his thumbs crushing her Adam's apple.

She tried to squeeze her fingers between his. Her rapid pulse was throbbing hard against his gloves. She reached out, grasping for something to cling to. He swung around to prevent being kicked by Lisa's thrashing legs.

She felt for her purse, but it wasn't there. The veins in her face and throat swelled above the surface of her skin. Everything seemed to be getting dimmer as she became starved of oxygen.

All went black.

Her eyes rolled into her head and her legs gave out. Lisa's limp body hung in his arms. He lowered her to the ground. Her legs were tucked under her knees, arms spread-out, and head contorted.

Out of breath, he wiped the sweat from his brow. He examined his kill, verifying no trace of himself was on the victim. He lifted Lisa by her ankles and dragged her to the back of the alleyway.

The backs of her arms were becoming bloody from rocks and broken glass cutting into her paper-thin flesh. He turned Lisa on her side and slipped off her gold wedding ring.

A car drove past and he jumped.

He reached inside his pocket and replaced her ring with another. Suddenly he fell back, swearing and covering his face as bits of gravel and rock pellets raided his eyes.

Lisa crawled away. Double vision impaired her sight for an instant. She spotted her brown purse on the sidewalk. If she could attain it she would have a fighting chance.

The man lumbered after her. She was yanked back by her hair. She screamed and grabbed his hand; the other came over her mouth. She bit the leather of his thick glove and could feel the heat of his hand sandwiched between her teeth.

He released. She fought to unfasten the clasp, but her fingers couldn't comply. Muscular arms elevated her back into the cavernous pit. Lisa thrashed, but his iron grip constricted.

"Let go of me!" she screamed.

He threw her into the trash cans. The earsplitting crash echoed. Blood trickled down from her nose over her lip. Her throat was raw and her head pounded from all sides.

He lunged his right foot into her stomach. She coiled and gripped her abdomen tight, shaking and unable to breathe. Those huge gloved hands came down. Lisa's raspy voice cried out and she grabbed his wrists.

She strove to take the strain off her frail neck by standing, but her legs couldn't seem to take the burden of her weight. She kicked more and more as the ground beneath her feet dwindled. The remaining strength in her was escaping her body. Lisa could feel herself blacking out again and the wild thumping in her chest slowing.

Using her last drop of energy, she sunk her nails into his left cheek. Lisa's eyes, bloodshot and distended, stared into the visible darkness of those dreaded black eyes. The veins in his forehead bulged. Saliva seethed through his clenching teeth. His face was flushed and dripping.

He dropped her. Lisa didn't know how badly she was hurt except from the streaks of red on the pavement. Before her were the straps of her bag poking out from behind one of the cans. It was far away. He booted a can aside and slammed her against the brick wall.

He wrapped her hair around his fingers and pulled her head to his. Lisa tightened her lips and pounded her fists on his shoulders, but he pinned them to the wall. She violently shook her head as he forced his tongue into her mouth.

Like an afflicting poison she could not escape, she whimpered in repulsion and sank her teeth into his lower lip. He recoiled and struck her. Lisa was determined, against all odds, to survive.

She kneed him in the groin and went for the bag. He was after her like a Tasmanian devil. She ripped it open and he knocked her down. The contents spilled out in front of her.

Up Lisa's back he climbed, ripping at her clothes, and pinned her head and neck to the ground. "You bitch!"

The derringer was out of reach. The weight of his bulging stomach crushed her back. She stretched out her arms, digging her nails into the ground.

"I always could tell you were a fighter. I like it."

Lisa felt for her metal nail file. It had to be close. She stabbed it into his hand; he screamed and fell off.

The gun was inches away. Lisa drug herself, pushing with her legs and pulling with her arms. He caught her ankle with his other hand.

"No! No!" She spread her fingers and could almost touch the edge of the barrel. She kicked and kicked and kicked until his grasp loosened just enough.

She seized the gun.

He froze.

There was a loud pop.

Wetness drizzled onto her face. His head dropped onto her shoulder. The pistol was warm in her hand. An immediate scent of gunpowder surrounded her.

In her ear was a gurgling sound, a death rattle, as his final breath escaped his lungs. She wiggled out from under him.

There he was – dead.

When the reality of it sank in, she lost control, kicking herself away from the body as if he was infected with the Black Death until her back touched the wall. Her breathing was labored. The cold sweat that dripped into her cuts burned like acid. She clutched the gun barrel to her chest.

*I killed him. I killed him. What-what am I going to do? I killed Joe.*

Mere instinct was her reserve and sole motivation. She tiptoed around the puddle of expanding blood encompassing his head, picked up her purse, and returned the contents one by one.

Lisa avoided looking at the body as she deviated around it. She had no clue how much time she had before the repercussions of the conflict found its way into the alley. She stepped over him, got down on her knees, and yanked the nail file out of his hand with a grimace.

With all her strength she rolled the lifeless corpse over to the wall. Lisa accidently looked. Blood seeped from the hole into his wide-open eyes, down his nose and mouth, and was beginning to trickle into his ears since she turned him right-side up.

Her stomach turned. She had to catch her breath. The trash cans would render good cover. She positioned them around the body.

Then, like a frightened mouse running into a vast labyrinth, Lisa escaped into the night.

PULSE RACING, BREATH QUICKENING...

Lisa hobbled with no destination in mind. Dogs barking in the distance gave her the feeling as a runaway slave with nowhere to hide.

She was lost. Running off and on for hours, she wasn't sure anymore. The subtle glow of dawn crept over the buildings. This area was at least dim and secluded.

*Get a grip, Lisa. You have to get a grip.*

Lisa avoided public places and spots of crowd dominance. She needed to stop, however challenging, to rest her exhausted body and frantic mind. Behind a vacant tenement house, she curled into a ball and concealed her head within the darkness of her skirt. Almost immediately she slipped into unconsciousness.

A baseball thumped her leg, stirring her awake. She lifted her head, dazed, squinting from the brightness of the sun. A boy approached to pick up the ball. He got an eyeful of her rough appearance before going back to his buddies.

"Oh!" Lisa grasped the sides of her head. The face of her watch was broken. 9:57 a.m., she guessed. She was out for four hours.

Lisa hadn't comprehended the magnitude of her circumstance, but then again, she hadn't had time. Lisa held onto the wall, gently rising to her feet. Her legs quivered.

She waited for her head to catch up and shuffled to the end of the street. People stared as they passed her. There was a café across the street. That would be a good place to clean up.

The bell jingled. Each head turned in unison. A man sitting at the counter sat his paper down. A passing waitress carrying dishes halted.

"What can I do for you?" asked the cook behind the counter. He was bald and chubby, not unlike her old friend.

"Yes...ahem," Lisa's throat was hoarse and it hurt to speak. "Restroom?"

"In the back to your left."

Lisa ignored the trailing eyes and locked the door. The small mirror facing her reflected a woman she had never seen. She inched closer, horrified at the image of the much-older woman, beaten and aged beyond recognition. This was the reason for staring eyes.

Dark bags hung under her eyes. Her neck was beginning to discolor. The dried blood on her face wasn't hers. Her beige top was speckled with red spots. She wet some paper towels and wiped her face and dabbed her sore arms.

The backs of her arms were red and badly scraped. It stung as the cool drops rolled down them. She lifted her top to check her stomach. There was no damage apparent, but it hurt like hell since Joe rammed his foot into it.

Lisa sat on the toilet. Her ring slipped down to her knuckle, but she paid no attention. At the bottom of her skirt was a gaping hole. Raising her legs, she saw both were bruised all the way down.

Lisa started to sob. "Everything was going so well."

*I shouldn't have run. I should have gone to the police. It's too late. I can't now.*

*It would incriminate me.* Lisa pulled out the blood-stained nail file from her purse. *Unless I got rid of incriminating evidence... no, if they found out it would make things worse.* She washed the blood off under the faucet.

*They can't connect me at the scene. I left nothing behind.*

At the moment she was safe. She contemplated what to do next. Options were limited. She straightened her clothes and fixed her hair as best she could, and went back out. Chatter remained at a low hum.

Lisa took a seat at a booth and told the waitress behind the counter, "I'd like a cup of coffee – black."

They were staring again. Lisa could see the reflection of their staring faces in the glass of the window. She spotted a telephone booth on the corner. The waitress sat a cup in front of her and poured.

Then something hit Lisa like a literal slap across the face. She rushed out of the café to the booth and took out a card from her purse. Her finger trembled as she spun the numbers on the rotary.

*"Mayfield Investigations – Gail speaking."*

"Is Mr. Mayfield in? It's urgent."

*"May I ask who's speaking?"*

"Tell him it's Lisa Mallory. He'll know."

# CHAPTER TWENTY SEVEN

Voices came out of the darkness, resonating to her as if from the end of a long tunnel. One spoke her name. She tried opening her eyes. Someone must have been compressing her head in a vice.

She struggled to move. The weight of her body felt like it had tripled, similar to being underwater. Her right arm particular was heavier than normal.

A soft deep voice whispered her name. "Lisa." It was close and it sounded familiar. "Open your eyes, Lisa."

She managed to pry one eye open. All she could see was a colorful haze. The world around her was blurry. Gradually, the blur started to fuse together in the shape of a face.

James beamed with joy and took her in his arms. "Darling!"

Was this a dream? Was this another wonderful illusion that her imagination, fueled by memory and circumstance, deceived her to forget what really was? She chose to go for it.

"You're here," breathed Lisa. James kissed her all over. He bombarded her neck, cheeks, and lips with an endless supply of stored up kisses.

"Yes, and I'll never leave. I thought I'd lost you, too."

"You love me."

"Always. Always."

There was the possibility that she would never again set eyes on her husband or hear the gentleness of his voice. She so relished the moment that she hadn't realized how badly she was hurt.

The frail state of her body combined with mental exhaustion made it difficult to speak. Faintly she said, "I've missed you."

"My Lisa." James's fingers grasped the sides of her waist tight as he kissed her passionately again. "You're so beautiful."

"You didn't forget me?"

"Life at the house has been hell." Lisa raised her left hand to his cheek and caressed his stubble. He was real. "I haven't been able to sleep in our bedroom. I've been staying in the guest room all this time.

"Lisa, do-do you know what the day before yesterday was? Our anniversary. One year we've been married."

Lisa had forgotten.

"You're here with me now. That's celebration enough."

A voice from behind James said, "Be gentle now."

"Lisa darling, this is Dr. Talbot. He's been taking care of you." James moved over to the chair beside the bed and laid his hand atop her head that was wrapped in bandages.

"Do you remember what happened to you? You were hit by a car yesterday evening. You sustained a nasty blow to the head and a broken arm."

Dr. Talbot shined a light into Lisa's eyes. "You are a very fortunate woman, Mrs. Mallory. Your arm will heal; it was a clean break. But it's your head I'm concerned about. How is your vision?"

"A little blurry. I-I'm dizzy, too."

He took Lisa's wrist to gauge her pulse. "What is your full name?"

"Lisa Rose Mallory."

"Maiden name?"

"Wells."

"What are your parents' names?"

"Um, Preston and Etta."

"Birthday?"

Lisa thought for a second. "January 27, 1921."

"You have a concussion. The dizziness and blurred vision should pass in a day or two. Do you remember the accident?"

"Last thing I remember is running...running. I don't remember why."

James and Talbot glanced at each other. "Well, I wouldn't worry about it. Whenever there's trauma to the head short-term memory loss is not uncommon. I'll leave you two alone," said Talbot. "Refrain from getting her excitable, Dr. Mallory."

Lisa stared into her husband's blue eyes. She tried to think of something to say. The flood of emotion she felt couldn't be condensed into words. Countless times she found herself savoring in his company, only to wake up in that dreary motel alone.

James slid over onto the bed and placed his hands on both sides of her pillow. Slowly he lowered his head to hers until their mouths touched. Lisa lifted her arms to put around him, but had difficulty lifting her right because of the cast.

"How long must I wear this?"

"I'd say about four to six weeks."

Lisa noticed an envelope sticking out of his jacket. "What's this?" she asked, pulling it out.

"Don't."

"It has my name on the front."

"I changed my mind. I'd rather you didn't read it."

"What does it say? Open it."

"No, Lisa."

"Please. If you didn't want me to read it then you shouldn't have brought it." James grunted. "Is it divorce papers?"

"What? No!"

"Then it must be something pretty awful."

"You always have to have things your way, don't you?"

He removed the single paper from the envelope and unfolded it. He cleared his throat. She knew he didn't want to read it and it amused her somewhat making him.

"My dearest Lisa," James began. "In the entirety of my life my heart has not beat as many times as I have thought of you since you've been away, even though it beats faster when your gorgeous face enters my troubled mind. I cannot help but wonder if you knew how truly I love you that you would come back to me or that I would come downstairs in the morning from another sleepless night to find you in our den listening to Bobby Darin.

"I understand that I'm not the best husband on occasion, and there may be times when you find yourself in a position where you question your reasoning for marrying me. However, no matter how you dissect the problems we face, love will endure."

James took his eyes away from the letter and recited the last lines by heart. "I'm hopeful that is what will get us through this terrible misfortune, but will also be what keeps us together. If I should see you again it will mean the whole of what I've written lacks in purpose, for it was a needless task to stray my mind away from the torment of not knowing where you are."

James stuffed the letter back in its envelope. "Ahem, I-I, uh, wrote it in a hurry."

Lisa took the letter from his hand and held it to her chest. "It's mine now." Lisa cried out suddenly in pain.

A different male voice entered the room. "I do hope you're not in too much pain, Mrs. Mallory."

Talbot ordered, "Keep it brief, Lieutenant."

Lisa heard the word "lieutenant." That word triggered it all to come back in a single second; disposing of her things, leaving the motel, the mad dash from police, and getting a head full of windshield. She was scared again.

"My name is Lt. Robson, ma'am."

She knew the name.

He stood at the end of her bed, larger than God himself. "You haven't met me, but I know you. Do you feel up to answering a few questions? Strictly off-the-record."

James barked, "No, she does not."

"I wasn't speaking to you."

James glared at Robson with certain hatred. "When concerning my wife, you answer to me."

"James, please. Yes, Lieutenant, I think I can manage."

Robson removed his hat and laid it on the bed, a definite indication he wasn't going anywhere. "Can you tell me what happened July 18$^{th}$?"

"You don't have to answer, Lisa."

"Stay out if this, doctor."

"James," Lisa said softly.

James charged over to Robson. "My wife isn't some criminal you can grill at your leisure. Where's your rubber hose, huh? Surely there's more than you packed into that suit."

Lisa called his name a little louder. "James, you aren't helping me." He returned to the chair and held her hand.

"July 18$^{th}$ – What happened?"

James patted her hand as Lisa thought hard. So much was happening to this one woman who dreamt of the simple life, but life never asked what she wanted. Blame came and went as always, tiresome and painful, solving nothing.

"It was my last day at the diner and I was on my way home. Joe attacked me and tried to kill me. He must have been waiting for me to get off work."

"Why would he want to kill you? For what reason?" asked Robson.

"I don't know."

"Correct me if I'm wrong. You killed him in self-defense?"

"Yes. I..."

Lisa saw Joe's head jerk back as the bullet penetrated, a visual she couldn't rid herself of.

"I had to shoot him."

"Why did you run?"

Lisa started getting excitable as her state of mind that night returned even though she was safe in a hospital bed. "I-I panicked. I was almost killed myself and I panicked."

"That's understandable. For three weeks you panicked. In all that time you couldn't go to a police station? Turn yourself in?"

"What do you mean?"

"If you knew you were innocent, why did you keep running?"

Lisa knew the answer, but Joe was gone, and with him, the proof of his malice. She couldn't think up a cause for his trying to kill her except that someone told him to. Better yet, someone hired him to. Why would he murder his best friend's wife just for the hell of it? Joe wouldn't have thought a woman of five-foot-four could kill him.

They looked when the door opened; it was the doctor. "He wants to see her now. Somebody's gotta go."

James said, "I'll go."

Donald appeared at the door. All she could distinguish was he was a tall man with dark hair.

"Donald!" Lisa held out her arm to him.

"Dear Lord, look at you!" The siblings embraced. "Are you okay?"

"I'll be fine. Where're Rebecca and the kids?"

"They weren't able to come. I'll bring them. I promise." Donald bent down to her ear, "I can't believe you ran."

"I'm not finished, Mrs. Mallory," said an impatient Robson. "You claim it was self-defense, yet against you are several witnesses that say you and Norris weren't the best of friends. You haven't explained why he would attack you. I see that you're not well and I'm not trying to put you on the spot, I just want the facts."

Lisa managed to sit up. Her entire right side, ribs and hip especially, were in excruciating pain. Donald put his arm behind her for support.

"Lieutenant, if I hadn't shot Joe I wouldn't be here. He tried to strangle me. That's all I know."

"Where's your proof? There're no bruises, no marks on your neck."

"It was three weeks ago."

"Exactly."

Lisa extended her good arm and showed him the cuts that were almost healed. "Look at these scars. I didn't give them to myself. And they didn't come from getting hit by the car."

"You could've got them when you were a kid for all I know. That doesn't mean Norris gave them to you."

The minor exertion of sitting up and arguing her case made her tired. With a long sigh, she laid back down.

Robson asked on his way out the door, "Incidentally, where is the gun?"

Donald closed his eyes.

"It's in my purse."

"No, it isn't. We've gone through your bag."

"I put it there."

Robson didn't believe her. He appeared to be growing aggravated by this feeling that Lisa was giving him the runaround. "I see you're going to stick to that story. Well, that's your prerogative."

As soon as he was gone Lisa shouted, "I can't believe this! What's happening?!"

Donald dropped to one knee and took her hand. He pleaded, "Forgive me, Lisa. Please, don't be angry. I-I did it with good intentions."

"What?"

"I took the gun." Lisa inched back slightly. "I thought it would help you."

"Where is it?"

"I threw it in the Hudson."

Her derringer was lost forever. She couldn't even tell police, because then she would have to tell them where she was hiding. If she told them *she* threw the gun in the Hudson, it might be taken as an admission of guilt. Was Donald trying to help or hinder?

The fact that he did it behind her back is what bothered her most. She wanted to convince Robson that she had every intention of cooperating.

"Aw, hell!" bellowed James when Mayfield poked his head in the waiting room where he was sipping coffee. "Who the hell told you?"

"Which room?" Mayfield asked.

"Last on the left. See the doctor before…" Mayfield was gone before he could finish. James muttered under his breath, "Asshole."

"Not you again," snapped Donald.

Lisa raised her head up. "Who is it?"

"The gumshoe," Donald answered.

"Edgar Mayfield?"

"That's the one."

"Come closer. I can't see you very well." Donald rose from the chair and went around the bed to get out of his way. "It *is* you."

"I heard you had quite an accident," Mayfield said.

Donald pointed with a derogatory thumb. "You've met this character?"

"Donny, I'd like to be alone with this man."

"You…*you* hired him?!" Donald was stunned and glared at Mayfield. "But-but you told me James hired you!"

Mayfield replied, "Young man, we both lied. Besides, it's not like you had every opportunity to ask her yourself. Right?" Lisa and Donald threw each other a look in alarm. "But that'll be our little secret."

"Please go, Donny."

Donald didn't waste any time getting out. His feelings were hurt and, with the apparent alliance of the two, he felt like an outcast.

"Tell me everything. I want to know everything."

"Now isn't the time. You need to rest." Mayfield sat beside her on the bed. "I wasn't sure at first how far I could run with what little you gave me. Boy, did I dig up the dirt.

"I kept in-depth descriptions on a recorder. I'll come back sometime tomorrow. We'll discuss it then." Mayfield lowered his head and his voice. "You're not going to like it."

James saw Donald outside Lisa's room leaning against the wall with his arms crossed. "Why aren't you with Lisa?"

"Mayfield's in there."

"You know better than to leave her alone with him."

"She hired him. Yep, my caring and thoughtful big sister hired a gumshoe to keep tabs on me." He bit his lower lip. "I can't believe she did this to me."

James snapped, "Why don't you shut up. This isn't about *you*. I don't like this. I'm going in there."

James barged into the room to find Mayfield by the window and Lisa apparently asleep. She was laying with her left arm across her stomach. He spotted the gold ring on her finger.

"This isn't your wedding ring. The police have it." He slipped the ring off her finger, stirring her into consciousness. He inspected the inside where he saw the monogram, *"E.N."*

"Where did you get this?"

"James, I'm so tired..."

"Where? Please tell me."

"Joe. It was Joe." James closed his fingers with the ring in his palm. Mayfield was scrutinizing him very close.

Dr. Talbot entered with Robson and Dodds behind him. "There are *way* too many people in here. *You*," Talbot pointed at Mayfield. "Whoever you are, go."

There was an awkward tension as Robson locked eyes with Mayfield. James appeared to be in some kind of trance and was paying no attention to what was happening.

"Mrs. Mallory," Robson approached the bed. "This is Sgt. Dodds."

"Ma'am," Dodds bowed his head.

Talbot examined Lisa's bandage. "She's had too many visitors today. You guys got five minutes." He walked between the two policemen and showed them his wristwatch. "I'm timing you."

Robson asked Lisa, "Do you understand what is happening?"

"James?" Lisa called to him. He didn't answer.

"Ma'am?"

Lisa's legs began to fidget under the covers. "It isn't fair. It..." She felt unprotected and vulnerable to anything that came at her, and there was nothing she could do to fight back.

"James?"

Robson gave Dodds a slight nod. Dodds removed his hat and read from the inside:

"Lisa Mallory, you are charged with murder in the 1st degree. You have the right to remain silent. If you give up the right to remain silent, anything you say can and will be used against you in a court of law. You have the right to speak with an attorney and to have an attorney present during questioning. If you so desire and cannot afford one, an attorney will be appointed for you."

# CHAPTER
# TWENTY EIGHT

**"I** missed you, Aunt Lisa," said Simon, cuddling up to her in the bed.

Lisa kissed the top of his head. "I missed you. It's been too long." Rebecca sat beside the bed and lifted Julia into her lap. Lisa ran her fingers through her nephew's silky dark hair and looked into an innocent little face that was unable to comprehend.

Lisa wouldn't let him go. It felt so good holding the boy up to her breast. His skinny arms embraced her neck.

"I love you, Simon."

"Don't forget this one," said Rebecca. Simon hopped over Lisa. "Julie spent a long time getting ready. She wanted to dress her best for you."

Rebecca sat her on the bed. Lisa put her arm around her and sensed something wasn't right. She took her chin and the girl jerked her head away.

"Julia!" Rebecca exclaimed.

Lisa shook her head for Rebecca not to scold. "What's the matter, Strawberry?"

"You don't love me anymore." Julia began to toy with a loose raveling on her dress.

"Now Julia, that isn't true. I love you with all my heart. You and Simon mean the world to me. I thought you knew that."

"Why didn't you come to see us?"

Lisa didn't know how to explain when not even she had the answers. It was far too complex for four-year-old ears. It was a painful truth knowing Julia felt neglected and heartbroken because of her.

"You're too young to understand. Aunt Lisa is going through something no one should have to, and because of that I was not able to see the ones most dear to me." Julia's eyes crept slowly upwards. "I cross my heart to my favorite Strawberry."

Lisa opened her arms. "Forgive me?" Julia smiled and jumped in her lap. "That's my girl."

"Do you like my dress, Aunt Lisa?"

"I do. It's very pretty." Lisa admired her tiny black frock with pink polka dots and ruffles.

"How are you holding up?" Rebecca asked.

Lisa laid back and rubbed her eyes. "Emotionally, I'm a train wreck in the works. I feel like a solitary passenger on a train headed into a ravine and it's too late to jump. Rebecca, I've been thinking about the near future. Once I'm back on my feet they'll rip into me like the Christmas turkey, I know it."

"I know what you're going to say. You know I'm not a trial lawyer. I'll help you as much as I can."

Donald came into the room, "Hi, girls." He went to Rebecca and whispered to her, "Does she know?"

Donald was referring to the cop that now stood guard outside Lisa's door.

"She knows. Come on, kids, let's go down to the cafeteria and get something to eat."

Rebecca was trying to be gracious and give the siblings privacy, but secretly, Lisa wished she would have stayed. Lisa folded her arm over her cast.

Donald rubbed the back of his neck. "How are you feeling?"

"Don't speak to me."

There was a long silence. "W-what?"

Lisa wouldn't allow her eyes to shift in his direction. Saliva seeped through the cracks of her teeth. "I can't believe you."

"What are you talking about?"

"You stabbed me in the back." Anger gave her the courage to look him in the eye. "Money means more to you than your own family." He put his hand over his mouth, realizing Lisa knew all that he had done.

"I gave you everything and you took it."

"Lisa, please."

"No!" Much softer she spoke, "You betrayed me."

Donald was speechless, and that in itself proved his guilt.

"Now, you sheltered me and I appreciate that, but...wait. Wait." A pressing thought came to her. "That's how you were able to afford me. God!"

Being in the same room with Lisa as his darkest secrets became exposed was torture. Donald would have run out in a heartbeat if his childlike attachment to his sister wasn't keeping him there. His entire world was crumbling.

"You didn't tell Rebecca."

"Your marriage is none of my business." Lisa wiped a fallen tear. "You have no idea what you put me through. All that time I thought it was me. I laid awake nights desperately trying to figure out what I did that would cause you to throw me out of your life.

"Little did I know it was money. It's always been about money, hasn't it?"

Never before had Lisa viewed her brother in this light. He was always the confidant, the friend, but now was reduced to a cut above enemy, for the little brother she raised would not have committed such a sin. She didn't know this man and didn't want to.

Lisa probed, "So...did it help?"

"Did what help?"

"The $250 a month you sold me for." Lisa's tone was cold and callous as she began to distance herself.

"James offered it to me."

Lisa slumped down into the bed and turned over. "I hope it was worth it, little brother."

All Donald could see was the back of her head. "Don't do this to me. It isn't what you think. I was desperate. The bills kept pouring in faster than I could pay them.

"This was long before Rebecca graduated. I didn't want to do it. I knew it was wrong, but..."

Donald was starting to show perhaps his true self to Lisa. She gave no sign that she was hearing him. "What was I supposed to do? Would you have preferred the kids went hungry? Would that have made you feel better?"

"Go away...*Donald.*"

Donald shuffled to the door. He wouldn't take his eyes off her in the hopes she would stop him, but Lisa let him go.

"IT APPEARS TO ME YOU KNOW ABSOLETELY NOTHING about your husband." Mayfield drank up the last couple swallows of his coffee. "You know nothing about his past or his family; very vague if you ask me."

"I married James because I love him. It didn't matter to me if he had family issues. I've had some of my own lately."

"Because of him. Admit it. You're blind to the man. You hired me to investigate and I have done so. It's not my problem if you don't like what I give you."

Lisa still made excuses for the things she couldn't explain. It would be a difficult truth to swallow knowing that again she fell in love with the wrong man, and again defended him. Mayfield attempted to bring her down to a more practical level where she could see it from his perspective. For Lisa, perhaps living with the mistake would be easier than admitting to it.

"Do you mean to tell me that you believe your husband is blameless?"

Lisa picked at the food on her tray. "I don't know. Joe did warn me about him before the wedding. What do you think?"

"Well," Mayfield tilted his chair back with his foot propped on the bed. "Your brother has many skeletons; a whole graveyard, in fact. Your husband, however...he's Snow White."

"If you couldn't find anything, then there's nothing to find."

Lisa said it with the intention of ending the matter, but Mayfield was persistent. "There are a few things I would like to clarify. Like your relationship with your ex-husband, if you'll pardon my being blunt."

"I have no relationship with Robert."

"I know he came to you for financial help, and I know you rejected him. He, uh, told me other things as well."

Lisa didn't see that coming. "I see. I'm not paying you to investigate me."

"Well, I kinda like to know who I'm working for."

"Mayfield," Lisa spoke slowly to ensure there was no misunderstanding. "I am not comfortable discussing this with you. It was a very dark time in my life."

"I understand, but it may pertain to what's going on."

For an instant, Lisa loathed every bone in his body. This was so deeply personal and disturbing to her that she shuddered to be reminded of it.

"It seems you already know all there is to know. It was a mistake and I regret doing it, okay?" Lisa shakily drew air into her lungs. "I couldn't afford a child, nor did I have the time to raise one."

Mayfield asked, "Does James know?"

"No! I told him I didn't want children and he left it at that."

"What about your brother and his wife?"

"They have two."

"I mean their relationship."

"Oh it's...um, they've had turbulent times. The waters seemed to have settled now."

Mayfield rubbed his chin. "The first time I was in their apartment I happened to notice a picture hanging on the wall; a wedding photo. Do you know the one?"

"Yes, behind the door."

"Did they really want to marry or were there other reasons involved?"

"Simon," she answered. "She was pregnant with Simon. She just turned eighteen. Donald wanted to make it right."

"But did they want to marry?"

"I think so. I don't know." Lisa waited to see if Mayfield had any more questions. "Any more loose ends in need of tying?"

"Just one – Henry Norris."

"I told you I've never heard of him. I don't give a damn about Joe's family."

"The police don't know Henry Norris. You don't know Henry Norris. I wonder if he even exists."

Lisa felt she was encountering every roadblock. The private detective she hired provided her with more questions than answers. The info he gave her was upsetting and prompted more questions.

"I'm sorry. I'm just scared."

She nudged her tray away. The tips of her fingers trembled. It traveled down her hands and into her arms. For three weeks she lived in motel rooms, only to downsize to a hospital room, and next a cell.

Mayfield scooted his chair closer. "I've been in the game a long time. I've been hired for any and every kind of seedy case you can think of. You have my vote, kid."

"Oh my God!" Lisa threw her hand over her mouth. "How could I be so stupid?"

Mayfield backed away. "What?"

"The letter – the-the threat."

"What threat?"

"I forgot. A while back I received a death threat in the mail warning me of what was to come. I dismissed it at the time." Lisa couldn't believe she overlooked her sole chance for a defense. A tiny spark was ignited inside her.

"Do you still have it?" asked Mayfield.

"Yes!"

He smacked his hands together. "That's great! Where is it?"

"At home."

"Good. All we have to do is call up your husband and..."

"No! James doesn't know about it. I never told him. Mr. Mayfield, I need you to bring it to me."

"You mean, go inside your house?"

"You'll have a key."

"But your husband..."

"Will be with me."

"You do realize this is going beyond my obligations."

"The house is mine, too, and you have my consent to enter."

Mayfield grumbled under his breath. Mayfield saw in Lisa a last morsel of hope. The fragility of her current state of mind did concern him. Neither James nor Donald knew all of what she was bearing, because she could only confide the entirety in him.

Mayfield couldn't refuse; he gave her a slight nod.

EVERYTHING DEPENDED ON MAYFIELD bringing the death threat back to her. All of her hopes were in this one act.

Mayfield waited until 4:00 p.m., when he was certain James would be with Lisa, giving him a two-hour window. He made his way up to Cos Cob and was giving himself one hour to find the threat. According to Lisa, James is an early riser and commutes to New York around eight, and is home around six. But that is under normal circumstances.

Lisa was anxious and wanted the note in her hand. It was already after four. Up to now he came to see her everyday like clockwork. The one day he needed to be there, he wasn't.

The door opened. It was a nurse. "Do you need anything before my shift ends?"

"The right side of my body is sore."

"Be back in a jiffy."

"Come on, James, where are you?"

Mayfield parked outside the gate. With key in pocket, up the driveway he walked with a steady stride.

"Thank you," said Lisa to the nurse, throwing the pills in her mouth. "Have you seen my husband today?"

"The tall, strapping gentleman who resembles Burt Lancaster? Not today. I would remember." The nurse opened the door to leave and there he was. "Speak of the devil."

"Pardon me," said James.

"You can run into me anytime." The nurse smiled as she went around him.

Mayfield inserted the key in the lock. This was just the second time he entered this elegant residence. He passed through the private entrance into the foyer and felt a heavy weight land in his chest. Lisa's absence from the house seemed to have drained the life out of it.

The house had taken on a different feeling since he was there last. A house may just be a house, but it does become the people that are living within its walls. James being its only occupant had completely transformed this former home into a gigantic shell.

It was the perfect opportunity to do a little snooping, but he chose to focus on the matter at hand. He was to find the master bedroom.

"What's the matter, darling?" James sat down at the foot of the bed.

"I know what you did."

"And what is that, may I ask?"

"I know you paid my brother to keep away from me. You led me to believe that Donny only wanted to use me, and it was you all along."

"Darling."

"I remember it like it was yesterday. We were leaving Sardi's and I asked you what it was that I did to deserve his rejection. You looked into my eyes and told me I was right in feeling betrayed. Donny betrayed me because of you."

Lisa gazed into the eyes she thought she knew so well. They still appeared the same, though under the radiance of a different light. She couldn't have imagined all of this going on at the same time she was feeling the effects of wedded bliss.

"I know why you did it. You didn't go about it the right way, but the thought was there."

James took Lisa's hand and kissed it.

"Never do anything like that again. I've thrown Donny out of my life. It didn't hurt as bad as I thought it would. He isn't the brother I remember.

"I guess after all these years I still saw him as the little boy I grew up with, the little boy that loved me."

James separated his lips from the top of her hand. "I am sorry. I-I couldn't watch him destroy you any longer."

Lisa stroked the top of James's warm hand, feeling the veins and soft hairs. "While we're on the topic of Secrets Kept from Lisa Mallory, would you clear up one more matter for me?"

"Of course."

"Have you had any affiliation with Alma? Recently."

James hesitated, but the word managed to slip out despite it. "Yes."

Lisa already hit rock-bottom and was anticipating a rescue. There wasn't another edge to send her over. She was strong.

"I know how you feel about Alma and the *only* reason I went to her for help is I thought she might've known something. She played me into letting her join in with me. She said she knew things about you and used that to lure me in like a fish on a hook. I thought maybe we could find you. I didn't know it was *you* who hired Mayfield."

*My abortion.*

Lisa rose up in a panic. "Did she say anything about me?"

"Whoa, whoa, lie still."

"Did she?!"

"No, she didn't!" He lowered her down to the pillow. "The partnership didn't last but a day. I couldn't take her longer than that."

"Are you angry with me about the PI?"

"I guess not."

"I needed someone to be my eyes, someone with an outside perspective."

"Well, at least he's out of the way. That's one less problem we have to worry about."

Mayfield followed the stairs, grasping the banister as he ascended the curved staircase. Lisa's instructions repeated in his head: *"Go up the stairs to the master bedroom. It's the last bedroom on the left."* He came upon the large wooden door.

He stepped into the room and went to the window. *"Under the bottom left leg of the chaise lounge there is a loose floorboard."* Mayfield gripped the base of the chaise and moved it aside.

James told Lisa, "I've been on the hunt for a defense attorney. We want the best money can buy and today I think I found our man. His name is Gregory Dodge. I requested a meeting for tomorrow afternoon.

"It's just a consultation. I must warn you, he's young. Thirty... maybe. But every person he's defended so far has been acquitted."

"He's no older than Donny. We're talking first-degree murder!"

It was behind the white sheer curtain. That had to be the loose floorboard. The spaces between the ridges were broader than those around it. Mayfield strained to work his nails into the crack.

"Damn."

His fingers were fatter and his nails shorter than Lisa's. Then he had the idea of using Lisa's key. With one swift flick of the wrist the board went flying and hit the wall. Mayfield looked into the small space and saw nothing.

He reached in the hole with his fingers and felt around. Had he pulled up the wrong board? Mayfield checked other surrounding floorboards, but each was secure.

The death threat was gone.

# CHAPTER TWENTY NINE

"What do you mean it wasn't there? Are you sure you looked under the right one?"

Mayfield was the bearer of the worst news and assumed the role knowing what was to follow.

"No one knew! I can't...I can't think." Lisa was fraught with lungs similar to an asthmatic, wheezing for the least bit of air.

Mayfield forced her back into bed. "Relax. Panicking won't help you." He poured her a glass of water and handed it to her. "What're your thoughts?"

Water trickled from the sides of her mouth. "My housekeeper? But I never told a soul."

"What about James?"

"What about me?"

James was standing at the door.

"James, you're early." Lisa signaled for Mayfield to go.

"I brought Mr. Dodge with me."

Mayfield asked, "Who's that?"

Lisa rolled her eyes. She mouthed for him to get out. Mayfield wasn't easily intimidated, and definitely not by James.

"Why are *you* here?" James asked the question to Mayfield, but looked to Lisa for the answer. "Out." He pointed at the door, "Out."

Mayfield lifted his hat to Lisa. "I'll be in touch."

"I thought we were finished with him. Never mind. Mr. Dodge, you can come now."

A tall, well-built young man in a gray suit entered the room carrying his hat in his hands. Though he was young, his face was developed and appeared older than his age. Lisa was expecting the fresh-faced youth of a kid just out of law school. This put her more at ease.

"Lisa, this is Mr. Gregory Dodge: Attorney at law. Once the doctor dischargers her it's off to jail she goes. We're pressed for time."

"If you don't object, I'd like to talk with your wife in private."

"I guess not. I'll be outside if you need me."

Dodge pulled up his trouser legs and took a seat. He had light brown hair coated with oil. He possessed a deep voice that carried. Command in the courtroom wouldn't be a problem.

Lisa wasn't going to tiptoe around his feelings. With the niceties out of the way she could get to the real issue on her mind. "My husband tells me you've won every case. How many would that be?"

"Not very many."

"Then...how do I know you can handle my case?"

"I guess you don't. Brass tacks, Mrs. Mallory. There's no guarantee I can get you off scot-free."

"I killed him in self-defense, Mr. Dodge."

"Greg, please," he corrected. "And anyone who takes a life is at fault unless they had cause and there is proof there was no other action left to take. If not, then they must forward their mail to the state pen." Dodge unrolled a piece of chewing gum. "Like some?"

He smacked his teeth together with the pink gum in the middle; wet, sopping sounds seeped from his mouth. "Chances for a solid defense are improbable." Dodge stood and paced from one corner of the room to the other, chewing and chewing as if his mouth was the engine for his brain. "What's your occupation?"

"Don't have one. Not anymore."

"What was your last?"

"I was a waitress."

"Where'd you work?"

"Larry's Diner."

"How long?"

"Nine years." Lisa spit the answers out as quick as she could, but not before he was asking the next.

"What kind of gun did you use on Norris?"

"A derringer."

"Is this your first marriage?"

Lisa huffed, "No."

"Give me the story."

"Is this really necessary? My ex?" Lisa was teetering on borderline frustration, but conceded given the fact she needed him. "I married Robert Frisco in 1950. We divorced after five years.

"Cheating from his part. The drink was a factor, also from his part. I met James March of last year and married him in August."

Dodge leaned on the bedrail. "Why do you think Norris would attack you?"

"I don't know."

"That's not an answer."

"He...he was an unpredictable, horrible man. I sensed it the first time I met him. He would whisper vulgar things in my ear, give me looks, stalk me."

"I take it there're no witnesses to these accounts. How long was it between when you met him to when he attacked you?"

"Um...about a year."

"That long, huh?"

"I hired a PI. You might've seen him a few minutes ago when he left. We think someone paid Joe to kill me."

"That may well be, but neither the police nor the DA is interested in conspiracy theories."

Lisa pushed herself up with her arms. "I've had enough of this back-and-forth, Mr. Dodge. When are you going to start helping me?"

"Call me Greg. And I am helping you. I must be apprised of the entire situation. We wouldn't want the opposition to blindside us, would we?"

Lisa sat there for a long minute that seemed to go on and on. "I think I'll have a piece of that gum now." Dodge dug into his pocket for another piece and placed it in her hand.

"Now, Mrs. Mallory..."

"Lisa," she corrected him in return.

"We need to devise a strategy." Dodge returned to his chair. "Personally, I believe you were justified in your right to protect your body. It's also what you didn't do that'll hurt you though.

"What you *did* manage to do is run, regardless of your reasoning. Because of that you're guilty of murder. Premeditated and deliberate."

"He came at me! Do you think I asked him to meet me in that alleyway?!"

Dodge pointed his forefinger at Lisa. "And for *that* reason, you won't be pleading guilty. Not yet anyways. Under the letter of the law, you have the right to fight before folding, and I will advise you if and when the latter approaches. It's up to you."

Dodge stopped chomping his gum long enough to smile at her. Stressing the importance of the words to follow, he leaned in closer. "Now, Norris was discharged from the force for brutality. What I will try to do is focus on his uglier qualities so the jury will sympathize with you. Understand?"

Dodge extracted the gum from his mouth and tossed it in the bin. "Why did you kill Joseph Norris? What can you give me?"

"Not self-defense?"

"Besides self-defense."

If only Mayfield brought the death threat back with him. If only her one redeeming piece of evidence hadn't disappeared into the blue, for it would validate all that she said and lived through.

*What to tell him...what to tell him...* "Joe blamed James for everything bad that happened to me. Just before our wedding..."

"Skip it. If you can't back up what you say then it didn't happen. You're sticking blame on a man who can't defend himself. The courts are particular about that. Keep trying."

*"Besides self-defense." Joe wanted me dead. By the grace of God, I survived. What does this lawyer want from me?*

"Oh, I filed a police report on the basis that several attempts were made on my life."

"Good. Good. Which station?"

"Greenwich Police Department, I guess."

"This adds credence to your self-defense plea. I'll get a copy of it as soon as I can. That is, if you want me."

He was young, but he was sharp. She was willing to take a gamble and hope that his winning streak would endure. "Yes," she replied.

"If at any point you feel I don't measure up to your expectations, fire me." Dodge pushed the chair back with his legs when he stood. "I think this was a good first session, don't you?"

Lisa made a grimacing face; the gum was already bereft of sugar. "I wouldn't know." She spit it out. "What about fees?"

"Your husband is fine with it." Dodge held out his hand. Lisa accepted it. "It was a pleasure meeting you. You let me do the heavy worrying."

Dodge was about to leave and realized he forgot to ask her something very important. "You've been charged, correct?"

"Yeah," Lisa replied.

"So, you've met Lt. Robson. Did you say anything to him?" Lisa didn't answer quick enough to satisfy. In a flash, Dodge was at her bedside. "How much did you tell him?"

"All I told him was that I defended myself. He-he told me it was off-the-record."

"No details? No specifics?"

"I told him I killed Joe in self-defense. He asked me why I ran and..."

"Damn. Lisa, you never, ever agree to an interrogation without an attorney present, especially when the rap is murder. Real sly. He won't do this again."

Dodge reached over and gripped Lisa's shoulders. "Listen to me very carefully. Under no circumstance are you to divulge *any part* of this case to anyone without me present, especially a police official. Understand?"

"Yes."

"Remember what I told you. You contact me," he uttered with a smile.

James popped his head in the door. "Do you want to hire him?"

"He's hired."

Dodge shook hands with James on his way out.

James sat on the bed and brushed Lisa's bangs to the side. He began to massage her left foot. James's face was stoic, much like one of those busts of Roman emperors. He would look at her and then back at her feet.

He squeezed a little harder to get her attention. She pulled her legs back to tell him she didn't like it. Between them, an unspoken conversation was taking place. James was bothered about something. Lisa didn't want to know.

He switched to her right foot. He had massaged her feet before and this time there was less massage and more gripping. She was resisting his insistence. He wanted her to make the first move.

"So..." James started. "Speaking of lawyers...Russell Sheridan called for you this morning." He positioned his hands on each side of Lisa. "This makes the second time."

James may have been treading on thin ice. "He wouldn't tell me the nature of your business. Would you mind telling me?"

"It was about my will."

James's posture slackened. Lisa didn't hesitate. She blurted the answer surely and quickly as if to get the inevitable over with.

"As in Last Will and Testament? You're kidding. Lisa, you're thirty-eight. Why would you make a will?"

"I didn't make a will. I simply updated the one I already had."

"I'm assuming this pertains to the money I gave you. Who's in this will?"

"No, James."

James crushed the pillow beside her head with one hand until it was flattened. Lisa wasn't going to tell him. This was one aspect of her life that belonged to her and no one else.

REBECCA WALKED UP THE STEPS TO HER APARTMENT to find James waiting by the door.

The rare occurrence took her mind to a worse-case scenario. "What's happened? Is Lisa alright?"

"She's fine. We found someone to defend her."

Rebecca reached into her clutch bag for the key. "Come in. I don't like chatting in the hall. Can I get you something to drink?"

"Thank you, no, I can't stay."

Rebecca went into her bedroom to put away her things. Something was bothering him. It must have been to bring him there of his own accord.

James didn't wait for Rebecca to come out. "You...you work for McGaffrey, right?"

"Yes."

"Have you met a Russell Sheridan?"

"Russell Sheridan? I don't believe I have. Why do you ask?"

"He also works for McGaffrey. Remember a while back when I asked you to talk to Lisa to find out why she was behaving strangely, keeping to herself?"

"Yes."

"Well, like you said, she was contemplating a will. Only said will already existed. I was wondering if you knew about it since you work in the same firm."

Rebecca emerged. She didn't appear shocked or puzzled. "It's large firm. Besides, he couldn't tell me even if I asked him."

James meandered to the sofa, but didn't feel comfortable or welcomed enough to sit.

Rebecca looked at her watch. She wanted James to leave. Donald would be home soon and she wasn't up for another agonizing encounter.

Donald pulled up in time to see James exiting the building. He took the key out of the ignition and remained in the car until he was gone. For all the money Donald accepted, he was now paying the penalty. Providence had at last conquered, making him compensate for what he took. Would he be able to win back the affection he put a price upon?

# CHAPTER THIRTY

It was Saturday morning. An officer came to take Lisa to the inevitable location.

Lisa wondered why he didn't handcuff her since, after all, she was a criminal. However, embarrassment was the least of her worries.

A nurse wheeled her down the hall with the officer beside them all the way. Lisa looked over and up her left shoulder to see the stiff, hulking policeman. She could only see the lower half of his face because the brim of his hat hung so low. She was looking up into his nose, really.

After an uncomfortable elevator ride, they were out the hospital doors to the black-and-white parked in the front. The officer opened the backseat door and helped her in.

In Lisa's mind, this was *it*. It was no longer an event to dread. She had built up in her mind what to be ready for, but it seemed surreal. She had never broken a law in her entire life. Now she was being fingerprinted.

"Good morning, Mrs. Mallory," greeted Robson, entering the claustrophobic, tiled room. He held a cup in one hand and a heap of papers wedged under his arm in the other. Lisa sat at the table as solid as the walls that enclosed her. Closer examination would reveal she was shaking like a shriveled leaf in autumn.

"How are we today?" he asked, dropping the papers onto the table with a thud. "Now, I don't want you to be scared, Mrs. Mallory. This is routine."

He pulled a chair up to the table. The feet made a piercing screech as it dragged the hard floor. "Before we begin, is there anything you would like to say?"

"M-my lawyer," Lisa mumbled.

"I'm sorry, I didn't hear."

"I need to contact my lawyer – Gregory Dodge."

"We've contacted your husband and he's bringing him along. Would you like some coffee? It's just outside – piping hot."

"Black."

"I wouldn't have it any other way." Robson tapped the one-way mirror on the door. The same officer that picked Lisa up came through. "Two black coffees."

Lisa hadn't eaten a bite since the day before. Her stomach wasn't prepared for the strain of digesting both food and first-degree murder. It was all she could do not to slump in her chair. Perhaps her old picker-upper would do the trick, and then she could think with a clear head.

Lisa threw her head back and downed the coffee given to her. The door opened and Dodds came in with a clipboard. He didn't say a word as he parked himself on a stool in the corner. Robson never acknowledged him. This was probably some tactic they used to heighten the anxiety in their suspects.

Robson loosened his tie. "So...how did you meet Joseph Norris?"

"He was a friend of my husband." Dodds began to write. Lisa recalled Dodge giving her strict instructions not to talk to the police without him.

"What was your first opinion of the man?"

"I think I better wait for my attorney."

"You got something to hide?" Robson was detached and cold. Lisa got the feeling it was going to get worse, attorney or no.

"Of course not," she answered.

"Then there's nothing for you to worry about." Robson pulled a cigarette from the pack with his teeth. "Why did you kill him?"

"I-I-I had to."

"That's a strange way to put it. What do you mean?"

"He attacked me, Lieutenant. He wanted me dead."

"Maybe he just wanted to talk. He startled you, and then you shot him."

"No, no."

Robson took a long puff and tapped the ashes into the tray. "You persuaded this friend of your husband to meet you in the alley."

"No."

"You didn't really want to kill him, but you felt...threatened."

"Y-yes."

"You had to get rid of him." Lisa shook her head. "He frightened you. He was a brutal, menacing man.

"He made advances to you, bullied you to the point you couldn't take it any longer." Lisa shook her head fiercely. "You tried telling your husband about it, but he wouldn't listen. This was his best friend. He couldn't fathom those despicable accusations.

"You were still newlyweds. He didn't know you *that* well. In the back of your mind, there was one option. It was the road to peace. Am I on the right track?"

Lisa hit the table with each denial. "No! No! No! You got it all wrong. That's not the way it was."

Robson signaled with the wave of his hand. "By all means..."

"Joe was all those things you mentioned, but..."

"Did you tell your husband?"

"No, but..."

Robson stood up. Lisa felt no bigger than an insect for the squashing. "You mean to tell me this man was making your life a living hell and you never told your husband?"

"I-I-I thought about it."

"You're giving me the runaround. That's what you're doing. I've been behind this badge for twenty-six years. You think I can't see when I'm being played like a worn-out record?"

It was hard concealing her fear, but she didn't want to feed into it, or give Robson the impression that what he was saying might be true. She fought to stay strong. Her shell was growing harder and it was becoming easier to combat attacks of every sort.

He meandered around the table. "You made three mistakes. Mistake Number one: You left evidence proving you were at the scene of the crime." He stood behind her. Not being able to see him added to her anxiety.

"Mistake Number two: You keep screaming self-defense and yet you never bothered to call the NYPD after you shot him. We have witnesses that can attest you loathed Norris." Robson was next to her ear. "That was your third mistake.

"You threw him out of your house during a party. "Get out you bastard," were your words to be exact; made quite a scene." Robson slowly returned to his seat and took the last remaining sip of his coffee. "You want to know what I think? I don't think you're a bad person.

"I think you were driven to this outcome. You seem like an intelligent woman...though that might be a ruse. Where did you hide all that time?"

Lisa simply stared at him. She knew he was expecting an answer, but he would have to keep on expecting.

Time passed and still no Dodge. Lisa didn't know how much longer she could hold out.

For the fifth time – "Why did you kill Norris?" Robson was relentless, tenacious to a fault, and stronger than her. Lisa repeated her story over and over again. It seemed both detectives' ears were plugged up with their own theories and opinions that they weren't capable of hearing anything that challenged them.

"Lieutenant, won't you listen to reason? I told you, I was going to see Russell Sheridan. I'll take a lie detector test."

"Sheridan is the lawyer handling your will."

"Yes! I wanted it to be a secret. I was on my way to keep the appointment when I was pulled into the alley. Obviously, Joe knew where I was going that night and waited for me."

"Why would he want to kill you, Mrs. Mallory? He's not in your will, is he?"

"Don't be stupid."

"Why then? He had nothing to gain from your death." Lisa glanced over at Dodds who was still in the corner writing away. "Don't look at him. Prove to *me* why he would want to kill you."

"Maybe someone paid him!" Lisa closed her eyes the instant she heard the words and realized what Dodge meant. It sounded ludicrous.

"Come on! You can come up with a better excuse than that. I admit the man wasn't the type to take home to Mother, but isn't that stretching it? I will ask you once again..."

"No."

"Why did you kill Norris? I want to hear you say it!" The room was getting smaller. There wasn't even a window. The light above their heads was so bright and so hot.

Dodds removed a plastic bag from his jacket and dropped it in the center of the table.

"My wedding ring!" Lisa snatched it without delay.

"Your husband already identified it as such," said Dodds. "It was found under Norris."

"Well?!" yelled Robson.

*Where are you, Greg?* Lisa wiped the sweat from her brow. *Please get here.*

"We know you purchased a Smith & Wesson .32 caliber derringer, but, as I'm sure you know, we don't have it. Would an innocent woman who's trying desperately hard to prove her innocence dispose of the murder weapon? Running scared, hmm? Scared of being found with the murder weapon on your person?"

"I lost it!"

Robson slammed his hands on the table causing Lisa and the table to shudder. "That's a lie! No one, innocent or guilty, would lose the weapon they used! No one! You hid it somewhere!"

"No!"

"You chucked it in the river!"

"No! No!"

"Yes! You buried it!"

"I didn't!"

The tip of Robson's nose touched hers. "Why did you kill Norris?"

"Because he was going to kill me!"

"Saturday, July 18th, you fixed it to where he would meet you in that alley!"

"Stop it!"

"You hid in the shadows, waiting for him to pass you. You called him out by name and he turned. Pointblank – Norris is finished!"

Robson reached into his stack of papers and slammed it down in front of Lisa. Before her was a black-and-white photograph of the body in all its twisted ugliness. A neat hole was bored in the center of his forehead.

Lisa threw her hands over her face.

"For a woman who just killed a man in self-defense you managed to tidy up nicely. You pushed the body flat up to the wall. You even positioned trash cans around the body to conceal it. Here's the puddle." Robson dug out a second photo.

"The blood left a trail when you moved him. Look at it." Lisa refused. The memory was more vivid than any picture he could show her. "I said look!"

Lisa took her hands down, but shifted her eyes away. She could still see much of it through her peripheral. She found the night of the attack returning to her like a raging torrent that couldn't be stopped. She could still feel his thick fingers clasping her throat.

"Tell me what really happened." A long tear fell leaving its trail down Lisa's cheek. Robson saw it and knew he was reaching her. "Let it out."

The door opened and in came the officer. "Lieutenant?"

"What?!" Robson shouted.

"Her attorney and husband are here."

Dodge barged into the room, his claws protracted and ready to pounce. "What do you think you're trying to do, Lieutenant? Railroad my client?"

Dodge pushed Robson's papers aside to make room for his satchel. "You think I don't know how these things work? You press her flat for six hours until you get a confession."

Dodds spoke, "She's been made her rights."

"I think my client has had enough for today, thank you very much."

Robson signaled to Dodds for them to leave. Both shared the same frustrated expression.

As soon as they were gone Lisa jumped on Dodge. "Where were you? I was beginning to think you weren't coming."

"Sorry, we were stuck in the traffic jam from hell. Hey, what did I tell you about talking to the police without me?"

"I know. They sucked me in."

Dodge sat in Robson's seat. "How much did you tell 'em?"

Lisa got up to stretch her legs for the first time in almost two hours. "Nothing more than he already knows. Oh, I did tell him about Russell Sheridan."

"Who?"

"He's the lawyer handling my will. That's where I was going that night."

"You didn't tell me about him. Can he back you up?"

"Absolutely. Speaking of which, I need to give him a ring."

Dodge took a piece of gum from his pocket and held it out for Lisa. She declined so he indulged himself. "You'll have to pardon my gum chewing. I'm trying to kick cigarettes.

"I got a copy of the report you filed back in June." He rammed his hand into his satchel and handed it to Lisa. "It mentions your encounter with the gray Chevrolet that ran you off the road.

"They couldn't do much without a license plate, but it demonstrates that what you say holds water." Dodge grabbed a pencil and paper. "What was the name of that lawyer again?"

"Russell Sheridan – McGaffrey Law Offices. My sister-in-law works there." Lisa was wringing her hands. "Greg? What's going to happen to me?"

"You will be transferred to a pretrial detention center where you will await arraignment."

"Where-where is James?"

"Outside, but you can't see him yet."

Dodge looked at her face and knew she was scared to death. Lisa adored James still. With all that was plaguing her mind she made room for him. She stroked the finger which once donned the ring that now occupied a plastic bag.

"You should contact Edgar Mayfield. He's been snooping around for me."

Dodge jotted the name beneath the other. "And who is he?"

"A private detective."

"MY NAME IS MAYFIELD. I'm a private investigator. Can we talk?"

Alma smiled, "First or last?"

"Beg your pardon?"

"Your name."

"Last, ma'am."

Alma eyed Mayfield favorably. She released the chain and let him in. "Let me take your hat. Sit anywhere you like."

Mayfield chose to sit on the left end of the sofa and Alma sat in the middle, flinging her leg up on the cushion. Additional apparel was to be desired as Mayfield fought the impulse to glance down. The majority of his questioning over the weeks ended with the name Alma George. He needed to see for himself the woman who was painted in this not-so-good light.

"What is your first name, may I ask?"

"Edgar."

"Tell me, Edgar, what is your reason for paying me this visit today?"

"Lisa Mallory." Alma rolled her eyes. "I've been told that you know her quite well."

"To my misfortune."

"What makes you say that?"

"By what authority do you ask these questions?"

"That's a valid point. If you would be willing to answer them, then perhaps I would be willing to answer yours. Quid pro quo, Ms. George?"

Mayfield's thinking was she was an open book. She was blatant and not ashamed to speak the truth about anything. According to Donald, Alma loved to gossip and spread it around like a bad case of the flu.

Alma was enjoying the stranger's company. She wouldn't have any problem telling him what he wanted to know, but why not make the most of a rare opportunity? Fun and games were her specialty.

"Agreed." Alma laid a hand on Mayfield's knee. "You start, darling. Isn't this fun?"

Mayfield didn't remove it providing it didn't drift north. "I've spoken to several people in Lisa's circle and one who used to be."

"You mean Robert."

"He mentioned that you spread around Lisa was…consorting with the landlord."

"Is there a question in there?"

"Do you deny it?"

"Not at all. I'll climb to the summit of the highest building in New York and confess it to the world. It didn't last, but it gave me satisfaction."

"Satisfaction for what?"

"No, no, my darling Edgar," Alma waved her finger at him. "It is *my* turn. If you're sniffing around Lisa's circle, then you must know what's happening. Has she been captured yet?"

Mayfield contemplated whether or not to answer. Would it hurt Lisa in the unpredictable future?

"Yes," he answered.

A crafty grin formed on Alma's maw, her eyes like Medusa, so cold they might've possessed the power to turn Mayfield to stone.

"Stella is your niece. You introduced her to Robert while he was still married to Lisa. Why?"

"For the same reason I spread the rumors." Alma's appeal was diminishing and something else was surfacing. Her gestures were more vicious and her tone venomous. "I enjoyed observing the little bitch as something she held dear was being taken from her.

"I don't know why you're questioning me anyway. Lisa's doctor-husband came charging into my apartment thinking little me was involved in her second disappearance. Not even I could've foretold she was capable of spurting a bullet into a man's skull."

"Why would he come to you?"

"Because I've known Lisa for so long."

"Spell it out."

"Well," Alma moved her hand from Mayfield's leg to reach for her cigarettes on the coffee table. "He was going out of his gourd when he called me that first time. I convinced him to call me back whenever he found out about his sweet wife." Alma lit her cigarette and added with a raised brow, "And he did."

"I don't like that word 'convinced.'"

"I told him we would exchange info, much like you and I are doing now."

"Mm-hmm. What was it you told him?"

"Don't you think it's my turn?"

Mayfield was becoming agitated with the duration of this questioning. Alma was shrewd, and it was difficult to get too much out of her at once. Alma returned her hand to his leg a little higher up this time.

"What is the charge?" she asked, the cigarette hanging from the side of her mouth.

"First-degree..."

"Not murder?!" Alma burst out with a loud and boisterous cackle, throwing her head back and kicking her legs up in the air. Mayfield was chuckling with her out of discomfort. "Oh Edgar, you have just made a redhead's day. I'll tell you whatever you want to know."

"Great. What secret did you tell James?"

"I told him about Lisa's abortion. He didn't take it too well." Mayfield's jaw dropped. He took her hand from his leg. "Come on, Edgar dear, don't tell me you caught the Lisa lovebug, too."

"Oh well." Alma pressed her cigarette into the tray. "Is that all? I've got the nightshift tonight."

Mayfield was still trying to absorb what he learned. "I can't think of anything."

Alma showed him to the door. "If you do, let me know." She played with the buttons on his jacket. "Or if you simply want to pop by for a little one-on-one. I wouldn't mind."

Mayfield showed Alma his ring. "I'm attached."

The second his feet hit the hallway carpet he cringed in disgust. What a relief it was to be out of that apartment. This further added to his suspicion.

Alma George was vindictive, bitter, and pitiless. A terrible combination of the worst human flaws found in one woman who had exercised each of these on Lisa. She wasn't shy. On the contrary, she was proud. Yet, if Alma wanted Lisa dead would she be so obvious, or was she just evil enough not to care?

James did in fact know Lisa's darkest secret. He's known all this time and has never uttered a word. This unsettled Mayfield also.

Alma rushed to her telephone and dialed. "Hello, Stella? It's Alma. May I speak to Robert, dear? I have urgent news."

LISA WAS LED DOWN A LONG CORRIDOR. Due to her cast, in place of handcuffs, the guard held firmly to her arm. The hallway seemed to go on forever, or maybe it was because she was watching her feet instead of her surroundings.

At last, she reached what was to be her new home for the foreseeable future.

The guard pushed open the sliding door made of iron and guided Lisa inside the concrete box. What kind of experience could she have when its history consisted of fear, loneliness, and isolation? Her freedom and her right of choice hung in the balance.

Lisa was frozen in place. A single light bulb dangled at the end of a wire from the ceiling. The iron door screeched as it was shut, so loud the echo resonated throughout. The cell was dark and disturbing, so she tugged on the pull string to turn the light on. It flickered for a few seconds and slowly increased to brightness.

Lisa was able to clearly see what she didn't want to see. The size of the cell appeared to be approximately six feet by twelve. To her right was a flat, iron bed that sat close to the floor.

In the corner to her left was a porcelain toilet and sink side by side, and a medicine cabinet with a mirror. The grayish concrete walls were stained with cigarette spots and unpleasant graffiti. Lisa took three shuffling steps backward to the bed. She could feel the bed through the thin mattress. There was a faint female whimpering coming from down the corridor.

Lisa stretched out on the slab. She wanted so bad to cry, so bad to release the hell accumulating inside, much like the woman whimpering down the hall. Her cries were gradually becoming louder. Her last waking thought: Hoping the guard would return with something to eat or drink, or perhaps a pillow.

The weight had grown heavier since last she slept this deep. The world was black. There was nothing behind and nothing ahead. Again, Lisa didn't know where she was trying relentlessly to get to, but that urge to get there was more powerful than she was.

Silence engulfed her, except for the faint whimpering behind her that was never there before. That, in addition to her own labored breathing, was all she could hear. The further she walked the heavier the weight became. Lisa was so familiar with this frightful place that she knew what to expect as the end drew closer. The burden upon her tiny shoulders was growing heavier and heavier.

She collapsed and the blinding light ignited above her. Where was the figure? It had always been there. And why had the gun not materialized in her hand?

She was surrounded by layers and layers of bricks that went on for miles. The whimpering ceased. Suddenly the weight was gone and right before her eyes.

She was dragging Joe. There was a hemorrhaging hole in the center of his head.

He grabbed her head and pulled her down to him. In a raspy voice he moaned, "You killed me." Lisa thrashed about to free herself. "You killed me," he repeated over and over and over.

"You killed me..."

# CHAPTER THIRTY ONE

Mayfield was growing very frustrated with Dodge who was paying little attention. He thought it would do some good going to Dodge's office.

"Are you listening, Mr. Dodge?"

"I am, but there's nothing I can do. You tell me that someone near to my client, maybe her husband, wants to do her bodily harm. Why?"

"Must there be a reason?"

"I think so."

"Well, I don't."

"She bumped off her enemy, remember? Aside from the prospect of spending twenty to life in the state coop, she should be safe."

Mayfield leaned on Dodge's paperwork from over the desk. "Lisa may well still be in danger. Who will be held accountable if something does happen?"

Dodge swiftly raised his head and tossed his black-rimmed reading glasses to the side. "What makes you think it's James anyway? I've never picked up anything..."

"James is at the heart of Lisa's troubles. He's domineering, jealous..."

"Save it." Dodge pulled his papers out from under Mayfield's hands and filed them away in his cabinet. "I have a to-do list as long as your arm and don't have the time or the interest to listen to shaky theories and speculations that have no bearing on this case. I will *not* bulldoze the courtroom with this garbage. Not to mention be made a laughingstock."

"Perhaps I can help." Mayfield walked around the desk to Dodge who was quite taller than him. "I have been sniffing around this thing for a month. I know these people."

"I don't need a gumshoe muddying up the waters. If the prosecution got wind of this, he would have a field day." Dodge pulled his jacket off the back of his chair. "Lisa tried to hand me some baloney about someone hiring Norris to kill her.

"What do you two want from me?" Dodge stepped around Mayfield and instantly felt guilty. "I'm sorry, sir. I truly am, but this case..."

Dodge struggled to find the words. "It's going to be an uphill climb as it is. Look, I'm on my way to see Dr. Mallory now. You can tag along if you like."

Mayfield was most eager and offered his car for the trip in gratitude.

They went to the hotel where James was staying. Dodge was there to obtain facts that could aid in Lisa's defense. Mayfield was there with different intentions. Dodge cautioned him on the way there to say nothing unless it pertained to the case, and then if it was crucial.

Dodge rang the bell of the front desk. The clerk came promptly. "Can I help you?"

"I need to speak with Dr. Mallory. Could you call his room?"

"Dr. James Mallory?"

"Yes."

"He's not here, I'm afraid. He received an emergency phone call from the hospital last night and hasn't returned."

Mayfield jumped in, "Do you know which hospital?"

"Mount Sinai."

Mayfield, like the little devil on Dodge's shoulder, began planting seeds of doubt as to the credence of the man that was paying Dodge's high-priced fees. He was doing so in the hopes one seed would take root and he would have someone on his side.

Dodge spoke to a receptionist at the hospital. "Is there a Dr. James Mallory here?"

The girl went to the other side of her desk and checked a chart on a clipboard. "Yes, Dr. Mallory is here. He was in the E.R. most of the night. He relocated to the CVU a couple hours ago with his patient."

They made a dash for the elevator that was closing and occupied both sides. Dodge thought to fill up the silence. "Most people don't like lawyers either, you know."

"I'm aware people don't like me, young man, particularly the police." Mayfield grinned, "Even you. Am I right?"

"Hey, I didn't mean..."

"Don't worry about it. I've been hauled into stations all over this city more times than I care to count for getting in the way. As a matter of fact, that'll probably be the title of my autobiography. *Get Out of the Way: The Secrets of Private Eyeing as Told by Edgar Mayfield*."

The elevator doors opened. The hall was overrun with medical beds, wheelchairs, orderlies, nurses, and candy stripers running in and out of rooms. They had to sidestep the rush to get though. Mayfield was nearly run down by a nurse pushing a medicine cart.

Dodge nudged Mayfield with his elbow. Halfway down the next hall was James wearing a white coat. "Ho, doctor! Come on," he told Mayfield.

A look of surprise and displeasure formed on James's face in seeing Mayfield lagging behind Lisa's attorney. It appeared to him Mayfield didn't want to be seen, using Dodge's height to his advantage.

"What's this all about?"

"This isn't a deposition, but I...*we* need to ask you a few questions, that's all."

James wasn't happy that Dodge was associating with Mayfield; he was paying him good money. "Follow me." James passed between them and led them up the hall to the break room several doors down.

James went to the table where hot coffee was simmering and paper cups were stacked high, and poured each of them a cup.

Mayfield didn't waste any time. "Shouldn't you be worried about Lisa?"

Dodge was dumbfounded. Zero tact.

"I got an urgent call last night. A patient of mine, lovely old gal, had a massive coronary. Or perhaps I should have ignored the call." James handed a cup to Mayfield full to the brim and it spilled on his hand.

"You do have other doctors in your employ."

It was a good time for Dodge to take over. "James, all I want from you is a few facts that could help me in the defense of your wife. You can start by telling me all you know about your friend, including what the police may not know." Both Dodge and Mayfield took out their notepads.

"I wouldn't know where to begin."

"Well, how did you come to know him?"

"He was a friend of my father's. He used to take me out on beer runs in my youth." James took a sip of his coffee and crossed his legs. "He even smuggled me in the back of his patrol car a few times."

"What was your take on his character?"

James thought about it. "He was a little rough around the edges, liked the drink too much, but I never imagined he was capable of something this horrible. I used to be quite fond of him." Mayfield was writing every word that billowed out of James's mouth.

"Were you aware of his involvement with the KKK?" James tensed up and threw his legs apart. "I guess that answers that question."

James shook his head in disbelief. "I-I never..."

"Did you pick up any hostility or bitterness between Joe and your wife?"

"I sensed Joe was attracted to Lisa, which made me uncomfortable, but that was normal for him. He took pleasure in the delights of many women. I was the same way myself once."

Mayfield tackled his statement. "Shouldn't that have been a big red flag for you?" Dodge threw him a look. "Why did you let her near him then?"

"Because *I* was there. The two of them were seldom alone together. Then out of nowhere one day she exploded and banished him from the house."

"Hence the party incident," Dodge concurred. "How was Joe with other relatives?"

"My mother didn't care for him. Joe kept to himself. He wasn't an outgoing man."

Whether or not James would take the bait, Mayfield cast out a line by asking the question that plagued his mind out of sheer curiosity. "Why did you combine forces with Alma George?"

James crushed the cup in his hand. "I think we're done here."

Dodge was in the middle of this ongoing feud between James and Mayfield. It was Mayfield's questions that worried him. It was also that the façade of the rich, distinguished doctor did not deceive. What did Mayfield see that he couldn't?

Dodge implored, "Don't go. Mr. Mayfield will leave. Won't you?"

"No, I don't think I will." Mayfield stared James down. "I have just as much cause to be here as you do, young man. I am here on Lisa's behalf."

James yelled to cover his true discomfort. "Why am I being talked down to…like…like…" He threw the smashed cup against the wall. "Like a goddamn threat?!"

"Neither of us meant to offend you. If you will…" Dodge indicated to the chair for him to sit back down.

Slowly they returned to their seats. Mayfield guessed James wouldn't answer his question. But it did get a rise, which was becoming easier to do.

Dodge continued, "The toxicology report verified your friend was not under the influence when he died. He attacked your wife with a sound mind. Speaking of which, were you aware of any history of mental illness or neurosis."

"No, but he was involved with the Klan, so he must have had something wrong with him. God." James covered his face. "I lost track of him when I moved to New York. Almost a decade later he looked me up and told me he was working for Apple Grove Life Insurance and making a decent salary. There is no feasible explanation for him to attack my wife!"

Mayfield muttered, "Unless someone paid him to." He didn't bother lifting his head up from his notes.

Dodge asked, "Why do you think he looked you up? There was a big gap between. He didn't have much family to speak of. His ex-wife died four years ago."

James exhaled heavily with his head down, "Yes."

Mayfield could read all over his face that he was deeply troubled. He had the look of a man who wanted to say something important and then changed his mind.

"I have to go, gentlemen. I'm needed elsewhere."

Mayfield tapped his fingers on the table, oblivious that he was doing it. There were two sides to James. Dodge was choosing to stay in the dark.

"It doesn't appear as if he's coming back, does it?" Dodge smacked his hands on his legs as he rose. "Let's go. I'll try him again some other time."

DODGE LET HIMSELF INTO THE DISTRICT ATTORNEY'S OF-FICE. He nodded to the secretary before going in.

"Hey, Al."

"Greg!" Al leapt out of his chair to greet him. "It's great to see ya, kid!" Their hands met with a firm shake. "How long has it been?"

"Since last Thanksgiving."

"How's your pop these days? Still retired?"

"Yeah, but not happy about it. It's only a matter of time before my practice will be *Dodge and Dodge: Attorneys at Law.*"

Al MacQuillan was the ADA assigned to Lisa's case. He was also old friends and prosecuting rivals with Dodge's father. It was to Lisa's advantage, this close rapport her lawyer had with other prominent lawyers.

"Libation?"

"No, thanks."

"Alrighty then, what brings you to my office today?"

Dodge sat on the edge of MacQuillan's desk. "I just dropped by to tell you I'm on the Mallory casefile."

MacQuillan had to think to remember. "Mallory...Mallory..." He snapped his fingers, "The woman who shot the cop. It's your hot potato, huh? If I were you, I'd drop out of this one, kid. It's open-and-shut."

"Ex-cop," Dodge corrected.

MacQuillan scoffed in amusement. "It's suicide, kid. You'd be jumping headfirst into shallow waters."

"I don't understand."

"Judge O'Neal." Dodge grimaced. "Would you like a continuance?"

Dodge exhaled, "No. Damn."

"You sure? I can try and get another judge."

"I don't want my client in jail any longer than she has to be." Dodge chose his words carefully. "Actually, I was hoping maybe you would, uh, drop the charge to manslaughter. That way I can get her out on bail. Her husband has more than enough money."

MacQuillan gave a cunning grin and leaned back in his chair. "Your father wouldn't have done that."

"He might've."

"I would like to help you, but it's non-bailable. *I* would like to have the murder weapon, but I'll make out. You just keep plugging away. I know you'll fare okay."

Dodge smiled, "I'll be seeing ya, Al."

"In court."

JUDGE O'NEAL took his time getting up the steps to his chair. He was a short, plump old man with a bald head and white hair on the sides. The arthritis in his knees kept everyone standing longer, awaiting his instruction.

Dodge sat on a bench close to the front with his secretary and father who chose to chaperon. Al MacQuillan was at the prosecution's table.

One of the clerks pounded his gavel. "Here ye, hear ye, hear ye. The circuit court for the district of Manhattan is now in session. Please be seated."

O'Neal, dressed in his black robes, felt it obligatory to introduce himself to the familiar courtroom with unfamiliar scattered faces. "My name is John O'Neal for those of you who don't know me." His voice was gruff and whispery. "In case any of you are wondering, I just celebrated my seventy-second birthday. I should be retired.

"I've come to the conclusion that I am still needed in a court of law. I tell you this because though my hearing isn't what it used to be and I can't see to sign my name on the checkbook, I am still sharp as a tack and can keep up with the most quick-witted attorney."

Judge O'Neal polished the lenses of his glasses on his robe and hung them on his ears. "Let's begin, shall we? We will commence with the criminal docket."

One by one each accused was brought before the bench, all of them entering a plea of not guilty. Over an hour elapsed before Lisa's time had come.

"Case Number nine: *The People v. Lisa Mallory*. The charge – murder in the first degree."

Dodge glanced at his father and rose up, buttoning the bottom of his jacket. "Gregory Dodge for the defendant."

O'Neal motioned for the bailiff. "Produce the prisoner."

The bailiff disappeared into the door on the side. When he returned, Lisa was at his side, her arm still bounded in the hard plaster that was becoming a part of her body. It was a relief to get out of the gray attire and wear one of her own dresses, except her hair was in a ponytail and she was barefaced.

The second she passed into the great room her eyes searched for an identifiable face. Dodge's was the only friendly one she could connect with. James wasn't there.

The bailiff ushered her in front of O'Neal. Lisa looked up at Dodge and he smiled. This was the world in which he thrived. As for Lisa, it was a terrifying place to be trapped. It was up to an old judge and twelve strangers to choose which path she was to go, and for Dodge to convince them which path was best.

Lisa had to stretch her neck to be able to see the judge sitting high up on his throne. He was the overseer of this world, and seeing as she occupied its lowest level, made him appear more so like the judges of old.

MacQuillan read the charges. "State of New York, court of Manhattan, I, Albert MacQuillan, prosecuting attorney, come into Manhattan for the court to understand that one Lisa Mallory be charged with murder in the first degree and be held without bail."

"Mrs. Mallory, do you know you are being charged with first-degree murder?" asked the judge.

"Y..." Lisa cleared her throat. "Yes, sir, Your Honor."

"Counselor, how does your client plead?"

"Not guilty, Your Honor. Your Honor, this is my client's first offense and her husband is more than capable of posting bail. I ask that my client be able to return home pending trial."

"Your Honor, Lisa Mallory is a flight risk to the max. She spent weeks eluding police, and as to Mr. Dodge's statement to this being her "first offense," murder is a mighty hefty first offense."

"Agreed. Bail is denied. The case of Lisa Mallory will be held first for trial." Judge O'Neal pounded his gavel.

LISA WAS LYING ON HER BUNK WHEN SHE HEARD THE CELL DOOR SLIDE OPEN and hopped out of the bed.

"You have a visitor," said the guard.

"Is it my husband?"

"Follow me." The guard led her out of the gloomy cellblock and showed her to a windowless room with a chair and a wire mesh divide. "You have fifteen minutes."

Lisa expected to see her husband, but instead saw the former.

"It's wonderful to see you," Robert spoke as he moved toward her from behind the mesh. Lisa's heart beat faster and her face glowed. "I would have come to see you sooner, but this was the first chance I was able to get away."

# CHAPTER
# THIRTY TWO

She offered him something to drink or eat as she always had before. This time he didn't accept.

Greta dabbed her neck and breasts with perfume and coated her cheeks and lips with rouge. She appeared at the bedroom door in a see-through negligée. The entire house was dark except for the light streaming out of her bedroom across the floor. It allowed Donald to see the outline of her legs.

He stood rigid like a military man and said, "Not this time, Greta. No more." He was planning to do this for a long time, but hadn't found his nerve until this night.

It was a complete jolt for her to hear Donald's abrupt assertion. "Where is this coming from?" she asked.

Donald sighed and pushed his hair aside. "I just can't participate in your bed games anymore. I've given you what you wanted and you've given me what I needed. It's over."

"May I ask why the sudden change?"

"Someone very dear to me..." Donald rephrased his wording. "There's a lot going on in my family right now. I need to give it my full attention."

"Can't we once more this nacht?"

"I don't know what your intention was when I agreed to this, but it was far from companionship, believe me." Donald feared that similar tactics used to lure him the first time would be used to keep him coming back. He couldn't allow himself to give in again.

Greta may have been attempting a different approach when she began to cry because she was not the type. "Stop blubbering," said Donald. "You're not fooling either one of us."

"Leave me!" Greta pulled two tissues from a box on the table beside her and dried her eyes that weren't wet. She grabbed his hand as he stepped away. "You know me so well. There is no chance of changing your mind?"

Donald kissed the top of her hand. "Goodbye, Greta."

From this point he didn't care what she did. If she told all, that no longer mattered to him. He realized at some point he would have to let go. Let go of his secrets and the fear they generated in him.

Rebecca was in the kitchen washing dishes when Donald returned. She felt her hair being lifted and his hot breath on the back of her neck.

"Donald, this isn't the time." He pulled her to him. "What's got into you?"

She saw in his eyes a tiny spark kindle, and it warmed her heart. In spite of her hands and wrists coated in lather, Rebecca threw her arms around his neck. He lifted her into his arms and carried her to the bedroom, together experiencing a tender and genuine contact from both. It was longed for and needed within this struggling marriage.

The sheet had worked its way down to their feet. Donald and Rebecca laid wrapped up in each other. He asked her, "How long has it been since I told you how much you mean to me?"

Rebecca gazed at him. "You've been so distant."

"You mean the world to me, Rebecca. You always have. I'm sorry if I've put you second to anyone. You're my lady."

Rebecca looked into his eyes for some time and began to see that he meant what he said. She moved her hand to his cheek and kissed him tenderly.

Donald tugged on the chain of the lamp on the nightstand. "I was considering going to visit Lisa. What do you think?"

"You should at least try, dear. I took the kids to see her last weekend."

"You think so?"

"Absolutely. She needs you." Rebecca drew Donald's head to hers so she could kiss him and nipped his chin instead.

"Ouch!" Donald shrieked. Rebecca snickered. "My little wildcat," he bit her neck.

A loud bang on the door startled them. "Mom!" It was Simon.

They heard the hinges of the door squeak and threw the sheet over them. "Close the door!" shouted Donald.

"Julie's in my stuff again."

Rebecca answered, "I'll be there in a minute, Simon." She got out of bed and stepped into her slip. "That boy!"

"Well, he did knock. Ha-ha."

"Our eight-year-old son nearly saw us with our asses in the air." Rebecca threw open the door. "Hilarious!"

Donald was feeling good. He couldn't put his finger on why. Perhaps it was because Lisa knew the truth about him, which removed the majority of the weight he was lugging around day-to-day. Now that he chucked Greta to the wind, he could rekindle his relationship with Rebecca with a devoted heart and a clear conscience, concentrating the whole of his youth on his family. He couldn't go back to old habits.

Lisa's dilemma seemed to be the instigator behind Donald's leaf-turning decision. The next day he called in sick to his day job at the cab company. He decided he was going to make things right with his sister, but not before paying a visit to two very important people that he neglected to see in years.

The sun was veiled behind a cloudy overcast that expanded the length of the city. Donald knelt down on the uncut grass and lowered his head in reverence.

PRESTON GARLAND WELLS
NOVEMBER 7, 1882 – MAY 24, 1939

ETTA JEAN THOMPSON-WELLS
JUNE 4, 1893 – MAY 24, 1939

"I miss you both so much. I've...I've done such terrible things. I should have come to see you sooner."

Donald yanked the weeds out of the ground that was covering the stone's inscription. He then rested his hand over his mother's name.

"Momma, Lisa won't talk to me. I can't blame her. Do-do you remember the time Lisa got mad at me for squealing on her about Peter and you sent us to our room. It didn't take long for her to forgive me.

"You knew, didn't you, Momma? You knew she would. Do you think she will forgive this time? What I've done is worse than anything I've done before.

"I'll be thirty in a few months. I want to make a clean sweep of my life."

*There is a knock at the door. Lisa rises to her toes to see through the peephole.*

*"Kincaid," Lisa mouths to Donald.*

*"Telephone for you downstairs."*

*"Stay here, Donny. I'll be right back."*

Donald takes advantage of Lisa's absence and bolts into the kitchen, not knowing how long he has, to steal a few of his mother's homemade cookies from the forbidden after-dinner sweet jar.

"Donny!" He rushes back into the living room, his mouth occupied with melting toffee. "We have to go. Right now."

"Go where?" Lisa runs into the kitchen, opens the cupboard, and stands on a chair to reach the teapot on the top shelf. "You can't use that money," Donald proclaims. "That's for the rent."

"We need money to get to the hospital." Lisa snatches his hand and tugs him down six flights of stairs. "Follow me." She takes off in a sprint down the sidewalk.

Donald's nine-year-old legs struggle to keep up. "Lisa, slow down."

Lisa spots a cab parked down the next street. She holds out her hand for Donald to take it and they run together. Donald pushes his legs as fast as they will go.

Lisa taps on the glass to get the driver's attention. "Bushwick – Wyckoff Heights Medical Center."

Donald pleads to his sister, "What's happening?" Lisa remains silent and is breathing hard.

The cabbie pulls to an abrupt halt at the emergency entrance. Lisa plops a five into his palm before he gets a chance to quote her the correct amount. She again reaches for Donald's hand. He resists.

"Take my hand, dammit!" They step inside a structure of chaos and are overwhelmed by screams of pain and panic-stricken doctors and families.

Lisa sits Donald down on a bench in the waiting room. "You stay right here, okay?"

"Lisa..."

"Stay here!"

He grumbles an okay and slumps into the chair.

His eyes grow numb to the clock, each tick and hour and each hour a day. He waits and waits. Large men in white coats pass the door in constant procession. Only the women wearing the white hats seem to notice the boy.

Donald decides to go to the door and stick his head out. Lisa is at the end of the hall alone. Agony takes over her calm exterior. Her head falls into her hands. Donald is frightened by the sight.

"L-Lisa?" he says.

She quickly dabs her eyes as Donny runs to her. "Donny..." Lisa kneels and takes a deep breath, "It's Mom and Dad." She is barely able to speak the words. "They're gone."

Donald shows great panic and confusion. Lisa takes his shoulders. He looks past her into the room behind. He cannot see the bed for the curtains.

Something tells him they are in there. Lisa pulls him into her embrace and Donald's body slackens.

*"W-what will happen to us?"*

*Lisa forces a smile before revealing her face. "I'm going to take care of you. You trust me?"*

*"I trust you, Lisa."*

Donald retuned to the present. "Thank you for reminding me. Lisa, don't you worry. It's my turn now."

"She doesn't wish to see you. Sorry," the guard informed Donald.

"Um…did you tell her it was Donald Wells who's here to see her?"

"Yes, I did. She was adamant. Sorry."

Donald was hoping for partial clemency, optimistic she would've shed some of her bitterness, but she was still holding on. All she was enduring was changing her. While she was becoming harder with the passing of each day, which was essential for her survival, the affection that Donald had come to rely on was dwindling.

Lisa had been taken for granted too long. It was time for her to think of herself for a change.

# CHAPTER
# THIRTY THREE

What is the law? Is it just some pointless scam to con the American public into believing that its citizens matter? Or is it an unbiased system of government to help and comfort those in fear of being wronged?

Her life had self-destructed. She still wondered if she was to blame in some way.

Lisa was shaking in her seat. She wanted to appear confident in her lawyer and in her own truth. She kept her hands clasped together in her lap so no one would see. The courtroom wasn't full, but it was soon to be as people continued to trickle in.

Who were these people? Were they here for the spectacle of a murder trial? How bored must they have been to go out of their way to spectate someone else's pain.

Judge O'Neal, with a slight crankiness simmering beneath the surface of his tone, turned to address the already-selected jury. "Ladies and gentlemen of the jury, before we proceed, I must examine your qualifications to sit as jurors. Remember you are under oath. Are all of you citizens? Raise your hand if you are not."

Lisa wanted to ask Dodge something, but he was busy getting his notes together and she didn't want to bother him just for reassurance and comfort. He wouldn't have been able to give it anyway.

"Are there any law enforcement officers among you?" They shook their heads. "Are any of you related by blood or marriage to a law enforcement officer?"

Lisa leaned forward slightly and looked across the room at MacQuillan. He was doing what Dodge was doing, and conferring with his secretary very serious like. *Jesus,* she thought. *I'm the one under the gun here.*

They were taking it so personal, as if either one of them lost the case it was going to hurt their standing. She didn't know if Dodge and MacQuillan had gone head-to-head before, but it felt like it.

"Do any of you have business with the prosecuting attorney, Albert MacQuillan?"

"No," answered the jury.

"Do any of you have any business with Gregory Dodge, attorney for the defense?"

"No."

"Are any of you acquainted with the defendant sitting on the left of Mr. Dodge?"

Lisa happened to look behind her in time to catch Rebecca coming in; she took a seat near the back. The sight of her reminded her of Donald, and bitter thoughts followed.

O'Neal took a long breath, "Will Dr. James Mallory, the defendant's husband, please stand." Lisa looked at her husband who sat directly behind her next to Dodge's secretary. "Do any of you know Dr. Mallory?"

There came several "nos" from the jury. "Thank you, doctor. Counsel may question the jury."

MacQuillan and Dodge examined each man and woman. MacQuillan first. James reached over and rested his hand on Lisa's shoulder.

*Nine men and three women. Let's hope sex isn't the majority vote. Five of them look over sixty. Three of them are over seventy.*

*That's good. Older people have forgiving hearts. Unless...unless they're set in their ways. Two of them look my age and the other two are in their twenties.*

*Can such diverse people agree on anything? How will they take me? What does a twenty-something have in common with a sixty-something? They don't wanna be here. It's obvious they don't wanna be here.*

One was obese and looked like the buttons of his suit were going to give at any moment. Three were bald and one gave the impression of being asleep through the entire examination, but neither attorney had thrown him off. The three women were of homemaker decent, decked out in their finest church attire, white gloves and lace shawls. One of the elderly gentlemen kept toying with his pocket watch.

Lisa closed her eyes in horror that these people, God knows the type of people they were at home, would be standing in judgment of her. As individuals they were most likely decent people. No one sitting in those twelve chairs would have been suitable to Lisa. It seemed to be a sound system, but would it be if in her shoes?

"YOUR HONOR, COUNSEL, MEMBERS OF THE JURY think back to July 18th of this year. I know it isn't easy, but try and recall what you were doing that night. It was a while ago, so I'll give you a minute."

MacQuillan began his opening statement using a casual approach to put them at ease. With the subject matter being murder, the jury would automatically perceive MacQuillan to be the guy in white.

"That night I was with my daughter and son-in-law. They have two four-year-old twin boys. I had the joy of putting them to bed."

Dodge scoffed in amusement.

"Saturday, 9:30 p.m. – That was the time the defendant left Larry's Diner, her place of work. Two blocks away the body of Joseph Elliot Norris was discovered. The state will prove that the defendant was in the alleyway of the victim's horrible demise *at the time* of his demise." He meandered to the jury box which was closest to his table.

"She hated Joseph Norris. *Hated* him. And the state will prove she, on more than one occasion, displayed that hatred, verbally and physically. You will hear testimony of an eyewitness at a party who observed the defendant dispel Norris from the house when he was there to join in the festivities."

Lisa covered her eyes. It was killing her inside. She wanted so much to stand up and tell her side of it, but she had to button up and let Dodge be her voice at the appropriate time.

"You may ask, "What does a party have to do with a murder?" My answer: Everything, for it was the trigger that would eventually lead to Norris' heinous murder. Two weeks prior, the defendant bought a gun that matches the bullet found in Norris." MacQuillan got in the jury's faces to stress the importance of his forthcoming words. "To top it off, the state will show that she confessed to the NYPD."

MacQuillan returned to his laid-back manner. "The justice of Joseph Elliot Norris will rest upon your verdict. I don't want you to go by what I say. The evidence will speak for itself, and then... then you can follow what your heart tells you. What you know, based on the evidence presented, is to determine the truth.

"The state's truth or the truth of the defense. In essence, that is what you're here to do. You are the most crucial part of the justice system. Take the jury out of the system and we have a dictatorship. You will meet many witnesses throughout the course of this trial, more than you can remember the names to, but it's what they say that's important.

"I'm asking you to return a verdict of murder in the first degree for Lisa Mallory for a crime that should *never* go unpunished. I know that you will make the right decision." MacQuillan signaled to O'Neal and ambled back to his chair.

After hearing MacQuillan's opening statement, Lisa again started worrying about the age of her attorney and his limited experience. Would he be able to stand up to his skilled and much older opponent?

"LADIES AND GENTLEMEN OF THE JURY..." Dodge walked around the table and sat on the edge. Not a sound was heard as everyone anticipated his next words. He folded his arms and lowered his head. "Ladies and gentlemen of the jury, I am not here to contend with any of what Mr. MacQuillan has told you today, because..."

He paused.

"It's true." Dodge lifted himself from the sitting position. "My client, Lisa Mallory, is more than a client. She's my good friend. In case any of you are wondering, no, I am not throwing her under the bus."

Dodge stood adjacent to the jury, his hands behind him with a slight grin. This was his style: Pause for effect.

"I heard Mr. MacQuillan say that Lisa left Larry's Diner around 9:30 p.m., which is true. Larry will attest to it. Joseph Norris was found in an alley two blocks away from the diner one quarter after midnight. And Lisa *was* in that alleyway."

He remembered everything MacQuillan said in the exact order. She glimpsed over at his notes and saw he had written down everything MacQuillan said in shorthand.

"Did my client hate Joseph Norris? She didn't like him, but she didn't hide it either. I'm not going to drone on and on about the guilt or innocence of my client. The truth is, Lisa did kill Joseph Norris, but in contrast to what Mr. MacQuillan has said, this is not a case of guilt or innocence.

"This is a case of right and wrong. Was Lisa in the right or in the wrong? Or was Norris in the right or in the wrong?"

MacQuillan stood, "Objection, Your Honor. The defense is implying guilt upon a man who can't defend himself."

"Sustained," answered O'Neal.

"My apologies. Ladies and gentlemen, while you are being bombarded with evidence, remember these words, "Right or wrong." It is for the state to prove, beyond a reasonable doubt, that the defendant willfully murdered Norris."

By their expressions and fixed eyes, the jury seemed to be warming to Dodge. He took another long pause. In the courtroom, words were powerful. They were the weapon of the attorney, and they could build or destroy.

"I will prove to you that Lisa had no other choice but to protect herself. Otherwise, I might've been defending the victim."

"Objection."

"Your Honor, this is what the entire case is regarding." Dodge frowned at MacQuillan. "We can play this game in cross-examination. Can I at least finish my opening statement?"

"Agreed. Let the defense finish."

"Ladies and gentlemen, take a good look at my client. She's not very big, is she?" The jury turned their heads. "Lisa, do you mind standing?" All eyes were on her.

"About five-four, wouldn't you say? Lisa shot Norris. And before there was a terrible battle for life. How could a small woman of five-foot-four murder a stocky man of six-foot-two without a gun? The answer is she absolutely could not.

"Then why was there a fight, I ask you. You can sit down now, Lisa. I will answer these questions later in the trial. As I said before, the burden of proof rests on the state. Which means Mr. MacQuillan must show you that Lisa Mallory, not just killed, but *murdered* Norris in cold blood, and there can be no doubt in your minds.

"If each of you had the opportunity to get to know this woman, I think you would find she is a good person, filled with compassion and sympathy, which she now needs from each one of you. In your eyes she's a criminal who sits across the room, and you would rather be someplace else, but Lisa can't be. She has a brand-new husband and a beautiful home in Connecticut in which to share with him, and it all rests on you whether or not she returns to them."

Pause.

"Thank you."

His opening statement bettered MacQuillan's. Dodge was a man of glib tongue and colorful words that glided from his mouth in the most perfect order. It contained a hint of compassion, and she could feel he meant every word. The proceedings were over for the day. Tomorrow was the official start of the trial.

It felt like being tied down on a train track with the train approaching in the distance. Each day the train advances. Dodge is able to loosen the knots to free her, but MacQuillan tightens them again. And those twelve strangers are the passengers.

TUESDAY, OCTOBER 13, 1959 – THE PROSECUTION

"Death was instantaneous. Norris sustained one gunshot to the head. The bullet passed through the brain and lodged in the back of the skull."

"Did you find anything else in your examination?"

"Indeed. I located a tumor the size of a walnut." There were expressions of surprise from the female jurors.

MacQuillan stated to the judge, holding up a folder. "I ask that the recorder mark this report as People's Exhibit One for identification."

"Noted and marked," said O'Neal.

"Let it be noted the people give the report to the defense. Counsel may cross-examine."

Lisa followed the advice of her attorney and kept her cast on the table in full view. Sympathy was the card Dodge was choosing to play at this time.

"Dr. Stevens," Dodge moved to the witness with the report in hand. "Your purpose was to ascertain the cause of death. You say that death was immediate?"

Dr. Stevens was a man whose hands did most of the talking for him. "When a bullet enters the brain, regardless of the angle, it's almost certain death. In this case it was fired at close range."

"Almost certain death?"

"There have been rare circumstances where a victim has survived, but they're in a vegetative state, a coma."

"That didn't happen with Norris?"

"No. The trajectory of the bullet passed directly through the center of the brain."

Dodge adjusted his black-rimmed glasses as he scanned Dr. Steven's report. "I see here in your report there were minor contusions and abrasions found on the body as well, and a stabbing in the right hand."

"There was minor nerve damage. The puncture was ¼ of an inch deep."

"And a bite mark on the lower lip. Don't forget about the bite mark. Tell me, all of these injuries, the stabbing, the bruises; is it safe to say there was a struggle?"

MacQuillan jumped in before the witness could answer, "Objection. The defense is leading the witness."

O'Neal was languid, resting his head on his fist. "Sustained."

"I'll rephrase the question. What do you think happened that would cause these wounds?" Dodge stood in front of Stevens, blocking his view of MacQuillan.

"A struggle would," Stevens responded.

"Who was winning?"

"Objection. It's obvious who won, Your Honor."

Dodge threw off his glasses and kept going. "That bite mark has me baffled. I've been to the movies, and the only time I see that is when the man is trying to have his way with a woman against her will. So, she bites him. Can you think of any other reason why a woman would bite a man's lip?"

Stevens thought for a moment. "No."

"In this postmortem you were asked to check for alcohol or drugs. What were your findings?"

"There was no sign of drugs or alcohol in the bloodstream."

"The deceased had a clear mind?"

"I don't understand what you mean."

"What I mean is Norris was sane when he died."

MacQuillan hit the table. "The defense is suggesting the deceased had a mental illness. The question is argumentative, Your Honor. There was no evidence of assault on the defendant."

"Overruled. I'll allow it. Answer the question, Dr. Stevens."

Stevens exhaled deeply, "Yes, Norris was, as you put it, sane at the time of his death."

"No more questions."

"No redirect."

Dodge returned to his table and winked at Lisa. He didn't seem all that concerned about MacQuillan's courtroom methods. MacQuillan seemed to be the type that objects more often than necessary in order to win his case, or at least disrupt the thinking of his opposition. Lisa found herself on the edge of her seat, wondering when his next outburst would be. Would Dodge be able to provide the best defense with his opponent interjecting at every junction?

MacQuillan announced, "The people call Dr. Gerald Richardson."

James got up and left without telling anyone. Lisa guessed it was the forthcoming testimony of Joe's doctor and the news he would divulge to the court that James already knew and didn't care to hear again.

"Dr. Richardson, please tell the court your background."

"I graduated from Temple University School of Medicine in Philadelphia. There I received my Bachelor of Medicine and Surgery, Masters of Surgery, and Doctorate of Medicine. Those are the required qualifications of an oncologist."

Richardson crossed his legs and entwined his fingers together. *What a snob*, thought Lisa. She figured it was all that education and the money that came with it. In truth, it was because he was Joe's doctor and was automatically allied with her attacker in friendship.

"If you will, Dr. Richardson, tell us about Mr. Norris's affliction."

"I object, Your Honor." This was Dodge's first objection. "What does the deceased's illness have to do with my client for whom this trial is being held? Unless Mr. MacQuillan is attempting to deceive the jury by tugging at their heartstrings."

"I find it is necessary, Your Honor."

"Objection overruled. I see nothing wrong with the witness. Continue, Dr. Richardson."

Richardson turned to face the jury with a somber voice as if they were his patients and he was giving them the dreaded diagnoses. "Mr. Norris had what is commonly known as a Glioblastoma. In other words – brain tumor. The symptoms differ depending on the location of the tumor. In Joe's case, his was in the temporal lobe."

"And where is this temporal lobe, doctor?"

"It's close to the skull base. His primary care physician in St. Louis located the tumor. Not but a couple weeks later he moved to New York and made an appointment with me."

MacQuillan asked, "How advanced was the cancer, doctor?"

"Not very. However, it's an aggressive form, and his was growing at an alarming rate. Joe's symptoms, even with treatment, were getting progressively worse with time. It began with severe headaches and blurry vision, but the last three months he was experiencing seizures. He had to quit his job because he was barely able to function."

"What was the treatment in Norris's case?"

"Chemotherapy and radiation."

"What about surgery?"

"He and I discussed that. The cost was exceptional. The tumor was in a volatile place, very high-risk. I told him I would be willing to take the risk if he was. He felt he had nothing to lose."

Lisa was remembering the night of the attack. *That's why I was able to fight him off.*

What was to her advantage that night was now working against her. MacQuillan was turning her into a coldblooded killer who took the life of a dying man.

Richardson added, "I was giving him morphine injections for pain."

"How long did he have?"

"My patients suffering from that form of cancer generally live up to one year, two if they're lucky. Joe was not. Two months before his death he came to my office in a cold sweat and demanded something be done. That's when we agreed on the surgery. Now, I don't know what the outcome would've been, but without it I say he had three months."

Then Richardson placed the icing on the cake by ending with, "In my opinion, the defendant did him a favor."

MacQuillan smiled, "Your witness, Mr. Dodge."

Dodge stood but remained in place. "I have one question. You being an expert in your field, is there a possibility this tumor would have triggered a mental change, one that might have been the cause of unusual behavior?"

"There's a possibility."

"So, if Mr. Norris did something abnormal, such as attacking a woman in a dark alley..."

"Your Honor!" MacQuillan shouted. Dodge persisted anyway and found himself shouting to outtalk MacQuillan.

"...his cancer could have been a factor in his behavior."

MacQuillan hurried around his table. "That is an accusation in sheep's clothing if I ever heard one!"

"I did say "if", You Honor."

O'Neal pounded his gavel. "Quiet! Answer the question, doctor."

"Joe's faculties are in question."

"Thank you." Dodge grinned ear-to-ear at MacQuillan as he sat back down. Lisa grabbed hold of his arm in excitement.

O'Neal said, "If the prosecution doesn't have any more questions..." MacQuillan shook his head. "You may step down, Dr. Richardson."

MacQuillan was so angry he called his third witness through gritted teeth. "The people call Milford Griffin."

The clerk called him to step forward. "Raise your right hand, please. Do you solemnly swear the testimony you're about to give in this case to be the truth, the whole truth, and nothing but the truth, so help you God?"

"I do."

"You may take the stand."

James returned to the courtroom at this time. On the way to his seat, he happened to spot Robert sitting halfway on the opposite side. He had no idea he was there. And Stella wasn't with him.

Lisa put her hand on her shoulder for James to hold it as before. He was reluctant, but fulfilled the wish anyway.

"Will you state your profession, Mr. Griffin?"

"I'm a forensic photographer."

"And were you called upon by the police to take photographs of the body of the deceased Joseph Norris?"

"Yes, sir."

"Do you recognize these photographs as the ones you took?" MacQuillan handed Griffin the same horrid pictures that was shown to Lisa in interrogation.

Griffin flipped through each one. "Yes, sir, these are the ones."

"I wish to submit these photos as evidence. The photos are given to the defense for examination. Your witness, Mr. Dodge."

"No questions, Your Honor."

Lisa leaned over and whispered in Dodge's ear, "Is-is everything alright?"

"We're only ankle deep right now." Dodge rapidly tapped his pin on the table. "Would you happen to have a stick of gum on ya? I'm dying for a smoke."

MacQuillan called, "I wish to call character witness, David Bundy." A portly gentleman with a cane took the stand. He walked with a limp, shifting his weight to his cane every alternating step to take the pressure off his bad leg. He placed his cane with a polished brass handle between his legs.

"What is your occupation, Mr. Bundy?" asked MacQuillan.

"I'm district manager for Apple Grove Life Insurance Company."

"How did you know Joseph Norris?"

"He was one of my salesmen."

"Why don't you tell us about him?"

"I hired him last year and he resigned in...May of this year, I believe. He was one of the top guys on my team. He had a way with people, a way of speaking to them. Losing him was a loss for all of us at Apple Grove. It's not every day that you come across someone who is as hardworking."

"So he was a dependable, levelheaded man."

"Yes."

"Thank you, Mr. Bundy. No more questions."

"No questions," said Dodge.

The prosecution called for Lt. Robson to testify next. Lisa grew apprehensive at the sight of him.

"I'm innocent, Greg, no matter what he says," Lisa pleaded.

"You are guilty unless I *prove* you innocent. The law dictates otherwise, but that's the cruel, actual truth of it."

# CHAPTER
# THIRTY FOUR

"**D**etective Lieutenant Marc Robson," MacQuillan began. "Yesterday you testified that you and Sgt. Dodds were in charge of the murder investigation."

Dodge interjected, "Your Honor, I object to the use of the word 'murder'."

"Granted. Could you use another word, Counselor?"

"Lt. Robson, you and your sergeant were the investigators handling Norris's death?"

"That's right. We were given the case by Capt. Brandon."

Robson looked so smug sitting in the witness chair, or that's how Lisa perceived him, his manner polite and his diction flawless. He had done this before and was gelling nicely with Mac-Quillan.

"When you arrived at the crime scene, what did you find?"

Robson talked with his hands as if he was making an oil painting of what he saw to MacQuillan. "The body was pushed up against the building. There was a trail of blood from the center of the alley to the wall, and there were trash cans surrounding the body. It was concealed adequately."

"Did you find anything else?"

Robson crossed his legs and folded his arms, comfortable with the questions he and MacQuillan rehearsed. Robson never stammered or hesitated once. "We found a shell casing to a .32 caliber derringer, which proved to be pertinent when we ascertained that Mrs. Mallory did in fact own a Smith & Weston .32 caliber derringer, purchased two weeks prior."

MacQuillan handed Robson a bag with the casing inside. "Is this the one you found in the alleyway?"

"It is."

"I ask that the recorder mark this shell casing as People's Exhibit Two for identification. What else did you find, Lieutenant?"

"Mrs. Mallory's wedding ring."

"I'm sorry, I'm not sure I heard you. Did you say her wedding ring?"

"Yes. Her husband identified it as such and so did the defendant." Robson looked at Lisa for the first time since he took the stand.

MacQuillan walked to his desk, took a second bag with the ring in it, and handed it to Robson. "Is this that same ring?"

"Yes, it was under the body."

MacQuillan held the ring out so the jury could see it. "I submit this ring as evidence. You also questioned the defendant, did you not?"

"After she was released from the hospital, yes."

"And what did she say?"

"She admitted three times to killing Joseph Norris. The first time we spoke she said, and I quote, "I had to shoot him.""

Lisa grabbed Dodge's arm in a panic. "He told me it was off-the-record."

James was alarmed also. "He did. I was there."

"Hold it. Objection, Your Honor. Whether or not my client killed Norris isn't the issue here. The question should be, "Was she justified?""

MacQuillan opposed, "Your Honor, the defense is trying to impugn the integrity of my witness."

"All respect to Mr. MacQuillan and his witness, but he is obviously trying to confuse the jury by dodging the issues that could hurt his case. My client was under the assumption of Lt. Robson that what was said was off-the-record."

"Your Honor, she was picked up on a first-degree murder charge and interrogated."

"But she wasn't read her rights until after."

"Approach the bench," ordered O'Neal. "Both of you." The squabbling attorneys glanced at each other in apprehension. "I don't much care for the conduct being exhibited in my courtroom."

Dodge hung his fingers over O'Neal's desk. "My client and her husband say Lt. Robson questioned her before she was read her rights and now he's spewing my client's private words all over this court."

"That's a technicality," said MacQuillan.

O'Neal scratched the back of his head. "I'm inclined to agree with Mr. Dodge...if what he says is true."

"Your Honor," MacQuillan nudged Dodge aside. "The defense is basing this accusation entirely on the word of a killer."

"Oh, are you the judge in this courtroom now?"

Lisa looked over at the jury. Certain members were watching her. Not directly because they knew she was watching them. Looking directly at someone with the prospect of conviction in the near future would be the equivalent of befriending the pig before slaughter.

O'Neal gnawed on his glasses to aid in his decision, further deepening the ridges from previous decisions. "A jury cannot disregard what it has already heard. I will sustain Mr. Dodge's objection. Do you know when your client was officially mirandized?" he asked him.

"Right after she was questioned, Your Honor. In the hospital."

"Mr. MacQuillan," O'Neal motioned for him to come closer. "From here on stray from asking your witness any and all testimony prior to Mrs. Mallory's arrest. I will allow what's been said, but no more. You may continue."

Dodge returned to Lisa who was anticipating an update. She vied for his attention and was promptly hushed.

"Lt. Robson, let's talk about Joseph Norris. You did a background check, correct?"

"I did."

"What were your findings?"

"Norris was born and raised in Springfield, Illinois, and was a police officer for the St. Louis Metro Police Department." Some members of the jury dropped their mouths slightly.

MacQuillan slipped in a question about Lisa. "To the best of your knowledge, did the defendant ever once attempt to notify police of her alleged attack?"

Dodge caught it. "That isn't a question, it's an assumption. Mr. MacQuillan is attacking my client."

"Overruled."

Robson answered. "No."

"What about friends or relatives?"

Lisa winced as Dodge called out again. "Objection! How could he *possibly* know who she did or did not speak to? Why doesn't he ask her friends and relatives?"

"Overruled, Counselor!"

"Not to my knowledge."

"I submit the shell casing and ring to the defense for examination. Your witness, Mr. Dodge."

Dodge was ill at ease and in a rush to question Robson as if it was his life that hinged on the answers to follow. Dodge stood over him, but he wasn't intimidated, for he had faced many defense lawyers.

"You testified that Mrs. Mallory purchased a .32 caliber derringer, and you say it was a .32 caliber derringer that killed Norris, correct?"

"I did."

"What qualifies you as an expert in firearms?"

"I have been around guns all my life and that's not including my involvement with the NYPD."

"So, because you're knowledgeable with guns that gives you the right to assume in this court?"

"I *object*. Defaming a good citizen such as Lt. Robson is an insult."

"Sustained. I would advise you refrain from such remarks, Mr. Dodge."

"I apologize. Well, Lieutenant?"

"Well, what?"

"I repeat the question."

MacQuillan was livid and ready to object, but Robson was becoming livid as well and responded before he had a chance. "I wasn't assuming anything. My sergeant and I hit the pavement right away. We left nothing to guesswork. Upon searching Mrs. Mallory's home, with the consent of Dr. Mallory, we found a bill-of-sale for the gun in the defendant's bedroom."

"Yes, I'm aware of that. What about the cartridge?"

MacQuillan interjected again. "Your Honor, is the defense going anywhere with this line of questioning? We've already established that Lisa Mallory owned the gun that killed Norris."

"Then where is it?" Dodge motioned to the jury as if asking them. "I would like to see this *"gun"* that Mr. MacQuillan won't shut up about. Do you know where it is, Lieutenant?"

"Mrs. Mallory told us she lost it, but I didn't buy it."

"I don't wanna hear about your doubts. The truth is you don't have the murder weapon. Right, Lieutenant?"

Robson bit the inside of his cheek. "Correct."

"Now," Dodge meandered over to the jury box and leaned on the railing. "Your background check on Joseph Norris; he was a police officer for how long?"

"Twenty-eight years."

"Wow! That's a mighty long time. Why did he quit?"

"Objection. I don't think this young man, in his limited experience, is qualified to be a defense attorney. He's shown little to no understanding of the basic principles of these proceedings that any common public defender would comprehend. He's spoken out of turn, disrespected witnesses, this court, and attempted to confound this intelligent jury."

Dodge rolled his eyes. MacQuillan yelled, "Right there! On top of that he's pointed fingers at the deceased, an already-dying man who was unjustly killed before his time!"

"Come on! Mr. MacQuillan may have sensitive feelings, but this is a court of law and feelings come second to the truth."

O'Neal tapped his knuckles on the desk. All was silent as they waited for his verdict. "Objection sustained. I see no bearing this line of questioning has on this case. Move on."

Dodge's face fell. MacQuillan seemed to have assumed the role of Joe's defender. But he had a plan, and he knew that what he was about to do was unethical, but the jury had to know. Once they heard, they wouldn't forget.

"It was you, Lieutenant, who told me Norris was thrown off the force for brutality."

MacQuillan threw his pencil down onto the desk so hard it bounced off. O'Neal slammed his gavel; it echoed to the far reaches of the room.

Dodge kept on. "He couldn't control himself. He had a terrible temper."

"That will be enough!" The sheer insolence of Dodge's gall made a thick vein arise in the center of O'Neal's forehead. "Will the jury disregard that last statement? And it will be stricken from the record."

Lisa found herself gripping the tables' edge.

O'Neal ordered him over. Dodge knew this would happen. "Another outburst like that and we are going to have words in my chambers. Do you understand me?"

"Yes, Your Honor."

O'Neal pointed his gavel at him. "Your father taught you better, I'm sure. I will not tolerate this behavior."

Lisa wasn't sure what had happened until Dodge turned around and she saw his face. She couldn't describe it, but there was confidence and self-assurance. Whatever it was, it made her feel good. By now she too was confident she found the right lawyer.

"I have no more questions."

MacQuillan was still on edge. "I have one more. In regards to the gun, your understanding of firearms is well documented, correct?"

"Yes, sir, it is."

"You would know a Smith & Weston .32 caliber derringer if you saw one, including the cartridge?"

"Yes."

"No more questions."

O'Neal stated, "You may call your next witness."

"The people now call Betty Marsden to the stand."

A shapely blond rose from the back wearing a pencil skirt and twisting her way to the front in her black three-inch heels, clacking up the wooden floor. At first Lisa couldn't remember where she had seen her before, and then it came to her – the party. She was Rebecca's friend.

"Raise your right hand. Do you solemnly swear the testimony you're about to give in this case to be the truth, the whole truth, and nothing but the truth, so help you God?"

"Yes, I do."

Rebecca was more than surprised. She hadn't spoken to Betty since the party.

MacQuillan began, "Will you state your name, miss?"

"Betty Marsden."

"You are a college student, Ms. Marsden?"

"Indeed. I'm a law student at Columbia University."

"In what way are you affiliated with the defendant?"

"I'm friends with Rebecca Wells. They're sisters-in-law."

"How do you know her sister-in-law, Rebecca?"

"We were at law school together, but she's graduated. I'm a few years behind Becky. That's why Mrs. Mallory threw the party. Not because I'm younger, because Becky graduated. Ha-ha-ha."

MacQuillan was taking his time with this witness. The others were matter-of-fact. "If I may clarify for the jury, your friend, Rebecca, who you met at school, is sister-in-law to the defendant, and the defendant threw her a party because she graduated."

"Righto."

"And naturally you were invited."

"Naturally." The dimples forming in each of her cheeks caught MacQuillan's attention. She crossed her legs and didn't bother covering her exposed knee, and MacQuillan didn't bother hiding the obvious eyeful.

"When was this party?"

"April 19th of this year."

"Would you mind explaining, in your own words, the events of that day?"

"Not at all. Mrs. Mallory held the party in her mansion up in Connecticut, beautiful place. We were all having a wonderful time. There was food and drink."

MacQuillan stepped off to the side so the jury had an unobstructed view of her. "Becky was opening gifts when Mr. Norris arrived. I don't know how long he'd been there before I noticed him. He was standing in the doorway of the living room watching for some time, I think."

"Who was he watching?"

"All of us, the whole gathering."

"Did he appear angry or troubled?"

"No. On the contrary, he looked to me as if he wanted to join in."

Lisa cursed under her breath, "What a load of horseshit!" Dodge shushed her.

"What happened next?"

"Mrs. Mallory noticed him before any of us did, and she made a special point to be as discreet as possible so not to disturb the festivities. I was closest. She stood in front of him and said, "You are no longer welcome here." When he didn't leave, she screamed at the top of her lungs, "Get out you bastard!"

MacQuillan faced the jury. "Is that true? That's what Mrs. Mallory said? "Get out," and she called him a bastard?"

"Yes, sir."

"And after that?"

"She pushed him."

"Pushed him?"

Betty nodded. "Mm-hmm, she pushed him with all her weight to get him out."

"What did he do?"

"He left."

Lisa couldn't take it. She stood up, shouting, "That's a lie!" Her chair fell back.

Dodge picked the chair up from the floor and sat her down. "I apologize for my client's outburst. It won't happen again."

"See that it doesn't," replied O'Neal.

"Are you trying to make things harder for me? I don't care if what you hear up there is false. You will sit in that chair and you will take it. Bite your tongue 'til it bleeds if you have to, but shut up."

Lisa sank in her chair like a scolded child. Dodge inserted a piece of gum into his mouth. He must have really been upset if her outburst made him crave a cigarette.

MacQuillan continued, "Is there anything else you want to tell the court, Ms. Marsden?"

"I don't want anybody here to think badly of Mrs. Mallory. I like her very much. I'm glad she invited me to the party. As a matter of fact, I spent the night there. I never met Joe, yet her actions that day, in my opinion, were unwarranted."

"No more questions. Council may redirect."

MacQuillan had barely finished his sentence before Dodge started in on his witness. "So...you're a law student."

"Yes, sir, I am."

Dodge realized he forgot his gum. He reached in his mouth and was at a loss where to put it. He glanced at O'Neal and slipped it into his pocket.

"I bet this is good practice for you."

"Objection. I don't like the sound of that statement," declared MacQuillan.

"Sustained," O'Neal answered with a long, breathy moan.

"You appear very chipper for a young lady who's testifying against a woman she professes to like."

"I object. Is the defense going to question the witness or play psychiatrist?"

"Please Your Honor, allow me to finish. Ms. Marsden, you told the court that you were sitting closest to...where was it?"

"The door?" she answered with a question.

"I don't know, you tell me."

"It was the door."

"You sure? Because I seem to recall you saying that you were closest to Mrs. Mallory and Norris, but not that you were sitting and not that you were by the door."

"Well, that's where it happened. That's where he was standing."

Dodge went and sat on the edge of his table. "I'm not picturing the scene. You were sitting."

"Y-yes."

"If Mrs. Mallory was causing that much of a commotion, wouldn't you stand up?"

"Maybe I did."

"What did the others do?"

"I don't know."

"You don't *know*?" He hopped down and sauntered toward her. "You seem to recall every word my client said, even the exact day this occurred. Okay, I'll deviate a bit. Who were you sitting beside?"

"Another friend of mine and Becky's – Madge."

"Is she in this courtroom now?"

"No."

"Why not? If she sat or stood next to you then she saw everything you saw and heard everything you heard. I'm forced

to assume the reason you're here is because you know more...
*or* you love the idea of gaining the experience in court."

"Objection."

"Would it give you some kinda extra credit?"

MacQuillan shouted, "The defense is trying to discredit my
witness all based on whether she stood up or not. This is ridiculous!"

"Overruled. You better be getting to the point soon."

"Ms. Marsden, I wanna know verbatim what my client said to
Norris that day, and it better be exact, because my entire career
hinges on my memory." Dodge and Betty stared eye to eye. "If
you see yourself in my place one day, the inability to recollect
might cost you the life of your client."

Dodge signaled to MacQuillan with his eyes so only she could
see. "It isn't your relations with the higher echelon that will win
your cases in the future. Tell me...what did Lisa say?"

"I'm not afraid of you." Dodge thought she was speaking to
him. Betty's demeanor changed to a solemn one. "Mr. Norris,
you are no longer welcome in my house.

"Leave now or the police will make you leave. Get out you bastard."

"She warned him beforehand?"

"Yes. Then she pushed...she tried to push him out of the room.
He got angry and pushed her back. He was a very large man and
she fell down."

"Objection! The defense is leading my witness."

Betty continued, "When he pushed her he made a horrible
sound, not unlike a growl of rage. Every one of us there jumped.
It was all so unexpected. We were having a good time."

"Was his behavior provoked in any way?"

"Not from what I saw." Lisa felt herself smiling. She marveled
on how Dodge knew how to reach her. He took a gamble and
won.

"Thank you. No more questions."

MacQuillan couldn't have run faster to the witness stand if he tried. He was furious. "Does it make since to throw someone out of your house and call them a bastard for standing there?"

"No, but I knew nothing of their relationship before that day. There was a reason, I'm sure."

MacQuillan got in her face. "You thought you'd lie to this court to make yourself look good, is that it? That's perjury, Ms. Marsden."

"I did no such thing. I-I never lied."

Dodge thought that he would help Betty Marsden. "Now don't lose your temper because I was able to refute your witness's testimony. And she didn't lie. Not really."

"That'll be all, Ms. Marsden," said O'Neal. She lingered there for a moment until Dodge nodded for her to go.

O'Neal called for a fifteen-minute recess for the attorneys to gather their papers and thoughts, and for him to rest up before the next round of verbal punches. James got up to use the restroom and saw Robert again. Rebecca was in her usual seat by the door. James threw her a glance on the way out.

Lisa looked behind her. Rebecca's face lit up, but she was looking past her. Then she found Robert. She mouthed to him a "thank you" which was answered with a smile and a wave.

THE BAILIFF ORDERED ALL TO STAND AS JUDGE O'NEAL RETURNED TO THE COURTROOM.

MacQuillan didn't waste any time. He must have built his confidence back up after having lost most of it in the last round. "The state calls Victor Brago as its next witness." A middle-aged man of Italian descent took the stand.

"Mr. Brago...you are the proprietor of Old West Guns on the West Side?"

"Yes."

"For how long?"

"Seven years."

"Do you know why I asked you here today?"

"Because the defendant bought a gun from my shop."

"That's *right*," MacQuillan hit the table with his fist. He took a small piece of paper from one of his many files. "I submit this receipt as evidence. Read the items from this receipt aloud to the jury, if you will, Mr. Brago."

"One Smith & Weston .32 caliber derringer and one box of .32 caliber bullets."

"And the date purchased?"

"June 30th."

"Two weeks before Joseph Norris's death!" MacQuillan was in the jury's face as he spoke that very important statement. "And do you recognize this receipt as one from your shop?"

"Yes, this came from my shop."

"One more question." MacQuillan walked to the defense' side with determined stride and stood beside Lisa. "Take a look at the defendant. Do you remember her?"

Brago leaned forward to get a clear view of Lisa. "Not specifically, but there is a spark of recognition. I remember her face."

"I have no more questions."

"Uh, no questions."

"Your Honor," said MacQuillan. "I feel compelled to divulge to you and this court that I have one more witness."

O'Neal pulled up his sleeve to check the time. "You have an hour before lunch. How long do you estimate it will take for you to get through your witness?"

"Not long, Your Honor, but I'm sure counsel will redirect and that may take longer."

O'Neal laid his head atop of his fist, the customary position it seemed. "Continue," he said with a sigh.

MacQuillan threw the bailiff a signal. "The state calls Louis Jacobi to the stand."

That big, sweet, baldheaded man hobbled in. His eyes met with Lisa's across the room.

"Larry," Lisa whispered.

# CHAPTER THIRTY FIVE

**M**ayfield was at a loss.

For some reason he felt obligated, a nagging urge of inner council telling him there was more for him to do. He had fulfilled his duties to Lisa. To do more would be going beyond the qualifications of the job.

The stumped detective had been sitting in his armchair for hours. Ruth knew all too well not to bother him when he was like this. It wasn't often that a case would get under his skin.

Mayfield had a backlog of cases at the office. Why not work on something fresh and clear his mind of this mess? Because Lisa was in danger. But that wasn't his problem anymore. Besides, she was in a place where no one could reach her.

Why couldn't he let go?

He had his suspicions. However, he didn't want them to be known to anyone of authority without proof. They failed the first time. Most killers always try again.

What more could Mayfield do?

"HE'S TESTIFYING AGAINST ME," said Lisa, a faint quiver in her voice.

Dodge whispered to her, "He had no choice. He was subpoenaed."

MacQuillan began, "Tell us your name and occupation."

Larry sat stiff in his chair the same as Lisa. "Louis Jacobi. I'm the owner and manager of Larry's Diner."

"What're your duties there?"

"A little of everything; I cook, serve the patrons, wash dishes."

MacQuillan asked the questions without even looking at his witness. Instead, he read from the deposition like he was reading a script.

"Why don't you tell us a little about yourself?"

"Like what?"

"Where you were born, your marriage, and so forth."

"Your Honor, do these questions serve a purpose?" asked Dodge.

"I see no problem," replied O'Neal. "Providing it doesn't take too long."

"Carry on, Mr. Jacobi," said MacQuillan.

Larry shifted his eyes ever-so-slightly, seeing Lisa with the quickest of looks. "I-I was raised in a small Jewish neighborhood in Brooklyn. I spent thirty years of my adult life as a bridge constructor and bridge maintenance.

"Every night after I'd get home, I would cook the family a meal with last week's earnings; that's always been my true passion. When I was in my late twenties, I met Genevieve who worked at the local flower shop. Six weeks later she was my wife."

Lisa knew the story by heart. She couldn't help feeling a tad jealous of his marriage. That's the kind of relationship she sought with Robert and James, and both fell short of those expectations. Larry and Genevieve were married for more than thirty years and couldn't have enjoyed each other more.

Lisa wasn't naive to the point she expected perfection, but she never expected the relationship to be tested to this extent. She saw herself devoted to this one man for the rest of her life.

"I had a hand in the Triborough Bridge. I'm proud of that. The diner came after I retired. Genevieve and I used up all our savings as a down payment on the place. That's when I met Lisa."

"After you bought the diner?"

"Not exactly. Lisa came to work for me in 1949 around Hanukah. She had just moved to Manhattan and needed the work, and I needed the help. I previously hired three young girls to wait tables and a dishwasher.

"Money was tight enough without having to pay out to dead-weight. Lisa did the work of all three, so I chucked the others and made her a constant full-time employee." Larry smiled at her. "She stayed with me for nine years. I would say it was a wise decision."

MacQuillan allowed him to talk even though he was praising the defendant. Dodge knew he had something up his sleeve. How would it look to a jury if a man who was open about his caring for Lisa presented the most devastating evidence against her? How would Dodge be able to refute that testimony? There was a reason MacQuillan saved this testimony for last.

"She sounds perfect. Why did she quit?"

"She never gave me a reason."

"That's odd. A woman works for you for *nine years* and then one day at random comes up to you and says, "Mr. Jacobi, I can't work for you anymore. I quit."

"That isn't how it happened."

"Enlighten me."

"I got the impression she didn't want to."

"Why would you think that?"

"Because I know for a fact she loved her job. She liked her customers, most of whom she learned the names to, and they liked her. The diner was hers as much as mine."

"When did this happen?"

"In April. She stayed long enough for me to find a replacement, and she also trained her replacement."

"Don't take this the wrong way, but it is a waitressing job after all. You're telling me she stayed for nine years because she likes people and then quit. No details, no explanations."

Larry exhaled. "Yes."

"Why?"

*Condescending jerk.*

James was growing anxious, recalling his last conversation with Larry when he blamed him for Lisa quitting.

Larry responded with, "I believe her husband was the cause."

James bit his upper lip.

"Dr. Mallory is a prominent, wealthy, somewhat snotty man, and I got the impression he didn't like his wife working such a menial job. Menial to him. You should have seen her face the second she laid eyes on him, and then you would know what I'm talking about. She would've quit if he asked her to."

"How do you know this?"

"I was there. They met at the diner. The following weeks she was off her game, because her mind was on him." Larry pointed at James with his eyes.

"You can't tell us what was on the defendant's mind. We'll come back to this later. Tell us about Mrs. Mallory leading up to that night."

Larry changed position in his chair. His eyes kept shifting to Lisa all the while he spoke. "She was bothered. Her performance in her work suffered. She even forgot to come in one day."

"Go on."

"For about..." Larry cocked his head as he thought back. "I'd say about a month before this dreadful mess, Lisa was deeply troubled. I tried talking to her."

"Is it possible she was anxious about her impending plans?"

"Objection!" Dodge's voice echoed up to the high ceiling.

O'Neal was in agreement. "Mr. MacQuillan, you must know that's wrong."

"I apologize to the council for the defense. To rephrase, in what way was she anxious, Mr. Jacobi?"

"She barely talked, which was unlike her. I called her every night after work to make sure she made it home safe."

"You must have been concerned for her state of mind."

"When you know someone as long as I've known Lisa, you would be able to tell when they are not themselves."

"Is it possible the defendant was worried about something, scared maybe?"

Larry gave a hesitant but truthful, "Yes."

"What do you remember about the 18th of July?"

Dodge, as with every witness MacQuillan introduced, took notes on their every word and minute mannerisms; anything that would assist in his redirect.

"I remember that night vividly because it was Lisa's last day. Susan, Lisa's trainee, was ready to hold down the fort. Lisa picked the 18th about a month in advance."

"Hold it!" MacQuillan called out. "You just said she picked her last day one month before. Correct me if I'm wrong, but isn't that around the same time her behavior changed?"

Larry stammered, "I-I-I don't know."

"That *is* what you said, isn't it?"

Lisa watched him with pity. He must have realized how it sounded and was struggling to come up with another motive other than some imaginary master plan of hers.

"Don't you remember, Mr. Jacobi? You said it not one minute ago."

Lisa tugged on Dodge's pants. "Wait," said Dodge. "The-the prosecution is bullying his own witness for God's sake. Surely there's a rule against that, Your Honor."

"Overruled."

Larry wiped the sweat from his brow. His head was sunk so low Lisa could no longer see his face. He spoke soft and faint. "You're right."

MacQuillan rephrased Larry's words louder to the jury. "So... Mrs. Mallory became distant around the same time that she chose the 18th to be her final day working at your diner. That night Norris is brutally murdered in cold blood."

Dodge threw his chair aside as he leapt up.

O'Neal stood and leaned over the bench. "You are out of line! I'm not gonna warn you again!"

"Yes, Your Honor." MacQuillan returned to his table. "Why do you think Mrs. Mallory chose July 18th?"

"I didn't ask."

"Didn't you have any say in the matter?"

"Should I have? I couldn't make her stay if she didn't want to."

"Fair enough. About July 18th – I interrupted you. Please continue."

"What? Oh, um...it was dusk. She was getting ready to leave. I noticed she was sad and went to see how she was doing.

"I assured her once more that she didn't have to go. Anyway, we said our goodbyes. She also said she had a lot of things to take care of."

"What things?"

"I don't know. She also said she was late. For what, I don't know. That was the last I saw of her until I went to visit her at the hospital."

Lisa wished now that she told Larry about her appointment with Russell Sheridan. The fact that James found out was upsetting enough without her privacy turning into an open book for all to hear.

"Let's back up a bit. You were at the party, correct?"

"I was."

"If I may remind the jury – the party I speak of is the one given by the defendant for her sister-in-law who graduated law school. Testimony of the party was given to us by Betty Marsden. I would like to hear your side of what happened."

Larry opened his mouth to speak but Dodge beat him to it. "Your Honor, with all due respect to Mr. Jacobi, we have already heard testimony of the party from another witness of the prosecution. Is it necessary to hear the same testimony from a different person?"

O'Neal considered Dodge's words as he chewed his glasses. "Objection overruled. Different witness – different testimony. You may continue, Mr. Jacobi."

"It was in April..."

"Again, in April. Mrs. Mallory, at the same time she gave you notice, was also preparing a party where there was a struggle with Joseph Norris. Go on."

Larry continued with a hint of dread in his voice. "Anyway, my wife and I were the first to arrive. Lisa and James were preparing the house. When Rebecca arrived, we toasted her achievement and moved into the living room for gifts."

"What was your gift to the budding lawyer?"

Rebecca gave a touch of a smile.

"A typewriter," Larry answered. "It was while we were in the living room that Mr. Norris showed up. I was sitting next to my wife by the fireplace when everybody got quiet. That's when I noticed Mr. Norris by the door and Lisa in front of him. She was saying something, but I couldn't hear."

"What happened next?"

Larry changed position again. "Um...well, she told him to get out."

"She didn't say, "Get out you bastard?""

"She-she might have."

MacQuillan paced in front of Larry with the intention of making him nervous. "Either she did or she didn't, Mr. Jacobi. Which was it?"

Lisa hated MacQuillan more and more. Larry, by his outward manifestations alone, was suffering having to throw her under the bus. Larry mumbled, "Get out you bastard."

"And then what happened?"

"He pushed her down and was gone in a flash."

"I have just a few more questions. Back to the beginning when I asked you why the defendant quit her job at the diner, you said it was because you thought her husband was the cause. Did it ever occur to you that Joseph Norris may have been the cause?"

"I didn't know the man."

"It wasn't a lack of thought on your part?"

Larry was growing tired, along with the frustration that follows. "I told you the truth to the best of my knowledge, which, as far as I'm concerned, *is* the truth."

"Consider the facts you've presented to this court today." MacQuillan walked back to his table and read from the deposition. "It says here the defendant, using your words, didn't want to quit her waitressing job at your diner but did so because of her husband."

"That's right."

"Yet, at the party around the same time she throws Norris out of her house for no good reason."

Larry stood out of his chair. "I never said that!"

O'Neal banged his gavel. "Sit down." Larry eased down slowly.

"What was the reason then?" asked MacQuillan, sustaining his composure. Larry pulled his tie away from his collar. "Did the defendant ever mention Joseph Norris to you?"

"No."

"I thought you were friends?"

"We-we are."

"It was Norris – he was the source of her quitting! She chose July 18th, the day Norris was murdered, to be her last day at the diner! Are you going to sit there and tell me that's a coinciden-ce?"

Lisa couldn't stand it. She lowered her head to the table and hid her face in her arms. Dodge told her to sit up.

"She had even become distant and reserved."

"Yes."

"And the night of July 18th she had a lot of things to take care of."

"Yes!"

"She quit her job of nine years out of the blue." MacQuillan locked eyes with Lisa. "Some coincidence," he muttered. "Thank you, Mr. Jacobi, you have been a very helpful witness." Larry slouched in his chair.

"You may cross-examine, Mr. Dodge."

O'Neal intruded as Dodge was about to start. "We will break for lunch and then the defense may cross-examine. Court will reconvene in one hour."

"HOW'RE YOU FEELING?" Dodge presented a pleasing smile to Larry.

"Aright, I guess," said Larry. "I've had better days."

"I'll make this as quick and painless as possible." For the first time in the trial Dodge took his notes with him to the witness stand. "Okay now...there is one thing I would like to clear up first. To use my client's words, according to you, you say that she had a lot of things to take care of. You don't know what those "things" were?"

"No."

"Mr. MacQuillan suggests "things" was the planning and execution of murdering Joseph Norris. My question to you is if Lisa Mallory was planning on killing Norris in cold blood, to use MacQuillan's words, would she be dumb enough to tell you about it?"

"I-I object, Your Honor," blurted MacQuillan. "How could Mr. Jacobi possibly know what the defendant was talking about?"

"Forgive me, Your Honor, but doesn't the question also apply to Mr. MacQuillan? He somehow knows she was talking about murder? The question was rhetorical."

"Refrain from asking rhetorical questions, Mr. Dodge."

"Do you agree "things" could've meant anything?"

"I do." Larry relished in the casual questioning. It was their side he was on anyway.

"Would you say that you and my client are close, as friends go?"

"Definitely. She's like a daughter to me."

"You know her pretty well?"

"I think so. There is a certain degree of trust between us."

"About this change that you detected in the weeks preceding Norris's death, that is your opinion, right?" Larry looked at Dodge curiously. "What I mean is, it is your perception that she was acting out of the ordinary."

Dodge turned to speak to the entire court. "There is not one person here, including myself and Mr. MacQuillan, who can distinguish a person's behavior from the way it should be. Not unless you're a therapist who's been working with Lisa Mallory for several months. Are *you*, Mr. Jacobi?"

Larry didn't know how to take the question or if Dodge was serious. There was a suggestion of uncertainty in his no. MacQuillan scoffed in delight at this bizarre detour Dodge was taking.

"If she was planning to murder this guy, why would she make a spectacle of herself?" Dodge started jumping up-and-down and waving his arms as if signaling for a plane to land. "I did it! Come and get me! I killed him!"

Excluding O'Neal, everyone, including the jurors, found themselves giggling. A rigid frown formed on O'Neal's puss.

"You get what I'm saying, don't you, Mr. Jacobi?" Larry nodded. "Maybe she *did* quit because of her husband. Why not? Maybe she didn't want to endure the exhausting commute to Manhattan every day.

"Whether she mentioned Norris to you or not isn't definite proof that he was the cause of her odd behavior. And I'm not saying you made it up. I'm just saying that often what we see is not always what is."

Dodge was grabbing at straws and hemorrhaging badly, and Lisa could feel it. It was in the air.

"Do you believe in coincidences, Mr. Jacobi?"

"I-I guess I do."

"That's what July 18th was – a coincidence. It was her last day of work and Norris was killed in self-defense by my client. No one can prove otherwise because that is the truth. Mr. MacQuillan?"

When Dodge returned to his seat, he tapped his foot on the floor to a thumping only he could hear and a faint squeak coming from his chair only Lisa could hear, and that told her how her case was going.

MacQuillan didn't bother standing. He knew he won this round.

"Mr. Jacobi," he began. "If you could read signs of love on the defendant's face regarding her husband, don't you think you could distinguish changes in her personality?"

"I think so."

MacQuillan put a pencil up to his lip with a flicker of enthusiasm in his face. "When were the Mallorys married?"

"August of last year."

"Was it a nice wedding?"

Lisa looked at James; he didn't understand either.

"I thought so," Larry answered.

"Let me ask you this. If her husband was the cause of her quitting, why did she take so long?" Larry couldn't find the strength to answer the simple question.

"Well?"

Larry mumbled, "I don't know."

"I can't hear you."

"I said I don't know."

MacQuillan stated to the jury, "I can tell you it wasn't her husband that made her quit." He glanced at each member of the jury before closing his case. "I have no more questions."

The anger, confusion, and the frustration were building up inside of Lisa like a dam in a raging flood about to burst. Her Lady Luck was drifting out on the ebb tide. She almost wished Joe succeeded.

# CHAPTER THIRTY SIX

**"S**ign here, Mr. Jacobi," said Russell Sheridan pointing to the dotted line. "And you sign here, Mrs. Jacobi." Sheridan stood over them to verify.

"It's all done, Mrs. Mallory." He gathered the papers into an even stack. "Signed and witnessed." He knocked on the door to alert the guard.

Lisa breathed a sigh of relief. The guilt Larry was enduring was great. It wasn't his fault and he knew it deep down. Still, he was made a spectacle of, and he felt responsible for her case going south.

"Come on, dear," said Genevieve. "We have to go." Sheridan held the door open.

Larry didn't want to leave until something was said. He just couldn't. If the worst came to pass, how could he live with himself? It was more for his peace of mind than Lisa's.

Lisa told him, "Go. It's okay." Larry looked at his wife and back at Lisa. "Everything is alright." And between them it was.

Instantly, the guilt left him. Larry was regarded to Lisa as a caring employer, devoted friend, and father figure, none of which was going to change.

James saw Larry and Genevieve leaving with a man he didn't know.

"How are you, Ms. Lisa?" Lisa leapt into his arms in that moment. She began to weep into his chest. "What brought this on?"

Lisa had trouble speaking as the welt in her throat grew. "You...you haven't called me that in ages."

James lowered his head down to hers. The simple kiss slowly evolved into a locked embrace while the connection remained strong. When they parted it took a couple of seconds for them to regain their thoughts. The spark was still there.

"Um, why don't you sit down?" James pulled out a chair for her to sit and took her broken arm. "Is your arm causing you any pain?"

"No."

"I saw Larry as I came in. Who was that man with him, if you don't mind my asking?"

"Russell Sheridan."

James now had a face to go with the voice on the telephone. He wanted to know more without pushing her since she was adamant about not disclosing details. "Why was he here?"

Lisa shot him a glance.

"I'm sorry, darling." James took her hand. "Forget I asked."

Lisa couldn't think of anything to say to him. She was thinking, however, of the future and her own well-being.

*If I'm convicted, he will divorce me. How would we sustain our marriage from behind bars? He isn't about to stay married to a woman in prison. I'll be alone again.*

Lisa blurted the question with no introduction. "Will you marry again?"

James pulled away from her. He may have been offended by the insinuation that a divorce would even be considered on his part, much less hers.

"I'll be surrounded by high fences, walls, razor wire, and armed guards. What kind of relationship will we have if you have to go through all of that to see me?"

"Knock off that kind of talk. You're not going to be convicted."

"How do you know that? The way things are looking now that is a possibility we have to face."

James released her and walked to the corner. Lisa heard the exhales of exasperated breathing. "You're innocent. You know it and I know it."

"Like an innocent person hasn't been sent up before."

"We shouldn't be having this discussion. This isn't exactly how I wanted us to spend our time together." James was visibly upset and was struggling with his thoughts of what he wanted and what he would be forced to confront. "We've been married for a year and you're sticking divorce on the horizon?"

James took her shoulders in a strong but loving manner. "People don't just belong to themselves, Lisa. It's people that make up people's lives. People belong to people."

Lisa curled into his arms and laid her head on his firm chest. She could hear the faint beat of his heart. Softly, he whispered, "Don't give up on me."

"James...I-I....I can't stand this cage another minute. P-please take me away from here."

James tried to be the calm in the storm, his voice holding at an unwavering tone as he rested his head on top of hers. "You're staying right here."

"Why do you want to throw your life away for me?"

"My little waitress. My innocent little waitress."

# CHAPTER
# THIRTY SEVEN

FRIDAY, OCTOBER 16, 1959 – THE DEFENSE

MacQuillan would be at the top of his game now that the proverbial ball was in Dodge's court. It had reached that crucial point and purpose of the trial.

Dodge called his first witness, Sgt. Gary Vallencourt, the policeman who filed the report of Lisa's alleged attacker. Dodge, with his head cocked to the left and a stern look, asked the first question.

"On Monday, June 22nd you filed an Assault and Battery complaint for Lisa Mallory, did you not?"

"I did."

"Would you mind telling us about it?"

"Not at all. I was working desk that day and your client," Vallencourt pointed to Lisa, "came into the station, clearly upset and with a legitimate complaint. I poured her a cup of coffee and asked her what was upsetting her. She proceeded to tell me of a mysterious gray Chevrolet that made numerous attempts to run her off the road.

"She couldn't tell me for sure if the assailant was trying to take her life. However, she did tell me they were experienced behind the wheel."

MacQuillan interrupted, "Objection. Your Honor, how would the defendant know what an experienced driver drives like, much less their technique."

"That sounds like a sexist remark to me," barked Dodge.

"I'll overrule the objection. Continue, Sgt. Vallencourt."

"Anyway, Mrs. Mallory told me she was unable to elude them until she reached city limits."

Dodge leaned against the witness box with his arms crossed. "What details did she give you of the assailant?"

"She knew the assailant was male because she caught a glimpse of his arm. From her description he was a large man with a leather jacket and a hairy hand."

"For the record, the prosecution has a copy of said report. Go ahead, Sgt. Vallencourt."

"I filed the A and B and informed Mrs. Mallory, in all honesty, not to count on much."

"That doesn't sound very encouraging."

"It was the truth. The vehicle described was probably rented, and without plates it would be impossible to locate."

"In your opinion, what did you think of Mrs. Mallory?"

"She was a polite, charming woman who was genuinely upset. I felt it was my duty to help her. I knew filing the A and B wouldn't do much good, but just the act of doing *something* was enough to take the edge off."

Dodge faced the jury. "She must have been frightened to go to the police in the first place. Your witness, Mr. MacQuillan." Dodge grinned at his father sitting a couple rows back, proudly or enviously watching his son and old friend on the battlefield.

MacQuillan had a copy of the report in his hands and was reading it. "Sgt. Vallencourt, how long have you been a police officer?"

"Five years an officer, eight years a sergeant."

"Do you get much crime in Greenwich?"

"Not as much as here, I bet." MacQuillan was not amused. Vallencourt tried to rescue himself. "I stay busy."

"So, out of the goodness of your heart, you took time out of your busy day to file a report which you knew would be a waste of your time and hers." Vallencourt took a breath to answer, but MacQuillan didn't allow him to. "Your Honor, I have a witness I asked here today in the event that I might need him and I wish to use him as a rebuttal witness."

O'Neal nodded. "You may step down, Sergeant."

"The state calls Officer Hammond to the stand. Bailiff, would you bring in the witness?"

Lisa had no idea who this man was; just another guy in a suit like every other man in the courtroom. It wasn't until she heard his voice that she remembered him.

*"What happened to your car, ma'am? Get in some sort of accident?" asks the deep-voiced cop in an irritated manner.*

Lisa, still clutching the wheel, is incapable of answering. "You were exceeding the speed limit by thirty mph. I'm afraid I need to see your license. That is if you have one."

How did the Prosecuting Attorney find out?

"I had to tell him, Lisa," Dodge whispered to her. "It's called disclosure."

"Officer Hammond," MacQuillan began. "Where do you work?"

"Springdale, Connecticut."

"How far away is Springdale from Greenwich?"

"Oh, to render a guess, I'd say around a thirty-minute drive."

"Not very far. Now..." MacQuillan meandered over to the jury. "Explain to this court the circumstances of your encounter with the defendant."

"I ticketed her with a fine for reckless driving and speeding. I was parked on the outskirts of town and saw her barreling down the highway, all while nearly running two vehicles off the road. It was at that time I switched on my siren and pulled her over." Hammond was hamming it up, siphoning all the attention he could.

"Did she give you a reason for her actions?" asked MacQuillan.

"She attempted to hand me some malarkey about a maniac in a Chevrolet trying to kill her. All I saw was *her* driving like a maniac."

James's face was a blank. She lied to him that day, but he knew the truth now. It was a long time ago. More than likely he was attempting to dredge up the details from the memory banks.

"I have here a copy of Sgt. Vallencourt's report and I see it's dated Monday, June 22nd. I also have a copy of the fine. It's dated Sunday, June 21st. What car was the defendant driving?"

"I can't recall the make, but it was a fine automobile."

"It was a Buick Lesabre. One would think such a car could easily outrun a Chevrolet. That is if there was anything to outrun."

"Objection!"

"No more questions."

Dodge rushed to the witness. "Mr. Hammond, what state was the car in when you pulled my client over?"

Hammond quickly replied, "I can't recall."

"But you can recall the quality of the car. Try real hard."

Hammond glanced over at the jury. "I do recall a bunch of dents and scratches, but I chalked it down to poor upkeep."

Dodge got in Hammond's face. "Is it possible you were so focused on my client that you never noticed a gray Chevrolet?"

"I guess."

"You guess?! I'm finished with this witness," Dodge uttered with a repulsed tone.

"Step down, Mr. Hammond," ordered O'Neal. "Is there more rebuttal, Mr. MacQuillan?"

"Yes. I call Michael Patrick to the stand."

Lisa tugged on Dodge's arm. "Where is he digging up these people?"

Dodge seemed as much in the dark as she was. His sturdy façade was crumbling little by little and revealing the true man behind the big words. He had his doubts just as Lisa, but it was his job to give her the best defense he could, and that goal was becoming more and more of a challenge.

MacQuillan was quick to begin. "Mr. Patrick, what is your profession?"

"I'm a mechanic."

"Where are you based?"

"Greenwich." He appeared to be a polite young man who didn't mind being there.

"On Sunday, June 21st a 1959 Buick Lesabre came into your shop, correct?"

"Yes, sir. That day that nice-looking lady came in and begged me to buff out the scratches and dents. It was badly banged up."

"Why did she have to beg?"

"We're closed on Sundays, but we do work on occasion to catch up. Our workload was piling up, but I made an exception. The interesting thing that stood out to me was she had to have it back within a couple of days. There was at least five days' worth of damage."

"Allow me to clarify for the jury. Mrs. Mallory, who went to the local police for help, thought it more important to fix her car first."

Dodge interrupted MacQuillan, "What kind of remark is that?"

The outburst angered O'Neal. "You will use the proper method of objection, Counselor!" Dodge sat back down.

MacQuillan erased the faint smile and resumed his poker face. "That doesn't make sense to me. If someone tried to run me down with their car, the nearest police station would be my next destination."

"Objection," said Dodge. "The prosecution is attempting to influence the jury."

MacQuillan's demeanor was one of arrogant certainty. "The defendant managed to outrun her assailant, so how good of a driver could they have been, unless they never intended on killing her?"

"Objection! Objection! Mr. MacQuillan is again making sexist remarks. There is no room in this court for those kinds of Neanderthal ethics."

MacQuillan maintained his composure. "Your Honor, there is also no room in this court for abuse. Verbal or otherwise"

"Enough!" O'Neal pounded his gavel. "I will not allow this childish bicker in my courtroom. I sustain Mr. Dodge's objection. Now go on!"

"It's not my opinion. It's fact. Lisa Mallory waited a whole day to report this "attack" and thought it more urgent to fix her car.

There is no proof there was ever a gray Chevrolet because, for whatever reason, she repaired the damage."

Two men on the jury sitting side by side in the back row nodded their heads.

It was Dodge's turn. Could he turn this around somehow? Still, it was important to look confident.

"Mr. Patrick, what was the damage to the car exactly?"

"There was no internal damage. The entire driver's side door was smashed. There were multiple scratches and scrapes, chips to the paint, all external. Even the back glass had to be replaced."

Dodge thought carefully before asking the next question as not to get ahead of himself. "What was your personal opinion of the damage?"

"Either she is the worst driver that ever hit the streets or she has an enemy."

"Why do you say that?"

"There's no other explanation, unless she took a sledge hammer to the car."

*Yes! Yes!* Lisa rejoiced inside.

"If she wasn't attacked, then why did she have to take her car into the shop in the first place?" Dodge spoke to the jury as well. It was an effective tactic to bring them to a more personal level. "I'm finished."

MacQuillan wasn't.

Dodge stopped dead in his tracks and closed his eyes in dread. After he ended on such a high note he didn't bother sitting down. Each witness was an individual battle and he was ready to fight for this one. No matter what MacQuillan came up with he was ready to think up something better.

"Is it so farfetched, Mr. Patrick, so fantastic to think that maybe the defendant *did* take a sledgehammer to her 1959 Buick Lesabre?"

Dodge pounced on MacQuillan, "How is the witness supposed to answer that?"

"I withdraw the question. When she brought the vehicle into your shop, didn't you ask about the condition of the car?"

"It's not my job to ask questions."

"I didn't ask you what your profession entails. I asked if you questioned the car's state. You shouldn't have to think too hard if you're telling the truth."

"I-I guess you can say I was curious. She was shaken up. My first reaction was that she was in some sort of accident."

Putting a finger to his lips in imaginary puzzlement, MacQuillan sat on the edge of his table and spoke aloud to himself, a cheap way of telling the jury what he was thinking. "Obviously, Mrs. Mallory thought up a reason for the damage that night and decided to report it as an attempt on her life the next day. It does help her case."

Dodge charged over to MacQuillan like he was going to belt him. "Are you trying to make this court believe that my client would file a fake report as some elaborate scheme so months later it would look good in court today?! Get real, Al."

"Counselor!"

"Sorry. Objection!"

O'Neal pointed his gavel at MacQuillan, "Keep your thoughts to yourself, Mr. MacQuillan. The jury will disregard that last statement. And finish up with this witness. We have a lot to get through." O'Neal plopped down in his chair with a swivel and a squeak.

Dodge ambled back to his table. Lisa kept her eye on him. He was livid.

MacQuillan resumed, "One more question. Why do a weeks' worth of work in two days? All because she begged you?"

"She paid me extra."

Lisa's head dropped. It was true, and she didn't tell Dodge.

"Thank you, Mr. Patrick." MacQuillan turned and grinned at Dodge.

Dodge could tell by Lisa's face that it wasn't a shock to her. She was frightened out of her wits at the time and trusted no one, and total secrecy was strived. Lisa didn't know what her husband's reaction was because she chose not to look at him. She felt an increasing feeling of unease in the air, and it was emanating from behind her. She couldn't bear to look at either of the men she was dependent upon.

Court broke for lunch. The moment the pounding of the judge's gavel reached everyone's ears the entire court stood in unison. James watched as the bailiff took Lisa out through the door on the side. It didn't take him long to discover Robert watching also.

This was turning into a bad habit and of concern for James. This time he was going to say something. There was a gridlock of people at the door. James wiggled and swerved around the people between him and Robert before catching him as he was about to exit.

James grabbed his arm. "Hey, I'd like to talk to you."

"Let's clear the path." Robert didn't seem nervous that James was confronting him. In fact, it seemed he was anticipating it. "Yes? Can I help you?"

"You're joking." James was a couple inches taller and used it. "Why are you here? Scratch that – I don't like it."

"You and Lisa are no longer married. She doesn't need you here."

"Mr. Mallory, there's no cause for jealousy here."

"No?"

"No. I'm a married man and expecting my first child soon. I don't want to steal Lisa away from you."

"You were a married man when you came to my house to see her, weren't you?" Robert lowered his eyes. "Why are you here?"

"Because she asked me."

MAYFIELD WAS ALSO IN THE COURTROOM THAT DAY waiting for the opportunity to speak to Dodge. As soon as court broke for lunch, Mayfield pushed through the people to get to him.

Dodge was putting away his papers into his attaché case and cursing under his breath at the staggering defeat he was facing with the day only half over.

"Mr. Dodge," Mayfield called out. "Hey, young man!" Dodge was surprised to see him there. "I have to talk to you."

"Have a seat." Dodge pulled out Lisa's chair for him to sit. "What's on your mind?"

"I don't need to ask you how the case is going. I saw enough."

"Yes, yes, get to the point."

"Okay, I'll get to the point and stick you with it. Lisa told me of a death threat she received months before her attack."

"Death threat? What're you talking about?"

"Just listen to me. This death threat was the start of multiple attempts on her life, a prelude as it were, and the only physical evidence proving there was danger to her life."

Dodge chuckled, "W-what kind of ding-a-ling would warn his victim before trying to kill her?"

"I've been thinking about that and I've concluded it must be money." Mayfield could tell by Dodge's face that he shrugged it off. "Open your eyes, kid! All of this started after she married that rich husband of hers."

"Here we go again." Dodge rubbed his neck in fatigue and frustration.

Mayfield spoke with candor and laid his hand on Dodge's shoulder. "Lisa isn't supposed to be alive. She killed Norris, but she has another enemy, a more dangerous enemy. I can feel it."

Dodge contemplated Mayfield's words. He was accustomed to hearing people make their cases. Whether or not he believed in the truth of the words is a different matter, but he believed the man.

"If what you say is true, then I must have it."

"I've already looked for it once at Lisa's request, but it wasn't where she said it was."

"What're you gonna do?"

Mayfield took out a key from the inner pocket of his jacket. "I still have the key to the house. I'm going back tonight."

# CHAPTER THIRTY EIGHT

**1** 2:32 a.m.

The house sat dead upon the hill.

Mayfield drove past the house to make certain no one was there. He parked about a block away and took only a flashlight with him. He made his way up the cobblestone driveway.

A warm wind brushed through the trees, breaking the silence with shaking leaves and twisting twigs. He kept his eye out for passing cars on the road. There wasn't a light or a soul for miles.

He slipped the key into the lock.

The stillness of the house gave Mayfield the opposite feeling. All he could hear was the faint ticking of clocks. He stood at the center of the foyer while he got his bearings. He was not to turn on any light, so he kept the flashlight at his side to guide him through the pitch darkness.

He took each room one by one, starting with the downstairs. 8,000 sq. ft. of house would take a while to cover. The den was first, and then the living room. He checked under cushions, behind pictures, under rugs, and inside every piece of furniture with a drawer. He even thought to look under the chairs and sofas, and found nothing but the accumulating dust bunnies that lived there.

Next was the kitchen. Mayfield wasn't expecting to find anything of importance there which is why he searched it. He looked in the cupboard, all the cabinets, behind every glass and plate. The remaining rooms on the floor were the dining room, three guestrooms, rec room, and a couple bathrooms, and Mayfield covered each one with a fine toothcomb. The garage and basement would be last if nothing turned up on the second floor.

The upstairs was next. The circle of light remained one step ahead of him and lit each step as he ascended the curved staircase. The individual rungs cast tall shadows on the white wall. Mayfield paused before reaching the summit; the long hallway was hidden in black. He shined his light, but blackness swallowed it.

Since he was in Lisa's room before he decided to start there. Mayfield checked under the loose floorboard once again to no avail. The grandfather clock chimed downstairs, echoing throughout.

It was 4:00 a.m.

He rummaged through Lisa's bedside bureau and saw a crumpled envelope in the middle of all the junk; reading glasses, lipstick, candy, loose change, notepads.

"Yonkers," he whispered. He took out the paper within and there it was.

You are hated.

I am hated.

Be ready.

"This is it!"

There was a creak out in the hall; Mayfield threw his light at the door. It was a large house with wooden floors that are bound to make spooky sounds now and then. That was his way of thinking. He stepped out to check anyway.

The farthest door at the end closed a couple of inches. His eyes may have been deceiving him. He had little light to see by. Mayfield slipped the death threat in his breast pocket and went to investigate.

He shined the light into each room and scanned right to left like it was a POW camp. Then he reached what appeared to be James's office. He couldn't resist.

It was a simple room. There was a desk with a telephone and a lamp, a chair, and a bookshelf partially occupied. The desk held nothing of importance but bank statements and a stock ledger. It wasn't until he reached the bookcase that he found anything of interest – a black metal box.

Closer inspection revealed a key was needed to open the box. Mayfield knew the key wasn't anywhere in the room, so it was somewhere in the gigantic house never to be found, on James's person, or in one of the several dozen books in front of him.

Mayfield moved the box over to the desk. To his good fortune, the key happened to be underneath. He inserted the key. The lid almost lifted on its own.

An aged photo of a dark-haired girl in a wedding gown was taped on the inner side of the lid. The first item to catch his attention was a gold wedding ring with the letters *"E.N."* monogrammed inside. There was a newspaper clipping dated Monday, April 15, 1940 concerning the disappearance of a young socialite, Elizabeth Norris.

This girl was someone of sentimental importance, a relative of Joe's it would seem. He continued down the page to read she was the daughter of the prominent banker Samuel Moran of Moran and Brewer Banking and Loan of St. Louis.

"I'll be damned," whispered Mayfield, "the tax return."

The tax return that stumped him made sense now. The date on the tax return was for 1940 as well, but who was Henry Norris? Further digging uncovered more clippings of Elizabeth, more searches for the beautiful young lady, but as the years went by the trail went cold, and by 1947 Elizabeth was pronounced dead. Her body never found.

It wasn't until the last clipping, Friday, July 18, 1947, when Elizabeth Norris was pronounced legally dead by the courts that Mayfield read the words,

"She leaves behind her husband of nine years, Henry Norris, and their seven-year-old son, James."

Mayfield thought it odd that in all those years of coverage there was not one photograph of her husband and child. There was plenty of her in all her elegant beauty and her big shot father, but none of the mysterious Henry Norris.

At the bottom of the box was a birth certificate for James Mitchell Norris. At first glance he assumed it was James Mallory, but the date of birth was December 2, 1939. This must have been the child that was referred to in the last newspaper clipping. He would be going on twenty.

Henry and Elizabeth had a son named James, bearing the last name Norris. Based on the tax return that the unknown informant gave to Mayfield, Henry Norris worked for his father-in-law and made quite a living. Somewhere along the way Elizabeth disappeared, and was, in all probability, dead.

Who was James Mitchell Norris? Who was James Mallory? Was Joe Norris really just a friend to him? Why would he have these items so carefully locked away?

Mayfield didn't know how to tell Lisa. He put his hands in his pockets. At least he had the death threat. He couldn't wait to show her and Dodge.

He felt something was missing, or it was what he couldn't feel – the key to the house. He felt inside his pants pockets, jacket, and inner pockets. It had to still be in the door.

He rushed downstairs trying not to let his feet get ahead of the light. Sure enough, there it was. He breathed a sigh of relief and cursed himself for his carelessness.

When he returned to the office the birth certificate was on the floor.

A weird feeling came over him.

In the corner he could hear faint breathing. Male or female, he could not tell.

Mayfield grasped his flashlight tighter, so wishing this time he brought his revolver with him. He didn't want them to catch on that he knew of their presence there. He pretended to rifle through the clippings as if he hadn't already read them.

Would they allow him to leave if he chose not to face them? Clearly, they didn't want to be seen. If he put everything back as it was and left the house, they would be none the wiser and he would still have what he came for.

He *had* to know who it was.

Slowly, he pointed the light to the floor at their feet. As quickly as he raised the light the intruder came at him and bashed him on the head with a blunt object.

Mayfield went down.

# CHAPTER THIRTY NINE

It was early morning. Mayfield was coming to.

From his perspective, all he could see was light pouring in through the sideways window, and the floor. His cheek was red and pockmarked from the shag carpet. His head throbbed with pulsating agony from the piercing sunlight. He rolled onto his back and shifted his eyes in a daze.

The ceiling wasn't familiar to him. It took him a moment to remember where he was. Instinctively, he reached for his breast pocket.

It was gone.

The events of that night were coming back to him. Mayfield got to his feet before his head could catch up and he stumbled. He had to steady himself by bracing the edges of the desk to stand. His clothes were disheveled, shirt un-tucked, and jacket unbuttoned. He scanned the floor all around him.

"Dammit!" Mayfield kicked the desk as hard as he could. Being short of breath and with his head pounding from all sides he tried to focus his mind. The time was 7:21 a.m.

Mayfield picked his hat up from the floor and rested in the chair. "Dear God, what have I done," he spoke aloud, feeling the developed knot beneath his hair.

He came to the decision very quickly that before he did anything, he had to tell Dodge what happened. Besides that, he wanted to get the hell out of that house. He returned the box and key to the shelf and did just that. The drive back to New

York was a struggle. He found difficulty keeping the car straight, yet a hospital never crossed his mind.

All he could think of was getting to Dodge. When he made it to Dodge's office no one was in. The hours on the door showed that he did work on Saturday. Mayfield was an hour early. At ten minutes to nine Dodge's secretary came clopping up the stairs and he traded the hard bench for a cushioned chair.

"What happened to you?" Dodge saw Mayfield bent over holding an icepack to his head. Mayfield slowly looked up at the young attorney. He looked every bit like hell and one of its demons had a go at him.

"We can talk in my office," said Dodge. He helped Mayfield to his feet and led him to the small sofa. "Here, lie down."

"I don't wanna lie down."

"Well, can I get you a drink of water?"

"No."

Dodge asked him with wide eyes, "Did you find it?"

"I did."

"You did? This is fantastic!" Dodge held out his hand. "Show it to me."

"Use your head, kid! What does my present condition tell you?" Mayfield threw the icepack on the sofa. "I told you Norris had help, didn't I? You remember I told you that."

"I don't understand."

"Lisa is still in danger. I knew it."

"You're not making sense."

Mayfield shouted at him, "The death threat is gone! *Gone*, you imbecile! You understand *that*?!"

Mayfield hobbled behind the desk and stared down at the street below. "Somebody clobbered me and took it. Twenty years in this game and I didn't see it coming." He looked over at Dodge and back at the street. "I'm sorry, kid."

"Do you know what it said?" Dodge asked.

"You are hated. I am hated. Be ready."

"What does it mean?"

"Well, I believe that "hated" is an anagram for death."

Dodge repeated the words aloud, "You (Lisa) are hated. I am death. Be ready."

"It was posted as well. Yonkers."

"Who do we know is from Yonkers?"

"Her ex is."

"You didn't happen to get a look at the person who mistook your head for a baseball, did you?"

Mayfield sat down and returned the icepack to his head. "Actually...it hadn't crossed my mind until now, but I wonder if the person who clobbered me is the same person who gave me the tip on Henry Norris."

"Unfortunately, my hands are still tied. I'm not about to introduce a death threat that I can't produce. It's not that I don't believe you. I guess your bump on the head was for nothing."

Mayfield smiled, "I wouldn't say that."

To Mayfield's delight and Dodge's fascination, he went on to tell Dodge all that he found in James's office inside the black metal box and how none of the contents had been taken by the intruder. Between them they made a pact not to disclose any of Mayfield's findings or their subsequent conversation, with the exception of Lisa, but with an added warning of a nameless threat still running loose.

"Oh shit," Mayfield said. "I forgot to call my wife. She's probably mobilized the entire police force." Mayfield lifted the receiver on Dodge's desk, "I need to use your phone."

"Go ahead. I have a lot of preparation to do. Before court reconvenes Monday, I'm going to have it out with Al and that judge."

"ABSOLUTELY OUT OF THE QUESTION," stated MacQuillan clipping his words.

In the judge's chambers the attorneys bickered as O'Neal reclined in his wide leather chair, rubbing the elbow of his right arm and absorbing both sides like a spectator at a tennis match.

"Your Honor," Dodge leaned over O'Neal's desk. "How can you sentence someone, *a woman* especially, to life imprisonment or-or death without examining all the facts?"

"It is a defaming of character and I want it on record that I am opposed."

"Duly noted," said O'Neal. "Continue, Mr. Dodge."

"Evidence was found in Joe Norris's apartment validating he was a member of the KKK."

"It has zero bearing on this case. What does Norris's personal life from thirty-something years ago have to do with his brutal murder?"

O'Neal paused for a moment before looking Dodge in the eye. "I'm inclined to agree with him."

This was why Dodge didn't want him presiding as judge. He had gone over-the-hill and back again, grumbled about the constant aching of his deteriorating joints, which at times impeded his judgment, and was set in his ways. Still, he would not retire. It had something to do with old friends retiring and kicking the bucket soon after from boredom and a feeling of futility.

"Your client was a child at the time," added O'Neal. "She didn't even know the man. Why should I allow it? Convince me."

Dodge came prepared. "The jury must know because this is a window into the man's mind. It's solid proof of his character and what kind of man he may have been. None of us here knew him. All we know is what he left behind.

"It's not my intention to crucify. I want to show the jury he had a violent side and my client had no other option but to protect herself."

O'Neal appeared he was pondering Dodge's approach with possible concurrence. MacQuillan was picking up the same vibe.

"I agree."

"What?!" MacQuillan shouted.

O'Neal raised his hand. "I sense your hunger for the profession. I was a young lawyer myself once. That being said, you have defied my rulings more than once. I did not allow Norris's dismissal from the force into this trial, and yet you felt your opinion to be greater than mine.

"Whether it's pomposity or passion I do not know. I *do* know that if you did it once you will do it again. So, I'm warning you now. You will abide by my ruling or I will hold you in contempt and throw you in jail.

"My arthritis and bursitis are killing me today; there will be no hesitation. I don't give a damn if you are the son of Harrison Dodge. Do you understand me?"

"Yes sir, I do."

"Now, if I didn't want the beating incident in the trial, why would I allow this Ku Klux Klan gibberish? It seems a waste of time. Not to mention it would sway the jury."

"At least let me present some of it, Your Honor. Please." MacQuillan was gesturing to O'Neal from behind Dodge, shaking his head with the upmost disapproval.

O'Neal stood up from his desk. "I'll allow the picture and the robes. Not the Capitol march clippings."

MacQuillan was furious. "Your Honor..."

"It was a long time ago in the victim's past. I've made my decision. Let's get in there and see how far we can get today."

MacQuillan and Dodge glared at one another as they followed the judge out of his chambers.

# CHAPTER FORTY

"The defense calls Lt. Marc Robson." Robson sluggishly made his way to the front.

"You're still under oath," O'Neal reminded him.

Dodge stood facing the witness box with an unimpressed Robson staring back at him. "Lt. Robson, in your investigation, did you find anything that caused you to question the innocence of the deceased?"

MacQuillan, without lifting his head up, mumbled, "Objection. Leading."

"Sustained."

"Do you recall the date you searched Joe Norris's apartment?"

"July 21st."

"What did you find?"

"I object, Your Honor. What's wrong with a direct question?"

"Make your point, Counselor."

"Alright." Dodge moved in closer to Robson. "Did you in fact find evidence that Joseph Norris belonged to a certain well-known hate group?"

"I did."

"And what was that hate group?"

Robson hesitated. "The Ku Klux Klan."

If that didn't put Lisa in good with the jury then nothing would. She was surprised that the judge allowed even the slightest hint of what could sway a jury in either direction. Gregory Dodge must have put up a great fight.

Dodge leafed through a folder of photographs at his table and dug out a small picture stained with time and presented it to Robson. "Do you recognize this photo as one that you found in Norris's apartment?"

"Yes," he answered.

"Tell the jury what you see."

"It looks to be an induction photo. There are four men wearing the white robes that they wear and they're holding their masks. The young man in the center has been identified as Joseph Norris."

"Will you read the inscription on the back, please?"

Robson flipped the picture over. "June 16th, 1923 – *"Today I'm..."*

"Go on."

"It's faded but it says, *"Today I'm an official member."*

Dodge took the photo from Robson and handed it to a juror and instructed the man to pass it down. Meanwhile, he motioned to his secretary who handed him a long box. Dodge stood in such a way the jury couldn't see.

"Are you finished?" Dodge asked the elderly lady juror on the end. She nodded and handed him back the photo. "Okay, now ladies and gentlemen, what I'm about to show you will resolve any doubt you may have about the deceased Mr. Norris. You can make your own conclusions."

Dodge slipped the conical mask over his head. Each member of the jury gasped in unison, as did Lisa.

"These were found in Joseph Norris's apartment." Dodge held the robe out in front of him. "As you can see Norris was a much larger man than myself."

MacQuillan charged at Dodge, yelling at the top of his lungs. "This is insanity! The insolence! This is an insult to the dignity of this court!"

O'Neal shouted, "Take that off now!" The entire courtroom was angered by this very effective demonstration. "I warned you!"

Dodge took it off and fixed his hair. "I didn't think it would cause such a reaction. I was merely trying to make a point. I apologize."

O'Neal fell back into his chair. "Alright, alright, continue."

Dodge asked Robson, "Are these the robes that you found?"

"Yes."

"Where did you find them?"

"In a box in the back of his closet covered in three inches of dust."

"So, there isn't much doubt that Joseph Norris was in the KKK."

"No."

"For those of you who may not know, the Klan is a secret society formed after the Civil War believed mainly to resist the growth of Negro rights."

Lisa hoped the jury was intelligent enough to work it out for themselves, the fact that Norris was discharged from the force for beating a black man, although that slip-of-the-tongue was deemed inadmissible by the judge.

"Your witness."

MacQuillan leapt out of his chair like someone lit a match under his foot. Lisa found it amusing in a way. "Lt. Robson, you may have just said something crucial to this case. You said the robes were found in a box in the back of his closet under three inches of dust. Obviously, they hadn't been worn in a long time."

"Objection," said Dodge. "How could the Lieutenant know when they were worn last?"

"Sustained."

MacQuillan fished frantically for a thought. Only Robson and O'Neal could see the angst etched on his face. MacQuillan switched gears. "If I may change the subject, I meant to ask you before, when was Mrs. Mallory captured?"

"Um, I'm sure it was August 9th, but I'd have to see the report to be sure."

"In what manner was she captured?"

Dodge couldn't believe his ears. "Your Honor, this is supposed to be cross-examination on the evidence presented. He-he's going way out in left field somewhere."

"Where are you going with this, Mr. MacQuillan?" asked O'Neal.

"Just give me one minute." MacQuillan spoke to the entire court. "I'm sure we *all* have noticed her broken arm by now. I mean, she has it sitting on the table in plain sight every day." Lisa took her arm off the table. "How did that happen, Lieutenant?"

"She was eluding police and got hit by an oncoming car."

"The defendant was on foot running from police when she was taken into custody?"

"No, she was unconscious."

"I'm finished, Your Honor."

Lisa turned to her husband, but he was focused on the man across the room that, by all accounts, should not have been there.

"The defense calls Donald Wells."

Donald came through the double doors dressed in his finest gray suit and marched down the aisle in long-legged stride. When he reached the defense' table he turned to Lisa, but as his head turned, she turned hers away.

O'Neal ordered, "Get a move on, young man."

The clerk began. "Raise your right hand, please. Do you solemnly swear the testimony you're about to give in this case to be the whole truth, and nothing but the truth, so help you God?"

"I do."

Donald kept his eyes on Lisa. She didn't know if Dodge asked her brother to testify or if he volunteered. Dodge couldn't have known of his betrayal, but either way she saw this as a cry for attention, an attempt at a reason for forgiveness on her part, and a cause to see her again, but they were merely in the same room together. She considered none of those.

Dodge approached him in a kind and gentle manner. "What do you do for a living, Mr. Wells?"

"I'm a desk clerk at a motel."

"For how long?"

"Not quite a year – eight months. I was a cabdriver for six years, but I quit a couple weeks ago."

"Why is that?"

"Because both jobs were too demanding and I wanted to be here for my sister."

"Mr. Wells, tell us your account of this...horrible mess. How and when did you first come to find out what happened?"

Donald spoke very matter-of-fact in a callus tone. "Well, it was very early Sunday morning. Lt. Robson and his Sgt. *Dodds* came banging on my door, waking up my family. After relentless questioning and the probing of our apartment, they finally elected to tell us that Joe was killed and my sister was missing."

MacQuillan stood up. "I don't much care for the way the defense is allowing his witness to talk about two decent men of the New York Police Department."

"That must have been scary," said Dodge.

"It was. We had no idea where she was. I didn't think much about Joe."

"Objection! The witness is adding unwarranted comment."

"He's just being honest, Your Honor, telling the truth like he swore." Dodge gave Donald a shy smile, speaking softly as if his next question was not for public display. "You love her, don't you?"

"Of course, I do." Donald again looked at Lisa to no avail. "Very much."

"As brother and sister, you confide in each other, right?"

Donald didn't hesitate despite the reply was less than truthful. "Yes."

"Did she ever talk to you about any problems she was having with Joseph Norris?"

"No, actually. But I never liked him from the start. He wasn't exactly a people person. I first met him at a little party Lisa and James gave prior to their wedding. He told dirty jokes and became belligerent with my wife when she politely asked him to pipe down. He had been drinking before he got there."

"Is it possible the defendant warned you about this man beforehand and therefore you had a prejudged opinion?"

"She never talked about him with me. Not once."

"Did you pick up anything was wrong."

"No. She was the same old Lisa."

Lisa tried to be more in control of her reactions. She may have confided in Donald *if* he was around, which he was not, and the reasons still made her blood boil.

*What a good liar he is. Nobody but me knows. If he looks at me one more time.* Lisa turned away.

It was all very safe up to that point, the prepared questions and rehearsed answers. Donald was at ease. "Your witness," Dodge told MacQuillan.

Lisa was curious as to how MacQuillan would handle him. His demeanor throughout the trial was one of brash intensity, as if he was speaking simply because he liked the sound of the words. He used his tongue as a weapon and ambushed each witness at the precise moment, all the while coming across as the good guy in white.

"It's nice to meet you, Mr. Wells. We haven't been introduced. I'm Albert MacQuillan. Are you nervous?"

"Not really."

"There's no need to be. Now...you told the defense that you and your sister, the defendant, are close."

"Oh yes."

"You also stated that your sister never told you about Joseph Norris, correct?"

"That's correct."

"*So...*my question to you is if you and the defendant are the close brother and sister you claim to be, why didn't she confide in you these troubles she was allegedly having with the deceased?"

"Objection!" Dodge dashed around the table.

"Overruled. I would like to know."

Donald was stammering and wasn't sure if he should answer since Dodge opposed, but he had to, and did in the safest way he could. "There're many things in my life I never told her, but that doesn't mean I love her any less or that we aren't close."

"There's truth in that. However, this man, according to the defense, was endangering your sister's life. That's a bit more serious than, say, having an affair with a co-worker. If someone were out to kill me, I'd tell the police or my wife first, maybe even my mother-in-law. The point is I would tell someone, unless you look at it from the angle in which there was nothing to tell."

Dodge pounded the table. "Now the prosecution is adding unwarranted comment!"

O'Neal took a deep breath. "Don't make me remind you again to use the proper method of objection. Sustained."

Donald was now gripping the arms of his chair.

MacQuillan persisted, "Your sister was missing for three weeks and you didn't see her all that time?"

"What are you saying?"

"Three weeks is a long time. Then again, it's very convenient. Plenty of time to concoct a cover story. Mr. Wells, you seem like a bright young man."

MacQuillan leaned on the witness stand, peering eye to eye with Donald and using a blasé tone of voice. "Do you honestly expect this court and me to believe that you never saw you sister once in that time?"

For the first time in over a month Lisa looked at her brother.

"I'm not blind, Mr. Wells." MacQuillan backed away and raised his voice for all to hear. "It's come to my attention that the defendant has not looked at you once. There has been no communication *at all*! She's conversed with her husband many times... but not you. She won't see you when you visit."

Donald glared at MacQuillan under his eyes.

"You're an upstanding young man; married, two kids, hard working. Your sister on the other hand..."

Donald stood, with his hands clenched into fists. "I'll have you know Lisa was beaten black-and-blue! That monster almost killed her!"

Lisa grabbed Dodge's arm. "Greg! Do something!"

"Ob...objection!" Everyone's eyes went to him, but he didn't know what to say.

"Sit down, Mr. Wells," said O'Neal. "You will quell any temper in my courtroom."

Lisa was now frightened for Donald.

"She came to you one night, frightened and alone, a warrant for her arrest, seeking sanctuary." Donald locked eyes with Lisa. Her expression begged him to stop.

Within the eerie silence Donald's weak voice replied, "I didn't see her."

"Then how do you know she was beaten black-and-blue?"

"She told me." Donald spoke with conviction enough that MacQuillan didn't take it any further.

"When could that have been?"

"I can't remember."

"I have one more question."

"No," said Donald.

"I'm sorry?"

"I will not answer any more questions unless they are legitimate ones. Not questions you've already made up the answers to. My sister did not murder Joe Norris. I know Lisa better than anyone in this room, maybe even her husband.

"She hasn't a violent bone in her body." Donald stood again. He wasn't speaking to a particular person, but venting to all who could hear his frustration. "Look at her!"

O'Neal banged his gavel repeatedly. "That will be enough, Mr. Wells."

Lisa warmed to him as he defended her.

"What's happening here is wrong! There is little evidence to warrant a conviction except what the damn prosecution has blown out of proportion, and instead of celebrating her survival she must face a jury? It is ridiculous."

O'Neal shouted at the top of his lungs. "You've made your point, Mr. Wells! Sit down!"

"No! What kind of man would make a martyr out of a bigot and a drunk, and a murderer out of a woman who served her country? You have no right condemning an innocent woman. There is no justice in slander."

O'Neal ponded his gavel so hard it made a cracking sound like the end was about to break off. He lost his grip and it fell to the floor. "Bailiff, take him away! I want him out of my courtroom!"

The bailiff forcibly led Donald out. He didn't resist.

O'Neal asked Dodge, "Did you know?"

"N-no, Your Honor, I didn't know."

A clerk handed O'Neal his gavel. "The jury will disregard all testimony from the last witness. I want it stricken from the record."

Rebecca left the courtroom to go to her husband. MacQuillan was taken aback by the verbal punches Donald threw at him. Everyone was staring at him to see what he was going to do next. The brief silence provided him adequate time to put his face back on.

O'Neal spoke out of a long whispering groan. "I don't know about anybody else, but I need a break. Court will take a fifteen-minute recess."

Dodge had been contemplating if he should tell Lisa what happened to Mayfield. If she knew it would only add to her fear. When the opportunity presented itself, he decided against it. Mayfield put his trust in him to tell her everything, but Dodge's foremost concern was Lisa's acquittal. What was next to come was to take precedence over all else.

"I CALL LISA MALLORY TO THE STAND." Holding her bad arm, she made her way to the dreaded chair.

Against Dodge's advice she chose to testify with the approach that no one could defend her as well as herself. In his words, if the prosecution made mincemeat out of her then it would be on her, and it would be a coin toss whether or not the jury would like her.

Dodge gave her a wide and encouraging smile, though his entire body said different. She was closer to the jury than ever, and as she was being sworn in, she could feel their eyes on her back – the contemplation, the doubting.

Dodge instructed her to keep her focus on him at all times and no improvising. Answer only what's been asked and embellish nothing. He situated himself between her and MacQuillan and asked the first question.

# CHAPTER FORTY ONE

**D**on't be scared, Lisa. Sit here and smile. No, don't smile.

Lisa sneaked a quick glance at the jury on her left.

*If they see that I'm not scared then they'll know.*

"Lisa, did you hear me?"

Dodge was waiting for an answer, and apparently, so was everyone else.

"No, I'm sorry."

"There's nothing to be afraid of. Be honest and answer each question to the best of your knowledge." Lisa relaxed somewhat. "Tell us about your first meeting with Joe Norris."

She knew her guilt or innocence hinged on her every word. The jury could have already made up their minds.

"Well..." Lisa began. "It was well over a year ago. James and I weren't married yet. He took me to his place one afternoon and Joe was there; he had let himself in. James introduced us and that was it."

"What was he like?"

"I remember feeling uncomfortable. He-he kept staring at me. I know it doesn't sound strange, but I had this feeling even then."

"He was attracted to you."

James lowered his head.

Dodge carefully and meticulously drove her testimony with his questions. "What was the first alarming incident to occur?"

Lisa thought about it and remembered the time Joe stopped by unannounced. She wasn't allowed to mention the death threat, which was a major factor in the confrontation.

"He-he stopped by unannounced one day and came on to me." The expression on James's face was solemn and forbidding. "Quite strongly. My husband wasn't in the room."

*Joe's thick, hairy hand brushes the side of her face. "Loneliness is one of the deadliest poisons." He peels off the shoulder of Lisa's lilac blouse. His hot breath moistens her bare skin.*

"I'd never encountered a man like that before."

"In other words, you felt threatened." Dodge treated Lisa, not as a witness, but as a friend. She found herself more relaxed than she thought she would be because she kept her focus on him as he instructed.

*"I know you fear me," whispers Joe. "When Jimmy introduced us, I sensed it."*

Lisa drifted in and out of the past as she recalled certain details that had left her amidst the storm.

MacQuillan interjected, "Your Honor, how much longer must we be forced to listen to this nonsense? It is a complete waste of time."

*"I don't blame you for not believing me when I tell you Jimmy is a threat to you, but I'm not the one being threatened, now am I?"*

It was a warning. James was focused on her. He looked so different than he used to.

Dodge chuckled nervously at the judge. "Ahem. Lisa? Lisa, are you with us?"

"Oh! Um, I started seeing him at other places. That's why I banished him from the house. I knew he was following me."

"Was the incident with the gray Chevy included in that banishment?"

"No, that happened after."

"Interesting. What was this party? I know we've already heard, but I think we need to hear it from you."

"It was a surprise party for my sister-in-law for passing the bar exam. James and I spent a lot of time preparing for it. And then *he* showed up. He knew, too. He knew I didn't want him there.

"I made it clear that I didn't want him around me anymore. Rebecca was opening her gifts and I didn't want to draw attention, so I asked him quietly to leave. I remember the strong odor of alcohol on his person."

Lisa looked at MacQuillan who was taking notes on everything she said. Dodge took a step to the side to block her view of him. "What happened next?"

"I threatened to call the police. I admit to calling him a bastard and getting physical, but I couldn't take him anymore."

"Physical? Meaning what?"

"I pushed him. He did push back."

"You have no idea why he would show up unwelcomed?"

"I think it was to scare me. He wanted to get a rise out of me."

Dodge stood by the jury. "Let's talk about the incident with the gray Chevy for a moment. How did it happen?"

"I was out for a Sunday drive when a gray Chevrolet starting riding my tail. I tried to elude him and that's when he smashed into me as hard as he could. I could barely stay on the road."

*She sees the red tractor approaching and swerves to avoid it, but she doesn't know the gray Chevy is there acting as a barricade. She crashes into her tenacious assailant, but he resists against her.*

"He continued to ram into me like some madman."

"Norris was a cop so he would know how to drive."

"Objection! Argumentative," said MacQuillan.

"Sustained."

"And after you filed the Assault and Battery with Sgt. Vallencourt?"

"Of course, my life was in danger."

"Let's fast-forward to July 18th, the night of the attack."

*She gasps for air. His grip tightens. Those awful eyes.*

Quick, horrid flashes assaulted Lisa's mind. She closed her eyes tight hoping they would disappear. "I-I don't know where to start."

Dodge appeared as nervous as her and sensed her hesitation; he helped her along. "It's after dark, around 9:30. You're leaving work, you just said goodbye to your boss. Then what?"

"Um, well, I had an appointment with Russell Sheridan. That's where I was going."

"Who is Russell Sheridan?"

"He's the attorney handling my will. I asked him if he could see me after work and he agreed. I never made it to the appointment."

The memory if that night was never going to leave her. She managed to block it out so she could sleep at night, but now, with no effort on her part, it came rushing in. She gripped the chair tight as if bracing for a scary ride. Her heartbeat was escalating in response; thump, thump, thumping inside her chest as Joe stood before her once again.

*She reaches out, grasping for something to cling to. He swings around to prevent being kicked by Lisa's thrashing legs. She fights to open her purse beside her, but it isn't there.*

"You were reaching for the gun?" Dodge asked.

"That was my reason for purchasing it. Next thing I remember is blackness. I-I thought I was dead."

Lisa never imagined how difficult this would be.

Dodge spoke softly to her. "Take all the time you need."

"I needed to get to my gun. It was in my purse and my purse was...somewhere. The sidewalk. Yes, it was on the sidewalk. I-I-I almost made it, but..."

*She is yanked back by her hair.*

"I didn't have time to get the gun out of the damn purse. He pulled me back in."

*Lisa thrashes, but his iron grip constricts. He throws her into the trash cans. Her face bounces off the metal. He lunges his right foot into her stomach.*

James had never heard her speak of this before, and his struggle to listen in all its graphic detail intensified his feeling of the neglectful husband.

*Lisa sinks her nails into his left cheek. Her eyes are bloodshot and distended and stare into the visible darkness of those dreaded black eyes.*

The jury especially seemed to be eating it up. Surely, they realized no one could make up a story as detailed and personal as this. The courtroom was dead silent.

"I knew that if I blacked out again, I wouldn't wake up. Somehow, I got the upper hand. I don't know how, but my purse was thrown to the opposite end, I guess in the struggle."

*She rips open the handbag, but a force knocks her down. The contents spill out in front of her. Up Lisa's back he climbs. The derringer is out of reach. Lisa stabs her metal nail file into his hand; he screams and falls off her.*

Dodge added, "That explains the stabbing in the right hand. Go on."

*The gun is inches away. Lisa drags herself, pushing with her legs and pulling with her arms. He catches her ankle with his other hand.*

"No!" She spreads her fingers and can almost touch the edge of the barrel. She kicks and kicks until his grasp loosens and seizes the gun.

*He freezes.*

"You didn't just shoot him? You warned him first?"

"It all happened so fast. I pointed the gun at him, but I didn't pull the trigger."

"This is important. You're saying you didn't pull the trigger when you got the gun and pointed it at him?"

*There is a loud pop. Wetness drizzles onto her face.*

"I-I don't know."

Each member of the jury exhibited a look of disgust. Dodge stayed at her. "If you were going to shoot him you could've done so as soon as you seized the gun."

MacQuillan interceded. "I object on grounds of pure speculation. The defense is guiding the witness."

Dodge stood over Lisa. "Think hard. What gave you cause to pull the trigger?"

"He was trying to kill me. Isn't that cause enough?"

"Something made you take that shot. What was it?!"

"Objection!"

Lisa felt Dodge was harassing her and she was confused. "I-I was scared."

"Then you would've shot him immediately. That's not good enough."

*Joe's face suddenly morphs into one of rage and he lunges.*

"He lunged at me. I remember now. Yes, that's why I shot him."

Dodge was pleased and gave her hand a couple light taps. "And then what did you do?"

"Well...I panicked. I hid the body, picked up my things, and ran."

"Why didn't you go to the police? If you killed him in self-defense, you had nothing to hide."

"As I said before, I panicked. I wasn't thinking straight."

Next came the topic that would end up being the most damning evidence against her, and no one but her was to blame. Dodge stood his ground and braced himself for the following. "Okay...so now you're running. What do you do next?"

"I just remember thinking I couldn't go home." James leaned forward. "I called a P...."

Dodge mouthed a direct "no" to Lisa.

"I-I decided to hide – motel hopping."

"What made you venture out into public then? That is how you were caught."

"I was caught because I ran."

Lisa realized the majority of her testimony was "I don't remember" and "I panicked". She couldn't reveal the whole truth. Dodge was insistent to not adlib, even if it included her friend Edgar Mayfield, which she thought would help her case. Was it because private detectives had bad reputations? Did the general public think all PIs were Sam Spades with a lit cigarette drooping from their lip and a revolver in their belt?

"What did you do before you were a waitress?"

"I was a secretary for an insurance company for a year. I was a welder at the Navy Yard from '42 to '44."

"Where did you live?"

"Brooklyn until after the war. By then I saved up enough money to rent a small apartment in Manhattan. I loved my first apartment, but it was too steep, so I had to move again to a smaller one. That was when I met my first husband."

Lisa's eyes found Robert.

"August of last year I married James."

Dodge turned to MacQuillan, "She's all yours."

Lisa instinctively held her breath. The mild-mannered prosecutor had every intention of going for the throat.

"If the deceased was your husband's friend, why would he flirt with you?" Lisa started to answer but he didn't allow her. "You're an attractive woman, but that isn't a reason unless you gave him one."

Dodge was at the ready. He hadn't even made it back to his table. "The prosecution is making aspersions on my client's character. So what if she's attractive! Does that make her guilty of murder?"

"I repeat the question. Mrs. Mallory, why do you think a friend of your husband's would flirt with you?"

"For one, he wasn't my husband yet, *and* I don't think he had any scruples whatsoever."

"It's clear that marriage wasn't a boundary to him if we're to believe you."

"It's not up to me if you believe me or not." Dodge eased down into his chair. So far so good.

"A dying man has nothing better to do than follow you. How come? You said you saw him following you on more than one occasion."

"I'm not the one to ask. Only he would know that."

"That's real cute." MacQuillan appeared as if he was holding back. He was getting at something and both Lisa and Dodge sensed it. "Were you scared of him?"

"Uneasy."

MacQuillan went to his table and held up an envelope. "Do you recognize this? Yes or no?"

"Yes," Lisa mumbled.

"Speak up."

"Yes!"

MacQuillan withdrew the paper inside. "Starting at the top..."

You are invited to attend a graduation party in honor of Rebecca Wells on April 19th at 2:00 p.m. at the home of James and Lisa Mallory. If needed, directions are enclosed. Gifts optional. We look forward to seeing you.

Regards,

James and Lisa Mallory

"You invite Joseph Norris to this happy little gathering after your alleged run-in of which there were no witnesses. You have the gall to sit there and talk about this dying man like he was an animal, knowing you invited this animal to your party."

Dodge marched up to the judge. "I protest to the harsh treatment of my client! I will not stand..."

O'Neal took a deep breath in old age and exhaustion of the two headstrong attorneys. "Mr. MacQuillan, you may now include yourself in my previous warning to your opponent. Proceed."

MacQuillan returned his focus to the witness. "You banned Norris from the house and then sent him an invitation. Why?"

"I banned him after I sent the invitation. I didn't want him at the party, but he and James were good friends long before I came into the picture. I didn't know he was dying."

"Mrs. Mallory, on what grounds were you divorced from your first husband?"

Dodge barked, "Objection. Reasoning. What bearing does that have with this case?"

O'Neal was curious as well. "Let's see where he's going. Answer the question."

Lisa didn't feel comfortable since Dodge was against it, but she had no choice. "Adultery and mental cruelty."

"On whose part?"

"His."

"You divorced him?"

"No, he wanted the divorce."

"You were willing to forgive him?"

Robert's sympathy for her was plain to see. No one there would understand. It was a bond only they shared.

O'Neal asked, "Where are you going, Counselor?"

"Are you Catholic, Mrs. Mallory?"

"I am, but..."

"As a Catholic, isn't it against your faith to remarry unless the first spouse is deceased?"

"Objection! This is incitement!"

"Overruled."

"How did you come to marry Dr. Mallory if you're Catholic?"

"We had to marry in a Methodist church."

"After you were nearly killed by the Chevrolet you went to the police." MacQuillan glared at Dodge who was standing a few feet behind him. "Your Honor, I'm uncomfortable with Mr. Dodge standing so close to his client. He may be feeding her answers."

"Return to your seat, Mr. Dodge."

"Anyway, you put your car into the shop and the next day you reported it to the police. Can you explain that? Were you hiding something?"

"Yes."

"Yes, you can explain, or yes, you were hiding something?"

"Both. I didn't want my husband to know. He bought me the car for my birthday."

MacQuillan got in her face. "You thought it more crucial to fix your car! Your own actions dictate that fact. You mustn't have been very scared."

"No, no, you don't understand."

"There are no witnesses. Officer Hammond didn't see anything. For all we know you could've taken a sledgehammer to the car."

"I object. He isn't allowing my witness to answer."

"Sustained."

"Surely your attorney has given you sufficient time to come up with an answer."

"The officer didn't believe me. I pleaded with him and he turned his nose up at me."

"Your entire account of July 18th troubles me, however graphic you paint the picture. This attack doesn't make sense. You were on your way to keep an appointment with your lawyer and you expect us to believe that Norris knew exactly where you were going at precisely the right moment to pull you into that alley and kill you. Do you make a habit of making appointments with your lawyer at night?"

"No."

"So, there is no way he could've known."

"I-I don't know. He was following me before."

MacQuillan pointed his finger in Lisa's face. "Ah, but he was in the alley before you got there. He would have to be, wouldn't he?"

"I don't know! Maybe he did know where I was going!"

"But you said you didn't tell anybody."

Lisa lowered her head in defeat.

"You ran, Mrs. Mallory...*after* you shot Norris in the head. You placed the burden of proof on yourself and admitted guilt the second you ran."

"I panicked!"

"Then how come you had the foresight to hide the body?"

"I-I-I...uh, I didn't think anyone would believe me."

"Okay, I'll bite. Why not call the police then?"

Lisa's eyes searched for Dodge, but MacQuillan was in the way. *What do I say? This is my last chance. I can't think. Dear God! I can't think of anything!*

"You planned Norris's death. I know this based on one fact alone. You went to the police after the Chevrolet allegedly tried to run you off the road, but you didn't go to the police when Norris attacked you, which would have been the time to do so. The gray Chevy no one saw and the gun you purchased prior to July 18th points to your killing Norris premeditated."

MacQuillan faced the jury. "Norris was far from sainthood, but that doesn't mean he drug her into that alley." He glared at Lisa like she was garbage. "You disposed of the gun as well, am I right?"

Lisa said nothing.

"I have nothing more to say to this woman."

"I do," shouted Dodge, eager to tip the scale back in their favor. "How was he dressed?"

"I'm sorry?"

"What was Norris wearing when he attacked you?"

"He was wearing black."

"How much black?"

"All of him."

"Did Norris normally dress all in black?"

"I don't think so."

"And the pictures taken verify he was dressed all in black. If we're to believe this guy's story, you instructed Norris to meet you and wear black so that after you killed him the police would think he was the guilty party. Ha!"

Dodge made a dash for the prosecution's table. "Or maybe she had time to undress him and change his clothes! Try that on for size, Al!"

MacQuillan acted amused. "Pure folly."

"That'll be enough!" O'Neal fell back with a sigh. "I've had about all the backbiting I can take for one week. Hopefully, if my blood pressure holds out, we can reach an end by tomorrow. Are you finished?"

Dodge asked Lisa plain and simple. No hidden meanings or suggestion. "Lisa Mallory, are you innocent?"

This time Lisa willingly looked at the jury. "I am."

"Step down, Mrs. Mallory," said O'Neal.

MacQuillan explained, "Due to extenuating circumstances my rebuttal witness will not be able to testify until tomorrow, Your Honor."

Lisa couldn't have been happier to leave that chair. James vied for her attention. Deep down, unknown to even herself, her trust in him was gone.

The atmosphere was changed, leaving what felt like a dark and spiteful cloud above her.

# CHAPTER FORTY TWO

Alma stood at the window, staring blindly at the busy street below as the faint glow of a red neon sign blinked off and on. The burning circle of ember of her cigarette was the solitary light within the darkened room. She held the cigarette to her lips.

The doorbell rang.

She was anticipating it. She exhaled the smoke from her last puff and extinguished the cigarette. She first checked her hair and makeup in the mirror by the door.

Robert pushed past her. "Alright Alma, what's this all about?"

"After you," she said sarcastically. "Can I get you anything?"

"This isn't a social call. Stella told me it was urgent."

"Stella tells me you've been attending Lisa's trial. She tells me you're keeping it a secret from her." Alma was fishing, but Robert was not obliging her on this personal matter.

She advanced slowly. "You wouldn't ask off work to be a spectator, not when you need the money." She stood so near to him that she stared into his neck. "Are you for the defense or the prosecution?" Robert became stiff. Alma laid her hands on his chest and indicated to the chair behind him, lightly nudging him backward.

Alma joined him and said with no hesitation, "I'm for the prosecution."

"That's no surprise."

"You misunderstand. I'm testifying tomorrow."

"What?"

"I told the prosecuting attorney what I know. He was very interested."

Robert screamed, "What the bloody hell are you doing, Alma?!" She leapt out of her seat. With each step he took she stepped back. "Why are you meddling this time, eh? Why can't you leave her alone?"

"She deserves whatever she has coming to her."

"What testimony can *you* give that would be of any merit?"

"My dear Robert, do you have to ask?"

Robert stared into her cold and telling eyes. In that instant he understood. He stumbled over to the window to free him from violent thoughts.

Alma embraced his waist. "Don't hate me, Robert. Why can't things be like they used to be?"

"You live in a dream world."

"You can't stand there and tell me you felt nothing for me. The long walks we took together, parties late into the night; we loved each other."

"There was only what you perceived to be love."

"I can't accept that. You wouldn't have stayed all that time if you didn't feel something. That is until she came along."

"Why do you think I left in the first place? I was tired of you, the lies. I only came to your bloody parties for the booze."

"It was her! She stole you from me!"

"You never had me."

Alma took his face with force. Her fingernails sank into his skin. "I see you in my dreams every single night. In all these years you've never left me and you never will."

Alma stood on her toes to kiss him. Robert pushed her away and she fell back onto the sofa. Alma lived under the delusion all these years they were once in love. The fairytale was over.

A black tear, stained with mascara, fell down Alma's cheek. She picked herself up. "You seem to be forgetting what I did for you. You should be thanking me – your beautiful wife, the baby just around the corner. *I* did that.

"Your marriage to Lisa was on the rocks before it began. She wasn't right for you and I knew it from the start. Darling, I know the pain you felt. I watched you every day." Alma went across the room and moved a small table aside so she could reach a painting on the wall.

"What are you doing?" Robert asked.

"I'm going to show you something four years overdue." Alma lifted the painting up from the nail, revealing a cutout in the wall five inches in diameter with a small hole in the center. Alma stepped back as instruction for him to look.

He stooped to peep into the hole that was the same size as his eye. All he could see was a dark apartment. "What is this?"

"Nothing of importance now. It was once a window into the world of Lisa Frisco. How did you think I came to know what I know?"

Robert raised his head. The ugly truth disgusted him when he thought of what she may have seen. "You-you spied on us? All those years?" Robert cringed like he was going to be sick and headed for the door.

"Don't you walk out that door! If you walk out on me again, I'll...I'll..."

"You'll what?"

Alma smirked, "You'll see tomorrow."

Robert could see past the façade of this woman. She carried a festering grudge around with her for a decade. He knew what she was capable of more than anyone. Alma fought to maintain her grin as her obsession's strong gaze pierced her like a sword.

"What do you intend to do?" he asked.

"I don't want to hurt you, darling. Hurting you is that last thing I want to do."

"Alma," Robert spoke in a soft tone, with rage boiling under the surface.

"Lisa wasn't worthy of you."

Robert rushed at her like he was going to attack. Alma stumbled over her feet and fell. "Quick saying things to make me hurt you!" Robert seized her and hoisted her up high; her toes barely touched the floor.

"Listen to me very closely. Are you listening?" Alma nodded. "Tomorrow you will testify and you're going to tell everyone what a kind and wonderful person Lisa is, and you're going to mean it.

"Lisa was a good friend and a friendly neighbor. In fact, you hated to see her go. That's why the two of you remained neighbors for so long. I doubt if you ever had a better friend.

"You could hardly fathom your friend planning the murder of a man and executing the murder of said man. Repeat what I just said." Alma pursed her lips tight. Robert shook her violently, "Repeat it!"

Alma fumbled over her tongue, like uttering such words was blasphemous. "Lisa was my best friend. I don't believe she is capable of committing murder." Alma hissed with the venom of a snake in Robert's face. "Lisa is innocent."

The red light outside reflected on their faces. Robert released her. He laid his hand on her shoulder and squeezed, and then bent down into her ear. "If Lisa is convicted you will be sorry. The other witnesses won't matter. I'll blame you."

Alma closed her eyes in discomfort as he pressed his fingers into her shoulder blade.

"I'll be watching you."

# CHAPTER
# FORTY THREE

The attorneys sat at their tables waiting for Judge O'Neal to arrive. Both were on pins and needles seeing as this was the last day. Lisa came in and took her usual seat beside Dodge and saw James was not there.

Robert squeezed through several knees to reach the aisle and then handed a note to Dodge's secretary, instructing her to pass it to her boss. "That man wanted you to have this," she pointed to Robert.

Dodge unfolded the paper containing a short message. "The rebuttal witness MacQuillan was talking about is Alma George. She testifies today."

"All rise!" announced the bailiff.

"This court is now in session. Judge O'Neal presiding."

O'Neal took no time in getting situated. "Let's get started. Call your witness, Counselor."

MacQuillan stood, "I call Alma George to the stand. Bring in the witness, please.

Lisa could already hear the clip-clopping of her heels on the marble floor. Alma was decked out in her finest for the occasion; a brown ensemble with matching gloves, fur hat and collar, and dangling on her arm, a tiny purse too small to hold anything except a compact and a handkerchief. Lisa went down the list of possibilities that could transpire from Alma's testimony, all of them bad. A certain toxin must have flowed within those veins.

Alma crossed her legs and pulled her skirt down to her knees, her bangle bracelets clinking off the other with every shift, and she smiled that teethy grin. "I'm ready when you are, Albert."

MacQuillan opened his mouth and Dodge cut him off. "Your Honor, I object to the testimony of this witness. We were never told and I am strongly opposed."

"Is this true, Mr. MacQuillan?"

At the same time the two attorneys were fighting it out, Lisa observed three interesting things happening: James arrived with Rebecca and chose to sit with her instead of behind Lisa as he'd always done. Donald was not with them. Meanwhile, Alma's eyes were on Robert who imparted a menacing stare in return. Something was going on. Why else would Robert, who had zero emotional or marital ties with Lisa, warn her of Alma's coming?

Dodge threw himself into his chair. "Well?" Lisa pressed.

"Quiet. I need to think."

MacQuillan started, "You've known Lisa Mallory for how long?"

"Longer than anyone in this room."

"How long is that?"

"Ten years. She was Lisa Wells when I met her."

"So, you know the defendant pretty well?"

Alma fussed with her hair all the while she was on the stand as if she was Perry Mason's star witness. "She and I were the best of friends. She was a darling young woman who came to Manhattan to start a new life."

Lisa couldn't believe what she was hearing. She found a pencil to transfer some of the hostility building up inside.

"I recall I threw a party around the time that she moved in next door to me and the poor thing was so shy she didn't mix with the other tenants. She sat in a corner the whole evening. I did find that very unsociable. However, that was the night she met her first husband, so it wasn't a total loss."

Lisa imagined striking her, stamping a deserved blemish upon that made-up face.

"Did you notice anything odd about her?"

"No."

MacQuillan became alarmed. "That wasn't what you told me, Ms. George."

Robert wasn't taking his eyes off of Alma. It was a powerful gaze of caution that Alma could not break free from. Would others catch on to these exchanges?

The heat was getting too hot for Alma, and she submitted to MacQuillan enough to get him off her back. "I did hear rumors."

"What kind of rumors?"

"Nothing good, but that doesn't make them true. The old man who managed the building liked her a little too much, if you know what I mean. But it's just gossip."

The brittle wood of Lisa's pencil began to crack.

"Would you say Lisa Mallory has been a woman of moral integrity, a law-abiding citizen?"

"Of course, Albert."

MacQuillan went and stood beside the jury box. It was coming. "The council for the defense would have us believing she's a woman who values life?" He could read the internal struggle on her face. "Do you deny what you told me in my office two days ago?"

"No."

"Then tell the court."

O'Neal added, "Or I'll hold you in contempt, Ms. George."

Her focus was on Robert. MacQuillan wasn't going to give up.

"Alright, let's try it another way."

"I object," said Dodge. "If his own witness has nothing but good things to say about my client, is it right to pressure her into divulging some sordid news which she obviously knows nothing about?"

MacQuillan blurted out in desperation, "Did you not come into my office and tell me Lisa Mallory had an illegal abortion in 1953?"

The pencil Lisa was grasping snapped in two.

Alma solemnly shook her head in agreement. The jury muttered amongst themselves. "Silence from the jury," O'Neal ordered. The judge's interest was piqued.

MacQuillan allowed the courtroom to quiet down. "You just said that Mrs. Mallory was a darling woman, to use your words. In truth, she committed an act of murder."

"Objection!"

"Overruled."

Lisa's insides tightened in agony as her darkest, innermost regret came out for all to hear. They all were judging her now. That personal scrutiny had been tormenting her since the day after the act.

"Lisa Mallory, for whatever reason, managed to locate some doctor, probably unlicensed, to do this horrible deed, for a fee of course."

Lisa was still tender in her heart. She thought of Simon and Julia and saw her own baby, what might have been. The possibilities were long gone. Suddenly their faces were all she could think of.

Dodge struck the table. "I *object* on the grounds of total speculation!"

"I'll sustain the objection. Stick to the facts, Counselor."

"I have nothing more to ask the witness. I think she said all that matters."

"How did you come by this information?" asked Dodge. "This isn't exactly something that is casually brought up in a friendly conversation."

"W-well, Lisa and I have been good friends for a long time."

"Some friend you are."

"Objection."

"Did she do something to hurt you?"

MacQuillan repeated his objection louder, "Objection!"

"How do you know this, Ms. George? I don't believe she told you."

Alma looked behind Dodge. He turned to see who she was looking at. Now the note Robert gave him made sense. "I see," he whispered. "Ms. George, did you know Robert Frisco before you met Lisa?"

Alma was fighting hard to keep Robert happy and satisfy Mac-Quillan at the same time, but she never took into account Dodge had a watchful eye. She was getting it from three sides and the panic came from within. Her heart beat wild like a drum out of control, hiding successfully from the world under the guise of the composed woman she was good at playing.

"How well did you know him?"

Alma licked her lips and drew in a deep breath, "Enough."

"Then my client married him, and today you happen to know something that only the two of them should know." Dodge pointed at Robert, "Did he tell you?"

Alma was somber. "No."

"Did Lisa?"

"No."

"I'm not going to press the matter. However, I find it disturbing that you know this very personal thing. Just out of curiosity, what made you move the rock and come all this way? Does it have something to do with him?" Again, he pointed at Robert.

"Go to hell," Alma muttered.

"I'm the one trying to help your best friend. I can't do that if I'm headed down there." Dodge spoke out as MacQuillan did before. "I want everyone to bear witness to this woman. She is a prime example of the prosecution's case and what he must employ to win it.

"He has put a woman on the stand that says one thing and means something else, a woman with obvious jealousy in her heart and ulterior motives in her mind, and uses what she knows about people to get back at them for something she thinks they may have done against her."

Dodge spoke candidly to her. "You must be one miserable human being. I bet you haven't a friend in the world."

Robert stood up and left the courtroom.

Alma turned to O'Neal, "May I go now?"

Dodge said, "I'm finished with her."

"No questions, Your Honor," added MacQuillan.

"You may go."

Alma rushed out of the courtroom and chased after Robert while calling to him. He wasn't stopping. She ran in front of him.

"Robert, it wasn't my fault."

There was no anger, no resentment or hatred. He stepped around her. The love of her life disappeared down the hall, and Alma was left standing with the realization that would be the last she would ever see him.

# CHAPTER
# FORTY FOUR

It came time for each attorney to present their closing arguments, a compilation of all the key points throughout the duration of the trial.

MacQuillan implemented his cut-throat technique. He appeared no less confident than he did at the start, despite Dodge's constant barrage of obstruction. Still, he was so very compelling. Like a professional actor he used words to impart feelings to his audience. When viewed in a certain light he was an actor on a stage.

He began by playing the pity card about Joe's unfortunate cancer and then switched to Lisa's purchase of the gun as proof of premeditated murder, along with her abusive behavior, however uncharacteristic. MacQuillan did his best to convey that Joe's many faults didn't mean he deserved to die. He was a human being who had problems and made mistakes like all of us. If he was already dying, Lisa had no right to take the remaining time he had, and his dignity.

Dodge agreed it was unfortunate that Joe was suffering from cancer, but it had no bearing on the real issue. MacQuillan made his case on tenuous circumstantial evidence. The prosecution failed to prove why Lisa would kill Joseph Norris. Unlike MacQuillan, Dodge's approach was candid, brief, a little less sensitive, but the facts were there.

The jury had been pulled up and down, backward and forward with many witnesses. Did MacQuillan succeed in making his case? Had Dodge given a secure defense?

Given what was at stake it would not be enough. There wasn't anything in this world Dodge could've done that would have pacified Lisa's mind.

HOUR BY HOUR, TIME TOOK ITS TIME.

The jury had been sequestered. That's when Lisa and Dodge began to worry. To ensure a verdict of first-degree murder all twelve minds must concur. Dodge was certain that MacQuillan's case was blown out the window and the jury would come through that door within the hour, but after five O'Neal called it a day.

If convicted she would face yet another hearing to determine her penalty. Life? Death? Maybe if MacQuillan or Alma had their way.

At least the cell she occupied was private. What happened to her was not a figment of her mind. Joe tried to murder her.

*If the jury decides I'm innocent of all charges they'll let me go.*

Is that what Lisa truly wanted? She would return to that big house on the hill with a husband she wasn't sure of anymore.

Each person that warned her of James Mallory, Donald in his own subtle way, Mayfield's intelligent deductions, even Joe in his most fearsome, she managed to blithely shrug it off.

*Could I have known all along what kind of man he was and his abnormal alliance with Joe?* Lisa was admitting to her own blindness.

She was also blind to the whole of her soul, her passion and humanity being chipped off piece by piece as it happened, and her loved ones being moved to the backburner all for a man. Since this trial she was coming to terms with that reality and was prepared to return things to the way they used to be if she made it through. She was a different person with different dreams.

*I wonder what they're thinking,* she speculated of the jury. *Are they sleeping? Will I cross their minds tonight?*

To sit down was an impossibility. She had to do something, even if it meant treading a path in her cell until sunrise. Lisa would pace the square perimeter the rest of that night. This was to be the longest night of her life.

# CHAPTER FORTY FIVE

The call came around 3:30 p.m. the next day. The jury was ready.

There was none absent this day. Donald and Rebecca were there, Larry and Genevieve, Robert, and James, returning to his supportive seat behind. It was a good day for Lisa in regards to loyalty. Mayfield was there as well in secret.

Lisa did her best to stay strong. The words "guilty, guilty, guilty," kept repeating in her head like a warped record. O'Neal sat on his perch overseeing his courtroom. Each member of the jury filed in one by one like soldiers on a march. Dodge took Lisa's hand and gripped it firm.

All nine men and three women stood before the judge. Following O'Neal's order, the clerk addressed them. "Members of the jury, which one of you is elected to speak on your behalf?"

An elderly man on the end stepped forward. "I am the foreman."

The thumping in her chest increased harder and faster, her stomach began to churn, and her head grew light.

"The defendant will rise," ordered O'Neal. Lisa's knees trembled. She didn't want to go down in front of everyone, but she didn't know if she would be able to hold out much longer.

The clerk asked, "What is your verdict?"

"We find the defendant..."

All Lisa heard was "not". The stone faces of the jury melted away revealing the joy shared by the rest. Lisa was in shock; she stood there staring at O'Neal beating his little hammer to a stub.

Dodge embraced her. "We did it! We did it, Lisa!"

Lisa gladly reciprocated the hug of the man who saved her life. "Oh Greg, I'm so grateful. I-I-I can't begin to tell you..."

"You don't have to."

She saw James. His was an old but genuine smile she hadn't had the pleasure of seeing in months. Disregarding her bulky cast, Lisa ran to him and threw her arms around his neck as he lifted her up and twirled her around.

"My darling, you're free!" He lowered her to the floor. "You're free." James noticed Donald and Rebecca standing beside them and moved aside. Lisa became rigid upon seeing her brother and would not look at him.

Rebecca said, "Congratulations. We're happy for you." Rebecca patted James on the back before going to speak to Dodge. James took the hint and went with her to leave them alone.

Donald tried to form words. All he could say was her name. He fell to his knees and embraced her waist. Her hands came up from behind and gently hugged his head.

He closed his eyes. Her forgiveness meant the entire world to him. From then on, he would do anything to protect their delicate bond. James was watching, and when they were finished, he walked over to Donald.

What happened next would shock Lisa. James extended his hand to him. No one saw it coming, least of all her. Was this a truce?

Donald glanced down at his hand and back up at him. Whatever this was, it was accepted. Donald willingly shook his hand. Perhaps this trial was the best thing that could've happened to her. James laughed and ruffled Donald's hair.

Lisa wasn't sure how to take it. In the not-so-distant past it would have made her so happy, but now...Her acquittal seemed to have instigated a domino effect of good fortune as her family was reunited and made whole again, except for Lisa who remained fragmented and troubled.

Dodge and MacQuillan shook hands as well. "You did good, kid," MacQuillan commended.

"I did, didn't I? I think I'll celebrate with a cigarette." Dodge pulled a single cigarette out of the inner pocket of his jacket. "I thought I'd come prepared." He inserted it between his lips. "This will taste so good."

Mayfield whistled at Donald to get his attention.

Donald rolled his eyes. "Oh no, what do *you* want?" Mayfield motioned for him.

As James held Lisa close, she spotted Robert across the room. He kept his distance but moved in close enough to make his presence known to her. He was an outsider. Lisa gazed at him with thankful eyes. With a warm smile he left to return home to Stella.

Lisa didn't know if she would see him again. Maybe one day. There still remained some affection for this man and there always would be.

By now Larry and his wife shared in the merriment. Lisa took her friend in arms. Meanwhile, Donald and Mayfield were engaged in a serious discussion about the future Lisa assumed would be waiting for her and the possibility of its end.

"Why tell me?" Donald asked. "You should tell the police. Tell them what you told me."

"I will, but right now I need your help. Lisa needs your help."

"Alright," Donald agreed. "What is it you want me to do?"

When Lisa was finally released her family and friends were by her side. They followed her down the steps of the courthouse. Mayfield was close by watching from his car.

Lisa expressed with enthusiasm, "I want to see Simon and Julia. Can I see them tonight?"

"Sorry," Rebecca replied. "It's a school night."

"I don't think it would hurt," said Donald. "This is a special occasion."

"Maybe tomorrow. I have a lot of work to do. I'm drafting a will."

James put his arm around Lisa. "Come, Lisa. Let's get you home."

Before James could lead her away, Lisa stepped over to Donald and took his hand. "Donny," she whispered, "will you please come see me tomorrow?"

Donald detected a hint of urgency in her voice. "A-alright, Lisa. I will."

James opened the passenger door. "It's time to go."

Lisa may have been unconscious of it, but she was crying out for help. Donald didn't like the look on her face as James took her away.

ALMA HAD SANK into a black hole of depression unlike ever before as the one remaining thing in her life that gave her pleasure was gone.

Exactly when it happened no one knew, but on the 24$^{th}$ of October Alma George was found by Stella naked and lifeless in her bathtub, her wrists cut, and floating in murky red water.

Written on the mirror in red lipstick was a message that read...

I'll always love you, Robert. Please forgive my selfishness.

Did she know the outcome of the trial? If given the time, would the miserable Alma George have been capable of starting a new?

The woman who caused Lisa so much pain had ended her life in defeat.

# CHAPTER FORTY SIX

The house was the same as when she left it, yet the warmth was missing. Now it was this empty, massive edifice with only two people to occupy it.

Lisa stopped at the bottom of the stairs to tell James something and he wasn't behind her. "James?" She walked up the stairs to her room. She kept expecting him to come through the door as she put away her things.

"J-James, could you come in here a minute? I need you." Lisa was starting to get worried. Where did he go? She rushed to the door and there he stood. Lisa clutched her chest startled. "Don't do that."

"Do what?"

"I-I noticed the room."

"I've been sleeping in the guest room down the hall." James reached for her; Lisa drew back. "I couldn't sleep in our bed without you in it." He leaned in to kiss her. He hadn't detected her discomfort, though the kiss was one-sided.

He lifted her up and carried her to the bed. "Oh James, I don't know." He pressed his lips to her neck.

Lisa felt powerless to stop him and didn't.

AS JAMES SLEPT the peaceful sleep of satisfaction, Lisa laid on her back staring up at the ceiling. All she could think about was the lost death threat and the office James didn't want her near.

Was whatever in there so horrible, so despicable that she couldn't be told? Up to this point Mayfield had done all of the footwork. After all, it concerned her future and her life. It was her turn to see for herself.

It was 3:17 a.m. She made certain James was asleep. She put on her housecoat, crept out of the bedroom, and softly closed the door.

Lisa tiptoed barefoot down the hall to James's office. She was afraid to turn on any lights, so she did her best without. She started with the shelf that was eyelevel and began by removing each book.

When it wasn't on that shelf, she started on the next shelf down. Time was in short supply. Lisa feared at any moment James would walk in. There were stacks upon stacks of medical books, homeopathic and naturopathic medicines, biographies, fine wines, how-tos, etc., all in the middle of the floor.

She kept glancing at the door. It was difficult groping around in the dark while remaining quiet. She was working on the bottom shelf when she saw it, a black rectangle in the corner.

*This must be it.* The key was underneath, right where Mayfield put it. Lisa eagerly carried it to the center of the floor and tripped over a stack of books.

She froze in place and shut her eyes tight, waiting for the thunder.

As Mayfield did before, Lisa inserted the key into the lock and turned it slowly. It clicked and the lid raised by itself. The first thing to catch her eye was the old photograph of the dark-haired girl in the wedding gown.

She was almost angelic as her flowing dark hair complemented the vivid white dress that dangled above the floor as if she was standing on a cloud. The picture's age made it difficult to see fine details. However faded, the face was that of a merry girl with a pristine smile. Lisa dug deeper into the box, rifling through the many newspaper clippings.

Each one concerned the Moran family or Elizabeth Norris, a former Moran prior to 1938, which was the year she married Henry Norris. Lisa speculated why James would have a wedding photo of Elizabeth, unless...

*James is not really James at all. He's been someone else this whole time,* Lisa thought while looking at Elizabeth's picture.

Lisa read aloud to herself, "Elizabeth Moran, wealthy socialite and daughter of a banker, marries Henry Norris."

*It doesn't say anything about him. If James is Henry, then who was Joe?* Lisa began to recall the times she asked James about his family and he would always get angry. From day one he was so elusive, so secretive, even concerning his own wealth, which Lisa had doubts as to its origins.

*"My old man was rich. I inherited everything,"* James once said of his prosperity. It was an inheritance, but his father had nothing to do with it. Lisa read of the lavish galas and luxurious balls Elizabeth hosted. After reading so many of these clippings Lisa felt she knew her.

Then she vanished. She went missing on a Saturday night and when she didn't return by Sunday the search began. Deep in her heart Lisa knew her husband was Henry Norris. In 1947 Elizabeth Norris was pronounced dead.

At the bottom was the same birth certificate that puzzled Mayfield – James Mitchell Norris born December 2, 1939.

*Born 1939? This can't be my James.* Lisa pulled it out of the box and a gold wedding ring fell into her lap.

Her heart stopped. It was the very ring with the initials *"E.N."* inside, and the very ring that James took from her at the hospital.

This was Elizabeth's ring.

Lisa was terrified that just a couple doors down slept a murderer. She could have easily gone to pieces right there, but by now Lisa knew composure was the one thing that could save her life. If James found her, that would be the end.

She needed to telephone the police. There was a phone in the office, but she was afraid he would hear. Lisa left everything on the floor and cracked open the door to make sure it was safe.

*If I could just get downstairs to the den, I'll be okay.* But it was a long way from the office. She would have to pass by their bedroom and descend the dreaded staircase without making a sound. With the picture of Elizabeth in hand she started off.

The hall was pitch-black. There was no light source whatsoever. Her eyes were adjusted, but barely enough for her to see past an arm length ahead of her. She followed the contour of the wall.

When it curved she would know she was nearing the stairs, so she felt of the wall, anticipating that curve. There was an eerie stillness in the house. Her heart pounded in her ears. The beating intensified the closer she came to their room as if it was beating away her existence on this earth with each step.

Out of the darkness resonated a sound – a breath that was not her own. Her eyes searched for a source. She reached out but felt only the air.

"What have you done?" breathed a voice, as if the ghost of Joe was mirroring her every move.

James came from behind. Lisa shrieked and fell back. She couldn't see him until his white face emerged.

Lisa looked up and saw Joe standing over her. It took her a moment to realize it was James. The look on his face was reminiscent of her attempted killer.

"How could you do this?" he growled.

His face was morphing more and more into Joe Norris. Was there really a transformation taking place or was Lisa becoming conscious of those clear similarities.

Lisa rose up from the floor. "You killed her. I know you killed her." He moved abruptly and she flinched. "I know who you are...Henry Norris."

James cocked his head.

Lisa backed away; he moved with her. "Joe was your father. And Elizabeth, she was your wife. I-I-I know how you did it, too, and why.

"You had your father do the dirty work while you plotted the whole scheme." Lisa kept backing away from him. "Once you got the money you changed your name to James, the name of your son, and moved here."

The heel of Lisa's foot touched the edge of the stair. "You murdered that girl...then you tried to murder me."

James whispered, "You don't know a damn thing."

Lisa drew nearer to the edge in fear of him. "Oh really?" She pulled out the picture. "Then who is this?"

James lunged at her and down she went, her body rapidly descending the steps with echoes of pain. The staircase curved and her head bounced off the wall. Lisa went limp. She hit the bottom of the stairs with a solid thud.

She cracked open her eyes in time to see the black figure of her husband coming down. She managed to get to her feet, but in an attempt to run she dropped. Her right ankle was either sprained or broken. She pushed herself up and limped all the way to the kitchen.

In hopes the darkness would shield her she took refuge in the pantry and peeked through the slats in the door. Lisa was pinned, unable to budge an inch in the cramped little room.

"Lisa! Where are you, Lisa?"

Lisa knew it was only a matter of time before he found her. A thin slit in the door to guide her vision made it impossible to determine where he was.

"Come out, Lisa!" His voice grew louder. Lisa cracked opened the door. Suddenly the kitchen light came on.

She threw her hand over her mouth to cover her breathing. What if he noticed the pantry door was open? She inched back as close as she could to the shelves behind her. The big shadow of her husband passed.

Lisa was shaking. The shadow passed again. Silence. It came back and this time stopped in front of the pantry. Darkness engulfed the little room. The head of the shadow looked up and then looked down. He reached for the knob.

She closed her eyes and prepared for capture. It didn't come. When she plucked up the courage to open her eyes the shadow was gone and the lights were out. She decided to stay where she was for a while.

It was nearing an hour and there hadn't been a sound from James. Lisa felt safe enough to make her getaway. The closest door was the front door. Unless James was upstairs it wouldn't have been a good idea to try to make it to the garage, and she had no way of knowing where he was.

She couldn't call the police, not in that house. There wasn't a neighbor in over a mile. Her car keys were upstairs and that meant no way out. It seemed her only choice was to exit through the front door and go from there – on foot and with a limp.

She wasn't about to venture out into the unknown unarmed. The steak knives by the sink would offer some protection. Lisa kept one close to her side as she stepped out of the kitchen. All the lights were still off.

A bluish glow from distant moonlight shined down the hall through the outside windows. She took that first step from toe to heel onto the wood floor and it creaked. The painful creak persisted until she released her foot. Lisa stretched her leg to the center where the floor would make less noise.

She was nearing the living room. She gripped the knife tighter. The room was dead. From there she could see the door.

The ceiling creaked. Lisa threw her head back. She stopped at the entrance of the den and listened for him. The ceiling creaked again as if there was a great weight bearing down on it.

Lisa poked her head out into the foyer and looked up at the top of the stairs. The den was next to her. He may have been in there all this time waiting patiently, but the longer she stayed in that house the more she put her life at risk.

Lisa bolted for the door.

She ran as fast as her bad foot would allow. She had a clear view of the road. Perhaps she would meet a car. Anything to get her away from there. She looked back at the house; he wasn't behind.

James came at her from the side. The knife fell to the ground. Lisa screamed as loud as she could.

James yelled, "Stop it! Lisa, stop it!"

Lisa kicked him in the shin. He released her and she got the knife. Lisa pointed the blade at him. In that second, he seized her wrist.

His strength was far greater than hers and she found herself losing her grip as his tightened. James got control of the knife. The shiny blade was now aimed at her.

Terror broadened her eyes.

There was a hollow sound and James dropped, revealing Rebecca clutching the barrel of a pistol.

# CHAPTER FORTY SEVEN

"**R**ebecca! Thank God!"

Rebecca noticed Lisa was not putting any weight on her right foot. "You're hurt."

Lisa stared down at her unconscious husband. "Do you think he'll wake up?"

"I hit him hard."

"I need to call the police. Watch him for me."

Lisa started to make her way back to the house. Rebecca stepped in front of her. She attempted to step around her and again Rebecca stepped in front of her with the gun pointed at her heart. Lisa looked over at James.

"He won't wake up. I'll make sure of that."

"Rebecca...I-I don't understand." Lisa did understand, but she just couldn't process it.

"Isn't it obvious? Since the first attempt was, shall we say, unsuccessful, I must carry out the second attempt on my own."

"And Donny? Won't he wonder where you are?"

Rebecca grinned. "He conveniently asked to work tonight. There's no help coming. It's just you and me."

The knife was under James's hand. Lisa went for it. Rebecca beat her to it.

"Try that again..." Lisa was staring directly into the barrel that was a few inches from her eye. "Oh, don't worry. I won't do it until all your questions are answered. I owe you that much."

Lisa gradually stood to her feet. Rebecca held up the knife. "Slowly now. I must admit I thought my plan was foolproof.

"A convoluted plan it was. After you killed Joe, I immediately had to think up an alternate one. It was that big oaf who bungled it. He was supposed to wait for your will to go through probate. He was a hothead. So impetuous."

"My-my will?"

"I was able to keep a watchful eye on your progress with Russell Sheridan. We even work on the same floor. His long lunches made it easier for me to snoop on a daily basis. He even keeps a desk calendar, so I knew all the appointments you made with him.

"I kept Joe on a long leash. I never objected to him putting the fear of God in you a little, but I *never* considered the buffoon would kill you prematurely." Rebecca bit the tip of the blade in contemplation. "When the police showed up at our door, I knew right then it was about you."

Rebecca let out a boisterous cackle. "But I was wrong. You were still alive. I didn't know what to do.

"Then a wonderful thing happened. You ran. And it came to me that you would be my out. I had no idea you hired a gumshoe.

"I thought James was your main source of capital. Imagine my delight when I discovered your wealth wasn't exactly chickenfeed."

"It was a small dowry from James."

"James signed over a fourth of his entire fortune to you. Seven hundred thousand plus is quite enough for my means. Poor Joe needed the money for his treatments. He quit his job a month before due to illness, and I needed him to focus his attentions on you."

"And James?"

"Oh, he wasn't involved."

"He-he wasn't?"

"Not at all."

Lisa looked down at him lying on the ground. *Wake up, James,* Lisa pleaded to him within the safety of her mind.

*Joe hands Rebecca a brown folder. She looks it over. "Is that proof enough for you?" he asks her. Rebecca nods her head in approval.*

*"If we're to proceed all that's important is the figures. Well, how about it? I don't have all the time in the world."*

*"Leave the thinking to me."*

*"It was I who gave the tax return to your PI that night."*

*"You pointed the finger at James."*

"I had to divert suspicion. Mayfield was getting too close." Rebecca chuckled to herself in recollection. "When Joe told me the truth behind your husband's wealth, it came to me as easy as turning on a light."

"But-but you were scared of Joe."

"I knew right off when he told me about Elizabeth that he's the one who killed her. He didn't admit to it, but I know. I'm certain James knows, too."

Rebecca was about to disclose she knew far more than Lisa about her husband all this time. "You see, many years ago charges were brought against James by the Moran family. That's why he changed his name and relocated here."

Rebecca reached inside her pocket. Lisa stepped back. "Do you recognize this?"

It was the death threat.

"It was I who sent it and it was I who retrieved it from this house. I overheard Mayfield plotting to get it back. One attorney to another, I simply asked yours what they were looking for. I couldn't have the one piece of evidence linking me to Joe's death floating around, so I waited for Mayfield to find it for me.

"Don't you see, Lisa? The death threat, the Chevy was all tactics to scare you into amending your will, and it worked!"

Lisa was numb inside. There was no anger or sadness, only a heightened sense of survival. Could she keep her talking long enough until she could think up an escape plan? Rebecca had six months to mull over her plan, six months from Lisa's marriage to James to the initial death threat. Lisa had mere seconds to escape it.

Lisa remembered the wedding ring. "What-what about the ring?"

"What ring?"

"That night Joe switched my wedding ring with Elizabeth's. Why?"

"To incriminate James or hurt him. Who knows?"

"Rebecca," Lisa's voice cracked. "You're my sister."

Rebecca lowered her gun. Was it sympathy or love that postponed the inevitable? Not love as we understand the word, but love as far as Rebecca was capable.

"My father was a compulsive gambler and he left us buried under so much debt that Mother died trying to pay it off. I was forced to marry when I became pregnant with Simon. Do you think I wanted to be tied down with a husband and a baby before the age of twenty? I had dreams and I had the ambition to fulfill them."

Lisa reached out for her. "Rebecca, listen to me."

She jerked the gun back up. "Now, according to your will, in the event of your death, James stands to inherit his money back. With James in prison, Donald and I are next in line."

Lisa said, "I wouldn't be surprised if you did away with him next."

Rebecca remained silent. In time she would kill Donald.

"James cannot be tried again for the death of his first wife. However, I do believe he will be tried and convicted for the murder of his second."

"Rebecca, I would've given you all that you needed."

"No! No! You still don't get it! It would be your money. No matter which way you dissect it, it is *still-your-money*. That's why it *has* to be this way."

Lisa was sizing up the situation. There were three factors against her: Her arm was in a cast, she now stood on a bad ankle, and she was barefoot. Her chances were better when she was up against Joe Norris.

Rebecca must have hit James hard. He showed no signs of coming to. If only he would wake.

"I love you, Lisa. Believe me. But I will not continue to live in that drab matchbox." Rebecca retracted the hammer.

Lisa screamed, "Get her, James!"

Rebecca looked away. In that instant Lisa pounced. Both women fell onto the dew-covered grass wrestling for the gun. Lisa grabbed Rebecca's wrist and the gun fired.

They rolled down a slight dip in the ground, coming to rest with Lisa on top. Rebecca still had hold of the knife and slashed her side. Lisa retained her grip. Her broken arm was giving Rebecca the upper hand.

Rebecca positioned her foot on Lisa's stomach and shoved her off. Lisa fell back. Rebecca let out a bloodcurdling scream and landed on top of her, restraining Lisa with both legs. She slapped her hard across the face and held the knife to her throat.

"I change my mind. Maybe I'll kill you this way. I *was* going to be merciful." Lisa could feel the individual ridges of the blade make contact with her thin skin.

"One sharp movement of my left arm and you're done." Rebecca put the gun to her forehead. "It's up to you."

Lisa swallowed hard. The knife was growing heavier on her Addams apple. This was the end of Lisa. All hope had left her. There was no sound she could hear except the loud click of the revolver. Lisa was eyelevel with James.

She needed him to be the last thing she saw. She mouthed "I'm sorry" to him.

Rebecca pulled the trigger. The shot pierced the silence for miles.

The bullet intended for Lisa was discharged into oblivion. Donald seized Rebecca's arm the second before.

"Drop it now!" he shouted.

"Donald, we need this. Please, think of what this would mean for us. All you have to do is look away."

Donald threw the gun away and dragged her off of Lisa. Rebecca began to weep uncontrollably and let go of the knife. Lisa struggled to her knees in time to see Mayfield running across the yard with the police.

The flashing lights illuminated the dark countryside, and the whining sirens were definitely the most beautiful noise she ever heard. Added to the chaos was a feeling of sickness at the sight of her husband motionless on the cold, hard ground. Mayfield helped her to her feet.

She ran over to James and fell to her knees beside him. She saw the back of his head was bleeding. "Help! Someone please help!"

Lisa turned him over. His face was stained with dirt and bits of grass. She brushed it off with her hand. "James?"

There was no response.

"I'm sorry I didn't believe you. I promise I'll spend the rest of my life making it up to you." She laid her head on his chest.

Mayfield placed his hand on her shoulder. "The ambulance is on its way."

Lisa did her best to speak through the growing lump in her throat. "How did you know?"

"I asked Dodge if he told anyone about my plans to find the threat. I figured somebody either must have overheard or he blabbed. Your brother and I have been watching the house all night. Sorry we cut it so close. We were around back when we heard the gunshot."

"She told me Donny was at work."

"He lied."

Lisa watched as police lowered Rebecca into a patrol car. No words could express her sorrow at Rebecca's deceit and malice. Her sister-in-law, best friend, and mother of Simon and Julia, was not the woman she thought. Her avarice was a hidden evil that must have been pent-up for years.

Perhaps even Rebecca didn't know about that side of herself. None of this would have happened if Joe hadn't come into Lisa's life. They were two people, worlds apart, with nothing in common except money. It was the desire for money that created a third person, a combination of both, and that person was the most dangerous of all.

The ambulance arrived to a screeching stop at the top of the driveway. James cracked open his eyes and moaned.

"James!" Lisa shrieked with joy and kissed him over and over again.

His voice was weak. "I knew it. You do love me."

# CHAPTER
# FORTY EIGHT

**"Y**ou reminded me so much of Elizabeth." James lay in his hospital bed with Lisa at his side. His head was tightly bandaged.

"She was absolutely flawless, in appearance and in manner. Liz made everyone the central part of her life...except me. Elizabeth the socialite never needed nor wanted a husband. I was there when she wanted to parade me around."

James took Lisa's hand. "All my life I wanted to be a doctor. Admittedly, I was swayed by her wealth and elegance, but I was young and wasn't cut out for the lifestyle. What I really needed was a woman who could take care of herself, but would still come to me, a woman who was beautiful, but didn't depend on her beauty.

"I found it in you. I married *you*, Lisa."

Lisa kissed the top of his hand. "What about the charges?"

"There was not one shred of evidence that could back up any of the Moran's allegations. After it was all over, I went into hiding to avoid further publicity and threats. And my son..."

He became emotional as he opened up about the secret closest to his heart. "I can still see his crumpled little face when I told him goodbye. I thought it would benefit us both. I left him with my mother who is gone now and sent money to them every month."

James covered his eyes. "I don't know where he is now. Try to understand, darling, I thought if...if I told you about my past that you would leave and you were the best thing to happen to me since.

"In any good person there is a little bad, and in any bad person there is a little good. My son and my wife are all the good in me."

Lisa leaned in to kiss him. His arms welcomed this special kiss, long-lost and long-awaited. James's candor warmed her heart with a feeling she thought gone forever. It was a good time to return the favor.

"I'm sorry I never told you about my will. I made a will after my parents died in case something happened to me. They had a small life insurance policy and I never touched a penny. Naturally all that changed when I married you. I hired Russell Sheridan and had him make some changes.

"First, I wanted everything you gave me to be returned to you. Certain sentimental items were to go to Donny, and if something happened to you, everything." Lisa braced herself, opening up about everything.

"In the absolute worst of circumstances, Robert and his family get everything." James pushed himself up with his arms. "It's not that I still love him or anything."

"Lisa..."

"I know it's unconventional to put an ex-spouse in a will, but after what I did..."

James took her face into his hands. "It's alright. Believe me, I understand."

"It appears neither of us was very forthright with each other." Lisa lowered her head so he couldn't see her face. "I can never give you a baby."

James raised her chin up. If he could forgive her then she could forgive herself. The internal condemnation that she had come to accept and live with would wither away. She and James were forgiving each other for sins committed against other people long before their story began.

"Things, people, aren't always what they appear to be."

It took Lisa a long time to learn that reality is what we make it. Whether you bury yourself in lies and gossip, or choose to ignore what you think you know and heed only to what is fact, the truth will become whatever you believe.

There was a quick knock on the door and Donald and Mayfield came in. "I hope we're not interrupting," said Mayfield.

Donald's eyes appeared so fragile. He was up all night with police, and Simon and Julia stood on both sides of their father. Simon could sense something was wrong. The time would come when he would have to tell them.

Donald asked in a soft voice, "How you feelin', James?"

James appreciated his concern. "I'll live. Thanks."

Mayfield twirled his hat in his hands. "It doesn't look good." Donald let out a sigh of despair at the heavy weight on his heart.

Julia spoke in her tiny voice, taking hold of her father's hand, "Don't be sad, Daddy. He'll be okay."

Donald forced a smile. "Well, we can't stay. I just came by to see how you two were doing. Come on, kids, let's grab a bite. I'm starved."

"Donny?" Lisa stopped him as he was leaving. "I'll be at home around seven if you...well, you know the number."

This time his smile was genuine. "Seven it is."

"Lisa, may I speak with you in the hall?" asked Mayfield. "This will only take a moment."

"Go ahead, darling. I'll just be bored until you get back." James kissed her on the nose.

Lisa followed Mayfield half way up the hall, quite a distance from James's room. Mayfield's fists rested on his hips as he exhaled heavily a couple of times and paced a small section of floor with short steps.

"Is there something the matter?" she asked. His head was bent over and all she could see was the top of his hat. "What is it?"

"No, not really. Well, maybe. I-I have one more loose end. A gut feeling."

"Oh?"

Mayfield kept tapping his left foot like there was a song playing in his head. Lisa was anxious to get back to James and the fact that she had never seen Mayfield this edgy was making her as uneasy as he appeared to be.

"Lisa, you're a smart woman."

"Thank you. I like to think so."

"And I think you're a strong woman. That goes without saying."

"Look, I'd like to be with my husband. You're gnawing on something. Spit it out."

"There's been so much going on these past few weeks I haven't had time to ponder seemingly trivial aspects of your case. It never made sense to me at the time, but I put it on the backburner until last night."

"What are you talking about?"

"The night Norris attacked you."

"What about it?"

"He knew your routine. You did the same thing every day for months, with the exception of that night."

"So? I don't understand. Am I missing something?"

Mayfield was indeed troubled and it was apparent. "Lisa...he knew where you were going that night. How did he know? That was the first time you deviated. Any other night you would have taken a cab to Grand Central and then home. You made that appointment with your attorney at a very strange time."

"I told you why. Because..."

"Yes, yes, I know. Secret. You knew your life was in danger. You were being threatened.  Why in the name of God would you put your life in jeopardy willingly?

"That office is quite a distance away from the diner, especially at night, alone, for a woman in fear of her life. Any *man* would have taken a cab."

"I was attacked. He tried to kill me. I thought you believed me."

"I do. But *you* put yourself in the position, and was prepared. Your intention..." Mayfield changed his mind on what he was going to say. "Meetings in the night, both parties with the same intentions."

Mayfield took her shoulder and squeezed gently. "You came to me for help when no one would help you. You can trust me. I couldn't touch you even if I wanted to.

"In this chaotic world we live in, especially in my profession, sometimes we have to take matters into our own hands."

Lisa stepped back and Mayfield's hand fell to his side. "Yes. Sometimes we do." They stared at each other. He knew. She knew that he knew.

"I have to get back." Lisa left him standing there. She stopped at the door and waved goodbye to him.

"We're alone," James said. "Get over here, Gimpy."

Lisa crawled up from the end of the bed to him. He held her close in his arms. "I wouldn't trade you for a million Elizabeths. You've ruined me."

"Wait," Lisa blocked his lips with her hand. "I want to leave the past where it is. I want to rebuild, this time on a foundation of truth. No lies, no half-truths from either of us."

"Ms. Lisa, you won't regret it. I'm going to show you the time of your life."

"Thanks, but I'll settle for nice and boring."

"You got it."

It was as if they were newlyweds again, with a kiss symbolizing their new hope for a promising future together.

CPSIA information can be obtained
at www.ICGtesting.com
Printed in the USA
BVHW062256251122
652756BV00003B/274